JUST PLAYING FOR KEEPS

HOCKEY EVER AFTER

LAUREN BLAKELY

COPYRIGHT

ABOUT THE BOOK

A grumpy/sunshine fake dating hockey romance from #1 NYT Bestseller Lauren Blakely!

Ever hear the story about the dating coach who got dumped on the hockey arena's Jumbotron?

Everyone did. But I *lived* it. Including the moment when Lake Axelrod, the team's broody, tattooed right winger, swooped in on skates to rescue me from public humiliation.

Even more surprising? When the famously grumpy (and ridiculously sexy) hockey star insists on being my fake boyfriend for my sister's high-profile wedding.

It's the perfect plan. His family stops pressuring him to settle down, and I'll get the ultimate revenge, since my ex is the best man. Bonus – I might even salvage my professional reputation.

We need rules though.

1 To pull this off, everyone from *his* teammates to *my* boss has to believe we're a real couple.

2 That means swoony touches and knee-weakening kisses are required.

3 When it ends, we walk away.

. . .

But the intensity in Lake's eyes after every post-game kiss makes me wonder if he's pretending. With each whispered secret, the line between fake and real bends. Until it shatters one night in a hotel room.

Soon, he isn't just playing the protective boyfriend—he's the only one who truly sees me.

If I'm not careful, I'm going to break the most important rule of all: **don't fall for your fake date.**

This is Lake and Remy's romance. Tropes include: grumpy/sunshine, fake dating, obsessed hero, workplace romance, best friend's brother

DID YOU KNOW?

To be the first to find out when all of my upcoming books go live click here!

PRO TIP: Add lauren@laurenblakely.com to your contacts before signing up to make sure the emails go to your inbox!

Did you know this book is also available in audio and paperback on all major retailers? Go to my website for links!

For content warnings for this title, go to my site.

JUST PLAYING FOR KEEPS

BY LAUREN BLAKELY

A Hockey Ever After Romance

1

I'VE GOT EVERYTHING UNDER CONTROL

REMY

Twenty-four hours' notice and I have everything ready. I can't leave a night like this to chance. Not after spotting a certain little jewelry box hidden among the sweatshirts in my boyfriend's closet.

Inside the arena, a peaceful warmth floods me, the bliss of thorough preparation for whatever the night brings.

Jameson gestures to the aisle in the arena, letting me go first. I move in front of him, walking down the steps toward our seats as anthemic rock music pipes through the hockey rink, pump-me-up tunes perfect for the players as they warm up on the ice.

Just look at Jameson. He's all dressed up, wearing his signature vest, of course, and a forest green checked shirt I picked out for him when he asked me to take him clothes shopping a few weeks ago. He's rocking an undercut, and his jaw is clean-shaven. When we reach the second row, he pats the cushy black faux leather aisle seat. "Isn't this great, Remy?"

His voice pitches with nerves. My chest tingles from that sign too.

"These seats are amazing," I reassure him, since he sometimes needs that.

When my boyfriend of eleven and three-quarter months surprised me last week with center-ice tickets to the one thousandth game the Golden State Foxes have played at this arena —seats I can't even get as the team's part-time community relations manager—I figured it was an early anniversary gift.

But then last night, I grabbed a hoodie to borrow, and a little gray jewelry box marked "Made by Fable" fell out of the front pocket.

I popped it back in its hiding place, borrowed a different sweatshirt, and shifted into planning mode, stat. A day later, here we are, at a place meaningful to both of us. And Jameson and I *did* meet by his craft beer brewery on the concourse, so it makes perfect sense he'd pick the arena for the occasion.

Once he settles into the seat, he waves a slightly shaky hand toward the boards. "I know how much you love these games."

I press my lips together so I don't burst into confetti. "I do."

Not the only time I'll be saying that in the near future.

I smooth a hand over my jeans as Lake Axelrod, the team's top right winger, glides past the glass, his gaze touring the stands like he's checking out who's here. I shed my jacket quickly, revealing my off-the-shoulder soft cream sweater.

Jameson's gaze strays briefly to my exposed shoulder, then he looks away, toward the ice. Eye contact must be tough when he's trying to keep a secret.

The game begins, and I focus on the action during the first period while mentally ticking off the arrangements I'd managed in one mere day. Like that slim videographer in the plaid beret weaving his way through the fans during the game breaks, asking them to share favorite memories of games in this arena, which are broadcast on the Jumbotron for all twenty thousand attendees to see.

I told Odin I'd help plan a special date for him and his wife if he'd stick near me during the upcoming fox toss when I think Jameson is most likely to ask the question.

And there's the curly-haired usher, Selena. I set up a hotspot on her phone once upon a time, and she told me she owes me (she doesn't), so she was happy to help. She'll have a bottle of Veuve Clicquot chilled to the perfect temperature and ready for her to bring over at my signal—a double tuck of my hair.

Then a row away is Savannah, the backup photographer I hired in case Jameson didn't think of it. What if he doesn't know I've always wanted a fun, frothy proposal, or that I'd want pics of every moment?

I stop myself from scanning the seats for photographers Jameson might have hired. It's best I focus on what I *can* control.

And I've prepared for everything.

I settle in for the rest of the game, trying to contain my excitement as the clock winds down to the second intermission. Finally, the loudspeaker warbles in the arena. "And now..." the announcer booms from the rink, "your Golden State Foxes are coming back to the ice a little early. Get ready to toss your stuffed foxes onto the ice as your home team collects them to donate to the local children's hospital."

The hockey stars fly through the tunnel in their purple and white jerseys, sticks in hand. The fans go wild, popping up in their seats to chuck their tawny stuffies over the glass and onto the rink.

The guys skate around, scooping them up with their gloves or sticks. I glance at the clock. The fox toss spans the final two minutes of the intermission—I planned the event. There are ninety seconds left. Plenty of time for Jameson to ask me to be his.

He rubs his palms along the denim on his thighs.

C'mon. You can do it, sweetie.

He reaches into his pocket.

My throat catches.

There's that tiny jewelry box-shaped bulge, right there.

Yes!

It's happening. And all I have to do is give the sign to kick off my embellishments. I tuck my chestnut strands over both ears as the music grows louder, the crowd turns wilder, and foxes fly over my head and onto the ice.

I glimpse Selena's curls as she carries a bucket of the best bubbly, then Odin in his beret, slinking down the row with his camera and mic, and Savannah, ready for the backup stills.

"So, Remy," Jameson begins, as he drags that box from his pocket. He curls his palm around it, and I can barely stand how fast my pulse is beating.

"Yes?" I ask, all my attention fixed on him. My cells are buzzing.

He reaches for my hand with his free one. "I wanted to let you know that I think you're really *great*," he says.

"So are you."

"And since you love this place so much, I want to ask you a question while we're here."

His words echo throughout the arena. Odin must have alerted the control room to switch to his camera feed and mic. We're live on the Jumbotron, like I'd planned.

"Ask me anything," I say to Jameson, but for the entire arena to see. I bet he'll be thrilled I engineered this. It'll be so good for his brewery, and he loves his little business like it's his pet.

Glancing at the screen where we're twenty feet tall, he

swallows roughly, then speaks again. "Will you still be friends with me?"

Wait. What? I choke back my half-formed answer to the question he *hadn't* asked. "Friends?"

"Yes. Will you consciously uncouple with me?"

He opens the Made by Fable box. But inside is not a diamond ring, like the designer makes. There's only a friendship bracelet, cheap and plastic, and it says *Friends Forever* on it.

My throat tightens. On the massive screen above the ice, twenty-thousand Foxes fans watch me struggle to breathe.

This is not a proposal. This is a Jumbotron dump.

2

MY FUN SIDE

LAKE

I rarely pay attention to the Jumbotron. But as I'm skating casually across the ice, scooping up another stuffed fox, something on the screen snags my interest.

I'm sure I've seen the guy around the arena. Right now, though, he's triple the size he should be and annoyingly earnest as he says to a girl not-quite on screen, "I can see it. You and me, hanging out, talking about our future partners."

What the fuck? Is some douchenozzle let's-be-friends-ing his girlfriend for everyone to see?

I drop a couple of foxes into a big laundry cart on the ice, then stop because...I know him. He's that jackass who works at the bar here and has somehow managed to date Remy, even though he doesn't deserve to lick her boots. And—fuck—that's her sharing the screen.

Remy, the chestnut-haired beauty with the upbeat smile and the snappy comebacks whenever I grouse about some event she asks us to do. Remy, my little sister's good friend. Remy, with the lone tear slipping down her shocked face.

Is the director in the control room ever going to cut to one of the other cameras for the Jumbotron? And why doesn't this guy on screen have the common sense to shut the fuck up?

"You could help me set up my Date Night profile," the fuckface continues with a too-sincere smile.

I bellow toward the control room, "Cut that off."

But the horror flick keeps playing as my new mortal enemy says, in all his pixelated gigantic assholery, "And I could help you set up yours."

Remy's lips part, and devastation rains down her pretty cheeks, just as a curly-haired woman arrives at her row with a bottle of champagne.

"Thanks, Selena, but—" Remy starts, and my god, she's thanking the usher while her heart's being broken.

This guy never deserved her.

There has to be another way to get the control room's attention off her.

I drop a stuffed fox onto the ice in front of me, swing my stick back, and launch that baby high into the stands. A few people in the crowd cheer as I make a game of this, and one of the camera guys on the ice to capture video for the Jumbotron feed swings his lens my way. Launching another fox, then another, I do what I despise—make myself the center of attention for anything other than the game itself.

"Here's your feel-good news clip moment," I growl.

Apparently, whacking a fox like it's a puck does the job because the impromptu demonstration of my stick skills replaces the douchebag's debacle on the overhead screen.

I send one more stuffed fox sailing into the stands for good measure.

Crisis averted, but only for now. The stuffed foxes are carted off the rink, and while we line up for the face-off, I steal a glance at the second row.

She's gone.

There are two empty chairs, and not a bottle of champagne in sight.

I wish there were something I could do for her. For now, I dig in and channel my rage toward the opposing team. The instant the puck is free, I snag it, chasing it down the ice.

A D-man slams into me, or tries to, but I shove him away. Nothing is going to stop me now.

This puck is mine, and when I spot an opening, I sneak it past the goalie and score my second goal of the night. Another point to pad the total.

But even though we win, I'm not happy.

I can't stop thinking about what happened to Remy. There's nothing worse than people assuming they know you from what they've seen of you in public.

* * *

In the tunnel, Miller yanks off his goalie helmet. "What the fuck was that?"

"I know, right?" I shake my head as we trudge off the ice. "What a dick."

That hardly covers it. If there's an insult strong enough for that prick, I don't know it. I need to spend serious time with a thesaurus—when I'm a little less angry.

Miller blinks, shoving a hand through his sweaty hair. "No, I meant—you were, ya know, fun and shit?"

I shoot him a look. "That's what you noticed?"

But maybe it's good he's not focused on the breakup. Miller has eagle eyes, though it's mostly for what's happening on the ice. And *I* was happening on the ice.

"It's nothing. We don't need to talk about it."

"But I kind of think we do, because it's like you just peeled off a brand-new layer of the Lake onion that we didn't even know existed," he says.

"Nobody needs to know about my layers," I warn Miller.

"Then you shouldn't have been so fun in front of the whole arena."

"I was *not* fun."

"But you were, Lake Onion. You were." He flashes a smile before he turns into the locker room.

But at least my fun side distracted him from what happened to my sister's friend.

The whole time I'm untying my skates and shucking my shoulder pads at my stall, I think about how Remy must feel right now. Hurt, heartbroken, ashamed. I can't believe some guy would be lucky enough to date her and then be dumb enough to let her go.

As I'm forced to talk to the media—where I give one-word answers that definitely don't show my *fun side*—I'm wondering what Remy's doing now. Is she curled up on her couch alone? Drowning her sorrows with friends? Torching the jackass's things? That thought brings a sinister smile to my face.

But as I walk back to the locker room, post-media scrum, I spot a brunette in a Golden State Foxes ball cap and hoodie at the end of the corridor, head down as she counts a basket full of stuffed animals.

She's...working.

That's just not right.

I march right over to her. When she looks up, she squares her shoulders and adopts a smile, but her face is paler than before, like she's washed off her makeup or something. Because that fucknozzle made her cry.

"Do you need a tissue?" I don't have one, but I'll find one.

But it's like she didn't hear me. She just turns up the

wattage on her grin. "Hey, I didn't know you were going to show off your stick skills tonight."

Hmm. Didn't expect a peppy response. "I didn't either." I narrow my eyes, trying to figure out how she's really doing. "Are you okay?"

"Of course." She pushes up the brim of the hat as if to show that she's absolutely, definitely, totally fine. "Also, thank you—I'm so grateful. You were very helpful with your attention stealing."

I call bullshit on her "fine" act. "You sure you're okay?"

"Of course. I'm just sorry that you had to deal with that. I feel bad that my whole situation ruined the fox toss for you."

That's a deflection if I ever saw one. "I'm all good. I was asking about you."

She waves a hand, like she can dismiss the whole night. "It might have been worse if you hadn't stepped in." Her tone is bright, with the no-big-deal-ness of, say, getting the wrong order at a coffee shop. "The Jumbotron operator probably didn't realize what was happening. I guess it seemed like a real—"

She can't utter the last word, but I can do the math—one ring box plus a Jumbotron screening equals proposal. Instead of finishing the sentence, she looks down at the basket full of stuffies. "I should go home," she whispers.

Her quiet voice twists something in my cold heart. I can't fix the night for her. But I can offer some small crumb of help. "Do you need a ride?"

The way I want her to say yes is a little ridiculous. Or, really, a lot.

3

HIS STICK SKILLS

REMY

Do I need a ride?

Such a simple, practical question. The same one my friends asked when they texted post-Jumbotron Dump. Did I need a place to crash, someone to hang out with, burn effigies with, binge noodles with—anything?

I couldn't face them, so I said I was fine.

I can't seem to admit to anyone that tonight is all my fault. That I should have done a lot of things differently after I found that jewelry box. It's extra embarrassing since I'm building a burgeoning career as a romance designer-slash-dating coach where I plan swoony romantic moments starring you and your beloved, not catastrophes starring me.

A fresh wave of tears pricks the backs of my eyes as I consider the offer from Lake. Jameson picked me up. Jameson drove me over here. Jameson didn't even ask how I was getting home after he popped the *will you still be friends with me* question.

Yes, I definitely need a ride, but I don't want to inconvenience my friend's brother, let alone a high-profile player on the team I work for. "Thank you for the offer. I'll just grab a Lyft."

His ice-blue eyes are no longer cold, but fiery, forged with determination. "Let me drive you."

I shake my head. "You really don't have to." He must have a hero complex.

A clatter from down the hall draws my attention. A reminder we're not alone.

Andre, the equipment manager, lugs some sticks and shoulder pads into the equipment room. He's a middle-aged gentleman with deep brown skin, the lines around his mouth creased from decades of smiles. I give him a wave, and he waves back.

One of the centers exits the locker room, checking his watch as he leaves. Like he's looking out for my privacy, Lake reaches for my elbow and guides me a few feet away, around the corner. My elbow is warm from his touch, and when he lets go, I miss the heat.

"Look," he says, "I know you can get a Lyft, but I don't want you going outside, waiting for a ride in front of everyone, with people asking you questions. You shouldn't have to deal with that right now."

I can picture the scene. It sounds so awful, my throat tightens. "Clementine would probably kill you if you didn't drive me."

He scoffs. "That's not why I'm offering. No—make that *insisting*."

I guess it wouldn't be asking too much...and he does seem to be pretty determined. "I need to go put these stuffies in a storage room for tomorrow's pickup. Can I have ten minutes?"

Lake gestures to his athletic shirt, his gym shorts, his slides. His dark, messy, still-sweaty hair hits his jawline, giving him a broody rock star vibe. "Good. I need time to shower."

Oh. Right. Of course. "Yes, shower. A shower's good."

His full lips quirk up the slightest bit. "A shower is very, *very* good."

"It is," I say, distracted in a way I didn't see coming.

The hockey star points to the stairwell door about twenty feet away. "I'll be waiting for you in ten. Right here."

"You can shower and get dressed in ten minutes?"

He laughs once. "I can."

"I'll be here. After your very good shower," I quip, mostly so he knows I'm not a total emotional wreck.

Even though I absolutely am.

"See you soon," he says, then waits for me to walk away first.

It's like having a bodyguard in the form of your friend's grumpy, strapping pro-athlete brother.

I push the cart of stuffies down the hall, still incognito-ish in the hoodie from my cubicle and the hat I grabbed from the swag shelf in the hope no one would notice me.

But Lake did, and he wants to help.

A hockey player I work with is kinder to me than the guy I'd thought wanted to marry me.

It's official—I have the world's worst romantic instincts.

4

OFFICIALLY TERRIBLE

LAKE

I fiddle with the console in my car, trying to find the right music for this moment. Do I blast a breakup tune? Some kind of your-boyfriend-is-a-dick song?

Correction: ex-boyfriend.

I fight off a stupid smile. Is it terrible that I'm glad my sister's clever, pretty, upbeat friend is suddenly single? But I push those thoughts out of my head, just like I've done with all the other Remy-centric thoughts that have landed in my head for the last year.

I find a promising playlist—something that sounds a little like the Arctic Monkeys and a lot like the kind of music you'd play after a really shitty day.

"Good?"

Remy nods from the passenger seat, clutching a bottle of champagne against her chest.

"What's your address?"

"I'll do it." She leans closer to punch the address into the car's GPS, and I catch a hint of her shampoo. Something floral and clean, and far too tempting.

I steal another hit of it.

When she's done inputting the address, she sits back and gives a small, apologetic smile. "It's not too far away."

"It's no problem." I'd drive her to the other side of the country if she needed me to.

"Thanks again."

She doesn't have to keep thanking me, but I don't want to correct her post-breakup etiquette. Or any etiquette. I pull out of the players' lot, nodding goodnight to Carmine at the security kiosk.

Remy looks away, purposefully, that hat still pulled low. But the second we pull out of the arena lot, she tugs off the cap, then runs her hands through her lush hair, combing out those gorgeous brunette locks.

"I'm not a hat person," she admits, like it's about more than the accessory.

I cruise onto the Embarcadero, the stars in the sky reflecting in the shimmering waters of the bay.

"What's the story behind this hat hatred of yours?" I ask.

As I sail past Fisherman's Wharf, still teeming with tourists, a tease of a real smile appears on her face. It's the best thing I've seen all night—better, even, than a goal. "Don't laugh when I tell you," she says.

"I won't laugh." It also feels important, this assurance.

"You promise?"

"Swear."

She exhales heavily. "They feel like they're squeezing my head."

I could point out *You can adjust a ball cap, you know*.

But she doesn't need a hat lesson. Feels like what she needs is maybe permission to be herself. I glance at her, holding her gaze for a short beat before I return my attention to the road. "You never need to wear a hat with me, Remy."

She's quiet at first, then says, "Thanks, Lake. And it's ironic, isn't it? Since my last name is Hatmaker."

I bark out a laugh as I slow at a red light. "I don't know how I missed that."

"My last name? Understandable. You don't have to remember it."

Oh, I knew her last name. And more details about her than I *should* know. "No, about Remy Hatmaker's hatred of hats."

She leans her head back against the headrest, then sighs. When the light turns and I tap the pedal of my electric car, she adds in a tone full of regret, "I can't believe everyone saw that."

I won't lie and say that no one noticed what went down on the Jumbotron. All I tell her is, "Yeah, it really sucks."

"It does," she says, slumping lower in the seat.

I drum my fingers on the steering wheel, tempted to keep up the convo and ask: *Did you actually want to marry that trying-too-hard asshat?*

Jameson always seemed like he was putting on a show when I walked past his craft beer stand on the concourse. Like everything was about being your cool brewmaster bud—from the vest, to the undercut, to the way he talked about *mindful brewing.*

Like that's even a thing.

I keep my mouth shut though. The GPS tells me to turn left, so I head into the Marina District, and my forearms tighten when the cool, modulated voice says we're less than half a mile from our destination. I don't want to say goodnight to her.

As I maneuver through traffic, she blows out another breath. "I shouldn't have..." she mutters, then purses her lips.

"Shouldn't have what?"

She rolls her lips together as if sealing in her emotions.

She looks like the bottle of Veuve Clicquot she's clutching, like she's ready to bubble over. Like she wants to.

"It'll stay between us," I add. Maybe she needs someone to confide in who's not a friend, not a family member—just some dude she works with occasionally.

Sometimes it's easier with people who don't know us, who haven't seen all our flaws, who aren't aware of all our mistakes.

We roll along a busy block where festive music plays from a tapas bar. When she shifts her gaze to me, her brown eyes are wide, swimming with remorse. "None of it had to happen this way tonight."

"What do you mean?"

She closes her eyes and covers her mouth like she's warring with herself to keep the rest locked up tight. After a few seconds of struggle, she drops her hand and blurts out: "I thought he was going to propose to me. Last night I found a little jewelry box in his sweatshirt. I figured it would be during our date, since our one-year anniversary is coming up, and the game was important. I hustled to arrange things at the arena. A big, fun mood. A declaration. On the Jumbotron, so everyone could see. I had a videographer lined up. I ordered the best champagne. I planned the elaborate, romantic moment I'd always imagined, and it went completely wrong. And it's all my fault."

There's so much to unpack in that confession, but we've reached her place. I slide into a spot out front, turn off the car, then shift in the seat to face her. "Nothing that happened tonight was your fault."

Remy just stares ahead through the windshield into the dark city night.

I set a hand on her knee, squeezing. I shouldn't, but I don't always listen to good sense. "He could have stopped once he knew you were broadcasting. And he fucking knew. You don't hear your voice reverberate and *not* know." Her brow furrows, like she's chewing on that thought, and after a moment, I add another. "You set it up, but you acted on a big fucking clue, and you were hoping for something. But he didn't stop when he should have, and that's just wrong. Fuck him. That guy is just a dick."

At last, she turns to face me, as a soft smile shifts her lips. "Thanks, Lake."

I let go of her knee. "I'll walk you to the door."

It's not a question. I get out of the car, walk around to her side, and swing open the door. Remy pops up, still holding the champagne bottle, with her hat and a friendship bracelet hanging around its neck.

I want to grab that bracelet, sneak over to Jameson's stupid beer stand, and shove it up one of the taps, far enough to fuck up his business. For now, I walk Remy toward the front door of an awfully nice Scandinavian minimalist-style place. She nods to the side of the townhome, though, and I follow her to a little porch leading to a guest house.

When she reaches the stoop, she looks up at me. "Thank you again. I really did need that. And I owe you."

She owes me nothing, but if there's one thing I'm good at, it's spotting opportunities. "Promise me something, then."

She tilts her head, her pretty eyes brimming with hopeful curiosity. "That I'll have a fantastic time hanging out with my plants while I avoid the world the next few days?"

"That. But also this. Promise me you're not going to take him up on that offer to make a dating profile."

"Are you offering to help me set one up?"

You're looking at your profile match, sweetheart. That's what I want to say, but I'm no good at romance. Instead I say, "When you're ready to set up your profile, call me."

She rolls her eyes. "Your phone will ring in a couple of years."

This makes me unreasonably happy. I tuck my finger under her chin and say, "Chin up, Remy."

"Chin up," she repeats, like it's the night's mantra.

I let go of her. As I lower my arm, I rub my thumb across the pad of my finger where I touched her. It's...sparking.

Hell, I am too.

She goes to tap a code on a keypad but stops after one button, then spins back, holding up and waggling the bottle. "Do you want this? I don't think I'm going to drink it—not tonight, at least."

"Save it. Crack it open when you're officially over that jackass who never deserved you."

"Deal." She pauses, brow knit, then her lips curve with some amusement. "How did you get a deal *and* a promise out of me?"

I flash a confident grin. "I'm just that good."

"Evidently."

As I walk away, I catch a widening smile, which stays with me down the steps and back to my car. The image tags along as I drive through the fog of late-night San Francisco, across the Golden Gate Bridge, and through the hills of Sausalito, until I reach my quiet home in Cozy Valley, away from all the madness of the city and all the mistakes I made there once upon a time.

* * *

Two days later, passing drills have my thighs screaming in the best of ways, and I skate behind the net, taking an easy lap. Riggs, our left winger, skates behind me.

"I hear you're an onion," he says dryly.

I snap my accusing gaze to Miller, who's guarding the net. "And you're a rat."

Miller just shrugs, shooting me a smile from behind his face mask. "I'm a rat. You're an onion. It's all good."

"We can call you Lake Onion and Miller Rat," Riggs shouts, racing ahead of me.

I catch up easily. "And I'll call you...Tortoise," I say, flying past him. Helps being the fastest guy on the team.

That speed helps us win that night's game, but even I'm not fast enough to evade the head of PR. After the W, he finds me unlacing my skates in front of my stall. With his tablet in hand and perma-grin locked in, Daniel launches his request with some butter: "Lake, of the two clutch goals. Can you talk to the media?"

Riggs barks out a laugh as he chucks his jersey into the laundry bin. "Lake? Talk to the press? More like grunt."

He's not wrong. Not usually. "I talked to them the other night," I point out.

"Two goals, my man. Two goals," Daniel emphasizes, staring at me with dark eyes.

"But, really," I bargain, "don't those goals speak for themselves?"

Daniel laughs lightly, then turns serious. "Nonetheless, you had the most impressive game."

Joking aside, I hate talking at these after-game interviews, but I'll be fined if I refuse. Reluctantly, I pull on an athletic shirt and trudge out of the locker room. Immediately, I scan the halls for Remy. I don't see her chestnut hair, her clever smile. How the hell is she doing? Is she okay?

I wish I knew.

In the media room, I weave past a table of snacks and a crowd of podcasters, bloggers, and sports reporters, then park myself behind the table on the dais at the front of the packed room.

Daniel announces, "We have Lake Axelrod for a couple of minutes," and before the final word is out, a baby-faced sports reporter in the front row shouts, "Why were you hitting stuffed foxes into the stands the other night? Was that a commentary on the Jumbotron Dump?"

Holy shit. It has a name? "No," I bite out.

"'No' to it being a commentary, or 'no' to it being about the Jumbotron Dump?"

For fuck's sake. "Why are we talking about something that happened two nights ago?"

"Because it's still news," he says earnestly. "The video has more than two million views."

It's like someone punched me in the kidneys. I guess that's a clue as to how Remy must be doing—awful.

Daniel clears his throat. "If you want to ask Lake about tonight's game, that's fine. Let's focus on the present."

Nice redirect. Answering dumb questions about the stuffie slap shots won't help Remy. People will talk about the Jumbotron incident, whether I comment or not.

If only I could distract them.

While answering perfunctory questions about tonight's game, I scan the room for inspiration. Then, yup, I've got it.

I wrap up my time, stand, and give a wave, something I never do. I say a polite goodbye as I leave the dais. Also out of character. Keeps their focus on me. As I pass the snack table, I grab a handful of Goldfish crackers, toss one high into the air, and dart out my tongue to catch it. Then another, then another. By the time I've reached the door, I've caught ten in a row.

I look back at the media gaggle, and they're all recording me. "To answer your question about the other night," I say, from the doorway, "I guess I just wanted to show off my fun side."

Then I exit. Maybe it won't go viral, but maybe it'll take some heat off of Remy, and she won't have to deal with more blowback.

But in case she does, I want to make her day a little better. On the way home, I duck into a shop and send a little something to her place, along with a handwritten note.

Hope this is keeping you in good company now.

5

WELCOME TO MY SISTER'S TED TALK

REMY

Caroline yanks a knife from the wooden block in my kitchen and holds it up to the window, where the mid-morning sun glints across the sharp blade. She stares at it with a cool green gaze that never suffers fools.

But, with a frustrated sigh, she puts it back. "He's not worth the waste of a good knife."

"Plus, you hate messes." I knock back another gulp of chai latte.

A tip of her head acknowledges my point. My sister's morning blowout is still gloriously intact after hosting her streaming lifestyle show, hitting the gym, and making a chai—which she'd brought to me as a lubricant for the *conversation we need to have,* as her text this morning put it. I've been bracing for the worst.

In the two weeks since the Jumbotron Dump, I've become known online as the Friendship Bracelet Girl. Because why have one name for your most embarrassing moment when the Internet can give you two?

That first weekend, I reorganized my closet here in the guest house where I live, just to the side of my sister's townhome. I devoured a few dark chocolate bars from my favorite shop (thanks to Mom's sympathy gift) and fixed a loose hinge on the closet door, touched up some paint in the kitchen, and watered the succulent Lake sent me. A lovely, thoughtful surprise. It's a Ruby Glow, rubbery green with red edges, and it fits my windowsill collection nicely.

Next, I wrote a note to my future self—my therapist would be proud—reminding myself not to fall for guys who just want to be friends.

Because that's kind of all Jameson and I were—companions. I wanted us to work so damn badly that I was holding us together with details and the duct tape of my own wishes, missing signs that seem obvious looking back.

Frowning, I finish the latte and set down the mug. As if she's been waiting for that, Caroline marches over to me, meets my gaze, and says, "It's time to talk." Her Machiavellian eyes flicker with strategy. "You should know, I have no problem kicking Jameson out of the wedding party before the festivities kick off."

"Why?"

"Because he broke your heart. Therefore, I hate him."

I laugh, but her expression remains serious. Also, I'm not so sure my heart's broken, per se. It's embarrassed, like the rest of me. "Caroline, you don't have to do that. He's best friends with Parker. You guys set us up."

"I know. And it seemed so perfect with him working at the arena and all," she says, regret in her tone. But it's replaced quickly with vindication. "And that's why I will boot him. I'll just tell Parker it's done, and he'll have to accept that."

But her wedding's in a month. I don't want my future brother-in-law scrambling to replace his best man on my account. That would make *me* the problem. I shudder at the thought. "Don't kick him out," I say, adding a smile to sell just how fine I am. "I'm completely fine with him being there."

"Good," she says with a decisive nod. "I'm glad *for you.* But also, I want everything to go smoothly since my brand manager just finalized the deal with Fresh Face. Not only do they want to sponsor the show, they want to sponsor all my pre-wedding events as long as I use their makeup and so does the bridal party."

I beam, like the sun. "That's terrific. I love their makeup and have been using it forever," I say, genuinely happy for her.

"And you have the dewy complexion to show for it," she says, and fine—she's not wrong. My skincare routine is top-notch. "Anyway, they're sponsoring all of the content I'm doing about the wedding for the show and of course for my socials. And they want you to do a few behind-the-scenes videos as the maid of honor, like the look you'll wear when we finalize the dress, or the perfect makeup for a bridesmaids' brunch, or the shower—that sort of thing. It might take the attention off *your situation*."

"I'm in," I say. "But it's because I want to help you."

"Great. That's why I've decided we need a preemptive strike."

I furrow my brow. "What's that?"

"You'll need a date for my wedding."

I recoil. I can't imagine anything I want less than a date. "Um, no."

"I get it. Dating sucks. But Jameson's single now, and my spies are telling me he's set up his dating profile. My friends have spotted him on the apps. His headline is...wait for it... *Hoptimistic About Finding My Match.*"

We mime gagging at the same time.

"That's awful," I say.

"Isn't it? And he goes on to say *Let's brew something special together.*"

"He can brew a batch of bullshit."

She stares at me with battle-ready eyes. "Do you see my point now? There's a very good chance he might bring someone else to the wedding. If your ex is at the wedding with a plus-one, you'll have to be there with someone too, otherwise it'll look like you aren't moving on."

"It's been two weeks. Am I supposed to have moved on? I was thinking I'd take maybe a couple of years to regroup. Figure out what went wrong. Learn from it."

"You don't need to sit on the sidelines and lick your wounds." Caroline paces around the island; she only needs a headset mic, and she could be presenting a TED Talk. "You need to get back out there and move the hell on like the fabulous babe you are." She pauses, levels me with a sharp stare. "And, let's be real, you don't want to be known as the romance planner who got dumped on the Jumbotron."

Or worse—the romance planner who screwed up her own Jumbotron proposal. "Valid point," I admit. Since it's not like the clients are lining up right now to hire someone who sucks at relationships.

I'm also not entirely in the mood to create jigsaw puzzle proposals or romantic movie scene reenactments for proposals, engagement parties, or big anniversary dates.

Imagine that.

But I'll need to get my mojo back soon. I'll need to move forward in my business, not to linger on what happened on the big screen. "You want me to change the narrative."

"Exactly. And what better way to show Jameson and everyone else that you're not hurt than by having a hot guy on your arm? You need a top-notch plus-one. And I already have an idea for your wedding date."

I give her my *I'm waiting* face.

My sister gives me her *I'm eight years older and know better* face. So, basically, her face.

"Okay. Who?" I ask, breaking the silence.

She sweeps a hand toward the new succulent. "The guy who gave you the plant to check in on how you were doing."

I blink. "You can't be serious?"

There's no hint of laughter in her eyes. "Do I look like I'm joking?"

"There's nothing in it for Lake. He's a superstar athlete."

A devilish grin shifts her lips. "A superstar athlete who helped you out of a jam."

"That doesn't mean he wants to be my wedding date."

"Please," she says, wearing confidence like it's her perfume. "You really think he did that whole thing because he's *not* into you?"

"I think he did it because he felt sorry for me. I work with him, and he's also Clem's brother."

She smiles again, without showing any teeth. "Then leverage the sympathy."

"Is that what you would tell your viewers?"

"No," she says, calm as a rattlesnake before a strike. "But this is what you need to do to live your best life. I love you madly and want you to move on. Also, I need this wedding to go off without a hitch. I have more than a hundred people working on my show, and I don't want anything to go wrong. I don't want Jameson to draw too much attention by showing up with a date. And I don't want Fresh Face worried about how it all might go down. It's a win–win. Especially since you get to look terrific, rebuild your business, and have a hot athlete on your arm as you do it."

Translation: *do it.*

I picture the broody, intense hockey star with the chiseled

jaw and cool eyes that never stray when he talks to you. The team's been on a long road trip, so I haven't seen him since that Friday night. But I vividly remember him here on the porch, under the midnight stars, with that cocky grin, saying, "I'm just that good."

What happens if he says no to being my plus-one? It would be embarrassing for a minute, but we don't spend that much time together at work.

But what happens if he says yes?

My heartbeat does something strange. Something wild it hasn't done in a couple of weeks. It speeds up.

"I'll ask him," I say.

"Do it tomorrow," Caroline says. "We have a picnic coming up for the wedding party. Fresh Face wants to show off outdoor makeup. I want to show off how well everything's going, including how well you're doing."

She leaves, taking the mug—and presumably, the rest of the sympathy—with her.

* * *

The next thing I do is write a list of possible outcomes in my Notes, Complaints, and Existential Crises notebook, then call an emergency meeting of my girlfriends, requesting their presence for Project Plus-One.

Mabel's the first to respond.

Mabel: Get your sweet ass up to Cozy Valley because for this type of meeting I need to ply you all with cake.

Clementine works down the street from Mabel's bakery, so she's game.

> Clem: I love it when you make things easy for me.

I touch up my makeup, toss on a light red cardigan, and hustle to the bus stop where I catch the next one out of town. Less than an hour later, I hop off the bus in Cozy Valley across from The Cheesery on Main Street, with its chalkboard sign featuring a drawing of Cupid shooting a heart through a block of Gouda. The air is crisp in mid-February but it's not too cold. As I turn onto Mabel's block, my gaze strays briefly down the street and beyond into the hills of this quirky, artsy small town.

Lake lives here on his family's equine therapy ranch that their older brother runs. Is he tending to a horse, or doing ranch stuff right now? The team just returned last night from their road trip, so it's possible.

But I push him out of my mind as much as I can. Best to focus on my mission.

I pick up the pace, marching toward the pink brick bakery with the Afternoon Delight sign on the garage windows of the former fire station.

Clementine's already inside, her blonde hair cinched in a long ponytail and she's laughing at something with Mabel. Heart-shaped cookies fill the display case, alongside red, white, and pink cakes for the holiday. My baker friend gestures for me to join them at the counter, sliding a red sugar cookie my way in the shape of a heart.

"Sweets help everything make sense," she declares.

"Truer words," Clementine puts in. "Now, tell us the ten million iterations you've outlined for this plus-one wedding project."

And all of them include your brother.

I take a bite, then lay out the why and the what of Caroline's directive, before I turn to Clementine. "And she wants me to ask Lake to be my plus-one," I say, with an apologetic smile.

She snorts. "Really? That's weird."

"It is?"

"I mean, he's weird. Brothers are weird," she says with a shudder.

"Is it weird that she wants me to ask *him* though?"

Clementine points at me. "No, it's weird that you're looking all apologetic. It doesn't bother me if you ask him."

My shoulders relax. "Oh, good."

She tilts her head. "Did you really think I'd be all *don't go after my brother*?"

"No. But also, I don't trust my judgment anymore," I admit.

"Don't let your asshole ex get you down," Mabel huffs. "Jameson's picture's going up on a wall of exes, and we can throw darts at it."

Clementine gives a sympathetic smile. "I will hit the bull's-eye so hard every day. Also, I kind of can't believe I'm saying this, but I agree with your sister's instinct. Lake would be a good plus-one since he doesn't talk that much. He'd just show up and growl."

"I don't mind a good growl from Corbin," Mabel puts in, with the secret smile of a happily coupled-up woman who gets good growl on the regular from her man.

"We know," Clementine and I tell her.

"And you do need a plus-one," Clementine adds, pointing

at me. "You can't show up to a high-profile wedding without one."

I return to the page in my notebook where I've listed potential opportunities to ask him. "I'll do it tomorrow before the game."

Mabel reaches into the display case, grabs a vanilla cupcake with pink frosting, and puts it in a box. "Give him this. It's his favorite."

Clementine beams proudly at Mabel. "Oh dude, good call. He loves free food."

I laugh. "Liking free food is so...*not weird*."

But I file that nugget away, thank them, then leave. Their support is the fuel I need to march into work tomorrow and execute Project Plus-One.

6

CUPCAKE PAYMENT

LAKE

After a long road trip, I'm more eager than I usually am to get to work. Because I want to get on my skates? Sure, I always want that. But maybe I'll finally run into Remy again. Haven't seen her since that night. Haven't heard from her since the plant delivery when she sent me a thank you text.

I grab my phone from the kitchen counter and swing into the living room to find my dad where I almost always find him—at the puzzle table.

"Do you need anything before I go down to the city? I've got time if you want to go into town and get a sandwich or something," I say, asking gently as I pose the same question my brother and sister ask him nearly every day too.

Sliding his reading glasses down his nose, he scrunches his brow, like he's really considering it. I wish he *were* considering leaving the house. But then he shakes his head.

"I've got one thousand problems, and not one of them is getting a sandwich," he says, pushing up the glasses and sorting through a pile of pieces in the corner of his puzzle table. "Gavin and Mira picked up the groceries for me."

"Let me know if there's anything else you need." I'm half

tempted to say we could go back to that puzzle store in the city, but there's no point.

Maybe he even knows it since he whips off his glasses, and a smile spreads across his weathered face. "Don't worry about me, kid. Just get to work. You're having a great season. I'll be watching the game tonight."

My heart twists. It'd be selfish of me to say *I wish you could watch it in person*. I pat his shoulder. "I'll see you during warmups," I say, then tap my left shoulder twice on my midnight blue suit jacket. It's the sign I always flash to the broadcast booth, but really to him.

He taps his shoulder, too, mirroring me.

I take off, heading through the front door and outside the home, sprawling on several acres at the edge of Cozy Valley. I have an apartment in the city too—sometimes it's just easier to crash there after games. But I'm here as much as I can to help with Big Steps Ranch. It was my dad's passion—he's a retired physical therapist, and he specialized in equine therapy and adaptive riding. My brother and his wife—also therapists—do the hard work of running it. I help out sometimes with the bird sanctuary on the edge of the property, though mostly I help by making sure we have enough funds to run it when times are tough.

I hop into my car, then swing by Miller's house a few miles away to pick him up. "Picture this," he says, the second he slides in. "A giga-coaster."

He chats the whole way about a magazine story he listened to about extreme experiences at theme parks, and the race now to unleash scarier and steeper and faster roller coasters. I don't have to say much, since Miller can hold a lot of conversations solo.

I just offer a word here or there as my thoughts drift to

Remy. Will she be working today? Did that prick and a half ask her to make his dating profile?

I stew on that till we reach the arena. As we're heading down the corridor toward the locker room, Miller regales me with a tale of an *exa-coaster* that's taller than the Statue of Liberty when my phone buzzes.

Her name flashes on the screen. Heat shoots down my spine. *So annoying.*

Remy: Hi!! Do you have a few minutes to talk before you start warmups? I have an idea I'd love to run past you. Maybe we could meet by the plant wall on the concourse? I have something for you too!

The plant wall—a section of the concourse covered in foliage native to Northern California—is out of the way. Which tells me this idea of hers probably doesn't involve a promo event. Is it about the dating profile? The fuck it better not be. She should just, I don't know, not ever date again. Or date me.

Except...no. She's too good, too kind, too upbeat.

I'd ruin her.

"Catch up with you in a minute," I mutter to Miller, but he's already joined up with Riggs as they turn into the locker room, telling him about the one-hundred-twenty-miles-per-hour speeds on the coaster.

I hustle down the corridor as I try to think of a response that doesn't reveal I'm scheming to halt her access to all dating apps. Is that possible?

Not without being a morally gray dickhead.

If the shoe fits.

I settle on a safer reply.

Lake: As long as it doesn't involve me doing a promo video about the plants.

Remy: What do you have against plants?

Lake: Nothing. It's the videos I don't like.

I bound up the stairwell to the concourse level, where vendors and concession stand staff are prepping for the game.

Maybe I'll tell her we can meet up later to work on her dating profile. That'd buy some time, right? Or, hell, I could even volunteer for some promo thing after all. That would distract her.

But maybe not. She's smarter than that.

The plant wall is on the other side of the arena, so I don't have to pass Jameson's beer stand on the way. That's probably for the best for him, since I'm clenching and unclenching my fists right now. My dress shoes echo on the concrete as I pass monster-sized posters of me and my teammates. Finally, I spot the chestnut-haired beauty standing by some dark green ferns and evergreens.

My pulse spikes.

Remy is stunning, dressed like she usually is on a game day. She wears trim pants that make her legs look impossibly long, and shoes with some kind of strappy little—I don't know —*strap* across the top of her foot. She's holding a pink box, and I think it's from the bakery that my teammate Corbin opened with our general manager's sister.

My mouth waters at the sight of it. And at the sight of her, since Remy's got on some kind of sweater that shows just the tiniest bit of shoulder—she wears that style a lot, and if I kept a gratitude journal, that sweater type would be listed every day.

A rumble works its way up my chest. The things I want to do to her shoulder with my mouth. The ways I want to run my tongue across her pale skin, bite down on her collarbone.

But I try to clear the haze of want from my head. I should not be thinking of her that way. The woman just had her heart broken. She doesn't need a hockey player with a black heart wanting to do bad things to her.

Or any other guy, for that matter.

Like a lane opening up on the ice, the confusion clears, and I've got my strategy. If she asks, I'll tell her it'll take a few weeks. Insist on a bunch of meetings to discuss dating profiles.

Stall.

I'm fucking brilliant.

I fight off a grin when I reach her, cutting to the chase. "What's your proposition? Is it about writing that dating profile?"

"Actually, no."

Hallelujah. "Good," I say before thinking the better of it.

She tilts her head. "Is it? Good?"

"Yup. Studies say it's best not to get back on the apps right away," I say shamelessly. I'm an athlete—we have to improvise.

She arches a pretty brow as her lips curve up. "I had no idea you were so familiar with research on dating apps."

I double down. "All the experts say it's best to avoid them for a good, long while."

"And to avoid dating in general for a good, long while?"

I carefully hedge my bets. "Just apps. On account of their being soul-sucking, mind-numbing and demoralizing."

"Oh. Wow. All three?" she asks, clearly amused, a little challenging.

With good reason. But I'm all in so I cross my arms. "Yep. Experts even suggest going cold turkey on the apps forever."

A small laugh gusts across her lips. "That's really good to know. And for the record, I'm totally not crying in my cereal over him. I'm moving on," she says, bright and upbeat. Don't know if she's just trying to sell it, but either way, that's good news.

"Good. He's not worth your tears or cereal."

"Words to live by," she says, then goes quiet for a beat when her gorgeous chocolate eyes stray to my chest.

Oh, well isn't that a plot twist? She likes what she sees.

Good. Let her enjoy the view.

She must collect her thoughts, since she continues a few seconds later in a professional tone, "About my idea. Now I know you already helped me the other week, and it was amazing what you did. So I hope this isn't too much, but since I promised that I wouldn't lean on Jameson to start a profile, I thought I could request something of you," she says with a bright smile.

I have no clue where she's going with this. But color me intrigued. "Go on."

"My sister's getting married next month. She has a bunch of events leading up to the wedding, and I was supposed to go to them all with Jameson," she says with a wince.

Say no more. "I'll be your date."

She blinks. "You don't even want to hear about it?"

Honestly, I've heard enough but I humor her. "Sure, you can tell me."

"My sister has a show on Webflix called *Live the Life You've Imagined*. It's kind of like an advice show, and she has a sponsor now for all of her wedding content—the event itself, but also a pre-wedding picnic, a shower, a dress fitting, and so on. Since I'm the maid of honor, I'm going to all of that. Jameson will probably be at a lot of those too, since he's the best man."

This wedding sounds like hell.

"Why would anybody want all this shit?" I ask, despite knowing I should keep that thought to myself.

"Some people think it's fun," she says with a sexy little shrug and a smile that slays me. I take it *some people* includes her. This woman seems like the type of person who enjoys everything. Who loves her daily latte, the cute little hummingbird that stops at her feeder—because I bet she has one—and the sun that peeks through the fog.

I stay stoic though. "Well, I'll do it."

She studies me quizzically. "Are you sure you want to do all that?"

I don't want to do any of it. But if it means helping her out and sticking it to her ex, I'm the man. "Yes."

"It's kind of a lot. But it'll help me as I rebuild my side business," she adds, then flips open the pink box and offers it to me. "That's why I wanted to offer you something in exchange."

"Is that the pink confetti flavor?" I ask, a little sheepishly.

"Mabel said it's your favorite."

I grab the box. "It is. Thanks."

"But that's not actually what I wanted to offer you. That's just a little extra. There's something else I want to do for you in exchange for being my plus-one."

I peel off a section of the cupcake wrapper. "What's your offer?"

A night to act out her greatest fantasies? No doubt that Jameson didn't deliver in bed. I'd deliver anything she asked.

She lifts her chin and smiles, those ruby red lips all glossy and kissable. "As you may know, I have a side business where

I plan huge romantic moments for people—proposals, engagement parties, anniversary dates, and just amazing dates in general. Of course, everything went horribly wrong when I attempted my own proposal. But if I haven't scared you away with that mistake, I'd love to plan some dates for you. If you have somebody you'd like to go out with. Free of charge."

She bounces on her toes. I stare at her like she's lost her ever-loving mind. Has she?

She seems to take my silence as a cue to keep going. "Maybe you haven't dated since..."

"Since my wife died," I supply. It's always a little strange to say, since Heather hardly felt like my wife at the end. Not that I can say that to anyone. But my failed marriage—a marriage that was breaking apart—doesn't factor into it.

There's only one reason I don't want Remy to plan a date —she's the first person I've had any feelings for in a while.

But I can tell she doesn't want this plus-one wedding favor to be one-sided.

I contemplate a suitable response as I take a bite of the cupcake. Buoyed by the sweetness of the treat and also of her, I make a spur-of-the-moment decision and execute it like a fast play on the ice. "I can see why you'd want to plan some dates, but what I really think you should do is not take me as your plus-one."

"Oh," she says, her face falling. "Really? I thought..."

I put the cupcake back in the box, close it, and step closer to her. "I don't want to be your plus-one, sweetheart. I want your ex, and everyone else, to think I'm your real date."

She's quiet for a long beat. Eyes flickering. Brow furrowing. "You do?"

That might sound fuck-all pushy, so I amend it. "Fake date."

She tilts her head, a small, curious smile forming. "You're saying you want to fake date me for *all* the wedding events?"

This makes perfect sense to me. A plus-one can be anyone —a friend, a rando, some guy who lives across the country and happens to be in town. But a date? That signals something important.

"What I'm saying is a plus-one is a cop-out. But being your new guy? That says your ex is a dumbass for losing you, and you're moving the hell on like the fucking goddess you are."

Maybe I've said too much with *goddess*, but the way her smile spreads is divine.

"Looks like you just got yourself a fake date then, mister."

I inch closer, tuck my thumb under her chin, like I did the night I walked her to her door. Her breath catches. I slide my thumb gently along her jaw. "See you soon."

"See you," she says, all breathy.

I don't leave yet though. When I let go, I ask, "Do you have a hummingbird feeder?"

She laughs, crinkling her nose. "No. Why?"

"You seem like someone who'd like hummingbirds."

"What gives you that impression?"

I shrug. "Just a feeling," I say, then turn around and take off since I need to hit the ice.

* * *

I finish the last of the pink confetti cupcake as I head into the locker room, like I'm walking on air. I ball up the wrapper, toss it into the trash can, then wing the cardboard box into a recycling bin.

"He shoots, he scores," I brag as I swagger over to my stall.

From in front of his stall, Corbin, our center, gives me the strangest look as he tugs on shoulder pads. "You were at my bakery today?"

"Maybe I was," I say, keeping the cupcake secret as I rip off my tie. The cupcake she got me. Because she fucking asked me to be her plus-one.

"Is that part of your pregame ritual now?" Riggs posits, always inquisitive, always poking holes as he laces up his skates.

I wiggle my eyebrows. "I guess we'll see if it becomes one when I get a hat trick tonight," I say. Then I line up my equipment on the bench in the order I'll put it on. It's the arrangement I've been using lately, and it's working this season, since we've been playing well. "Anyone wanna bet against me?"

"I don't know—is that even allowed, dude? Hate to break it to you, but we're on the same team," Miller says, tugging on his leg pads.

"Everyone owes me dinner if I get a hat trick," I say to the guys.

"How about you just get the fucking hat trick," Corbin says.

"I would hope a hat trick is incentive enough," comes the cool, even-keeled voice of our coach as he strides through the locker room.

I cut the trash talk as Coach Ahmed chats about strategy and how to beat the Boston Blizzards. I listen to every word with the thrill of a secret in my chest.

But soon, it won't be a secret, once we're pretending to be together. Yep, I'll get to spend time with the woman I've had a seriously inconvenient crush on for a while.

I hit the ice for warmups, feeling like I'm flying, stopping only to tap my shoulder for my dad.

Then, it's time to focus solely on the game.

I race down the ice, flanking Corbin as he snags the puck

at the face-off. He sets the pace, slicing it to me, and I race around the back of the net, lasered in on the rink, hunting for an opening and slipping it back to Riggs.

He shoots, but their goalie blocks it.

It's a tight game for the first period, but in the second period, I attack, attack, attack till I finally send that bad boy past the goalie's legs.

The lamp lights, and I punch the air.

We cheer, and when I hop over the bench, I down a swig of water from my bottle, ready to hit the ice again soon with all this energy.

Maybe it's the internal boost that comes from knowing I get to be Remy's "new guy" for the next few weeks. Whatever it is, I feel unleashed.

When the line changes and I'm back out there, Riggs feeds me the puck in a routine pass. I'm already moving, and even with the Boston D-men bearing down on me, my skates eat up the ice. I blow past their defenseman, then line up for a wrist shot. But nope. The goalie will be expecting it. I deke to the right and send a backhand...right through the net.

Yes! Riggs skates over and we high-five—with gloves on.

I skate hard always, but especially tonight. My cells are buzzing. Maybe she's watching. Maybe she's working. Either way, I'm going to play the part of her temporary boyfriend as well as I've scored in tonight's game.

I don't even grumble when she texts me that night with the first set of instructions. The attire for a picnic.

It sounds like hell, and yet I can't fucking wait.

7

UPPING THE ANTE

REMY

"So you're really fake dating my brother? My complicated, owl-loving, superstitious brother?"

Who's also unfairly hot. But I keep that to myself as Clementine and I hunt through sweaters at a stuffed-to-the-gills thrift shop. "Yes." My voice pitches up as I explain how Project Plus-One became Project Fake Date. "It was his idea. I said plus-one, and he said fake dating is better for sticking it to my ex. Are you sure that's okay?"

She meets my gaze across the vintage sweaters. "Like I said, it's fine, but if there's any fake kissing you need to tell me about, bring earmuffs."

I smile, relieved she's good with this escalation. "It's a deal."

"But," Clementine adds, drawing out the one-syllable word as she peers around the shop, checking for eavesdroppers before she whispers, "what are you going to tell everyone else?"

I tilt my head. "About us dating?"

"Yes. You need a story."

Shoot. She's right. I think fast, cycling through options. "Should I say you suggested I go out with him?"

She cringes. "I'd never set you up with my brother. He's far too...*complicated*."

"You think I can't handle a complicated man?"

She frowns, but her expression is full of both compassion and fondness. "No, Remy. I think you deserve a man who adores you. A man who cares. But I also think you deserve a man who isn't so...shut down."

Something aches inside my chest for several seconds. Maybe it's the reality that she's probably right about her brother. "It's all good since it's not like I'm going to real date anyone now," I say as I spot a teal cardigan that looks perfect for my sister's wedding picnic. "All my focus will be on faking it for the wedding. That means we need rules, a plan, and a story."

Once I find an outfit, I do just that—focus. As Clementine returns to Cozy Valley, I return to my place. I may have messed up my last romance, but I've got a chance to do things right in this fake one. Better get my ducks in a row.

I head to the kitchen, and I send Lake a text.

Remy: Apparently we need to establish rules for fake dating. I've got some ideas. Do you want to hash them out here over text?

I yank open the refrigerator to grab a raspberry bubbly water from the neatly arranged shelf of bubbly waters when his reply lands.

Lake: As opposed to you showing off your great date-planning skills when you plan a non-date during which you tell me the rules of our fake dating?

I can't stop smiling as I read his note. Or as I crack open the can, and it fizzes, sounding like I feel inside. But I don't take a drink right away. I lift my other hand and touch my cheek. It's warm, and I wonder where Lake is right now and if he feels a little flush as well. He did just up the ante again—from texting to hanging out.

Remy: So it's a real non-date to prep for our real fake date?

Lake: Whatever you want to call it, I'm there. Can't wait to find out where you take me. I love surprises.

Remy: I hate them. Maybe even more so now after that game a couple of weeks ago.

Lake: That is very understandable.

Remy: Thanks. Appreciate you saying that. Also, I guess we're opposites then.

Lake: We are. Good details to know about my new…woman.

Remy: Why is that good to know?

Lake: Maybe I'm keeping a list of things I know about you.

My fingers pause. I'm not sure how to reply. He's teasing me. He has to be teasing me. And besides, if he's keeping a list, it's probably because he wants to be good at fake dating.

Nothing wrong with that.

I do too.

As I crack open my World Domination notebook, I review the list of things I know about Lake Axelrod even though it's scarily small. He's superstitious. He's ridiculously handsome. He's known as Axman on the ice, partly because he's so tough on opponents. He likes free food and, it turns out, owls. He loves surprises. He's unruffled.

And then it all comes together, especially the part from Clem about him being a little weird. This might be the weirdest date I've ever planned. Or is it a non-date? I don't even know what it is. But Lake and I make plans to meet after practice tomorrow.

I'm kind of counting the hours till I surprise him with the non-date for our fake-date prep.

8

YOU SPREADSHEET NERD

LAKE

After I finish practice and Remy finishes her work in the office at the arena, we meet in the players' lot. Miller drove himself today, so I don't need to worry about him. But as I walk Remy to the passenger-side door, our D-man Ivan shoots me a curious look from a row away as he hops into his truck. Tomorrow, he'll be asking questions about why I'm holding open the door for the community relations manager as she slides into the car, no doubt.

But today I don't care.

When I drove her home the other week, it felt like a goddamn gift to be the one to help her out. To see those long legs stretched out in my passenger seat, her hair touching the faux leather of my car, her flowery scent lingering when she was gone.

I walk around the car and turn on the engine. It's a little surreal she's here again, just weeks later. Didn't see this fake dating twist coming. But I don't want to let on how stupidly excited I am simply to spend time with her one day after work. "How are you going to surprise me with this date, Remy?" I ask, keeping my tone even as I tug on my seatbelt.

"Lake, don't you know I can't tell you till we get there," she says, sounding pleased with herself as she meets my gaze with a smile.

Good. I want her to feel good.

I start to back out of the spot when she holds up a hand. "Wait."

I stop. "Did you forget something?"

"No. What's that?" She's pointing to the back seat, where there's a black mesh box strapped to the car.

"Oh, that's just Thor's car seat," I say, offhand.

"Your cat?"

"I see his reputation precedes him."

"I've seen the players and their posts with their pets. He's the majestic Siamese?"

"Majestic and knows it. He travels a lot from my family's place in Cozy Valley to my apartment in the city. Dude likes to look around. His harness clips into the car seat."

"I need a photo of that," she says, and I make a mental note of the request. "I want a cute little car seat for my future dog."

"Let me guess—little purse dog for you?"

"I like little purse dogs," she says, lifting her chin.

"And I bet they like you," I say, then pull out and head to the gate. "Tell me where to go," I say as I cruise past Carmine, giving him a nod.

"Toward the Bay Bridge," she tells me. I tense briefly. That's farther away from my place *and* hers. I don't want to be away from my dad too long. He's fine alone, of course. But he asked me to pick up some books at the library, and they close at seven. Gavin and Mira have a date night, so I can't ask them. Besides, I want to do my share.

I scratch my jaw at the light then ask the uncomfortable question. "How far are we going? I should..." I pause, reluctant, for a second, to share any detail about my family. But I push past it. "Spend time with my dad tonight."

She lifts a finger like she's got this. "One second." She whips out her phone from a purse, fingers flying across the screen. "Easy enough. There's one on the way to Cozy Valley."

"One what?"

She waggles her finger. "You want to be surprised, don't you?"

"I do."

"Then, go toward the Golden Gate Bridge and don't ask questions."

I seriously appreciate her quick thinking. "Thanks, Remy."

"No, thank you for doing this with me," she says, sounding grateful, almost too grateful.

I can't stand the thought that she thinks I'm doing her a favor by pretending to be her guy. That's so not how this situation is. It's an honor to show her how she should be treated by a man—and more than just not being friend-zoned on the Jumbotron. But I don't have a clue how to rappel into that conversation. Admitting I need to see my dad is vulnerable enough, so I keep my mouth shut as I maneuver through afternoon traffic.

Fortunately, I don't have to say anything since Remy moves full speed ahead. "I've been keeping track of how to make this pretend romance work. I created a spreadsheet," she says.

My brain short-circuits. "You have a spreadsheet? For fake dating?"

"Usually I write lists and sub-lists in a notebook, but a spreadsheet's a little better for tracking an event, as well as the timeline," she says, and holy shit, she's serious. "It's what I use for event planning so I'm trying to treat this the same."

I'm not even sure what to say, so I grunt something that vaguely sounds like *okay* as I turn onto Lombard Street.

"I wanted to list each task and account for any potential issues or hurdles we might encounter so we can address them before they become problems. First, we're going to have to say something at work. At least I am," she says, apologetic. "About..." She clears her throat, then gestures from me to her. "Us."

I tighten my hands on the wheel. "Why?"

"Considering the way Ivan was looking at us when I got into your car, I think people on the team and in management might start wondering."

Okay, so she saw that.

"And that means we need to, what—make a statement?" I ask. It comes out irritated, maybe because the idea is fuck-all irritating.

"No, but I kind of need to tell my boss about it, at least, since there are going to be videos on my sister's show," she explains. Out of the corner of my eye, I catch her scraping her teeth across her bottom lip like she's worried.

Shit. *I'm* worrying her. Because *I'm* being a dick. "Sorry, I'm just kind of private about that stuff." But what even is stuff? "Dating, life, and all," I say, trying to explain, even though it doesn't really make things better.

"Oh. Right. Okay," she says, then goes quiet and thoughtful again.

A question hangs thickly between us, unasked. *Why did I agree to fake date if I'm going to be a grumpy ass about screaming it from the rafters?*

Because you don't fake date in private. You fake date in public. That's the fucking point.

My chest tightens as I remember the way the media wrote about me after Heather died, the stories they told about us as a couple, the assumptions they made about how I felt.

But Remy's not asking me to talk to the press, or the fans,

or anyone, really. Fact is, Remy only asked me to escort her to a few wedding events. I'm the one who wanted to stick it to her ex by making a whole deal of this. Calling her my date. Saying I'm her guy.

I really didn't think this through, I realize, as I approach the Golden Gate Bridge.

"Are you sure you're okay with this whole thing?" she asks, breaking the silence. "It's not like we've announced we're dating or anything. We can just...go back to being co-workers again. I can go to all the wedding events by myself. I'm a big girl."

Or she could find some random dude to be her arm candy.

The thought grinds my gears. I yank the car over into the visitor center and park at a scenic overlook by the water, the majestic orange arches rising in front of us.

I can't believe it's our first non-date, and I'm already fucking up. Then again, maybe I can.

I blow out a breath, look her in the eyes, and speak from the heart. "Look, I'm pretty private, so all the planning and stuff threw me. But of course you can tell your boss."

"And what if Ivan asks you something? Or another guy on the team?"

"I'll say it's none of their fucking business who I date," I say.

She hitches in a breath like that answer worked for her. "Good."

She was probably worried her fake boyfriend was backing out before this even started. No fucking way am I going to be that guy. "I'm in, Remy," I tell her, making sure she knows I mean it from the bottom of my scarred heart. I meet her eyes, lingering for a few seconds, wishing I could touch her shoulder, her arm, her wrist to reassure her. But I resist. "That's a promise."

Her shoulders relax. Her gaze softens. "And don't worry about Daniel. He's pretty cool about all things, and he kind of likes me a lot," she says with a *go figure* shrug.

"What a shock," I deadpan.

"Hey, what does that mean?" she asks, teasingly.

"Remy, everyone on the Foxes likes you. You're just... likeable. And I'll go along with whatever you need to say. I don't want it to be weird for you at work. Or when it ends." Not that I want to think about that right now. "I'll make sure everything is accounted for in your spreadsheet," I tease, pulling back on the road. "You spreadsheet nerd."

"There's a lot more to cover from that spreadsheet."

"Can't wait to find out."

"In due time, Lake," she says, smiling, and everything is right in the world again.

I head onto the bridge, across the gleaming water, then through the rolling green hills of Sausalito. "Thanks," I say.

She gives me a curious look. "For what?"

"Just for this," I say.

This being *putting up with me.*

I focus on driving to the surprise date this woman planned for a broody, closed-off grump.

And I know why I insisted we fake date. I just want to spend time with her, and this feels like the only way I can. I'll take what I can get, and I better not mess it up.

A few minutes later, she points to an exit, and I follow her lead. At the end of the off-ramp, she directs me until she has me pulling into the parking lot of a...Costco.

Weird. "Do you need to run some errands?"

She shakes her head. "Nope."

"Do you need a jumbo size of something?"

She turns to me, a devilish grin on her gorgeous face. "I

heard you like free food, so I thought what better place than the home of all the samples you could possibly want?"

I'm speechless for a minute. Speechless because that's kind of an amazing thing to do—to figure me out.

* * *

I'm carrying a reusable grocery bag that I keep in the car and staring at something irresistible up ahead. "You're telling me I can get a sample of cereal, the world's greatest food, here?"

She guides me to the mouth of a cavernous aisle where a woman with curly hair and a blue apron smiles broadly at anyone passing by her table. She waggles a cup of some kind of granola at potential customers. Couples and families and solo shoppers stream past her, though some stop.

"Have you never been to Costco before?" Remy asks.

"I don't really do the shopping in the family." I don't know a lot of pro hockey players who do, but I don't say that since I'll sound like a privileged dick. Truth is, I haven't been to a big warehouse store like this in ages. Decades probably.

"We'll talk about that another time, but for now, would you like a sample of cereal, Lake?"

"I want nothing more," I say, locking eyes with her, even though that's not entirely true.

I do want something more. But that's something I can't have, so for now, we stride past the hordes to the table.

"Would you like to try some granola that's been elevated by a dusting of chocolate?" the curly-haired woman asks.

"You just named two of my favorite things," I say.

"We even have milk."

I turn to Remy, bringing a hand to my head, the sign for mind blown. "You didn't tell me they had milk with their cereal samples."

"I didn't think I needed to."

I turn to the woman. "Is this place heaven?"

She smiles. "No, it's Costco."

The woman picks up the milk and waggles it, as if asking permission to pour the oat milk on the cereal, and I say yes. She does, then hands me a small cup of chocolate-dusted granola along with a wooden spoon.

I take a bite, and my taste buds sing. "It's crunchy, just a little bit sweet, and the perfect amount of wetness," I say, meeting Remy's eyes. A blush spreads across her cheeks. And, damn, it looks good. I offer it to her. "Want some too?"

"I'd never let my date eat cereal solo," she says with a twinkle in her eye.

The certainty in her statement knocks the breath from my lungs.

Date.

She's getting into this fake date plan. After bringing the spoon to her mouth, she takes a bite. And I don't even attempt to look away as she drags the spoon past those ruby red lips. I don't attempt it because I can't do it. She has the prettiest lips I've ever seen.

She closes her eyes briefly. "Mmm. That's delicious, and I clearly need to get some."

The sample woman pumps a fist. "Mission accomplished."

But the real mission apparently is the rules of dating, because as we head down the cereal aisle in hot pursuit, Remy says, "Column D in my spreadsheet. How we began."

"What's in columns A, B, and C?"

"A is for the date, as in the day of the week. B is blank for ease of reading. And C is for the timeline, as in the number of days since we theoretically started seeing each other."

I laugh. "That's...adorable."

"It's not adorable. It's organized."

"Same thing."

"Aren't you the hockey player who's known for putting on his gear in the same order each time?" she fires back.

She's never in the locker room when we dress. "How did you know that?"

She laughs, like *really*? "Your teammates tease you about it. I have ears!"

"Fine," I grumble.

"Which makes you organized, too, then. Is organization still adorable?"

"I'm superstitious," I mutter.

"Adorably, superstitiously organized," she says, then squares her shoulders, passing a towering stack of Cheerios. "In any case, when someone at the picnic asks how we started dating, obviously the timeline is going to be quite new since everyone knows I was just dumped," she says, owning it. "We need to figure out what feels most reasonable."

We stop in front of a box of Corn Flakes so large it looks like a bicycle could fit in it.

My answer is decisive. "When you realized I was really the man for you and not that jackass who doesn't deserve you."

"That's what you want me to say?"

"Sounds realistic, doesn't it?"

She pauses, looks down at her shoes—they're strappy again, and I want to undo the little strap—and seems to give it some thought. "As good as that sounds, I'm not sure it's on brand."

"On brand for who?"

She gives an apologetic smile. "My sister. I want everything to look good for her wedding, so I can't really insult the best man."

I shake my head. "That guy's a douche."

"Why do you think he's a douche?"

I scoff, since it's obvious. "Because he broke up with you. It's that simple," I say, continuing a few more steps to the granola of our dreams. I grab two boxes, tossing them into the bag. "One for you. One for me."

"Wow. You're a good grocery date."

"I'm a good everything date." I'm thinking about our origin story as we round the corner, where I spot a mustached guy an aisle away offering cheese and crackers at a sample table. I stop in my tracks. A smile forms as I turn to her. "I think you should say I asked you out every single day since he broke up with you, and you finally said yes this past weekend."

"You do?" Her tone sounds enchanted, like that's a delightful way to have been pursued.

"Sounds realistic to me."

"And it's kind of romantic," she says. Clearly, she likes this direction.

Might as well pad the lead. "Why don't we just say I've been pining for you from afar, and I wasn't going to miss my chance the second you were single," I say as if I just came up with that on the spot.

Her smile spreads, matching the sparkle in those brown eyes. "That's perfect."

She sounds so sweet and happy, and those are beautiful sounds. I want to hear them again and again, so I ask, "What else is on that spreadsheet? We need to figure out where we went on our first date."

"Well, obviously, we went to Costco for the samples." She nods toward the cheese guy, who's wearing some kind of red and white old-timey shirt with an old-fashioned candy store vibe.

We head over to his table, where Remy says hi, then grabs a sea salt cracker with a slice of Monterey Jack and offers it to me. I take the cracker then bite into it, and holy shit, it's good. "It just gets better and better. Like this date."

"Guess I haven't entirely lost my date planning touch," she says, then snags a sample for herself, thanking the guy, then moaning approvingly after she crunches into it.

"We're both going to need those too," I say.

The man smiles, like he's pleased his cheese brought us together or something. "Like I always say, there's nothing cheesy about a date with Monterey Jack."

Remy gives a kind laugh. "Thanks again for the sample."

"You're welcome. Sometimes, you just gotta cheese the day."

"Words to live by," she says, and waves goodbye. Yep, that's her style—chatting with everyone. It's sweet, though definitely not my style.

We head down the cracker aisle, then stop by a woman offering olive samples, then I discover—yes, this is heaven—someone offering mini pizzas. I inhale two, but I rein it in. Though we do go down the frozen aisle and snag some mini pizzas. As we walk, I have half a mind to set my hand on the small of her back.

Which brings up a critical question. "What does your spreadsheet say about physical affection?"

She turns around in front of the cold case, her brow furrowed, gaze thoughtful. "I guess we'll have to be reasonably affectionate."

"Define *reasonably affectionate*," I say.

Please say it involves spreading you out on the bed and making you scream harder than you ever have before.

Her cheeks pinken again.

From the way she stared at my chest to her breath hitching, I'm wondering if Remy is on the same cell in her spreadsheet that I'm on.

"Hand holding," she begins, like she's checking off items on a list.

I don't waste time. I reach for her hand and slowly, teasingly slide my fingers through hers. Her hand is soft and warm, and when I run the pad of my thumb across her palm, a tremble seems to move through her. Her eyes flare. Such a good fucking look.

I clasp our hands tighter. "How about an arm around your waist?"

She nods. Quickly. "That sounds like a good idea too."

I let go of her hand and set down the bag, then move closer to coast an arm across her lower back. Goosebumps erupt on my skin. It's dangerous how good this feels. To breathe her in. To inhale that clean, floral scent of her hair. To touch her.

I need more.

"And this?" I take the lead as I shift closer, tuck a strand of hair over her ear, the move making her dangling earrings sway. They're little stars, and I touch the point of one, then barely brush my finger against her earlobe. I'm burning up already even in this chilly aisle. "Is that reasonably affectionate?" I rasp out.

She slides her teeth along her lower lip, then whispers, "Very, very reasonable."

Heat roars through me, a low, persistent buzz. I'm dying to ask about kissing. But she's so fantastically flustered right now that I'm thinking it's best to leave her wanting more.

"Let's figure the rest out later. I should get you home."

We grab the pizza boxes and head to the checkout, where I don't even give her a chance to take out her phone.

"Lake, I was going to pay," she says as I swipe my phone across the tap screen.

"No, you weren't," I say, emphatic.

"Lake, seriously. I don't want you to have to pay for anything," she says on the way through the lot. "You're doing me a favor."

I stop at my car, where I pop the trunk. "There's nothing about this that's a favor," I say in no uncertain terms.

I drive her back to her home in the Marina, not far from the bridge, giving me enough time to easily get home to Dad before the library closes. When I cut the engine, I say, "Hold on."

"Right. I need to grab my groceries."

"Yes, but that's not why I said hold on." I reach into the back seat and grab a gift bag from Whiskers and Kisses in Cozy Valley. For a hot second, nerves dart down my spine. It's kind of a romantic gift, and who the hell knows how it'll go over? I'm no dating expert. But I'd bet the puck from my first ever pro goal that her douchey ex sucked at gifts. "I got you a hummingbird feeder."

I offer it to her, but she makes no move to take it at first. Just kind of looks at me curiously. "Lake Axelrod," she says, as if she's speaking my name for the first time.

"Yeah?"

"I wasn't expecting a gift. I'm not used to them."

Called it. "Get used to them now. You're dating me." I check the time. I've got a few minutes to spare, and giving a gift isn't always enough. "I'll hang it up."

"I can do that."

"But it's what a good fake boyfriend would do." I'm not losing this battle with her—I intend to show her what she deserves.

She gestures to the porch. "I'll be sure to add it to my spreadsheet for tracking our dating history—hung up a hummingbird feeder after our first date."

"Good idea," I say, even though it's not the fake boyfriend in me that's doing this.

Not one bit.

* * *

When I return home, my arms are laden with hardbacks, the well-worn scent of old paper from the library books drifting past my nose. Ironic, since my sister runs a bookstore, but it's a romance shop and my dad's still into the hard-boiled mysteries he's always loved.

"Got your latest Damon Cross right here," I say, patting the new release, as a big, burly Siamese cat leaps from who knows where onto the middle of the table, his white paws skidding across the wood, hellbent on the almost-done puzzle.

"Thor," I call out to the little shit, who clips the edge of the puzzle, knocking loose a corner piece and some friends.

Dad chuckles. "He's such a turd."

"He's a cat, so yes," I say, then bend to pick up the pieces, but Dad's already waving me off.

"I got it." He doesn't like me to help him with things he can do for himself.

I step back and let him. "Almost done," he says, grabbing the remaining pieces that my asshole cat knocked off.

"Has he been bad?"

"Course he has," my dad says, but it's with affection. Dad sits back down and in no time Thor leaps onto his lap and proceeds to play the piano on my dad, like he's saying *all is forgiven, right?*

Dad pets him like yes, he's still the best boy, then he looks at me. "What have you been up to?"

"Just went to the store," I say evasively, since I don't want to get into the details of the Remy situation. It's far too complicated. "Got some cereal and mini pizzas."

He arches a dubious brow. "You don't shop."

"But I know how to."

He scoffs. "Was there a woman involved?"

"Dad," I warn, but inside I'm thinking how does he see through me like that?

"It's been three years."

I want to tell him it's been a while for him too. Mom left a long, long time ago—when Clem and I were in high school—and Dad dated some after that but not much. There's no need to point out the dearth of dates for him since it's not like he's going to go on a date here in the house. "I'm fine," I say.

"You should date again, Lake," he says, and there's a twinkle in his blue eyes—a twinkle I haven't seen in ages. He was fond of Heather, or really, fond of Heather and me. He'd even venture outside on the ranch with us to say hi to the horses or check out the egrets—even to look for the owls. A pang of missing lodges into my chest for those days, those moments of sunshine and fresh air for him. "Really, you should," he adds, just shy of plaintive.

I flash back to the moment in the car earlier with Remy, to my own reticence about what to say to my teammates or to her boss about dating. Would it make Dad happy if I was dating? Maybe, just maybe, it would. I like that spark in his eyes.

It's not a lie, really, to say, "There's someone I'm kind of into."

He pats the chair. "Tell me about her."

9

REBOUND PLAY

REMY

The next morning, I finish dotting all the i's and crossing the t's for an upcoming event at Doctor Insomnia's Coffee and Tea Emporium where the guys are going to be serving drinks, with proceeds that day benefitting a neighborhood job training program. I save the spreadsheet. Double check that it's in the correct folder. Email it to my boss.

With that done, I practice what I'm going to say to him in a few minutes when I swing by his office. It's not against the rules to date a player, but I want to be upfront. That's what I did last year, too, when I told Daniel I wanted to start a romance design-slash-dating coach business. I already had my podcast, so he knew I had some side gigs. His response was *As if I'd hire anyone but you to plan a date for my tenth anniversary*.

I step away from my standing desk in a cluster of cubes in the marketing department and head down the hall to his office. The door's ajar. He's on the phone, the receiver cradled against his black hair. "Right, sure. See you soon." He adds something in Chinese, then ends the call.

When he hangs up, he waves me in. "Rems, the herder of hockey baristas, what's happening today?"

"You reviewed the event plan already? I just sent it," I say, amazed he's already checked it out.

He checks his watch. "Five minutes ago. And yes. It looks good." He gestures to the chair across from his desk. On the corner sits a photo of his husband and their young son, adopted from Taiwan, where Daniel's from originally.

"It's going to be great for socials too," I add, feeling a little frothy from the praise. "I lined up Leighton to take pics. She's the best, though I wish we could get her to work just for us."

"Things I say about you every day. Or did you finally come here to tell me you want to work full-time for me?" He clasps his hands together as if in prayer.

"You're never satisfied, are you?" I ask, teasing him, and maybe evading the question too, since I don't want to work full-time for the team, though I love that he asks.

"I'm not ever satisfied. But that's a story for another time. And look, I get that you want to do your own thing. Brinkley's the same way," he says, referencing the other part-time community relations manager who he *also* asks to work full time on a regular basis. "He wants to be a sports talk show host. At this rate, I'll have to post a job listing since you'll all be leaving me soon."

"I'm very happy with my thirty hours a week," I say but that's not why I'm here, so I take a breath. My mind churns with all the ways this conversation can go wrong, but I think I've familiarized myself with them. "And along those lines, I want to give you a heads-up that I've started dating Lake Axelrod, and he's going with me to my sister's wedding."

Wow. That felt more uncomfortable to say than I expected. Probably because it's not entirely true.

Daniel gives me a look like I can't quite be serious. "Really?"

"Is that such a surprise?"

"No, it's just..."

Too soon? Too much? I want to say *are you disappointed in me* but that's a weird question to ask my boss, even though we were friends first before boss and employee. Still, I prepped for this, so I add, "It happened quickly. And my friends thought it would be a good idea to get back out there."

There. That's true enough. I don't feel terrible for saying that.

"Oh sure," he says. "It is. Trust me. You'd never get any judgies from me about getting back out there. I met Clay three weeks after my ex, who shall never be named, left me."

I breathe a sigh of relief.

But it barely lasts, since Daniel pushes up from his chair to shut the door. When he returns, he sits leaning forward, hands clasped, assuming the caring older brother role he's taken on with me. "It's just, you know the media made a big deal about him being a widower a few years ago," he says. "You weren't working here when his wife was killed. But with her being a hockey player too, and them being—"

"The first couple of hockey," I supply since I know what he's getting at. Even though I didn't work for the Foxes back then, I researched the team when I applied for the job. Lake met and fell in love with his college sweetheart their freshmen year. She was a center for the college team. They both went to the pros. Even played in the same city for a while. Heather Hadley Axelrod rose to fame as one of the fiercest women in the game, and her team finished one season with a championship. They were a beloved couple, until a motorcycle accident took her life a few years ago.

"Exactly and when she died," Daniel says with a reluctant sigh, "let's just say the press was a little obsessed with him. *How was he doing? Was he okay? Was he wearing an armband with her number on it?* Every move he made was under a microscope."

And soon after, Lake made fewer and fewer public moves. "I get that."

Daniel takes a beat, offers a small, thoughtful smile. "You could come under a lot of scrutiny, especially after what you just went through. That's all I'm saying."

I hate that he's not wrong, but I do appreciate his concern. "I know. But I think it'll be fine. Really, I do."

"I don't want to see you get hurt," Daniel warns, "again."

Like I did with Jameson. But no one will get hurt this time around. No one will be humiliated. Because it's all fake.

"Thanks for understanding," I say brightly, flashing my biggest *isn't dating fantastic* smile, even though my stomach twists with guilt. "It's just fun, really. That's all."

Daniel leans back in his chair, eyebrows wiggling. "Everyone needs a rebound now and then. Good for you."

I do need a rebound, and later that night, I slide into one of the suites for the employees so I can watch my rebound play.

10

THE REM-I-NATOR

LAKE

I'm flying down the ice, past the blue line, ready if Riggs passes the puck to me, ready if he doesn't.

On the ice, I'm ready for anything. Always.

I'm amped up from our early lead, my focus narrowed to the scrape of blades, the chill of the rink, and the action in front of, behind, and around me.

A Phoenix D-man swoops in out of nowhere, trying to cut Riggs off.

Riggs slips the puck to me.

I snag it and cruise behind the net, Ivan flanking me, looming like the beast he is.

Corbin's calling that he's open, so I lift the stick, sending it to our center, right as their D-man tries to knock me into the boards.

But I slip away from him, and he barrels toward Ivan, who knocks the guy into the glass. Like he's saying *stay the hell away from my boys.*

Which is precisely what he's doing.

I fucking love our D-men. They save our asses every night.

Like right now, as our other D-man protects Corbin, who can't get a good shot.

I race toward the net, where Corbin flicks me the puck again. I wrestle for it, then try once more to sneak it past the Phoenix goalie.

Nope. There's a snarl by the net, and I just can't. Back it goes to Corbin, who slams that bad boy in for a goal.

The lamp lights! The crowd goes wild.

And my heart jackhammers. I'm lit up, adrenaline coursing through my veins, excitement flooding my cells.

This, this feeling, this thrill never gets old. It only gets better, and it has ever since—

But the thought scatters when Ivan thumps me on the back and Corbin knocks fists with me.

Life changes, emotions, and other complicated shit stay behind when I hop over the boards. Glancing up toward the press box, I hunt for a sign of *her.* Sometimes she's there with Daniel. It's far away, but my eyesight's better than twenty-twenty, and I catch a hint of lush brown hair and a bright smile.

I give her a chin nod, just in case she can see me, then sink onto the bench.

When I grab my water bottle, Ivan's cracking up. Loud, boisterous, and directed my way.

I look at him as I down some H_2O. He doesn't stop laughing.

"What the fuck?" I ask him.

He waves his stick at the press box. "What's up with you and the Rem-i-nator?"

I cringe. "Is that what you call her?"

"Yes, because she's fierce. It's fitting. Answer the question."

Good thing I know what to say. "It's none of—"

"Remy?" Riggs supplies nonchalantly as he taps his stick on the floor. "Oh, the Axman's been into her for ages."

Are you kidding me? My teammate is ratting me out to my other teammate.

"That so?" Ivan asks with a smirk.

Best to cut this off at the head. I snap my gaze to Riggs as if he's lost his mind. "What are you even talking about?"

"Don't play the innocent. We all know you've had it bad for her since well before the fox toss," Riggs says, turning to Corbin and elbowing him. "Right, Nighty-Night?"

Corbin looks up. "Right, what?"

"Just say right."

"Nope. Not gonna just say something. What is it?" Corbin leans closer, curious now.

"Is Lake into Remy?" Ivan asks.

I groan. This is like tossing a steak to a pack of lions.

Corbin grins. "Oh, fuck yeah. At the bakery opening, he was like a dog salivating for—"

I smack the back of Corbin's helmet.

"Watch it, kid," he says to me.

"You were gonna say bone."

"And that bothered you because it's true?" Corbin counters.

Ivan laughs more. "This just gets better and better. I can't wait to give you hell at the next Lawn Men Club meetup."

"It's not a club," I say, since this is a perennial topic—we get together sometimes for lawn games, and the guys call it a club. I hate clubs so I refuse to use that word.

Riggs claps me on the shoulder pad. "Don't deflect."

"How's Sapphire?" I ask, deflecting the fuck out of this as I ask about his girlfriend, a reality TV star.

Riggs just shakes his head with a wry smile, clearly amused. "And the answer is...Axman's obsessed."

"And now you're giving her rides and what—going out with her?" Ivan pushes, since Ivan hates being left out of the news, and clearly no one is going to let this go.

"Yes," I say.

Before they can utter another word, I'm saved by hockey since it's time for a line shift. *Saved by hockey* is the story of my life. I hope it always will be.

* * *

When the game ends, I'm the first one through the tunnel. On the other side, I spot Remy walking the corridor, heading toward the stairwell, her chestnut hair swishing down her back.

Impulsively, I call out. "Hey, Remy."

She spins around, and something flickers in those brown eyes. Amusement? Flirtation? I'm really not sure, but I dive in anyway, peeling off my gloves as I go and catching up to her while I'm still in full gear.

"Hey," I say, ripping off my helmet as I reach her. "Saw you in the press box."

"And I saw you get an assist."

But I don't care about the assist I earned in the game right now. Something else is driving me on. Maybe the realization that our first *practice date*—if you can call it that—didn't go quite perfectly. It started a little wobbly, with me being taken aback, and her wondering if I was all in. Pretty sure I got my footing and convinced her, but this time around I want her to feel certain. Hell, she deserves to know I'm not a waffler like her asshole ex.

"Did you catch me giving you a chin nod?"

Her lips quirk up. She looks away for a second, a flash of

shyness on her pretty oval-shaped face before she turns back to me. "I didn't want to assume."

I square my shoulders and stand a little taller, which isn't hard since I'm already six-two and right now I'm wearing skates. "Assume, Remy. *Assume.*"

"Then it was a very nice chin nod."

I scoff. "Nice? C'mon. We can do better than nice."

"Can you though?" she taunts, and oh hell, Remy does have a flirty side, a challenging side. And I like it.

"Don't make me give you a smoldering-hot chin nod," I warn.

She curls her lips together, like she's holding in laughter. A few seconds later, she says, "Fine. Show me what you've got, Axelrod."

I rake my gaze over her, taking in her long legs, pretty lips, lush hair, and her creamy skin. I imagine kissing that slope of her shoulder, then pushing her sweater down, and with that lust-drenched image in mind, I give my date a long, slow, lingering chin nod.

Her breath hitches. Like it did yesterday. Her chest rises and falls. Her lips part. This is so fucking fun.

"Better?" I deadpan.

She blows out a breath as she nods, slow and purposeful, like she needs to get her bearings after that eye-fucking. "Very smoldering."

"Good. Will that work now for boyfriend material?" I ask, my voice low, just for her. "Is that in your spreadsheet? Cell C49 or something?"

"C69, but close enough," she replies.

She went there. Holy shit, she did. "My favorite cell," I add.

I could leave now. Really, I should. I'm a sweaty mess, and I need to change and shower. Coach'll be in the locker room in a few minutes anyway to give his attaboy speech since we played like gods tonight. But I don't want to leave Remy. I make another split-second decision. "Do you need a ride tonight?"

She points her thumb broadly in the direction of the arena entrance. "I was going to take the bus."

"No, you're not."

"Oh, I'm not?" she challenges.

I shake my head. "Nope."

"And why's that?"

"Because my teammates just gave me hell about dating you," I say, and lest she think that's bad, I hold up a stop-sign hand. "Because they're assholes. It's not because of you. That's just what they do."

"Okay," she says, like she maybe believes me but not completely. "But what does that have to do with giving me a ride?"

I'm no good at this stuff—romance, courtship, and what-not. I haven't dated since Heather died. But I treat it like a play on the ice and throw myself into it. "Because if I had to put up with them giving me a hard time, then I want to spend a few minutes with the woman I'm dating." Because she gave me permission, I lift a hand, tuck her hair behind her ear, and add, "Let me."

She's hesitant, like a cat unsure of the person offering her a treat, wondering if it's poisoned. She takes the treat but doesn't bite into it yet. "You can drive me home."

I move almost as fast as I do on the ice, setting a speed record as I shower and change, then meet her at the car.

11

A HOCKEY BIRD

REMY

I said yes to the ride because I wanted to steal another minute with him, or ten. The way he gave me that sinfully hot once-over in the corridor was so different from how Jameson would look at me, like I was his buddy. I was his binge-watching friend, his food-ordering pal, his let's-hang-out-tonight person. But I also don't want to get fooled again. I need to know what's behind Lake's comment.

Because my teammates just gave me hell about dating you.

As he drives away from the arena, I jump straight into the deep end. My therapist taught me that's often the best approach to a tough conversation.

"Why did your teammates give you a hard time? I know you said it's what they do. But is there a reason?" I keep thinking of the grieving widower comment that Daniel made. Are his teammates trying to protect Lake from getting hurt? Is he...too broken, like his sister warned me? Too shut down?

Lake's quiet as we drive along the starlit water, calm and still. "They said it with an eye roll, like *we know*."

I furrow my brow. "Like they know we're, what, dating? That doesn't make sense. It's pretty new."

He works his jaw back and forth for a beat. "Like they knew I was into you," he bites out, but with a sneer.

That knocks me even more off-kilter, and I let out a big laugh so he knows I know better. "Well, of course you're not."

But he grips the wheel tighter. "How do you know?"

The directness of his question keeps me off balance. "Well," I begin, but really, I don't know. I just assumed. "Because you're not."

He shrugs, his lips quirking up. "I could be."

I'm so thrown off now. Is that an admission?

He turns quiet again, and I do too. It almost feels like Lake's telling me something, but he's probably just having fun. I relax into the seat, and as we drive through the Marina, I tell myself I don't need to know every detail. This is a fake relationship. It doesn't matter what his teammates say or what he says to them.

When he stops at my house, he says, "Were there any hummingbirds?"

That is a much easier topic. "Yes. This morning. A few."

"Send me a picture of one tomorrow."

"Okay, I will." This conversation feels more natural—hummingbirds and rides home and making sure we nail the first wedding event this weekend.

But one thing nags at me. Something I've been wondering since he insisted on being my fake boyfriend. It nips at my heels as he walks me around the townhome to the porch of my little place. "Lake, what's in this for you? It's not like you need a fake girlfriend for your reputation. Or do you? Is this your way of moving past..." Should I say it?

"The way people see me?" he supplies, and that's close enough.

"Yes."

He scratches his jaw, giving it thought. "Not really," he

eventually says. "I just honestly couldn't stand how that guy treated you. Breaking up in public. Not even giving you the fucking courtesy of alone time and space. I mean, what if you had cried? It's just thoughtless." His tone is filled with vitriol for Jameson. "And I wasn't okay with what he was doing. Also, a friendship bracelet? Asking to make dating profiles? No. Just, no."

Lake said as much the first night, and that meant a lot to me—his bone-deep sense of what's right. His willingness to offer a hand and more. But how do you go from helping out to serving up dating services? "And I seriously appreciate that. But do you get anything out of this arrangement? Do you just feel sorry for me?"

"No. Not a chance," he says, the answer instant. He steps closer, licks his lips, then brushes a strand of hair off my shoulder. I fight a shiver. He's really good at these small touches. So good that my knees go a little weak, and I do my best to steady myself.

"What do I get out of this? I'll tell you. I get to spend time with a strong, sassy, clever woman who cares about other people, who keeps me on my toes, and who likes cereal too," he says, and I smile. "And birds. Or she will. I promise she will. Birds are awesome."

"Because they can fly?"

"Course. Flying's just cool."

"You wish you could fly, Lake?" I tease, glad to be back to the lighter stuff.

"I can fly on skates."

I laugh. "Are you the rare breed known as a hockey bird?"

His full lips curve up, and he nods, like he's saying he likes that term. "You know, I think I am." He exhales, unfinished thoughts flickering in his eyes. He turns quiet. Circumspect, really. "And my dad..." He scratches his stubbly jaw. Swallowing as if it's hard to say, he continues, "It makes him happy to hear that I'm spending time with you."

My chest warms from the sentiment and the admission. "I'm glad to hear that."

Lake's close with his father. I know that from him, but I also know from Clem that their mom's been out of the picture for a long while, so I understand why making his dad happy would be extra important. I'm relieved that he's not selflessly chivalrous, though I wholeheartedly enjoy his *good growl* brand of chivalry. I want to trademark that term and use it on my *How We Met* podcast, or as I dispense romantic advice from time to time with clients—because I'm determined to rebuild my business.

The thought reminds me that I should do some work tonight.

I reach for the door, but Lake's voice stops me. "Remy." It's all low and smoky, full of rasp, and seems to slide down my spine.

"Yes?"

"Yesterday, when we set the rules of affection, we missed something. We left out one important detail."

Heat rushes through my body as I turn, meeting his gaze. "What is it?"

"We said holding hands is fine. So's an arm around the waist." He pauses, moonlight streaking across his handsome face, a sliver of light illuminating the cut of his jaw. "But what about kissing?"

Well, that's direct.

And...effective. The mere mention of his mouth on mine sends my pulse hammering. A flush crawls down my neck and coasts over my body, and my imagination runs wild. Lake pushing me against the door, Lake caging me in, Lake kissing me possessively.

I fight off a shudder, then say at last, "If the moment calls for it."

He tucks a finger under my chin and lifts it. "Good to know."

He drops his hand and leaves.

I rub my chin, wanting this fizzy feeling to last.

12

BOYFRIEND STYLE

REMY

"Smile for the camera."

The directive comes from a pale, lanky, British guy in a porkpie hat, a Nikon slung around his neck. He's the photographer Fresh Face hired to shoot the picnic, starting with the wedding party members and their plus-ones. Caroline's brand manager, Margot, circulates here too—she's over by the tables, fussing with napkins—while a woman named Fallon from Fresh Face stands next to the photographer. Fallon's stern as a sentry with her tight bun and no-nonsense expression.

Caroline was right about finding a vibrant color—the teal cardigan I'm wearing looks great with the flowers behind us at the Botanic Gardens, and the khaki pants I'm wearing don't steal focus.

Lake, though?

He steals focus so hard in his untucked white linen button-down and tan pants that hug his thick thighs and strong ass. The man doesn't miss glute day, that's for sure.

Has Clementine's hockey-playing brother always been this hot? Sure, empirically Lake's criminally handsome. But he's also just plain hot. Like sex hot, like do-bad-things-to-me hot, like bend-me-over-the-bed-and-pull-my-hair hot.

And...I really need to be careful about these filthy thoughts running wild as we pose in front of the white snowdrops and yellow and purple crocuses.

Lake's arm is draped around me "boyfriend style" as he said earlier with a husky whisper in my ear. A whisper that sent a hot rush through me. Like what's happening now as his fingers curl around my shoulder.

The problem is we're part of the wedding party, and we're next to my sister and Parker. My parents are here too, and I did a quick intro with them and Lake before Fallon ordered us over for pics. I haven't seen Jameson yet, and I'm half dreading and half psyched for him to see the arm candy I've got.

Oh, was that petty of me? I don't even care.

"Lovely," the photographer coos, as he lowers the camera to check the display. "How about just the maid of honor?"

Is that part of the plan? I snap my gaze to my sister. "Do you want that?"

"Yes, that's on the shot list from Fresh Face," Fallon interjects. "Proceed."

Caroline squeezes my shoulder. "I told them you're a devotee. And it's good to show how great the makeup looks on someone of a different gen."

I scoff. "I'm eight years younger. That's not a generation."

"In wrinkles it is, my gorgeous little sister," Caroline says, practically ebullient for her, then grabs Parker's hand, leading him off with a "Let's say hi to some of the bridesmaids."

He smiles dotingly as he replies, "Whatever you want."

He's everything she wants—someone who happily lets her take charge.

With them gone, Fallon shoos Lake out of the shot. "Just the MOH," she says, as if uttering the words maid of honor takes too much work. Then, something must catch her eye across the gardens. "The MIL's lipliner!"

She sprints to triage Parker's mom's makeup.

The photographer smiles my way. "Don't worry. I've got you, love."

Lake deals him a dark look that does something dangerous to my insides, then steps out of view of the camera. But he stays close as the British shutterbug lifts his lens to capture me. "Now, love. If you can just give me a nice pout, yeah?"

Is that really on the shot list—a pout from the MOH? But Caroline wants everything to go smoothly, so I don't protest. Instead I get creative and say, "This is my best pout."

Then I *don't* give him my sexiest expression. Fresh Face can have mild vamp only.

"Brilliant. Just brilliant." He keeps clicking. When he's done, he says, "Thanks again. You're fun to shoot."

It's said with a gaze that lingers a little too long on my chest. An uncomfortable feeling slithers through me, but I've handled moments like this before. I can do it again, by maintaining my professional distance.

"You're welcome," I say, my tone distant and clipped, and right as I'm about to march off—since you should always march off from leery men—Lake materializes at my side, setting a strong hand on my arm. "Fallon said she wants FP now."

I furrow my brow. "Full wedding party?"

"Yup."

"Why not FWP?"

"I have no idea." He smirks like he's in on this too—the silliness of shortening everything.

"They'll certainly need me, then," the photographer says. I guess we can't quite shake Mr. Leery.

Lake turns to the photographer, shifting to full game face

—all stony and don't mess with me. "Yes, they will." And when Lake returns his gaze to me, his blue eyes flash with warmth, maybe even heat, as he says, "I'll walk with you, beautiful."

Oh.

I just acquired a pet name. One that sounds possessive and private rolling off his tongue. Lake ups the ante once more, dropping a quick but firm kiss to my cheek. My skin buzzes, whether from the *beautiful* or the kiss, I don't know. Probably both. I smile up at him.

"The moment called for it," he says.

Is it wrong if I hope the moment calls for a kiss again? "Good thing you listened to the moment."

"I always do." The man is seriously delivering on the fake boyfriend role. Like above and beyond.

We make our way to the picnic table, leaving the photographer in our wake. Lake keeps his hand on the small of my back, like we outlined at Costco, but somehow it feels like bending the rules of fake dating. Maybe because it's delicious and tingly, and I want so much more of it.

But you can't have it. Or him. That's not what this is. This is fake.

Reality is seriously irritating.

As we near the party, Lake brushes my hair out of the way and says, "If it's FWP, then fucknozzle will be here."

I wince. "I know."

Lake circles his arm around my waist now, like he's kicking things up a notch. "Have I told you that you look stunning?"

He said as much when he drove me over here. He's probably saying it to keep my spirits high. But I like Lake's compliments, so I eat this one up happily. "A few times," I say, as we pass purple hellebores on the way to the enemy.

"Because it's true," he says.

My heartbeat dares to speed up. But I can't let my mind be

tricked into thinking this fake thing with Lake is real, like my body seems to want. I lean into the playfulness instead. "My, my, you are very super boyfriend-y."

He pulls back for a second to look at me, like he's measuring my words and weighing if they add up, but his gaze snaps to the crowd.

I catch an annoying glimpse of Jameson and his floppy undercut, his light blue shirt, his ever-present vest. He's chatting with Parker, smiling, laughing in that gregarious way he has. He's twenty feet away now, and any second, we'll have to do the FWP photos together.

Jameson's head turns my way, and a second later, he's taking me in, then boom—he pads across the grass toward me.

Grinning.

Like I'm his long-lost bud.

My stomach churns with dread. This is my first time seeing him since the Jumbotron Dump. I knew this moment was coming, but it doesn't make it sting any less. That's the man I was going to say yes to. The man I thought I loved. The man who only wanted to be friends.

But as Jameson comes closer, I don't feel any more than the residual singe of embarrassment. I don't feel...much of anything else. Immediately, I know two things. One, we weren't sparky, fiery, passionate lovers when we were together. And two, I don't miss him now that we're apart.

When he reaches me, I go first, since it feels important to set the pace with a cool and professional tone. "Hi, Jameson."

My ex smiles, glancing from Lake to me and back. "Hey, Remy. Is this your new dude?"

"Yeah," Lake says, standing taller even though he towers above Jameson. "I'm her boyfriend."

My cells shimmy from the way he throws down. No bullshit. No games. Just a clear message. The preemptive strike my sister wanted.

"That is so awesome," Jameson says, and he sounds like he's happy for me, but almost a little too much. "I was really hoping you'd find someone quickly. And look at you. You did it. Go you."

I rewind his words and there's something a little...overly gregarious about them. Maybe he's trying to keep the peace? I just don't know. I *suppose* it's better than the alternative—him being a total dick. "Yay me," I say.

Lake cinches an arm around me, nodding to Jameson. "And thank you, man. Remy's a goddess, and I wasn't going to miss my shot to be with her."

And hello, possessive man stealing focus once more. I want to run my nails down his chest. To grab him by the shirt collar. To say *mine, mine, mine*. "You're the best," I say, then what the hell? I give a little tug of his shirt collar.

Who is this possessive demon inside of me? I was never possessive with Jameson. But I like it.

"This is just so great," Jameson gushes, ruining my demon glow-up. "I love this for you. I started seeing someone too."

I glance around, looking for the hoptimist. "Where is she?"

"Oh, Chelsea couldn't make it. She had a thing at her brewery. But hey, why don't we all set up a double date?"

My jaw comes unhinged. Jameson's leaning seriously hard into this *I'm a good guy and let's be friends* image. I bet it's all for show. For his bar. For the optics.

I'm tempted to tilt my head and say in a too-sweet tone, "Do you want me to break out the bracelet kit and we can make a matching pair?"

But if I activate my sarcasm, I'll look like a serious jerk at my sister's event. I don't have to, though, since Lake tugs me closer so I'm flush against him. He heaves a sigh, like he regrets this so damn much, then shakes his head at Jameson. "Thanks for the invite, but I don't share. Even our dates."

On that mic drop, the hockey stud cups my cheek, drops his mouth to mine and brushes a tender kiss across my lips. My brain goes whoosh as he claims me in front of the whole wedding party, but especially the guy who broke up with me in front of the whole hockey arena just over three weeks ago.

The kiss starts out innocent enough—just a hint, a tease, a promise. But it's also not at all innocent, since I'm learning Lake smells like cedar and tastes like fresh mint. I discover, too, that his stubble scraping my face makes my nipples stand at attention. That his hand on my back is nothing short of foreplay.

He murmurs against my mouth, a rough, sexy rumble that thrums through me. When he breaks the kiss, he shoots me a sly smile, just for me. "The moment called for it."

"It did," I think I say. I'm not sure if I'm speaking or thinking. It's hard to do either now that I know there's a world where knee-weakening, toe-tingling kisses exist. I don't think I knew of this planet's existence before today. But I'm an intrepid explorer and I want to traverse it. Map it. Study it. What else can he do with that mouth? His hands? His hard, cut body?

As I'm contemplating this new universe, I spot Jameson slinking off, his back to us.

And everything feels right on Earth too.

I recover speech, so I lift a hand toward Lake's handsome face, pushing some soft, thick hair away, then whispering in his ear, "Score one for the fake daters. It's one point every time you successfully nail a dating hurdle."

"We're going to run up so many points, beautiful," he murmurs back against my neck, sending a shiver through me again.

"I'd like a hat trick, please."

"Consider it done," he says, then we pull back and he gives a wry smile, mutters *fuck it* and comes in for one more kiss. On my cheek. It's tender and swoony, and I'm seeing stars.

But when he pulls back from my cheek, I'm seeing Caroline, staring bug-eyed at me, with a million questions in her eyes. And zero patience.

She grabs me by the elbow and marches me past a gurgling stream, around some bonsai trees, then out of sight of the guests.

Uh-oh. I'm in trouble. When she finally stops by a pagoda, she's grinning. "Well played. That was a brilliant preemptive strike. You went above and beyond the call of duty with tongue and everything." She parks her hands on her hips. "But what the hell?"

"What the hell what?" I ask, playing innocent.

She jerks her thumb toward the scene of the strike. "You didn't tell me you and your plus-one leveled up."

She's staring. Waiting. Tapping her espadrille. "Oh, well," I say, buying some time because I don't know that I want to start telling anyone that our dating is fake, especially Caroline. The more people know, the more likely someone will let it slip. What if she whispers it to Parker one night in bed? What if he tells Jameson, and then Fresh Face finds out, and then Caroline's perfect wedding is a mess? But I don't want to lie to her either though, so I repeat her words back to her. "You wanted me to neutralize the threat with a preemptive strike."

She arches the most well-groomed brow in the land. "Nothing looked neutral about that. Does that mean you're dating for real now?"

I give a non-answer. "Everything just happened so quickly."

"Really?"

But I feel completely truthful as I say, "Yes," since this past week has been a whirlwind.

She beams with pride. Just positively glows. "It was because of me, right? When I said you should get back out there. That I didn't believe in licking your wounds."

Thank you, big sister, for taking credit. "Yep. You're my inspo."

"Good job," she says with a nod. "I told you you'd need to show you're moving on and you did. All I can say is keep it up." She inches closer, narrows her eyes. "Because I want him to suffer, and you having the time of your life with a hot athlete is the best kind of suffering we can wreak on him."

Sounds like a good kind of suffering if you ask me. "So you want me to keep making out with Lake in public? Just making sure I'm clear on this."

"Public, private, wherever," she says breezily, but then dips a hand into the pocket of her pressed navy slacks and fishes out a tissue. "But wipe that kiss off your lips and go get a makeup refresh from Fallon." She freezes for a second, then smiles strategically. "Maybe we need to show how well the lipstick holds up with a kiss." Her eyes turn to moons. "That's it! I'm a genius! We're going to do a segment on the true lipstick test of a bride and groom—the wedding kiss. Let me go tell Margot about my brilliance."

And she's off, returning to her domain. I follow her, and when I reach the patio where the picnic tables are set up, I find Fallon, with her tablet and stern expression. "Hi, Fallon. Can I get a reapplication?"

Like a robot, she dips her pale hand into her makeup bag, and hands me a disposable applicator. "Now, be sure to smile and show how well it holds up against an ex test."

As I slick on some lipstick, it takes a few seconds for me to realize what the Ex Test is—the pictures with Jameson. Which means Fallon knows we were together. And Fallon's probably seen the Jumbotron Dump. And Fallon doesn't want anything resembling that at the wedding her brand is sponsoring.

A flush of embarrassment crawls up my neck. "Of course," I say, feeling chastened, like I'm the loser little sister.

I check my reflection in the phone camera. It looks perfect, like I know she'll want it to be. "Thanks."

She stares at me, appraising the application. At least I think that's what she's doing. "Yes, that's good for a glow-up."

That word sticks in my gut. That's why she wanted the pics of me with a sexy smile—to prove I'm not the loser. That's what Fresh Face gets out of me being here, showing off their makeup. To prove that rebounds work.

My stomach twists, but I understand the assignment. I drop the applicator into a bag Fallon offers for makeup recyclables.

Time to ace the Ex Test. I join the full wedding party for pics, flanking the bride on one side, with Jameson standing next to the groom. As the photographer snaps photos, I think of Lake. I imagine my plus-one making out with me in public, in private, anywhere. And I smile so hard, so well, so vibrantly.

Take that, Fallon. I'm the MOH who doesn't even care that her ex is in a photo with her.

I'd like my A-plus right now.

* * *

Once the pics are done, it's time to eat. Lake and I slide onto a bench at the picnic table across from my parents and near my sister and Parker. The photographer circles, taking pics of the meal, the laughter, the vibe.

As I reach for some spring salad to spoon onto my plate, my mother shoots me a thoughtful look, her light brown eyes crinkling at the corner in curiosity. "It's such a treat to sit with you, Lake," she says.

Lake flashes her a smile that surprises me with its size, its wattage. It's warm and bright, and he's not really a smiley guy. But evidently today he is. "And you as well, Mrs. Hatmaker."

Mom tilts her head, studying us once more, her dyed brown bob barely moving. She's a put-together woman who does cardio every day, who plays brain games each morning, who misses nothing since my mother doesn't permit failure. "So this all happened quickly?" she asks the two of us, and I'm not sure what she's getting at.

But I'd better answer quickly.

"Sure did," I reply, like the speed of my response will hide the way my pulse kicked up just there.

Mom shakes her head, like she's trying to work something out. After a beat, she swings her shrewd gaze back to me. "Remy, I'm just surprised you never mentioned anything about Lake even though we talked nearly every day for a couple of weeks there."

Oh, shoot. She's right. Why didn't I mention Lake to her then? I gulp, then try to improvise. "Oh, I thought I had."

"No," she insists, and she's a lot like Caroline, strong-headed—no surprise. My mom stood by my father's side while he battled some mental health demons while I was a kid. She was fierce, resolute, and determined to help her man. She's still that way. No wonder she became one of the country's most sought-after wedding planners before her retirement—she believes in the *I do* with the power of a thousand suns, and if she had to be the glue in their marriage, then dammit she'd be sticky. "I even asked if you were ready to date again," she points out.

"Can confirm," my dad puts in, with a flash of a smile for her, always for her. "Well, she told me about every call as soon as she hung up. She said you were taking some time off from dating."

Mom pats his hand as if thanking him for backing her up.

I rub my palms along my khakis, trying to figure out how to explain this discrepancy. "That was the plan at the time," I say evasively, hoping that throws them off the scent.

I steal a glance down the table at Jameson, and he's watching us like it's a tennis match.

Great. Just great.

I'd assumed his presence might dent our fake dating armor today, and I was ready for that interaction. But I wasn't prepared for my parents to give me the third degree, while my ex watches...like he's eating it up.

As I picture my spreadsheet and the details Lake devised about how he asked me out every day, Lake reaches for my hand under the table, threads his fingers through mine, and squeezes. It's like a balm. More so when he cuts in with, "But it's a good thing plans change. Because I was determined to get Remy to go out with me."

He gives my hand another squeeze under the table. It's like he's saying *remember, we planned for this?*

And...I do. "He kept asking me. He was very persistent."

"But why didn't you tell me?" my mom presses, like she can't quite believe I'd leave that out of a check-in call.

"A lot was going on," I say, hoping that covers it for her.

"The thing is, she didn't think I was serious," Lake supplies, talking to my mom. "All the times I asked her." He pauses, giving a self-deprecating grin. "I kept leaving these little stuffed foxes on her desk."

"Like the ones you hit on the ice?" my mom says, enthused. But then she stops, like she's embarrassed now, or maybe secondhand embarrassed at the mere mention of *the incident.*

But Lake doesn't give in to that lore. He barrels forward like the foxes were always part of our story. "Yup. Any kind of stuffed fox. I'd leave them with little notes. Sometimes with cookies. Other times with cupcakes. Sometimes, even a plant. A succulent, of course," he says, and holy smokes. This is *not* what we planned. It's...better.

It's fun.

It's delightful.

The pressure in my chest eases. The blaring in my brain dissipates.

And I want some fun in the middle of this tense picnic, so I jump into the fray. "My favorite was the one that said *For fox's sake, will you have coffee with me*?" I say to Lake, smiling dopily, like I'm recalling that imagined moment perfectly.

"Yeah, you liked that one. Even though you still didn't say yes," he says, and wind him up and watch him go. "I'd wanted to ask her for so long."

Lake blows out a pleased breath—like he's thrilled the entire table is eating out of the palm of his hand, from my parents to Jameson to Caroline, who's watching this with avid eyes. "I finally left a big stuffed fox on her desk with a note that said *I don't give a fox about anything but taking you on a date*."

I blush. I smile. I freaking giggle. It's such a ludicrous tale, but he tells it with one hundred percent commitment and I nearly believe it.

"So I said yes at last," I say to him, and Lake leans close, swiping a thumb affectionately across my cheek, then smiles contentedly before he lets go, leans back in his chair, and meets my mom's enraptured gaze head-on. "That's probably why she didn't mention it to you. It took her a while to know I meant it."

"But when I knew, I knew," I say.

He squeezes my hand once more under the table. "And she finally planned a perfect date," he says, and I feel bubbly everywhere from the save.

He gave us a whole new story. I give him a smile that says *thank you* and *I want you* all at once.

"And what was the date?" Jameson interjects, and can't he leave well enough alone?

Caroline waves toward a server heading our way with a picnic basket full of sandwiches. "Oh look, more lunch is coming."

But her deflection tactics don't deter the conversation, since Lake's already answering my ex with, "Costco. We had the best time eating samples."

Jameson chuckles under his breath.

Lake looks at him sharply. "Don't laugh till you've tried their granola."

"It's so good," I second.

Lake turns back to my mom, flashing a supportive beau smile that just slays me. "Honestly, it was a perfect date, Mrs. Hatmaker."

Damn, this man can fake-boyfriend ridiculously well. I'm surprised he's so upbeat, so sunshiny, but I'll take it. I bump my shoulder to his, getting in on the affection.

"A perfect date," Mom says happily, then looks at me with fondness in her eyes. "You were always so good at that! Remember that candlelit game night you set up for your father and me?"

I sit up straighter. All the tension slams right back into me. My muscles are tight everywhere. I remember those nights all too well—nights when I tried to fix their marriage. When I tried to help repair whatever was broken for them at the time. But I don't want to think too long about the dates I crafted for my parents, how long I planned them, how much time I spent making sure everything was just so. "I sure do," I say tightly as the server sets a tomato and avocado on focaccia bread in front of me and Lake shoots me a curious look.

"Now comes the true test of our makeup," Caroline declares from her end of the table, once more taking the reins of the moment, like the host she is.

"Can the lipstick withstand the sandwich test?" I ask, grateful for the chance to talk about something else. Something besides the fake dates with Lake and the very real ones I arranged for my parents once upon a time. Or the look my fake date just gave me.

I bite into the sandwich, and it's delicious—so good in fact that it distracts me from the bloom of feelings for my fake boyfriend that I didn't anticipate either.

He takes a bite of his sandwich, chews, and finishes, then leans closer to me, saying, "Score two."

And I like scoring with him even though I shouldn't.

* * *

After lunch, Lake tips his forehead to the edge of the gardens. "They have a succulent garden here."

"They do?"

"Yeah. Want to see it?" His tone is intense, like he really wants to do this.

There's a tug in my chest. I'd like to see it too. I glance around the scene, unsure if I can just slip away from my sister and everyone else. "I do, but can we take a rain check?"

"Yeah," he says, all casual. "Another time."

"Definitely," I say, then make a mental note to add this detail to my World Domination Notebook—Lake knows there's a succulent garden here.

Margot calls my name, and asks me to join her and the

other bridesmaids. Good thing I didn't sneak off to the succulents. I meet them at their table, and we *ooh* and *aah* over all the wedding events coming up, saying *we can't wait* and *that's going to be so fun* more times than I can count.

When the picnic winds down at last, Parker's chatting with Lake about the Foxes' chances this year, so I say goodbye and hug the bridesmaids. As I'm saying goodbye to the last one, the photographer sails past me again, stopping to catch my attention with a tip of his forehead. "One last shot," he asks, waggling his camera. "Fallon said to get one more."

She needs another one to show I'm not the pathetic *MOH*? Fallon's off with Caroline, reviewing something on her tablet by the hellebores, so I'm going to have to trust that she wants this even though my Spidey senses are tingling. This seems like a bit much even for the stick-up-her-ass stickler.

"Sure."

"Lovely," he says, then guides me to a nearby bush bursting with gold flowers. He takes a few more shots, and when he lowers the camera at last, he drops his voice too. "Listen, I'm only in town for a few days, but I'd love to give you my hotel card—"

Out of nowhere, a possessive hand lands on my back and a man appears by my side. "She'll be with me."

Then, to emphasize his point, Lake gives me one more kiss.

Hand holding my face.

Lips claiming mine.

Beard leaving its mark as my fake guy scores a hat trick after all.

And I didn't really doubt it earlier but I'm dead certain now. I want my fake boyfriend to do very real things to me. And that's a bit of a problem.

13

MY GAME PLAN IS NO GAME PLAN

LAKE

"Are we going to talk about the elephant in the car?"

Remy's looking at me with curious eyes as I drive through the Haight on the way to her home, the afternoon sun dipping lower in the sky.

"My hat trick back there?" I deadpan.

She laughs. "Yes, but also your sunshine personality. What bag of tricks did you pull that from?"

I scoff, like she's being ridiculous.

"No, I'm serious. You were pure cinnamon roll."

I play dumb. "What are you talking about?"

"You were a different person at the picnic," she presses, and she sounds...amazed.

But I rewind all the way to her first comment. *Talk about the elephant.*

If Remy wants to talk, that might mean I can finagle an extension of this time together. There's no hockey game or practice today. I don't need to return to Big Steps for a little while longer. And I happen to know a great puzzle shop not far from here.

"You free right now?"

"Um," she says, then holds up her hands. "Since you haven't tied me up, I'd say yes."

It's a miracle I don't crash my car from the fantastically filthy images flashing through my mind of her pinned to my bed, wrists bound, chest heaving. "I mean, do you have someplace else to go? Like another—"

I choke on the word *date* as a dark storm cloud hangs over my head. We never talked about whether this fake boyfriend arrangement meant we'd date other people. It better not.

"We have more rules to discuss," I bite out.

"Okaaaay," she says, thrown off but rolling with it.

I scan for a spot and find one at the end of the block. I pull over, then hop out and grab her door.

"What rules, Lake?" she asks, as a line digs into her forehead. Remy doesn't let things go easily. She wants to understand everything and doesn't want to be duped.

I seriously respect her tenacity, but I'm too irritated by the unwanted thoughts of her dating to have the convo this second. "Coffee," I mutter. "They have coffee."

Coffee will center me.

"C it is then," she says, talking like Fallon in initials. I'm irritated, too, that I find that endearing.

Irritated because I've got to get my act together with her. On the one hand, I'm jealous about the possibility of her dating anyone else while she's fake dating me. On the other hand, I'm annoyingly captivated by every little thing she does.

I drag a hand through my hair as we head to the yellow door of the Puzzle Me This shop. I grab it and hold it open for her, when a third emotion wallops me.

Missing.

My chest aches. I'm taking her to a shop I used to go to with my dad. A place I still go *for him*. I'm stepping into a place that's deeply personal without thinking about it, just because I want to steal another moment with her. But that seems to be my game plan these days—if a game plan can be not thinking things through.

I watch her take in the store's offerings, turning in a circle as she gawks at the displays. A 500-piece cat quarantine puzzle is perched on one shelf, featuring cartoon cats lounging across a living room, bingeing shows, knitting, and reading. Then a frothy pink one called Sugar Rush featuring photos of jars of candy, then a "dogs with jobs" puzzle, where mutts wear lab coats or type at desks.

She spins back around and stares slack-jawed at me. "I could send couples here on their dates."

I wish I could say that's why I brought her here. But see above—my game plan is *act on instinct.*

Instead, I try to see the shop through her eyes—the eyes of a woman wanting to make other people happy. "Yeah, I could see this being a good date spot."

"A terrific one," she says, perhaps soaking in the warm cozy vibe, the well-worn couches in the shop, then the tables in the café where couples and friends work on puzzles as they sip coffees and lattes.

That's an opening if I ever saw one. "Better make sure," I say, with a wiggle of a brow.

A slow smile spreads across her face. "Okay then, you puzzle nerd."

"You're a spreadsheet nerd."

"And you didn't deny you're a puzzle nerd."

I hold up my hands in surrender. "Can't deny it."

"Birds, puzzles, free food. You're an interesting man."

And you're the most fascinating woman I know. We head toward the café, and...what the hell? I grab her hand, then give a shrug. "The moment called for it."

"The moment is making a lot of calls today," she muses, as she looks at our linked fingers.

"So damn many," I say as we get in line. A few people are ahead of us, and briefly it occurs to me we're out in public *again*.

Sure, we were at Costco, but that didn't look romantic. Yes, we attended the picnic, but that was a closed event. I haven't really been out on a date like this in a long time. Hockey players aren't always recognized in public, or even often recognized at all, but you never know.

One part of me hates the idea of putting myself out there.

Another part of me can't stop wanting to be with this woman. I also don't want her to have to lie to her family, so as I thread our fingers more tightly together, I say in a low voice, "Next time you see your mom, you can tell her you planned another great date for us."

"Aren't you strategic?"

"Yep. Since this is date-worthy. Or so the romance designer tells me."

"It's so DW," she says, and I don't let go of her hand as we walk to the counter, as we order, as we wait.

It feels too good to touch her, like it did earlier at the picnic.

But all good things come to an end, and I have to let go when the barista places the cups onto the counter. I grab the coffee and the chai latte, and we slip into a booth with our beverages. There's a half-completed puzzle of San Francisco's Golden Gate Bridge on the table. Maybe two hundred pieces total.

I scan it, instantly spotting a few pieces of cables, and sliding them in easily. She spots one and slots it in. I feel a little like I've pulled off a bank robbery. I stole some more time with her on what feels like a real fucking date. I roll up the cuffs of my shirt a few times, and her gaze snaps to my right forearm.

"You have an owl tattoo," she says, staring right at the fine black lines of the bird.

"I do." I wonder if she's seen it before. I wear T-shirts—most of the guys do—during media interviews. Maybe she's never noticed. No big deal.

Right. You wish she'd catalogued every detail of you.

She leans closer, studying the linework. It's a simple drawing, more stylized than realistic. "It's so minimalist and pretty."

I'm about to ask if she wants to touch it, but I don't have to. Because there she goes, reaching for it, her hand coming closer, so close my skin is tingling with anticipation. But she stops when she's an inch away, pulling back her hand and taking a drink. "It's a great tattoo," she says when she finishes.

"Thanks. I like it a lot too."

She glances down at it once more, and I swear her breath catches. And I file that reaction away, too, as I take a drink, hiding a sly grin.

But the grin vanishes when she wags a finger at me. "We have a lot to discuss. Starting with your acting."

I groan, slumping back in my chair. Not sure why but I don't really want to dive into the alleged sunshine side of me. Or the acting, since it was hardly acting. Tattoos are more fun to talk about. "What about it?" I ask, all gruff again.

"You were so upbeat. It was...a contrast."

"You saying you think I'm, what? A grump?"

She gives me a gentle look. "You're kind of...broody."

"Understatement," I say under my breath.

Even though I really want to say *And do you like that?* But I'm not going to fish for compliments. I drink some coffee, and she takes a swallow of her latte, then adds, "I was kind of surprised."

Yeah, I was too. I wasn't expecting to have to go full simp today.

When I set down the mug, I scrub a hand across my beard, then answer her with honesty. "I figured you didn't want a grumpy-ass hockey player who despises people-ing as your fake boyfriend."

She laughs, snorting out some of her chai, and holy shit, it's the most adorable thing I've seen.

More so when her pretty brown eyes sweep down her shirt, checking for spots. Grabbing a napkin, she shakes her head and says, "Pretend you didn't see that."

"Nope, can't unsee it," I say. "You totally snorted it right out of your nose. That was...impressive to say the least."

"It's your fault. You made me laugh," she says, pointing a finger.

"By speaking the truth?"

"Yes."

"I'm not wrong though. About any of it."

"I don't know," she says, her tone doubtful. "You were pretty social there at the picnic. You talked to everyone."

"I talked to the people you wanted me to talk to. I did it for you," I say plainly, then grab a piece of the orange pylon and slide it into place.

She stops with the drink halfway to her mouth. "You did?" She sounds shocked, but delighted too. It's a good sound.

"Of course I did," I say.

She's quiet for a beat before she says, in a softer voice, "I don't even know what to say."

Say how much you liked the kisses. Say you want another one.

"I was just doing what you asked me to do," I say, nonchalant. "Being your plus-one."

"Lake," she says, gently correcting me. "That was above and beyond. You were so much more. You had my parents eating out of the palm of your hand. You handled it all so well. The photographer too. I used to think I was good at handling surprises, but you? You meant it when you said you love surprises."

"I'm an athlete. I'd better be able to handle them."

"You handled my ex too," she adds, and her smile spreads so fast it's like a comet. But then it vanishes into the night sky. "But something seems off about him, don't you think?"

"Oh, you mean because he's a complete and utter fucknozzle?"

"Well, there's that, but why is he so intent on being friends with me? It was almost like too much. What was all that 'Let's go on a double date' about? It felt a little like he was—"

I whip out my phone. "Up to something."

"Yes!"

"Let's check his socials. See if we can figure it out."

Her eyes flash with excitement. "I haven't checked his socials once since we split up."

That makes me outrageously happy, but I smother all semblance of a smile. "Good, let's keep it that way," I grumble, then type in his name, wishing I didn't know it but glad I do because I need to know what his deal is. I roll my eyes as soon as I get to his feed. "Are you fucking kidding me?"

"What is it?" she asks, her tone wary, and nervous too.

I shake my head at the schmoozebag in the pic. "He brought one of his own beers to the picnic. Look at this."

I spin my phone around and show her the screen. It's a selfie of Jameson at the outskirts of the botanic garden lifting one of his bottles with the label facing the camera and the caption reads: ***So great to be celebrating with Caroline Hatmaker and her fiancé with the most refreshing drink there is. Excited for the wedding!***

"And he tagged them both," I add.

She cringes, but then narrows her brow. "It's like he's trying to use my sister as a celebrity endorsement in some way."

"And trying to get them to what—carry his beer at their wedding?" I knew I was right about this guy. He's such a poser. "Why not just ask his bud?"

Remy breathes fire as she says, "Because he knows Parker has no say. We even joked about it when we were together. He said *I know weddings are for champagne but if they need beer, I'm their guy and I told Parker as much.* I just laughed and said *He's not making any wedding decisions and besides, my sister runs everything past me.* So Jameson probably figures he has to suck up to me."

I burn with loathing for this guy, but I don't need to let more of it show. That won't help her move on. Instead, I take a drink of my coffee, then set it down and meet her eyes. "Like I told you the other night, you deserve so much better than him —someone who tries to be friends after you split to get some social credit with your sister. Plus, the way he ended things tells me a lot about who he is." I shove my phone away, like it offended me simply by revealing his picture.

She winces, as if she's a little embarrassed. "I think the breakup kind of made it clear to me who he is too. I wish I'd seen it sooner, while we were together. But hindsight and all."

Well, I can't leave that tidbit alone. "What do you wish you saw?"

She takes a moment, clearly thinking. "There were things I liked about him when we were together of course. He *seemed* super self-aware and all. And friendly. He was friendly," she says, and I bite back all the bitter words I could say about the poser, letting her share. "But I think, looking back, I'm not even sure I missed him during the mandatory post-breakup hermit days," she says with a self-deprecating laugh.

I give a small smile at her characterization, then wait for her to say more.

"I missed the *idea* of him," she continues. "I missed *not* being embarrassed on the Jumbotron. I missed *not* feeling like a fool with an Internet nickname. I missed all that more than him."

And I can't hold back now. I lean closer, speaking from the center of my damn soul. "You deserve someone who treats you better. Someone who's honest. Someone who's passionate about you."

"I appreciate you saying that," she says, like I just gave her a compliment about a promo she put together, or the way she organized an event.

But this moment isn't about appreciation. It's about action. Before I know it, the words are coming out of my mouth. "I want to show you how you should be treated. Before, during, and after a relationship. I want to be the best rebound you've ever had. Nope—make that the best rebound anyone has ever had."

She looks at me like she can't believe I'm saying this. But I can. This new game plan—one I devised seconds ago—makes perfect sense to me.

Tilting her head, she asks carefully, "What do you mean exactly by rebound, Lake?"

I go full-speed ahead. "It was hardly an act today at the picnic, talking you up, treating you well, lifting you up. The story I told about asking you out every damn day felt real. You deserve someone like that. Someone who's relentless in his pursuit. You deserve someone who sends you stuffed foxes and leaves you notes. You deserve someone who messes up your lipstick," I add, and a slight tremble seems to run through her. That tremble drives me on. "Someone who defends you against douchey photographers and lying exes.

You deserve passion and honesty and to be put first in a relationship."

She lifts her hand, sets it on her heart, like she's touched. "Thank you. Seriously."

But nope. That's not enough. *Thanks* isn't the point. I hold her gaze, making sure she knows I'm dead serious. "While we're doing this, while we're fake dating, let me show you what it means to be treated with passion and honesty. That social-climbing fuckwad should not be your last impression of romance. I want to be. I want to show you what it means to put you first. That's what I mean by rebound."

She dips her head, like she's hiding a smile, or maybe emotions, since when she raises her face, her eyes are shining. "Show me how to rebound, Lake."

This is the real hat trick. "I will."

I slide another piece into place, feeling better than I do on the ice. There's just one more thing. "About those rules. I don't think we ever established an important one. So let me be clear. While you're fake dating me, I won't be dating other people and—"

"You better not!"

I jerk back. I wasn't expecting a little jealous dragon in Remy, but I like it more than her chai latte snort. "Tell me what you really think, Remy," I tease, feeling a little cocky too.

"Will you?" she asks sharply, not playing games.

I don't play either as I look her in the eyes again and say, slowly and clearly, "No. Fucking. Way."

She lifts her chin. "Same for me." She slides in an orange puzzle piece with a flourish.

God, she's hot when she's jealous. But her anger seems to cool as her eyes go thoughtful. "But what happens when this ends?"

My chest squeezes sharply, like someone's tied a rope

around it. I know it'll have to end. That's always been the plan. And the plan is to treat the end with the respect she deserves. "It'll be controlled. It'll be easy, since we've planned it. It won't be on a Jumbotron. I won't make you a fool," I say, in a promise that feels as important as any other one.

"I'd like that," she says, then takes a sip of her chai, sets it down, and hunts for another piece, finds it and puts it in place.

I do the same, and soon we've finished our drinks and completed the puzzle.

I can't stop the clock anymore. "I should go...get a puzzle for my dad," I say, a little sheepishly.

"I like the dogs-with-jobs one."

"I'll get that." I grab it and buy it.

On the way out, she turns to me and says, "Will you tell your dad we spent time together here?"

It's an easy answer. "I will."

"Will you tell him it was a date?"

"Unless you don't want me to?"

Her mouth goes soft. "If it makes him happy, you should."

It's said as if she already cares about this person she's never met. The person my mother left, along with my brother, Clem, and me.

I swallow roughly. "It will," I say, and that's more vulnerable than I'd planned to get tonight. But my fake girlfriend seems to have that effect on me.

14

SUCH A BAD LIAR

LAKE

My dad's already sound asleep when I get home.

But Gavin isn't. He's in the stables, checking that stall doors are closed for the night, and after he tells me that Dad went to bed, he asks, "You got any time in the morning before you go to practice? There's a new owl box for the bird sanctuary. Can you hang it?"

"Course I can," I say as he secures the stall door for Nutmeg, then pats her on the muzzle.

He brushes one hand against the other then tugs off his gloves. "Good. Just don't fall, like you fell on the ice the other night."

I flip him the bird. "Why don't you try to do your job in skates? Also, the D-man slammed into me. I got back up like that," I say with a snap of my fingers.

Gavin cracks up, bending over at the waist. "Oh, man, it's so fun giving you hell. You're so sensitive."

"I am not sensitive," I say, my brow narrowed.

He stops laughing, but keeps smiling as we head out of the barn. "Right, sure. But if you're worried you don't have the balance to do it, you can muck the stalls instead."

"I said I would hang the owl box."

"But if you can't manage it, there's horseshit to shovel," he says as he yanks one big door closed.

I pull on the other one. "Why have enemies when you can have a brother?"

"Might as well have both. More fun for me," he says with a wiggle of his brows as he strides across the grass, away from the home.

He stares at the property in the dark, then sighs, the satisfied sound of a job well done.

"You know—I'm happy to help around here," I say seriously. "If you want me to do more."

"I know," he says, kind and full of understanding. "But the bird stuff is more than enough."

Is it though? Sure, I know he and Mira like running Big Steps. A familiar pang of guilt twists inside me. Like I could help more. Or maybe it's just a memory of how happy my dad was before things started breaking. When Heather used to stay with me at the ranch before we fell apart.

Back before Dad stood in the open door one day, then said quietly, "I don't think I can go out."

My heart aches thinking of that moment.

I pull myself out of those thoughts right as Gavin looks me up and down with skepticism. "Why do you look like you're a frat boy?"

I'm wearing slacks and a white linen shirt. "I don't look like a frat boy."

"Country club guy. Same thing," he says with a hint of derision since we are neither. We didn't grow up with enough money for golf courses and tennis matches, and I never joined a frat, nor wanted to.

"I hate clubs."

"Again, why are you dressed like you're going to one?"

As we walk up the stone path to the house, I answer, "I had to go to a thing."

"A thing? What kind of a thing?" he goads, reading me instantly. *Brothers.*

I grind my jaw. Am I telling Gavin I'm fake dating someone? No, that'd be a bad idea. He'd mock me in front of Dad, and the point of fake dating is, well, to fake it. If Remy could tell her boss, I can tell my brother. "I had to go to a picnic. With a woman," I say.

Gavin's eyebrows shoot to the moon. I brace for him to say *you found someone who'd date you*, but instead he just claps my back as we reach the porch. "Judging from the smile when you got out of your car, I'd say it went well."

"I wasn't smiling."

"You're such a bad liar," he says, and we go inside, where I set the puzzle on the kitchen table, as Remy's pretty voice replays in my head saying, *"I like the dogs-with-jobs one."*

I replay other things as I head upstairs alone, thinking of her.

* * *

I have just enough time before morning skate for food and for a certain asshole cat who likes his morning walks. When I head downstairs, the scent of scrambled eggs and buttery toast floats toward me, making my stomach growl. My dad's at the stove, moving some eggs around in a pan.

"Morning," I say, then ruffle his hair. "I'm going to take Thor out for a walk. Want to come with me when you're done?"

It's rote. I ask it every day I'm here.

Dad blows out a thoughtful breath, like he's considering it.

"I have some things I need to finish up in here. But thanks for the offer."

My heart clenches. "Got it."

"It's pretty funny to watch him go for a walk though. A cat on a leash."

"Yeah," I say with a smile that hurts my chest.

"Why don't you take a video for me?"

I swallow roughly, then nod. "I will."

He waves the spatula at the pan. "Want some eggs? You need to eat before you work out.

"Sure," I say, since he likes to be the dad and, well, I like to eat.

He tips his forehead to me as he turns down the heat. "I heard you were dressed up last night."

"Word travels fast around here."

"It sure does," he says as he plates the food. "Dressing up—was it for the woman you're into?"

I picture Remy last night on the street asking if I'd tell him. I can see the curiosity in her brown eyes. "Yep. You want to know where we went?"

His eyes sparkle, and it gives me so much dangerous hope.

Before we sit down to eat, I grab the granola too. In between bites, I tell him about the puzzle store and the coffee and the woman who loves to ask questions.

"She's smart and curious, and she sent me a picture of a hummingbird in the hummingbird feeder, and she took me to get granola, and she's..." I hold the spoon midair.

"Pretty?" Dad asks.

"The prettiest," I say, then narrow my eyes. "And no, I'm not going to take a picture of her for you."

He laughs, knowing it was a joke.

After I clean up my plate, I wrangle Thor into his harness,

one white paw after another, but it's not hard since he loves his outdoor time.

The little stinker walks beside me, sniffing the path through the meadow, past the creek, to the edge of the property where a blue heron lands by a small lake, and a big owl watches high above in a black oak tree. A ladder rests against the fence, since it's easier to keep one out here in the sanctuary.

I tie Thor's leash to the fencepost so he's safe. He lifts his furry face to the sun.

A portrait of contentment.

I snap a picture of him, stuff my phone in my pocket, then climb a tree and hang a new owl box. When it's good and secure, I take a moment and look around. A stream snakes around the rolling hills on the property. Trails crisscross those hills, dotted with a few horses with riders on them, and their equine therapists leading them along. It's peaceful, green, and lush. Nature at its best with humans caring for it with respect. When I climb down, I snap a photo of the owl box, then I set the ladder against the fence.

Once we're back at the house, I say goodbye to my dad, then open the thread with Remy on my way to the car.

There's the picture of the hummingbird she captured the other day, wings a blur, beak dipped in the sugar water, the morning sun glinting off the glass. What did she wear when she went out there? Sleep shorts and a little button-down sleep shirt? Leggings and a hoodie? Or was she all dressed up in those trim pants she wears that make her legs look incredible, checking on the feeder while looking like she's about to slay the day?

I hit reply and drop in the photo of the cat, then the owl box.

Lake: Thor's very interested in the owl box I installed today.

Her reply is instant.

Remy: Wait, wait, wait. You have a cat on a leash? You hang owl boxes? This is on top of your hidden sunshine side and your puzzle mastery? What other secret talents do you have?

Lake: What secret talents do you have?

Remy: I can cut hair, groom a dog, assemble any piece of furniture in under an hour, fix a router, hang a picture, and plan the best dates 😊

Lake: Let's go back to that haircut thing. Can you give a haircut because of the dog grooming?

Remy: Nope. I taught myself when I was younger since I was convinced I wanted to be a stylist for a while. It's not the most useful skill since I don't cut my own hair.

I want to know more, but I have to get to work. I put the phone down in the console, doing my best to ignore the thoughts of her as I head to Miller's home to collect our goalie.

I pull into his driveway right as he's tossing a basketball into the hoop above the open garage. The man never stops moving.

I honk the horn because we're assholes like that.

Spinning around, Miller glowers at me, then trots into the garage, littered with his teenage brother's band equipment, and deposits the ball on a shelf. He grabs his gym bag and hops into my car. "Did you know studies show people who honk horns are dickweasels?"

"Yes. I knew that," I say as I back up, then flash an asshole grin to match the honk.

"But do you know the only thing that sucks about being a goalie?"

It's a setup, but I wade into the shark-infested waters anyway as I pull onto the road. "What is it?"

"I didn't get to give you a hard time on the bench the other night about finally, fucking finally, going out with your long-time crush."

"Fuck off."

Miller leans back in his seat, slides on a pair of shades, and just grins. "It's hilarious."

"What part?" I bark.

"The idea that she might like you."

I bristle. Is it really that hilarious?

Oh shut up, brain. No need to think about that stuff. You know this has a beginning and an end.

But I might as well make the most of the middle. When we reach the arena, I fire off a text to her.

> Lake: Are you working today? If you get a break, I want to steal you for a few minutes to go over what's next for the wedding.

As I stride into the locker room, a reply lands.

Remy: You bet I am! I'm going with some of the guys who are serving coffee at a local shop in between morning skate and the pre-game warmups. I can meet with you after?

Suddenly, I change my tune about promo events.

Lake: Got room for one more?

* * *

"Florence, here's your gingerbread nutmeg soy milk latte with—"

I stop trying to read off the list of what's in it. Florence damn well knows. She ordered it.

The friendly, curly-haired woman on the other side of the counter at Doctor Insomnia's Coffee and Tea Emporium just laughs. "It's all good, as long as I can take a picture with you?"

As if on cue, Remy slides by right next to me, smiling at the customer. "Take as many as you want."

The woman turns around in front of the counter and snaps a selfie of us—with me behind the counter, wearing a leather barista apron and serving lattes. Wait till my dad hears I socialized just for a woman.

Florence lowers her phone. "Thanks again for doing this," she says to me, her tone heartfelt. "Neighborhood Works is such a great organization."

"They are, aren't they?" Remy says, and I second her with a nod. Remy told me a bit about the non-profit's jobs program, and it's pretty cool that the team helps out.

But helping out also means serving another drink.

This one's a chai latte, so I hand it to a man on the other side of the counter who thanks me. Miller's serving some old dude a coffee and listening to his life story. Riggs is offering a hot take on whether koalas are cooler than foxes to a customer. And Corbin is riffing with a guy on what it'll take for us to beat the Chicago Barn Owls tonight.

When the guy with the chai leaves, I turn to Remy, who's managing the whole event with a certain kind of...pep. It's cute, really, the way she likes telling us where to go, what to do, when to be where, her tablet like a clipboard the whole time. She's in her element. I nod to the guy leaving. "Is that your favorite drink? Chai latte?"

"It is at the moment," she says. "I change it up each month."

"You do?"

"Life's too short for one drink. Sometimes I'm a matcha girl, sometimes a vanilla latte, sometimes a tea drinker."

I'm filing this away in the Remy folder. "Noted."

The conversation is short-lived since another customer appears, and the team photographer lifts her camera to snap more pics of us serving. I don't smile for the camera, but I'm glad I crashed this event. Which is weird.

Really fucking weird.

When it's over, we head back to the arena, and once everyone disperses to get ready for warmups, I catch Remy right before she heads into the stairwell. Her palm is pressed to the door.

"So what are the other wedding events?"

"Right. We were going to talk about that," she says, but she pauses, licks her lips, then says, "thanks again for coming today. We were able to donate even more to the org just by having another server."

"That's great. I'm glad."

"Me too," she says, then seems to breathe a sigh of relief before shifting gears. "Okay, wedding events. There's a cake tasting this weekend. I set that up for Caroline with Afternoon Delight, and she's already picked her three favorite flavors. But she wants to finalize the winner, and of course Fresh Face wants to get it all on camera. Can you come to that?"

"Yep." I lick my lips to show my excitement—for the cake, not the cameras.

"And I also have my *MOH* event," she says, sketching air quotes, "where they want me to pick up my maid of honor dress, but I can do that on my own."

"Got it." I try not to let on I'm disappointed.

"Then, there's the shower I've been planning—co-ed of course. We're calling it the Something Shared Shower, since Caroline thinks traditional showers are outdated, anti-feminist, and grubby. Hers is a totally different type of shower," Remy says, then explains more about the couple's plans, which include a donation angle.

Appreciate the change-up and the charity, but a wedding shower in any form sounds about as fun as wrestling Thor into a cat burrito when I have to clip his long-ass nails. I maintain my poker face as I say, "I'll take you."

"That would be great. And there's a spa day too, but we haven't finalized the date yet."

How can one couple have so many events? Never has there been a better advertisement for elopement than this wedding. "They're actually having a spa day?"

"She wants to treat the whole wedding party and their dates to a day of relaxing."

I fight off a cringe. Love a massage and all, but I am not a spa dude in any way, shape, or form. “Is there a rehearsal dinner too?”

Remy shakes her head. “Nope. She felt that was enough stuff.”

Ya think? “Send me the details,” I say, then she lifts a hand to wave, and fuck, I hate that I can’t grab it and give her a quick cheek kiss in the hallway.

But as she walks up the steps, an idea hits me. There is *something* I can do for her. In fact, it’s something I promised I’d do.

You evil genius, you.

I check the time. Perfect. I can squeeze this in before warmups. Damn, I’m brilliant. I hustle to the concourse, slip into the souvenir shop, and handle it quickly.

On the way back to the locker room, I flash back to our texts from earlier as I run a hand through my hair.

Lake: With all these pics coming up at the cake tasting, it seems like a good time for a haircut. You up for showing off those skills?

15

FOR FOX'S SAKE

REMY

Confession time—I had to read one of those *Hockey for Dummies* books when I took this job.

I had zero idea how the sport worked. I got the gig here since I was friendly with Daniel from an event planning agency I'd worked at. He asked if I wanted to interview for the community relations manager role, and I said yes.

Then I tunneled down into the rabbit hole of hockey for a crash course, watching videos, researching the sport, and devouring the book.

I want to say I love the game, but I'm not obsessed with it like I am with setting up an event, or planning an amazing proposal for a couple. I don't often slip away to watch some of a game in the press box. But tonight...after I answer Lake's text with a ***Yes***, I feel an almost inexplicable pull in my chest to learn more about hockey when it's game time.

If I'm going to study the gameplay, maybe I want to do that alone.

When I'm done with my work—planning an upcoming event with a youth sports clinic where the players are going to teach the kids for a day—I head up to the concourse, passing the plant wall, weaving through the food court, then flashing my badge at ushers. I don't need a seat. I can simply stand at the top of the bowl, watching from there, blending into the crowd.

First period's underway and already the arena seems to be vibrating with energy. The Foxes had a wobbly start to the season but they've been on a tear recently, firing on all cylinders.

Rowdy fans in purple jerseys sail past me carting nachos and gourmet pizza, sodas and cocktails. Determined to expand my hockey knowledge, I narrow my gaze to number seven. With the ends of his hair spilling out just past his helmet, Lake's racing down the ice, flanking Corbin, flipping the puck back and forth with him. Jostling for an opening, Lake finds none, so he passes the little black disc to Riggs, who flies around the back of the net.

That makes sense. It gives Riggs a chance to scan the ice for a teammate to pass to. In a nanosecond, Riggs sends the puck zipping right to Lake. My breath catches as Lake lifts his stick, swings, and aims for the goalie's legs. That's a wrist shot.

"C'mon," I mutter, crossing my fingers, hoping so hard.

But the goalie blocks it, and a D-man gets the rebound, then ferries the puck toward Miller.

The game goes like that for the rest of the period, tight and scoreless, as I file away the details of each play and each penalty. But soon, my shoulders are tight. Must be because I've been focusing so hard, trying to record all the info.

No, you wanted Lake to score. You wanted it so bad.

I blow out a breath, tear myself away from the stands, and tell myself to go home and focus on Romance By Design.

I have a new client at long last. A referral, and that's such a relief. I should plan his upcoming special date, but as I ride home on the bus, I'm staring out the window, watching the waterfront roll by and daydreaming about the haircut I'm going to give the hockey player with the finest flow on the ice.

* * *

When I arrive home, I bound up the steps to my porch on the side of the townhome, ready to punch the code into the keypad, but I stop in my tracks.

In front of my door is a huge gift bag from the Foxes gift shop. Tissue paper spills out of the top, and anticipation bubbles inside me.

This could just be a work gift, maybe. Something from Daniel? I pull back the paper, and once my fingers brush across soft, plush material, I don't think this is a gift from my boss after all.

I grab the bag, punch in the code with lightning speed, and carry it inside. Once the door snicks shut, I drop my phone on a table, sink to the floor in a squat, and paw through the bag like a ravenous dog.

I pluck out a stuffed fox.

A tiny ferocious one, and he's holding a note. My breath catches as I reach for the small white card in the fox's paws.

I unfold it and read.

For fox's sake, will you have coffee with me?

Tingles rush down my arms. I fish around for another fox. This one, in a cute little purple jersey, holds a card tucked under its arm.

I don't give a fox about anything but taking you on a date.

I'm grinning so stupidly, so broadly it should be illegal. I grab another fox and open another note.

Zero foxes given about anything but taking you out...for cake.

I feel deliciously carbonated now, a soda bottle all shook up.

I dip my hand in again and again, pulling out more foxes from a nearly never-ending supply. Finally, when I'm surrounded by tawny stuffies, I reach inside the gift bag and find a bigger card. This one has today's date on it.

I flip it open.

There. It did happen.

He recreated the story of how he asked me out to make it real. After I send him a thank you text, laden with exclamation points, I spend the rest of the night redecorating with a dozen stuffed foxes, enjoying it more than it feels I should.

* * *

I rattle off the details of the wedding for my therapist, Elena, the next day at our early evening session. "And Caroline has her own wedding planner, but I've been managing some things for her too. Don't worry though—I want the things I'm planning to be perfect, but not *too* perfect," I say, a nod to one of the things I've been working on with her.

"That's good to hear because we can't control everything. Or most things, but it's good to remind yourself that you can handle the outcome regardless of what happens. Just like you handled the Jumbotron situation," she says. With warm bronze skin and a grandmotherly attitude, Elena Alvarez has seen a lot as a therapist. A Jumbotron breakup was a first though. "I'm wondering if all this wedding planning stirs up anything about how a younger you had to deal with planning?"

That's a damn good question. That's also why I came to her office in the first place even though I don't entirely love talking about how my sister and I grew up differently. Those eight years made a big difference. Mom and Dad were happy when Caroline was a kid; they'd nearly split up by the time I was ten and she was in college.

"Sometimes," I admit, with a sigh. I didn't love the way I felt at the picnic when my parents praised me for the dates I planned for them when I was in grade school.

But if I dive into that with Elena, I'll have to tell her I have a fake boyfriend, and I doubt fake dating is one of the approved cognitive behavioral therapy techniques.

I keep my pretend romance to myself for now, and I kind of like my secret.

* * *

I'm grabbing my to-go cup and slinging my canvas bag on my arm a few days later, ready to catch an early bus to a meeting with an animal rescue we're partnering with for an upcoming event, when someone bangs on my door with a battering ram.

I swing it open, and yup. It's my sister. In full TV makeup and sporting a luminous blowout, she brandishes her tablet triumphantly, with the words *It's done* on the screen.

I squint to see an email from Fallon. "What's done? Does she mean she booked everything for the cake tasting tomorrow?"

Shaking her head, Caroline's eyes gleam with retribution. "The photographer who was a little too frisky with you? I made sure he was fired from the assignment. No one treats my employees that way, let alone my sister."

Oh.

I'm oddly touched, though it's wholly unnecessary. "It didn't really bother me that much," I say, since my maxim for the wedding is *don't rock the boat.*

"Please. He was asking you to go to his hotel. Fallon overheard him."

I didn't realize Fallon was skulking around, but that seems on brand for her. Plus, I was distracted when Lake swooped in with a kiss. "True, but it didn't seem—"

She holds up a stop-sign hand. "Look, this is better than the alternative. I was strongly considering wringing his neck with my bare hands. Margot talked me down."

"It's good to work with a pacifist who wants to keep you out of prison."

"No one fucks with my people. There will be a new crew coming for the cake tasting." She spins around, ready to march down the steps and back into her townhome in her ethically sourced eco-friendly kitten heels when she stops and wheels back around. "But they want to stop by here first."

"Sure. So you can get ready," I say, gesturing to her townhome.

"So *we* can," she corrects. "I told them you've been using their makeup forever. The brand is all about real people and authenticity, so they're going to grab some quick B-roll of you first, then me."

"Okay," I say, trying my best to sound excited, but likely failing. Being chronically online is so not my thing, but it can't be too hard to do a get-ready-with-me video.

"And make sure Lake is there."

My chest flutters. That's an awfully inconvenient reaction to his name. So's the shimmer of heat rushing through my veins.

"I'll let him know," I say evenly, since I don't want to entirely let on how excited I am for a little extra time with him. But hold on. He's theoretically my real date, and a good fake girlfriend would be glad about that. Right?

Shoot.

Real girlfriend.

A real girlfriend would be glad about that, I repeat in my

head. Man, it's hard keeping track of what's real and what's not. I really don't want to mess anything up.

All day long at work the next day, I keep my head down and focus on the animal rescue event, but when a text from him lands in the early afternoon, all thoughts of work vanish.

Lake: My place or yours?

He's asking about the haircut. Of course he's asking about the haircut. But I tug at my shirt collar and fan my face before I answer with ***Mine.***

* * *

Everything's ready. A towel, scissors, a comb. A spray bottle of water. A chair in the kitchen. I pace around my home, checking to make sure the counter is clean. I do a quick online check, making absolutely sure I have everything for a haircut.

I scan the site and my supplies. Perfect. I've got this.

But maybe I should practice some breathing exercises since my pulse is rocketing to the freaking moon. It's just a haircut. That's all. There's no need for my heart to beat so infuriatingly fast.

I close my eyes, take a deep breath and—

The doorbell trills, and I jump.

"Shit," I mutter, then I check my reflection in a mirror in the hallway. Minimal makeup since I'll need to touch it up for Fresh Face.

I stride down the hall, smooth a hand over my T-shirt, and open the door, all while trying to hide the racing of my pulse.

16

MAN BUN FAN

REMY

Lake looms in my doorway, filling the space ominously. The afternoon sun halos his face, highlighting his strong jaw, lined with a beard that looks trimmer than usual. It's operating at scruff-level now, and that's unfairly hot. I try not to stare, but my mind's going haywire, and my gaze bounces all over him. He's wearing jeans that hug his thighs, a maroon Henley that shows off the shape of his big biceps and the outline of his strong pecs, and a glimmer in his blue eyes. He's the portrait of the athlete post-workout, his hair slicked back, and wet.

"I just took a shower after practice. It dried a little," he says casually, running a big hand through his wet hair, almost, *almost,* in slow motion. "But you can just get it a little more wet, right?"

I blink, trying to process his words. But it's hard with the way he looks right now, all muscular and clean, and the way he sounds, too, all gravelly and flirty.

"Yes, it's wet," I say slowly, like I'm mesmerized. Because I am.

His lips quirk up in the hint of a grin. "It is? Wet?"

"I mean, I'm wet," I correct, then panic shoots through me

at my faux pas. "I mean, you're wet. Your hair is wet. Your hair is plenty wet. For a haircut that is. Wet enough for a haircut."

That grin grows wider. He cocks his head. "So everything's wet, Remy? That's what I'm hearing?"

I clench my thighs, even though they ache. "Yep."

I turn around so he can't see the heat spreading across my cheeks. Not that it matters. Pretty sure he knows it's there, and he's the one responsible for it.

"Come inside," I say, but then my mind replays my words. *Come inside*?

I need to get it together.

"Oh I definitely will," Lake says, too amused, and I only have myself to blame. He shuts the door, then asks, "Shoes off?"

At this rate, seeing his socks would probably arouse me, so does it even matter? "Yes, please."

He toes off his sneakers, then pads quietly into my home.

"Sit, please," I say, gesturing to the chair.

I'd really better keep this businesslike. Friendly. Coworker-y. I don't want to cross any lines with him. He asked for a haircut, not a blow job.

Great. Just great. Now I'm thinking of getting down on my knees and my brain can seriously screw off.

Before he sits, he nods to the windowsill with my family of succulents. "Looks good there."

"It does," I say, a little warm all over again as I glance at the Ruby Glow. "It was sweet of you. And, in retrospect, it's helpful for the whole backstory."

"I wanted to cheer you up." He holds my gaze in that intense way he has. It's so disarming, the steadiness in his eyes, and the passion too.

"It definitely made me feel good. Someday, my plants will become real pets. Four legs and all."

"I like that plan." He glances at the plant, then me. "And this one suits you. Ruby lips and all."

Heat roars inside me once more as his gaze drifts to my mouth, to my lips outlined in ruby red.

We're talking about a succulent, and I'm definitely wet. The irony.

He parks himself in the chair at last, relaxing casually, legs slightly spread, smirk in full force. "Want to make sure it's wet enough?"

I close my eyes briefly, fighting off another onslaught of inappropriate lust, fighting off the urge to take him up on his offer. Trying to figure out, too, if he's just taunting me.

But whatever the answer is, I want to do a good job. I want to earn an A-plus in cutting his hair. I open my eyes. "Yes, the scissors will slide so much more easily through a nice wet head of hair."

After I set a towel around his shoulders and neck, I grab the water bottle, move behind him, and spray his locks, dampening them once more and taking control at last.

When I'm done, I set the bottle down, grab the scissors, then say, "What's the plan, Mr. Hockey? Buzz cut? Undercut? Messy and short? Just a couple of inches off the bottom? Or stylist's choice?"

He cranes his face, looking up at me, his eyes glimmering darkly. "Surprise me, Remy."

This man and his love of surprises. He's hard to keep up with. But when someone says *surprise me,* you ought to deliver. I drag the comb through his hair, making sure everything's even as the ends hit his shoulders. As I'm sliding the teeth through a chunk near his ear, I try to remember a time when Lake had short hair. I'm coming up empty though. "So tell me, what inspired you to chop off the *finest flow* in hockey?" I ask as I set down the comb and reach for the scissors.

"Just trying to impress my girlfriend," he says, all cocky and nonchalant.

I move around him to meet his gaze. "And you think she likes short hair?"

"I don't think she wants to ever picture her wedding date in a man bun, so…yeah."

I huff out a laugh. "What makes you think that?"

"Call it a hunch. My hunches are usually right." He pauses. "You a man bun fan?"

I snap the scissors open and closed. If he's going to have fun I am too. I move behind him once more, line up the scissors at the nape of his neck, and slice off a healthy four inches. I hold up the chunk of wet hair to his face. "What do you think?"

I can feel him smile, rather than see it as he says, "I think I was right. You like short hair."

That fluttery feeling descends on me once more. Like butterflies are setting up camp in my chest. *Must ignore.* I open the blades again, position them against another section, then snip. "Maybe I do," I say, as the hair falls to the floor.

I move along the back of his head, working meticulously, painstakingly as I cut his hair, giving him a neat, trim look. Then I move to the front, where his hair falls in a swoop near his ear.

"Time to trim this up too," I say, but then pause, standing in front of him, assessing where it's best to position myself. The problem with trimming the front of his hair is I need to get a little closer to him.

Lake must sense it since he widens his thighs. "Just stand between my legs. I won't bite."

But what if I want him to? A blast of heat roars through me, as I step between his spread legs, running my fingers through the hair I need to chop off, my hand lightly sliding against his forehead as I go.

He sucks in a breath. The temperature in me rises. I take a beat, steadying myself.

"It's a tight space," he says quietly.

Everything is dripping with innuendo. "It is," I say, breathy.

"I'd better make sure you're...steady," he says, then raises a hand and lifts his face, meeting my eyes as if asking for permission.

I give a faint nod. His right hand comes down gently on my hip, holding me in place as I stand between his thighs. I glance down at his hand briefly, the outline of the owl peeking out beneath his shirt sleeve. My fingers itch to touch it, to trace it. Tearing my gaze away, I cut the rest of his hair.

Soon enough, I'm done. "There you go."

"Do you like it?"

I look down at him. His blue eyes are patient, but hopeful. "I do. Want to see it?"

"Yes, but first..." He drags a hand through his hair again. His eyes widen. "That's short."

"Too short?" I ask, hoping he likes it.

"You'd better check," he says, then reaches for my hand, gently guiding it up toward his head. I take the permission slip he's giving me and run my fingers through his short, wet hair. A full-body shudder runs through me as I do so, like I'm checking my handiwork when I'm just seizing the opportunity to touch him.

His body is tense as I go, like he's keeping everything bottled up.

I move my hand away, turning around to grab a mirror, but he's standing. "Let's go check it out in a bigger mirror. Okay?"

The word mirror reverberates in my skull, as ideas—filthy ones—flash before me. "Okay."

I walk to the bedroom, then show him the full-length mirror on the back of the closet door. He considers his reflection, then turns to me. "This what you like?"

I liked his hair before, but I like it even more now. "I do."

His lips curve up in a small grin, as if he's never been more pleased than to give me what I want.

And right now, in my bedroom, alone with Lake and his newly shorn locks that I want to grab hold of, I want...him.

His smile burns off though as his eyes roam over me. "You're wearing a T-shirt," he says, noting my outfit.

"It's just for the haircut."

"I figured," he says, then swallows, pausing. "Are you going to wear one of those shoulder things?"

"Shoulder things?"

He steps closer, brushes his fingers along my collarbone, lighting me up. "Those tops you wear."

I know what he means. "An off-the-shoulder sweater."

"Yes. That."

"I can wear one."

"Good idea," he says, all raspy and heated.

Lake likes my sweaters, and this should not delight me so much. But it does.

I remind myself I'm only one month post-breakup and anything, anything at all, with my fake boyfriend who I work with would be a bad idea. I can't risk something else going wrong. Being another joke. Messing up my sister's wedding.

Caroline would be hurt. My parents would be disappointed. And I'd be so unbelievably upset with myself.

I can only imagine how much more therapy I'd need. That thought brings me down to earth, and so does a knock on the door. Fresh Face is here, and I'm both irritated they've ruined the moment and grateful I'm saved by the bell.

17

THE DISTRACTION PLAY

LAKE

If I'd thought the view from an owl box was great, it has nothing on the view right now. I'm leaning against the wall in the narrow hallway that looks into Remy's tiny bathroom. She's standing in front of the mirror, putting stuff on her face. Words like foundation, concealer, matte, and primer float in the air like they mean anything to me. A videographer shoots from the doorway, while another woman stands nearby—a producer type, who'd earlier set up a ring light and made sure Remy was mic'd.

I watch it all go down from a few feet away. Never knew that this was missing from my life—watching someone put on makeup.

Heather wasn't a big makeup person. Sure, she did hers before we went out on dates, but I never deliberately watched her put it on. No real reason, other than maybe it felt like something private.

But today I'm invited, and I'm damn glad I RSVP'd.

Because Remy's so absorbed in dusting on the powder that she bites her lip. She stares in the mirror, checking out her work with such intense focus, all for a date with me.

It's intimate, and I've been invited.

Fine, fine, a fucking camera crew is here too.

But I'm the only civilian, and I'm transfixed by the way she grabs a tube of mascara and meticulously swipes some on. As she does, her lips are parted, and I fight off a groan from that view of her mouth.

Soon, she's done and declares, "And there you go."

The videographer stops shooting. "That was great," she says, friendly but efficient. "We need to go shoot the bride now. But we'll catch up with you at the bakery. We can see ourselves out."

They leave as quickly as they came, the door snicking loudly shut.

When they're gone, and it's just us and the quiet of her home, she locks eyes with me. "You were watching the whole time?"

It's more curiosity than accusation. "You were doing something important to you," I say, owning it. "What'd you think I was going to do? Look at my phone?"

She leaves the bathroom, joining me in the hall. "I guess I hadn't thought about it."

You're much more interesting than anything I could scroll through.

But I keep that thought to myself. Don't need her worrying that I'm obsessed with her.

She nods to her bedroom, then in a playful voice, says, "I guess I should go grab one of those so-called *shoulder things*."

"Off-the-shoulder sweater, Remy; that's what it's called," I say, teasing her right back.

She rolls her eyes, and heads to her bedroom but stops at the door. "And do you also have a request for what pants I wear?"

"I get to make requests? This is my lucky day."

"It sure is." She doesn't know the half of it.

"What are the options?"

"Want to come see?"

Because every damn thing with Remy is a yes, I nod and follow her into her bedroom again, this time gobbling up all the details of her. Including my own surprise. I guess I'd thought it'd be super girly. Red bows on the wall, pink bedcovers. But it's a little more earthy. Muted greens and beiges on her bed. Black and white photographs on the walls of cities like Paris and Tokyo.

Framed shots of her friends too. A small little jewelry box. I want to pick everything up and ask her questions. Instead, I follow her to the closet.

She opens it and then whips out hanger after hanger of jeans and pants, and all at once I'm overwhelmed. Maybe there's a reason I've never really participated in this pre-getting-ready thing before. How the hell am I supposed to choose what pants she should wear?

"Everything looks good on you," I say, speaking the truth plainly.

"But I need to pick. My sister said something fun. That was the dress code."

"Okay," I say, scrubbing a hand across my beard, scanning for something fun.

But then I spot it—a short little skirt on a rod behind her. My neck blazes. "That," I rasp out.

She grabs it, holds it at her waist. "This?"

Holy shit. It's short and black, and I'm just dead. "Is that a trick question?"

"Why would that be a trick question?"

I flail my hands at it. "Because *yes.* That. Wear that," I say, more emphatic than when I tell my team *let's fucking go.*

She shakes her head, smiling, then shoos me out of her room. "I'd better get dressed then."

It's like it's Christmas Eve as I wait for her to emerge.

A minute later she walks out wearing a sweater that reveals the most enticing amount of pale flesh at her collarbone that I just want to kiss and lick and bite. That skirt that makes my jaw come unhinged. The way I've wanted her before is nothing compared to how much I want her now. Those legs. Those long, toned legs. Muscular calves, strong thighs...

The whole way up to Corbin and Mabel's bakery in Cozy Valley, I'm well aware this thing between us is all fake. I'm her fake date for this whole series of videos on her sister's show about her wedding and all its countless, ridiculous, over-the-top events.

But every glance at the curve of Remy's calves, every time her eyes meet mine, makes the word "fake" feel like a goddamn lie.

* * *

The look Corbin gives me when I walk into his bakery with a hand on Remy's back is the definition of "I told you so."

I shoot him a look that I hope says *shut the fuck up*.

When Remy steps away from me to go say hi to Mabel, Corbin stares me down. "Dude."

"Dude," I reply.

"You look—"

"What? Am I not allowed to take her on a date?"

"No, what the fuck happened to your head?"

"Oh, right, that." I lift my hand to drag it through my hair, but there are only phantom locks there. "It was time for a change."

"Damn, you were proud of that hair. Best flow in hockey, or some shit like that."

"Aw, you keep up with me."

"It's hard not to when you brag about it all the time."

"Don't worry. I still look fucking awesome. Remy cut it," I add.

Corbin smiles like he's caught me red-handed. "So that's how it goes."

I shrug off the comment, like it's no big deal since that's easier than facing the bigness of the deal. "Yep. That's how it goes," I say, then survey the scene in the Afternoon Delight bakery. The camera crew is here. Remy's sister stands in front of a mural of a fox and a llama sharing a cupcake, the whimsical scene a stark contrast to the intense look on her face as she talks with two other women—one with a tight bun. Both were at the picnic. Pretty sure one is from Fresh Face and the other works for Caroline. But as soon as Caroline spots her sister, she beelines over and hugs Remy.

The crew captures it on video.

Parker's here too, checking out some of the shop's popular "F*ck Mornings" merch, and Jameson is also here with his dumb undercut and stupid smile, and...hold on. What's that? Is he actually holding a bottle of his beer? Just like at the picnic. He's probably going to try to hold it up and get it casually in front of the camera.

Fuck that guy.

But then—yes! Let's fuck with that guy. I motion for Corbin to come closer, then say out of the corner of my mouth, "Help a teammate out?"

Corbin nods. "Always."

I tell him the plan, and he says dinner's on me for the rest of the season.

"Fair," I say, as I knock his fist in agreement.

Corbin calls Mabel over and whispers to her. She nods with something like glee in her eyes.

A few minutes later, the bride and groom settle in at a white table, with Jameson and Remy nearby. Everyone's in place. Mabel grabs the first slice of wedding cake for the couple to test and heads over to Caroline and Parker. Since the camera is focused on the couple, I take my chance.

I catch Jameson's eyes and motion for him to join Corbin and me behind the counter. Jameson's brows scrunch and he gives a *who, me* look. I nod, mouthing "*Yeah*."

And that's all it takes to reel him in. The status seeker heads over to us.

"Hey, my buddy wanted to hear more about your beer. You know Corbin Knight? He's on the Foxes too," I say, casual and nonchalant as I jerk my thumb toward him.

"Oh, yeah. For sure," Jameson says, excitement flickering in his beady little eyes. "Great goal the other night."

"Thanks, man," Corbin says, then nods to the ever-present bottle Jameson holds like it's his security blanket. "Tell me more. Because I'm thinking a bakery that serves beer is the next big thing."

Jameson buys it hook, line, and sinker. "You're speaking my language. What goes better with cake than brew?"

Anything. Literally anything.

But Corbin dials in an Oscar-worthy performance, setting an elbow on the counter, looking like he's all ears. "Tell me what you got, my man."

Jameson launches into a long-ass description of every excruciating detail of his beers, while I slip away and join Remy.

She gives me a silent look, asking *what's up*.

I just flash her a satisfied smile, one I hope reassures her that I've got this handled. She doesn't stop though. Her eyes are imploring.

Right. She hates surprises. Don't want to stress her out, so I lean in, brush some strands away from her ear, and whisper, "Just taking care of the best man with a little distraction."

It takes a beat as she watches them, then she puts it together, her brown eyes sparkling as she seems to fight off a smile. When Caroline slides the cake her way, Remy lasers in on the maid-of-honor job. She takes a bite of the vanilla and buttercream concoction. As she licks her fork, she moans her approval. "So good," she says to Caroline, but I'm hearing it in other contexts.

Imagining it.

Heat flares through me.

Remy hands me a fork, saying, "Try it."

I take a bite of the cake, and it's sweet and moist. "Delicious," I say, but I'm looking at her pretty mouth, remembering the taste of her at the picnic. Craving another one.

"Told you cake tasting would be fun," she says.

And so is fucking with her douchey ex. I sneak a glance to the counter where Corbin peppers him with question after question about beer he's never going to carry.

When I turn back to Remy, she's smirking at me. Partners in crime.

The videographer is busy shooting Caroline and Parker as they discuss whether the buttercream and vanilla is better than the chocolate ganache or the one with strawberry. The bride and groom quickly eliminate the chocolate ganache, and since we're in the background of the shot, I presume, I drop a kiss to Remy's cheek.

Possessive.

Lingering.

Her breath hitches, then she blinks off her reaction as I pull away.

Remy nods to a slice of cake in front of us. "Have some more. You've earned it."

I dig in, then nod my approval as I give her the fork again. The videographer backs up, widening the shot while Caroline asks Remy to weigh in on the options.

She points to the one with strawberries. "This one. It's so good," Remy says.

"Isn't it?" Caroline replies with a proud smile, like she's genuinely glad Remy agrees. She turns to Parker. "What do you think, babe?"

He gives a doting smile. "It's the best, honey."

I flash back to Remy's words that he's not in charge of anything. Seems so, but the way he listens to Caroline and focuses on her tells me he likes his life that way. That he knows his role and seems damn content with it.

I know my role—making sure Remy gets to experience the opposite of her ex. I flick my gaze to the counter, confirming Corbin's still distracting him.

Yep. He is.

I return my focus to Remy as she takes one more bite of the strawberry cake. When she sets down her fork, the gods of fake dating smile down on me since there's a smudge of something white and sweet on the side of her lips.

"You've got something here," I say, and sure, I could motion to her lips. Yeah, I could offer her a napkin. But I didn't say yes to being her guy to half-ass things. I'm all the way in. With the videographer turning the lens toward us, I say to Remy, "It's just a little frosting."

Her eyes glimmer. "You'd better kiss it off then, Lake."

As if I was going to do anything else.

I lean in, flick my tongue across the corner of her lips, and taste the sweetest treat ever.

She shudders as a soft murmur ghosts across her pretty lips. That quiet gasp thrums through my body, vibrates in my bones. And sets up camp in my head.

It's a sound that's going to stay with me all night long, and then when I get on a flight for an away game tomorrow and leave all this fake romance behind.

I definitely owe Corbin dinner for the rest of the season, but it's so worth it as Jameson pitches his beer to Corbin the whole damn time we're cake tasting, and I've made sure the fuckface didn't get his product placement in this wedding segment after all.

After the event wraps up and her sister and team leave, I linger with Remy in the bakery.

"You don't mess around," she says, something like wonder in her voice.

I give a cocky shrug. "I'm a full-service kind of boyfriend."

"Seriously. That was so extra," she says, then licks her lips. "But in the best of ways."

"You deserve extra. Like I told you."

"And you delivered, Lake." My name comes out soft on her lips, but full of meaning, full of appreciation.

For a few heady seconds, I'm tempted to lean in, kiss her mouth for real, and thread my hand through her hair.

But the cameras are off, her sister is gone, and Jameson has left the premises. It's just Corbin and Mabel, along with Remy and me, and we're not fake dating for us or for them. We're fake dating for others.

There's no need to perform, so I don't touch her again.

* * *

I cock my arm, stare down the pallino, and then take perfect aim, tossing the red ball in my hand.

"C'mon, baby," I urge, coaxing it along the court with the power of my words and will till it smacks the target ball.

I thrust my arms in the air, victorious. "Pretty sure I'm undefeated now," I tell my teammates at The Gameyard, a new Cozy Valley bar and grill that's known for its good food, but also its lawn games. My teammates kidnapped me a few months ago and forced me to join them for their *excursions*. I've made them regret that every day by beating their asses every time I play. Like I did just now.

"Why did we want him to join our club again?" Corbin asks with a groan as he records my winning score on a piece of paper. "It's bad enough I had to see him at my bakery last night."

"It's okay," Ivan says, then lifts his phone and snaps a picture of me. "We have blackmail power now. We can release photos of you being social."

"No one would believe they're real anyway," I say with a scoff, then sink down into a lawn chair, relaxing. It's good to chill for a bit after we all met for a hard workout this morning at Miller's home gym. We'll hit the road tonight for some away games.

"That's true," Riggs says thoughtfully, twisting at the label on his bottle of bubbly water. "Everything is fake these days."

I flinch. Does he know about my fake romance? Do they suspect it's all a ruse? But how could they?

"And I'd deny it," I say, keeping the focus far away from my inner thoughts and my outer dating life. "And thank you for inviting me to your Lawn Men Club so I could eviscerate you."

"Feel free to leave now," Miller says, nodding to the bar. "And don't let the door hit you on the way out."

"You're stuck with me schooling you now," I say.

"And since we're stuck, let's talk Montreal," he says, shifting gears to chat about the team we'll be playing next on their turf. "They lost their star forward and their offense has been weaker this season. We need to control the blue line and be aggressive with puck possession."

"And that also means the D-men need to keep *their* D-men off the puck too," Ivan puts in.

We dig into a game plan, something we'll share with the other guys on the plane and the coaches. When we're done, Ivan turns back to me, stroking his chin.

"You went to the coffee shop the other day. For a team promo."

It doesn't sound like a harmless observation. More like a setup. "Yeah," I say, nonchalant.

"What's that about? Is this another layer of the Lake onion?" Riggs asks.

"Just wanted to help," I say.

"More like help your new woman," Ivan says with a satisfied grin, then wiggles his bushy brows. "You've got it bad. Admit it."

"Please," I say, adding a scoff to sell it.

Riggs pats me on the back. "Our boy is smitten."

I turn it right back to him. "Like you too, Fanboy," I say, using the nickname Corbin gave him when he pursued and fell for a reality show star—now his girlfriend.

"Yep. I'm calling it," Ivan says, then reaches for his wallet. "Here's a grand on Lake falling in love."

I double scoff. They have no idea how far off they are. "I'll bet against it."

Corbin whistles, then shoots me a sharp stare. "You really want to go there?"

Remy deserves the world. She deserves a man who's not broken. She deserves someone who believes in romance.

And that's just not me.

"I do," I say, and I bet against us.

18

THE PERFECT SQUISH

REMY

I'm finishing up my podcast in a studio in the Mission District, reading a How We Met story about a couple who were reaching for the same avocado at the farmers' market.

"And then, we debated how ripe it should be," I say, recounting the tale a listener submitted to me of how she met her wife. "And she insisted it should be almost squishy. I said 'not quite squishy' and we discussed the squishiness of avocados over the display at the farmers' market for a good long time till I asked her out."

I pause and sigh happily into the mic. "Listeners, is there anything better than the perfect squish of an avocado? Wait. You don't even need to answer because the only answer is yes."

Then I return to my computer and read the rest of the tale the couple sent me. "And now as I wrap up this week's episode, I have the term of the week for you. It's...good growl, as in a good growl brand of chivalry. It's when a man—or hey, a woman can growl too, because I'm all for equal opportunity growling—makes that sexy, rumbling sound in their throat and goes all possessive for you." I shudder at the memory of

Lake's sounds. "And let me tell you, once you hear it you don't ever want to go back to a time without growls. Until next time, don't forget to send me your cutest meet-cutes to share on the air."

I hit end on the computer and save the recording. I glance up at the window for the studio and wave at Skylar, my good friend who records her podcast here too. She hooks me up at the end of her hour-long slot here and since my show's a shortie, weighing in at less than ten minutes, I can just slide in for free. That is the only way I can afford the studio.

I gather my computer and head out. In the hallway, Skylar's holding her Doxie mix in her arms as she says, "For the record, perfect squish applies to butts too."

"Dog butts?"

"And hockey butts," she says, since her fiancé is a retired hockey player. "They should be hard enough to bounce a quarter off of and soft enough to squish in your hands."

I can't help but wonder if the squish of Lake's ass is perfect.

"Duly noted," I say as Simon shoots me the side-eye he's famous for, but I scratch his chin anyway, then say goodbye to my redhead friend, telling her I'll meet her in a couple of hours for pickleball. I've always loved playing with my friends, but Elena reminded me when I saw her this morning to do the things I *love still. Spend some time dating yourself. That'll help you move forward.*

And that wasn't the best opening either to tell her about my fake boyfriend.

Before I can see my friends though, I pop into my mom's favorite coffee shop in the Marina, finding her already at a table, peering through her reading glasses at her phone, then tapping the screen. A brain game, I bet. She spots me and waves me over.

"Did you make it to the top of the diamond league today in your app?" I tease.

"Please. I own that spot in the leaderboard," she says, then asks what I want to drink.

Nothing, honestly. But it'll make her think I didn't want to come to this impromptu review of the wedding plans if I say that, so I opt for a vanilla latte.

Once it arrives, she pins me with a more serious look. "Let's make sure we haven't forgotten anything for Caroline's big day. Is there anything we might have missed?" She clicks on her phone again, opening a calendar app. "I have a tracker from when I was planning weddings. We have to make sure she's all set with the wedding favors she ordered. Then we'll want to confirm the spa knows exactly how many people are coming. We want it all to come together without a hitch."

"Of course," I say with a crisp nod, ready to do my part to make sure everything is just so.

An hour later, I'm more than ready to leave the shop and am gathering up my things when she flashes me a knowing smile. "So...the hockey player," she says, in a *tell me more* tone.

Ah, of course she'll still want to know why I haven't said much. "What about him?"

"He's quite taken with you. Sending you foxes and plants. That's going to make such a good story someday."

Seriously? Is she already planning my wedding? "Mom!"

"But it will, Remy."

"We're just dating," I say, to try to call her off the scent.

"And you're already planning wonderful dates," she says, and something twists uncomfortably in my chest when she says that.

"That's what I do," I say, evenly. "Or at least what I'm trying to do."

"And you're so good at it." The twinkle in her eyes vanishes though, and with some concern, she asks, "But are you sure you're ready to date like this again? Is it the right time?"

It's like whiplash. She literally just said our romance would make a good story, but now she wants to know if the time is right? But that's my mother. She wants everything to be done in a certain way, on a certain timetable. Caroline's the opposite. She marches through life like a vengeful goddess, taking no prisoners, and making no excuses for living the life she wants.

"Yes, Mom," I say, holding my ground, wishing I were a little more like my sister.

* * *

Once I'm home, I put the encounter with my mom out of my mind. I edit the podcast file, then post it and get ready for the game with Mabel, Skylar, Trevyn, and also Clementine, who doesn't play pickleball but likes to watch while she knits.

As I'm tugging on a pickleball dress, my phone pings. I grab it as I pull the skirt down, and a little thrill zings through me when I see the name.

Lake: There are a few things better than the perfect squish of an avocado.

He listened to my show? Already? He's in Montreal, and game time is soon. Did he listen to it during his pre-game workout? I picture him on an exercise bike at the visitors' weight room, or lifting weights, headphones on, my voice in his ear, him sweating. I'm breathless, both from the news and from the images, and it's ridiculous how much I want to hear what's better than a perfect squish.

Remy: Do tell.

Lake: The quiet of the sun rising over the hills in the morning. A hard workout. And a catnap. Ideally with a cat.

Is Lake a secret poet? As I grab my racket, I dictate a reply.

Remy: I wish I were a napper. They sound delightful, but they make me more tired.

Lake: Then you're not napping right.

Remy: There's a right way to nap?

Lake: Yes. I can show you.

I run a hand through my hair. Do I want to take him up on that offer or is he teasing?

Remy: You're actually offering nap lessons?

Lake: I am.

. . .

He's so straightforward, it makes me feel wobbly in the best of ways. I'm so not used to a man like him. Blunt, confident, no bullshit.

Remy: Far be it from me to say no then.

I head to the door, feeling frothy. All from imagining...a nap? Who even am I? When did naps become flirty?

When Lake Axelrod told me he'd give me a lesson.

I picture him tugging me against him, spooning me, running his nose through my hair. The zing rushes down my chest, straight to my thighs where a sweet ache builds.

Lake: Nap lessons are a go when I return.

I'll see him in a few more days, and I kind of can't wait. But I also need to return to topic number one.

Remy: You listened to my podcast already?

Lake: It's what a good boyfriend would do.

Jameson never did.

Remy: I'm not used to that.

Lake: Remy, you watch my hockey games. Of course I'm going to read, listen to, and watch what you do.

I'm warm everywhere, but I remind myself not to get caught up. This is all part of him showing me how a man should treat a woman. That's all this is. It's not about me per se. It's some kind of, well, point. A point I like a lot. But a point, nonetheless.

Remy: Thank you. I appreciate it.

Lake: Besides, I was your inspo on the episode.

A blush creeps across my cheeks. He knows? I gulp then reply, coyly I hope.

Remy: Were you now?

Lake: You know I was. And now I know you like a good growl. If you're a good girl, I'll do it again for you.

I'm on fire, and I think I can be very, very good.

Remy: During a nap lesson?

Lake: Yes.

Maybe I'll find out about the perfect squish of his ass then too.

19

ALWAYS TOMORROW

LAKE

The loss in Montreal chases me on the plane to Denver. It was a sloppy, lazy game, especially after we strategized for it, and especially since we should have won. We can do better. Hell, we can dominate. That's my plan when we land in the mile-high city, when we hit the arena for morning skate, and when I line up my gear in just the right order in the locker room later for the game.

Wait. Should I switch out the shoulder pads for the elbow pads this time? Yeah, that's a good idea. Best to break this losing streak before it even becomes one. I move them around in front of my stall.

"You're switching things up already?" Riggs asks from his stall across from me.

"You memorized my routine. That's sweet."

"Yeah, it's sweet that I'm observant," he deadpans.

"Fair point. I'll allow it."

"Gee, thanks."

"And yeah. I'm switching it up. Don't like losing," I say.

"Me neither," Riggs seconds.

"Gotta do whatever it takes."

Riggs sits back on the bench in front of his stall, his brow furrowed like he's giving that some thought. "I hear you," he says, then lines up his gear in the same order as mine right when Miller strides in.

His gaze swings from me to Riggs and back, adding up the evidence. "I'm in."

As a goalie, he's got way more gear, but he follows the same basic order and the three of us are getting ready and lacing up our skates in sync.

It's going to be a good game. I just know it. Even though when I hit the ice, my gaze snags on a banner hanging in the rafters. One that has my last name on it. A reminder that I have a late dinner tonight. One I wish I were looking forward to.

But for now, I have a game to play, and once I'm on the ice, I'm free.

The game always clears my head.

Hockey, only hockey.

* * *

We're down by one. That's nothing. That's one goal to even it, and one more to pull ahead. We've got this. My heart is pounding against my rib cage and my thighs are screaming as I charge down the ice, flying toward the Denver goal. I'm jostling for the puck, and I've almost got it. I lunge for it with my stick but wind up pulling Denver's center with it.

Fuck my life.

The ref shoots his arm above his head and calls for a hooking penalty.

I curse up a storm as I skate toward the penalty box. The second the door closes, I rip off my helmet and slam it down.

Fuck, that was amateur hour.

I should have done better.

When I look up there's a shot of me on the Jumbotron in the box. I'm still not used to seeing that guy with short hair looking back at me even though it's been more than a few days now.

Maybe the haircut is fucking me up? I haven't won since Remy took the scissors to my head. Is that why we're losing?

But there's no way, since the mere thought of her loosens the tension in my jaw, the pressure in my head. Remy can't be anything but the best of luck.

This is just one of those games, and it sucks. But there's time to turn it around.

The clock ticks interminably down, and I make sure I don't look at their banners again. Don't want to think about the dinner. Don't want to think about anything but owning this game. I yank my helmet back on, and when the clock eats up all the time, I fly out of there.

* * *

But the best laid plans of hockey players don't always work out, since we trudge off the ice with an L. Two in a row, and I'm pissed.

Hockey is my happy place. It's where I don't worry about my family, or injury, or the past, or the future.

Daniel catches up with me as I turn into the locker room. "Good game. Tough loss," he says, and there are no playful nicknames on nights like this, when we lose.

"Yup," I say, then brace myself in the doorway for whatever's coming next. I doubt he tracked me down to give me a sympathy pat on the shoulder.

"There are some local press who want to chat with you. Since you're from here and all."

"Right," I bite out. I went to college nearby, so even though I doubt that's the only reason the press wants to talk to me, it's hard to turn him down. I don't like talking to the media, ever, but maybe it'll be good for Remy at work if I come off as a nice guy and not a standoffish jerk. I'm thinking of her as I say, "Sure, I'll talk."

A few minutes later, I sink onto a chair in the media room, ready to share some PR drivel about missed opportunities, cleaner play, and avoiding penalties, when a reporter shoots up a hand and clears her throat. "Andie Blackwell with *The Sports Network.*"

Tension shoots down my spine. That's Heather's old coach from college. I'd heard she was a color commentator for the Denver team now, but I never dug deeper into that.

I meet her gaze across the room, and it's eerie. Surreal even. I remember going to Heather's games in college, seeing her huddling with Andie and the other coaches.

"This is where Heather Axelrod used to play when she was in the pros," Andie says. "Did that make tonight's game harder for you?"

No.

But I can't say that. I'd sound like a calloused dick. They want me to say it's hard. They want me to say it's always tough playing in the arena where my deceased wife was the star of the women's pro league. Where her number was retired and hangs from the rafters. They want the same story they always have—the golden hockey couple.

"It's tough whenever you're on the road," I say.

"Of course. But here she left quite a legacy," Andie pushes. "Was that on your mind during the penalty or at any other time?"

I feel like I'm wearing a straitjacket. My jaw clenches as I chew on what to say. The truth is, I hardly ever think of her.

The truth is, I'm a cold, heartless jerk because I was falling out of love with her when she took her motorcycle out, driving fast and dangerously. And she was falling out of love with me too. Of course I was devastated when she died. Of course it upended my world. Of course I grieved. I cared deeply about Heather, and I wanted her to live a long, beautiful life.

But no one wants to hear that we were talking about divorce at the end. That we'd decided to separate the day before the accident. Least of all her parents, who I'm having dinner with tonight.

I meet Andie's inquisitive gaze.

"My mind was on scoring. On trying to be a good teammate. But yeah, of course I think of the legacy Heather left, and I know her family would be proud."

And that's true enough.

* * *

Later, I leave my teammates behind at the hotel and head to an Italian place Heather's parents loved, finding them at a booth with a red-and-white checked tablecloth and a parmesan cheese shaker. It's where they always took us out to dinner after games.

"Lake." Her mother stands to give me a warm hug. "So good to see you. Bummer about the game, but we were rooting for you."

"We always are," her dad says.

"Thanks. Just sorry we didn't win tonight. Especially since you were there."

"There's always tomorrow," he says jovially. Then something painful flashes in his eyes—the same green as Heather's. Maybe it's the awareness, for her, there was no tomorrow.

"Yeah, there is." I sit and grab a menu so I can avoid the truth about tomorrows.

I barely notice the menu as guilt sits heavily in my gut. They think I'm grieving more than I am, but correcting that assumption would hurt them more.

They like to talk about their only child. And I'm not going to deny some grieving parents the chance to take a trip down memory lane to better days.

Once we order, her mom talks about the game, then says, "Heather really loved playing at that arena." She's wistful and understandably so.

"She did," I say, and so it begins.

I do my best to honor her memory. For them and for the eight years I spent with Heather, both in college and after.

Chiming in now and then, I listen as they talk about her, what she was like, what she enjoyed, what made her laugh.

I eat my pasta primavera and nod, but my thoughts are back in San Francisco, with the woman I can't wait to see again.

20

VACATION FLING

REMY

"They love the MOH."

The bus just dropped me off and I'm walking into the arena with my sister in my ear, her voice a little husky as she tells me how her audience is liking the videos.

"And are they saying MOH too?" I tease.

"Argh! I can't believe Fallon is rubbing off on me like that."

I breathe a sigh of relief. "Thank god. I was worried you were going to start talking in abbreviations."

"Nope," she says, then must tug the phone away, since she's now coughing faintly in the background.

"Are you okay?"

"Perfect. I've got vitamin C, some tea with honey, and my mind vise to put this cold into."

"Where you'll crush it in seconds?" I ask as I grab the door to the employee entrance and tug it open. The second I'm inside the arena my chest flutters, as I wonder if Lake's here too. But I try to ignore those feelings, and those questions. I'm just going to work. That is all.

"Ideally. I don't permit sickness," she says, all stoic and badass.

"Dude, I can't stand germs."

"I know, Remy. Your mind vise is stronger than mine. Miss Perfect Attendance who was never sick."

Well, the youngest had to excel at something. But I don't say that out loud, since it'll sound like I was competing against Caroline as a kid. We were too far apart in age to have that dynamic. "I'm sure your mind vise has already destroyed it," I say, then tell my sister to give me a second as I stop briefly at security, where I say hello as they scan my bag and I walk through the turnstile.

On the other side, I tell her I'm back.

"Good. And as I was saying, they love the maid of honor. They being Fresh Face, my viewers, and the producers."

"That's nice," I say, since I don't want to get too excited over something I have zero control over—whether my sister's fans like me or not. And sure, I'm vaguely tempted to suggest that maybe Fresh Face will sponsor my fledgling podcast too, but I'm not going to start poaching my sister's sponsors or begging for them.

"And," Caroline adds, with a little flirt in her voice now, "I don't mind the hot hockey player in the shots too."

And those flutters take off, flying on little wings inside me as I head to the personnel doors, half wishing I weren't hoping to run into Lake, and half hoping I will. This is so annoying.

"Want to know why?" she asks.

"Sure," I say, intrigued.

"Because we're showing that jackass. Our plan is working. The preemptive strike," she says.

Oh right. That. The whole reason for the fake date. My sister is Machiavellian. "Yep. It totally is."

"Jameson's bringing Chelsea to the wedding now," she says, venom in her tone.

My nose crinkles. This shouldn't bother me, but it does. "His new...girlfriend?"

"I don't know. All I know is he said she's his plus-one, and I hate him."

That is so very my sister. "Understandable."

"But also, this is precisely why you needed that plus-one. To beat him to it and you did. So let's keep beating him. Keep showing him that you're not even thinking about him, or that damn Jumbotron. Why don't you bring Lake to the MOH—shit fuck damn—the maid of honor fitting after all?"

My lips threaten to curve into a smile. It's embarrassing how excited I am for extra time with him beyond the next wedding event. Extra time like...nap lessons?

Get that out of your head.

Ever since he teased me about those, it's not come up again. It was just fun—that was all. So ridiculous of me to even think I'd be having nap lessons. Who does that? Who wants that?

And yet, I'm practically giddy as I say, "Sure, I'll ask him."

Since I have a good excuse to reach out.

"All right. I have to go shoot a promo for tomorrow's episode. Wish me luck."

"Good luck with the germ-crushing brain."

I hang up, and start to head straight to the stairwell that'll take me to my floor, but before I know it my strappy shoes are taking me someplace else.

The long way. I pass the locker room, the weight room, the game video room, hoping to get a glimpse of the players.

But it's quiet, no one's here yet, and when I reach the stairwell at last I feel foolish.

This feeling is an excellent reminder that as much as I want him to go to the fitting with me, there's nothing real between us.

I reach my cube, settle in at my standing desk, and get to work on the event with the animal rescue. As I spend most of the morning working on it, I nearly lose track of time. Coordinating the details, checking on the venue, planning for the photographer and then lining up everything in a new spreadsheet gives me a sense of purpose I enjoy far too much.

I'm about to head down to Daniel's office and update him on how it's coming together when footsteps grow louder and there's a rap on the corner of my cubicle. I spin around to find Devon, our go-getter intern from the local university's sports MBA program, carting a gift bag. "Delivery for Remy Hatmaker." Her eyes spark with curiosity. "Looks like someone likes you. Also, I'm guessing it's from Lake."

My stomach swoops once more from the possibilities of what's in the bag, but worry chases it. This is what Daniel warned me about. People will assume things about Lake and me. They'll be excited for me for this "real romance." But what will she say to me when it "fake ends"?

I don't want to think about all the sympathy looks I'll get, the sad faces, the elbow rubs, the *you'll get through this* comments.

Even if he is a gentleman. Even if I control the narrative.

But right now I'm consumed with wanting whatever's in that bag. It's overwhelming, this urge to open the bag. I reach for it as calmly as I can. "Thanks, Devon."

She lingers, like she wants me to open it in front of her, but I won't. I don't know what it is. And I'm not sure I'll be able to hide my copious excitement when I do. Or that I want anyone to see it.

She rocks on her shoes. "What do you think it is?"

"I don't know," I say, honestly, trying to strip emotions from my voice.

She sighs happily. "I love it when my boyfriend sends things to the office. It's like peak boyfriending."

Then she leaves, and I breathe a sigh of relief and count down the interminable seconds till I can open the bag. Finally, I do, the crinkle of the tissue paper like a prelude. I dip my hand inside, then gasp, purse my lips, and fight off a squeal.

It's a blanket, soft and fleecy and the color of sage and sweet dreams. There's a card attached. With shaky fingers, I flip it open.

First, you'll need a nap blanket.

I don't want to be this excited. Really, I don't. There's no place for these silly emotions to go. So I don't pick up my phone right away to thank him, or ask him to the dress fitting. I've got to figure out how to maintain some semblance of... chill.

Yes, that's it.

I am chill. Super chill. So unbelievably chill that I find myself slipping into the ladies' room, cautiously checking behind me, then locking the door. Solo bathrooms for the win. I dial Mabel's number before I think twice.

"Girlfriend Emergency Line. How may I help you?"

I hesitate, then ask, "How did you know it was an emergency?"

"Easy. You picked up the phone and called. What's going on?"

The sound of the bakery on her end of the line drifts by—the clatter of a tray, the closing of an oven door. I blow out a breath, grateful she picked up in the middle of the day. But what do I want to say? All the things I can't tell my sister. For sure, the details I wouldn't even begin to share with my therapist.

"This whole fake dating thing," I blurt out.

"Oh, this sounds good. Give me ten seconds to set the

timer on my Sweet and Salties 'cause I don't wanna fuck that up." There's a pause as she works on her pretzel bars, then she's back. "What's going on?"

My heart is beating uncomfortably fast. "I'm not even sure. That's the issue. Lake sent me a gift. Well, another gift. He's given me a bunch."

"Oh, I love a gift giver."

"I know. I mean, it's all good. It's fine. It's just that I don't want to enjoy this so much. This fake dating."

"And, are you enjoying it?" she asks, inquisitive, like a curious reporter.

"Yes, so much, and it's scaring me."

She sighs sympathetically. "Oh, honey, why is it scary? Because he's nice to you?"

I close my eyes, lean against the cool tiled wall. "Yes. It feels good. These little things he does to make it seem real. The stuffed foxes, and the bird feeder, and the texts, and now this—a soft blanket. I don't want to get used to it."

"Because it's not real?"

I swallow roughly, then whisper in an unsteady voice, "Yes, that's it exactly."

She hums thoughtfully. Taking her time, it seems, before she speaks again. "Think of it like a vacation, then. You don't go on vacation and spend the whole time thinking about all the work you have to do when you get back, or all the chores waiting for you, right?"

"Right."

"You try not to think about how much it's going to suck to get on that plane when the trip ends. Instead, you swim in the ocean, lift your face to the sky, and soak in the rays."

My erratic pulse starts to calm. My breath comes more steadily as the words sink in. "He's just a vacation from my real life," I say.

"Exactly. You're allowed to enjoy it. And now go enjoy the hell out of your vacation."

That's what I needed to feel in control again of my wild emotions.

I say goodbye and tap out a text, starting with the first order of business.

Remy: Do you think you could come with me
to the maid of honor dress fitting after all?

His reply is instant.

Lake: Do you think you can come downstairs
to the training room right now?

Electricity shoots through me, and I say yes.

* * *

A few minutes later, I round the corner toward the training room, but I stop in the doorway, taking in the scene.

Lake lies face down on a blue massage table, with the team's massage therapist—Jaden—kneading the hockey star's shoulder.

Worry wings through me. Did he get hurt on the trip? I would have heard about it, though, through Daniel and internal reports. But what if something's come up?

Jaden's back is to me, his T-shirt with the crest for Howard University, his alma mater, stretching across it, as he digs in on Lake's right side, pushing with his whole body. Seconds later, the therapist lets go and says, "Better?"

"Better," Lake grunts.

Jaden backs away, nodding toward me with a "Hi, Remy" right as Lake pushes up, rolls to his side, and sits. His blue eyes connect with mine across the room and twinkle. "Hey."

Worry morphs into want.

"Hiiii," I say, but is that a word coming out of my mouth, or are there grunts too? Because Lake Axelrod is shirtless, his muscular arms on full display, his carved torso here for the gawking. I've never noticed when I've seen him shirtless before at the arena, but the owl has company.

A small herd of tiny, inked horses runs across his biceps. And a little cat is lucky enough to curl up on his lower abs. After I take in the art, my eyes help themselves to a tour of his body. A sprinkling of chest hair covers his strong pecs, travels down past that kitty, and disappears into the waistband of athletic shorts.

He's in ridiculous shape. Of course he is. He's an elite athlete. But it's one thing to know that and another thing to see it. To check out his bulging muscles after he's sent me a blanket. Not just any blanket, but a blanket he wants me to nap under. With him.

Heat shoots down my spine. My chest burns as I try to tear my gaze away from the sheer heft of his biceps, the sinews of his forearms, the cut of his shoulders. My fingers ache to roam down his stomach.

I clench my thighs and focus. First things first. "Are you okay? Did you hurt your shoulder on your road trip?"

He shakes his head. "Nope. Just a regular massage. Jaden makes me get them."

Jaden laughs. "Dude, you need them. You all need them."

My brain snags on another detail. "Were you texting me from the massage table?"

The corner of his lips lifts in a playful grin. "Jaden, was I texting from the massage table?"

Jaden rolls his eyes as he types into his tablet. "You? No. Of course not," he says, then mutters, "I only told you ten times to stop."

Lake smiles like he's busted and doesn't give a damn as he nods to the therapist. "Thanks, man. Feels better. Guess that science stuff does work."

"Gravity. It's a thing."

After Lake grabs a T-shirt and tugs it on, we leave the training room and head into the corridor. At the other end, the equipment manager heads toward us. Some of the arena staffers are nearby. We're hardly alone. Makes sense, since the team has a game tonight. I'm not sure where we're going, but Lake sets a hand on my back and says, "So you decided you want me there after all?"

I'm thrown off once again, like I was when he texted me the other day. But is it from the hand or the words? Or both? Or maybe from the way I *like* both. I remember Mabel's words —*enjoy it*. "I do," I say, feeling daring and breathless.

Something like a rumble seems to come from Lake. "So you missed me when I was gone."

I blink. He went there? Talking about missing? "I—"

I don't even know what to say.

"It's okay. I know you did," he says with a smug smile, then barely gives me a chance to answer since he adds, "what time do you want me to...come?"

I swallow, processing his naughty words, parting my lips, trying to speak without sounding like I'm thinking filthy thoughts as I give him the time of the dress fitting tomorrow.

"I'll pick you up," he says, then guides me toward the stairwell, opens the door, and lets it close. It's just us now in the echoey landing, a set of concrete stairs a few feet away. He nods toward me, his expression shifting to something less cocky, more needy. "You never mentioned the gift."

"Sorry. I was—"

He steps closer and presses his finger to my lips. "Don't apologize. I just want to know if you got it. That's why I was checking my phone on the massage table," he says, his voice stripped bare now, more vulnerable. "I got a text that it had arrived."

He's touching me at work. He's touching me in the hallway. He's touching me, and he checked his texts while he was getting worked on. And I'm melting into a liquid woman since he's desperate to know if I received his gift.

"Yes." And I loved it unreasonably. "Thank you. It's perfect."

"Good," he says, then drops his finger from my lips but doesn't let go of me. Instead, he coasts his thumb along my jawline up to my ear. I'm shuddering from the contact as he whispers, "Wish me luck tonight, beautiful."

I can't think straight, but somehow I manage to say, "Good luck tonight. I'll see you tomorrow."

And I turn around, head for the stairs, but then before I think twice, I do something terribly impulsive. Something unplanned. Something completely unlike me.

I spin around. "Lake?"

With a hand reaching for the doorknob, he turns back. "Yes?"

Impulsively, I close the distance between us, my shoes echoing loudly against the concrete floor as I reach him, cup his cheeks, and press a quick, featherlight kiss to his lips. "Here's a good luck kiss."

He looks shell-shocked and woozy as I back up.

Mabel was right. I am enjoying myself. *A lot.*

* * *

The next day I'm grabbing my bag, checking the location twice for the dress shop, and racing back into the bedroom to stare into the mirror one more time and make sure there are no blackberries from my lunch stuck between my teeth when my phone trills.

It's Caroline. She knows my fitting is in a few minutes. She must be checking in. Of course she is. That's so her. Even though she can probably see me leave from her house one hundred feet away.

"I'm on my way. I'll send pics, like I said. I promise," I say, brightly reassuring, hopefully before she can start to worry.

But she doesn't answer with words. She answers with a scratchy, loud bark. "I'm sick!"

"You are?" I automatically slide into nurse mode. "Want me to bring you some soup? Popsicles? Do you need more vitamin C? Some cough drops? Some medicine? Need me to take you to urgent care? I'll call a Lyft for us."

"Noooo," she says, wheezy and sad and so not her.

"Okay, what can I do? Name it."

"I need you to do the lipstick test for me."

I stop in the kitchen, set a hand on the counter to steady myself. "What do you mean?"

"Remember at the picnic? Margot and I decided to do the lipstick test? It was supposed to be tomorrow. But I'm too sick, and I don't want to get Parker sick, and I have to get it done soon. So can you do it today? With your date?"

My mind whirs with the thrill of more kisses. But also the

fear of asking Lake to kiss me. That good luck kiss in the stairwell was fun, spur of the moment. This would be planned.

The last time I thought I knew what a man wanted, I became the Friendship Bracelet Girl. Sure, Lake has kissed me on camera, but when my ex has been around, at the picnic, at the bakery.

Jameson isn't going to be present at the maid of honor dress fitting. It'll just be us. Just me and the flirty guy who wants to show me how a good boyfriend behaves.

But would he want the lipstick test as much as I do? That's my biggest worry—that it'd be one-sided. So I need to be crystal clear on what my sister expects. "What's entailed in a lipstick test?"

On a raspy cough, she says, "It'll be easy. Kiss him like you mean it."

21

ANNOYING DICKS

LAKE

In the passenger seat, Remy's fidgeting with her necklace the whole time. It's a silver pendant of a sun. She can't keep her hand off it as I drive along Van Ness toward the dress shop in Hayes Valley. Out of the corner of my eye, I catch her flipping it over like it's a coin, then back again.

She rolls her lips together, blows out a breath, turns the sun back over.

Something's up, but her self-protective streak is a mile wide and ten miles deep. I've got to start slow and easy to figure her out. "That a new necklace?"

"Oh, this thing?" she asks, like she's just noticed she's wearing it.

"Yeah. I haven't seen it before."

Her lips quirk briefly, then she says, "Your sister gave it to me just because."

"That's very Clem," I say.

"She's a gift giver," Remy replies but her brow knits, and she's thinking so loud, only I can't make out the words through the static. But something's on her mind.

Don't know what though, so I stay on topic for now. "She

likes to give me gag gifts. Last year for my birthday she sent me my face on a potato."

Remy bursts into laughter. "I had no idea that existed."

"Everything exists," I say.

"What'd you get her for her birthday?"

"A Congrats on Being My Sister candle," I say.

"I think she won that gift battle," Remy says. "But the candle is a nice touch."

"The potato is hard to beat," I admit, then nod toward her necklace. "That's pretty. And it suits you," I say, slowing at the red light at the top of a hill.

"Yeah," she says, a little distant. Then, maybe realizing she's elsewhere, she whips her gaze to me, flashing a closed mouth smile. "Thank you."

"It looks nice on you," I add, and I want to smack myself. *It looks nice on you*? That's so weak. I'm off my game now too. I tap the gas when the light changes.

She goes quiet again. Stares out the window.

I need to figure this out before we go into the shop. Don't want to walk into the store with this strange tension hanging over us before she has to deal with all her sister's people and all her sister's wishes.

The GPS chirps at me that we're nearing the store, so I turn at the next light, heading into the fashionable, trendy district. The second I find a spot on a side street, I cut the engine, turn to her, and ask plainly, "Are you okay?"

Right as she says, "There's something I have to ask you."

I'm grateful she wants to say something, but I brace myself for whatever it might be. "Ladies first."

She swallows, rolls her lips together, and meets my eyes. "Caroline's sponsor wants me to do a lipstick test. Today," she adds, the words piling up on top of each other. "Us."

My brain overloads. Wires short-circuit. They snap and

pop. Doesn't take a genius to figure out what a lipstick test is, but just in case, I say, "Like a kiss test?"

A tiny laugh falls from her lips. "Yes."

I smother a smile so it's not obvious this is making my fucking day. "On camera? To test the makeup or something?"

"Yes. It was Caroline's idea at the picnic, and she was going to do it with Parker—like a stress test for wedding makeup. And now she's sick, and of course doesn't want to get Parker sick before the wedding so she's on a strict no-kissing diet, but she asked us to stand in."

Somehow, in a past life, I was a very good boy. "You need to give me more than a good luck kiss," I say, then wiggle my brows. "Which, by the way, worked last night."

"I noticed. Five to three," she says, recapping our win last night.

"So we're the Fresh Face fill-in?"

She fiddles with the necklace one more time, bobbing a shoulder. "Yes. Is that okay?"

I could answer her truthfully with a *fuck yes*. But some moments call for a little...gamesmanship.

Some strategy.

Like it's a play I can see unfolding from all the way on the other side of the blue line, I scrub a hand across my beard, like I'm really considering this kissing test. "This would be for the cameras, right?"

"Yes."

"For Caroline to run as part of her wedding programming?"

"Yes," she says, her voice pitching up with worry.

"You want it to be perfect, I presume?"

"Yes!" She sounds desperate, and it's almost enough for me to put her out of her misery sooner.

But I'm not that nice. "There's something we're going to need to do first then."

She gulps. "What is it?"

I unhook my seatbelt. Unlock hers. Tuck a strand of hair behind her ear. Whisper against the shell of it, "Practice."

She trembles, a full-body shudder that I can feel. That I can hear. That drives me wild.

I pull back, pin her with a hot stare. "We should do it now."

"Before we go in," she says, jumping on board.

"Don't waste a second."

She grabs my collar, twists it, and tugs me close to her.

On the side of a busy San Francisco street, in the early evening, with the sun falling behind the horizon, I dip my face and kiss her sweet mouth.

I tell myself it's just a test.

That this is simply the kind of practice a fake romance requires.

But nothing feels fake about the quiet gasp she makes when my lips brush hers. Or the softness of her mouth. Or the grip of her fingers around my collar.

There's nothing false either about the way my mouth captures hers. Our lips slide together. My hand cups her cheek. My thumb coasts along her chin. Remy parts her lips for me, asking for more. Pulling me closer. Whimpering.

Heat roars through me, a heavy sort of ache as I follow her lead. Inching closer, kissing more, roping my hands through her hair, whisking my beard against her cheek.

She murmurs, then grabs my shirt even harder, a tight fist holding on. She picks up the pace, her mouth seeking more contact, her hands hungrier.

My greedy woman needs more, and I won't make her wait for it. I give her everything she asks for, snaking my hand around to the back of her head and cradling her skull. Nipping the corner of her mouth. Slipping my tongue between those plush lips.

Then guiding her eager, roaming hands away from the neckline of my shirt. As I take over the kiss, I peel her hand from the fabric of my shirt, then spread her palm wide open, and place it square on my right pec.

Well, she was checking me out yesterday. Might as well give the lady what she wants.

"Oh god," she moans softly against my mouth, then she takes what she desires.

She slides her hand down my shirt, her busy fingers traveling from my chest to my abs. It's decent, since I'm dressed, but it's wholly indecent too, the path she's taking, where she's headed, the hazy sort of lust that seems to consume her.

It's addictive, too, the way she responds when I show her where to go.

I could spend all night like this, wordless, just a touch here, a brush of my hand there, a reassurance that I want this.

But I'm keenly aware that Remy's a woman who likes to keep her commitments. And she made one to her sister. The more I kiss her like tomorrow won't arrive, the greater the chance she won't walk through that door to the shop. That'll make her mad at one person only—herself.

I summon all my resistance, cover her hand with mine, and wrench apart.

"We should go," I say, bluntly.

Her eyes are glossy. She gives me a funny look like my words don't compute.

I repeat it again. "You really should go," I say, maybe a little more forcefully than I meant.

Something seems to click inside her. "Right. Yeah. We

should." She's brushing her hands along her slacks, smoothing out her hair, and rearranging her features.

And fuuuuck. I was too harsh with the ending, with my tone. I don't want her to think I didn't like that kiss.

"Remy," I say, trying to cut through her worries.

But her phone trills. She snags it from her purse at the speed of sound. "Hi, Fallon. Yes, I'm on my way in right now."

She grabs the door handle and ejects from the car onto the sidewalk.

I'm up and opening the driver's side door in seconds when it hits me.

I'm sporting wood.

Great. Just great. Dicks are so annoying. "Remy," I call out, standing by the driver's side door as it shields my annoying erection. "I'll be right there. I need...to answer a message first."

She flashes a smile that I just know is fake. "No problem."

Then she rounds the corner and disappears.

22

CAN YOU SAY AWKWARD?

REMY

That was the most abrupt ending to the world's hottest kiss, and now I'm replaying every single second and wondering what went wrong as my shoes click on the sidewalk and I near Fallon.

The Fresh Face producer stands outside Champagne Taste, a consignment shop that specializes in upscale dresses for black-tie affairs.

Her lips are pinched. Her expression is stern. And I feel even more unsteady. From the kiss that felt like it ended with a correction on both ends—Lake's and now Fallon's.

He stopped that kiss abruptly, and I can't help but wonder why. Did he not like it? Not want it? Maybe I just can't read him. Or men for that matter.

But Fallon is an open book, tapping her ballet flat. "The MOH is here," she says into her walkie-talkie. She's talking to the videographer on a freaking walkie-talkie?

"I'm not late?" I say, but it comes out as a question.

She gives me a false smile. "Only by eight minutes. But I'm sure we can manage."

Was that an eight-minute kiss? I lost track of all time. Did

Lake? Something coils tight in my chest. I ignore the tension, the way I feel like a jack-in-the-box. "What order do you want to do things in?"

"Let's get you in the dress first. Then the kiss," she bites out as she opens the door with the Closed sign on it then peers behind us, scanning the sidewalk. "Did you bring a subject?"

"My wedding date," I say, but I feel foolish all over again. That kiss scrambled my brain.

"And where is he?"

"He'll be right in," I say, but I feel like I'm covering something up, like a girl making an excuse for a guy. I switch to problem-solving mode, trying to wrest control of the situation with a quick answer. "I'll get the dress on though."

Before I can take another step, she darts out a hand, her bony fingers circling my wrist. "The same one as before?"

I give her a look like she can't be serious. "Yes, of course it's the same guy."

Her lips twitch. "Good. We love a glow-up."

There's that word again. And I get it. Really I do. It's just so surreal to *be* the glow-up. But this is what I got myself into when I told my sister I'd get a date for her wedding.

I march into the shop, greeted by soft floral perfume, tasteful lighting, and Ella Fitzgerald music setting the vibe. I nod at the videographer, who's waiting with mini lights already set up around her phone camera, then say hi to a gray-haired woman at the counter wearing a shimmery blue dress. The shop owner, I remember from my first visit here. I flash my *I'm Caroline's sister and I'm not going to mess it up for her* smile. "Your shop is so pretty," I say to her.

"Thanks, love," she says to me in a warm voice that sounds like she's from London. Her cheeks are rosy in her pale complexion, and her silvery eyes twinkle. "Your dress is ready for you. It's in a dressing room at the back. The one with the red heart on the door."

"Thank you." I head straight past the racks of clothes to a hallway at the back of the shop.

There are two dressing rooms, and a wreath-like heart made of dried rose petals hangs on one of them. I yank it open. My black vintage dress with spaghetti straps hangs on a padded pink hanger.

"I'll just get this on," I say to no one, but really, to me, as I zoom into fix-it mode.

Inside, I tug off my sweater, skim off my pants, and shimmy into the dress. I'm zipping it up when the zipper snags.

"Crap," I mutter, right as the heavy sound of footsteps grows louder. Strong, purposeful footsteps. I pretzel my arms behind my back a little more, trying to loosen the zipper. But its stubborn metal teeth refuse to budge.

"C'mon," I grunt, fighting with it.

"Remy." Lake's voice is clear, like an order from the other side of the door.

It sends a zing through me, and I wish it didn't.

"I'll be out in a second," I say, all chipper and upbeat.

His big hand curls over the top of the dressing room door. "I didn't want it to end."

I freeze, my hands on the zipper. "What?"

"That kiss," he adds, lowering his voice, like he knows we can't act in public as if there might be any questions about our romance, any confusion.

"Oh. Okay," I say, my heart beating irritatingly faster.

"*At all*," he adds, emphasizing each word.

I purse my lips. I don't want to let on to Lake that I was doubting him. Or really, me. I don't want him to know that I thought—and it felt so important a few minutes ago—that he didn't want to kiss me with the same ferocity I wanted to kiss him. "It's all good," I say as breezily as I can muster.

"Are you dressed?"

"Yes, but the zipper is stuck."

"Let me in. I'll help."

I sigh, but I don't fight him. I let go of the naughty zipper and open the door. He joins me in the dressing room, closing it shut behind me with a decisive click. The sound of footsteps floats past my ears, but they don't sound like Fallon's ballet flats. More like heels, but they fade quickly enough.

Lake looks me up and down, his icy blue eyes like midnight flames, his voice rumbling in his throat. "Your dress," he says, raw and guttural.

"It's stuck," I whisper.

He moves behind me, runs a hand along the fabric, then gently, carefully wiggles the zipper from side to side. I try not to tremble from his fingers on me as he slides the zipper up, up, up.

He reaches the top, then clasps the eye hook together. "There," he says, low and smoky. He drops a soft, tender kiss to the space between my shoulder blades. It sparks from his touch. *I* spark.

"I didn't want you to be late. That's why I stopped."

I close my eyes, let out a shaky breath, more relieved than I want to be. "I thought you didn't..." I can't even finish.

"I do. I fucking do. But I was kind of a dick."

"You weren't."

"I was curt."

He *was* brusque when he ended the kiss. Still, I wish I didn't feel so bruised. So tender. I wish he didn't feel like I'm this damaged woman.

But maybe I am.

Maybe I don't have to be all the time though. I think of his words from the night Jameson dumped me in front of twenty thousand fans at the arena. *Chin up*. I can be brave again. I lift my chin, look in the mirror in the dressing room, and meet his gaze. "Thank you. For coming in here."

"Only place I want to be." He lowers his face, gazing at my body as he runs his hands over my bare shoulders and coasts them down my arms, slow and sensual. When he reaches my hands, he slides his fingers through mine. A double clasp, and it feels like a reassuring embrace from behind me. I'm fizzy everywhere, bubbles popping in every cell.

He meets my gaze straight on in the mirror again. "You'd better go put on some lipstick, Remy. I'm going to do everything in my power to absolutely fuck it up on camera."

All that tension, all that tightness, unwinds and slinks out the dressing room door, a jack-in-the-box unsprung. I turn around in his arms. "Thank you. For telling me all that."

He frowns, apologetic, then his lips return to a straight line. "I'm not always good with words."

I don't think that's true though. "You are."

But also, I think I need his reassurances more than I want to admit. And maybe that's okay.

Shoes click, flats this time, and a throat clears from the other side of the door. "Are you ready for the LT?"

"Yes," I say, opening the door, focused on why I'm here. The LT, or lipstick test.

With disappointment, Fallon points to my mouth, then dips her hand into her ever-present bag of makeup tricks. She extracts a lipliner and a tube of lipstick. "You were supposed to be wearing both."

"Oops," I say, while Lake coughs like he's fighting a laugh as he slips past us. I guess we know no lipstick can withstand an eight-minute side-of-the-road kiss that leaves you with a sweet ache between your thighs. "Give me the L and the LL then."

For the first time ever, the dour woman looks a little pleased as she hands over lipstick and lipliner, then tells Lake to wait by the wedding dresses.

When I finish applying the makeup, she marches over to the doorway leading from the dressing rooms back into the shop, motioning for me to join her. "You walk in from here, and the videographer will record you showing your dress to your date. You'll join him by the *wedding dresses*. Just talk naturally about the dress. Then I want you to say, 'But can this lipstick withstand a hot kiss?'"

I nod, repeating the line in my head. I didn't realize there was a script. But I also can't resist, saying, "Confirming you want an HK?"

Lake shoots his arm in the air from his spot near the dresses. "Or should it be a VHK?" He tilts his head, the most adorably quizzical look on his face as he asks if she wants a hot kiss or a very hot one.

The woman behind the counter hides a chuckle as she attaches tags to stacks of clothes on a pink, cushioned chair next to her.

"HK will suffice," Fallon says crisply.

"Got it," Lake says, then blows out a breath and murmurs to himself like he needs to remember every detail, "HK. Give her an HK. You've got this."

Fallon turns to the videographer. "Ready?"

"Always," she says.

Fallon backs me up to the dressing room area. "On three."

The videographer counts, and on cue, I emerge.

When I turn into the shop this time, Lake stares at me like he did the first time he saw me in my black strappy dress, with desire in his eyes. I walk across the store, the videographer following alongside me. It's so weird that someone's filming me, but I try to ignore her and act natural.

"Stunning," Lake says when I reach him.

And I forget the cameras. "You like?"

"Love," he says, as if he's mesmerized.

I strike a pose. I hardly feel like I'm acting. Lake's heated eyes journey up and down my dress, then he reaches for my hand. "I won't be able to take my eyes off the maid of honor."

"Good," I say, then he looks to my mouth.

And I forget my line. I forget the script. I forget everything but what he said to me about messing up my makeup.

Neither of us says a word. I don't know who makes the first move, but we collide. In mere seconds, he's kissing me fiercely, passionately, hands roping in my hair, hungry mouth devouring mine. He's relentless—determined, it seems, to destroy my makeup. As he kisses me, he dips me in the middle of the secondhand dress shop, his strong arm wrapped around me.

When the kiss ends, he tugs me back up, studies my lips, and smirks. "Sorry, Fresh Face."

There's no makeup that can withstand that kind of kiss.

23

IF YOU'RE READING THIS

REMY

After a few more takes, since of course Fresh Face doesn't want to show the kind of kiss that can decimate lipstick, we finally get one that shows off the lipstick's staying power even after a ten-second, knee-weakening kiss.

Fallon dismisses us, then leaves, the videographer dutifully following.

I change back into my clothes, then bring the black dress to the front of the shop, where the owner's working at the counter. "You did a great job taking it in. It fits perfectly."

"I have a brilliant seamstress. I'll let her know," she says, then pauses, her silvery gaze wise and curious as she glances from me to Lake, who's a few feet away from me. "You two are quite cute."

Lake turns toward her, then steps closer to me. "She is," he says, answering her as he looks at me, only at me. For a few breath-held seconds, it's as if the world spins away.

I blink, trying to come out of the haze as I tear my attention from him. "He *is* pretty cute."

Lake snarls. "I'm not cute."

I tap my chin, considering. "Handsome? Hot? Smoking? Strapping? Studly?"

"All of the above," Lake answers.

The shop owner laughs, then her laughter fades as she gestures to the two of us. "This is nice to see. He's a much better choice than your ex."

My cheeks burn for a few seconds, but for some reason I don't feel so embarrassed anymore by the Jumbotron incident, and how far and wide it's spread. I'm not sure if it's because of Lake or this woman, and the genuine sparkle in her eyes. She seems to really mean it. Like she's the kind of human who legitimately roots for redemption after a public heartbreak story.

Like mine.

Lake wraps an arm around my shoulders, then meets her eyes. "Couldn't agree more. Been wanting to see this myself for a long time too."

There he goes again. The man is seriously committed to this origin story of the long-standing crush. It gives me butterflies.

The shop owner arches a curious brow, then nods toward the back of the shop. "Give me a few minutes to hang it in a garment bag so you can take it home."

"Sounds great."

"I'm about to set out some lovely new sweaters and such. Clothes from an estate sale," she says, then waves to the pink chair. A mountain of neatly folded items sits on the chair, with dresses strewn over the back and jackets across the arm. "Feel free to take a look while you wait."

"Sure," I say, wandering over to the chair as she strides to the back of the shop, leaving Lake and me alone.

The store is quiet now; there's a lull in the traffic outside. The Ella Fitzgerald music from earlier has shifted to something newer, poppier. Ivy May, I think, a twenty-five-year-old pink-haired Brit who can dance and sing about heartbreak.

"Mind if I look? Maybe I can find that dream argyle sweater for your sister," I say as Lake leans against the counter.

"As a good BF I'd never get in the way of you thrifting."

I roll my eyes. "I see you're committed to the role."

"So committed," he says.

"Like I said, you're cute."

He growls. "Not cute."

"So cute."

He growls more deeply. "Cute things don't give good growl."

I smile as he drops another mention of my podcast, then paw through the sweaters, but there's nothing quite right for Clem or me. I riffle through the dresses on the back of the chair, when something rustles under my hand.

Feels like paper maybe, but it's also lacy. It's so different from the rest of the clothes.

I tug on the fabric, pulling more of the material, and something catches my eye and my hand. There's a piece of paper pinned inside the bodice of the dress, and it's—a wedding dress.

And it doesn't look old. It looks new and stylish.

The air whooshes from my lungs—estate sale. Did the bride die? I stare at the bodice of the dress and the piece of paper folded up inside it, pinned, with the words "Five Things To Do Before I Say I Do" on it.

I swallow, my mind racing, my eyes darting around the shop. I peer toward the back, looking for the shopkeeper. She's still busy.

I'm about to say Lake's name when he's moving toward my side, bending. "What did you find?"

Would this even interest him? But I remember his words

when I put on makeup last weekend. He's interested in what I'm interested in.

"Look," I say quietly. "It's like a letter pinned to the wedding dress."

"Open it," he says, quick, decisive.

"Okay," I say, needing no more permission than that. I'm dying to know what this says.

I unpin the letter, then unfold it.

And gasp. The first words are in a different handwriting from the rest of the note. They say: *If you're reading this, please treat it like the adventure this bride never got to experience.*

I glance at Lake. He nods urgently, then moves closer. My breath catches as I read the list with him by my side. As promised, it's five things this bride presumably wanted to do before her wedding. It's dated two months ago. I read it, and it says her wedding is this summer.

My stomach falls. Sadness grips my throat.

"She must have died," I whisper, meeting his eyes. His fill with sadness, sympathy. "Before she could do these things."

I bring my hand to my mouth, sealing in tears, or trying to.

"It's okay, Remy," he says, softly, reaching for my shoulder, squeezing it.

"It's not," I whisper, then choke out. "She wrote a list and didn't get to do it. She wanted to do this."

I squeeze my eyes shut, trying to block out the waves of emotion for someone I don't even know. There's no name on the note.

I should say something to the store owner. I really should. Her shoes are clicking and as they grow louder, she calls out in her warm, grandmotherly tone, "Find anything?"

Panic grips me. Do I tell her?

I don't know what to say, but Lake clears his throat. "We'll take this dress."

I flinch. He's buying a wedding dress? For me? What is even happening?

The shopkeeper smiles, a knowing, almost matchmaker-like grin as she glances from him to me. "I had a feeling."

But my stomach craters and it's not from the assumptions she's making. I can't take this. What if someone's looking for the note?

My gut churns, but I cut in. "There's a letter inside."

The woman smiles kindly. "I know. It starts with *If you're reading this...*"

She's read it. "Do you know the family? The bride? Did they give this to you?"

"They want to sell everything. Including..."

This is almost too much. But if they know, if they want this, this is meant to be. "Including the dress?" I ask, just to be sure.

"Including the dress," she repeats, then shrugs.

"Then, it's supposed to happen this way," Lake says, decisive, firm. He turns to me. "Do you want this?"

Four words and they feel like they're heavy, important. They hold the weight of this woman's last wishes. Her unfilled wishes. I don't know why exactly, but there's no question in my mind. I want this.

"I do," I whisper.

And that's it. He takes out his phone to pay, like buying a wedding dress for his fake girlfriend is just part of a regular day.

As he pays, he says to the shopkeeper, "Good thing we were here today."

"It's a very good thing," she says as she rings up the unused wedding dress. She gently folds the gown and the letter up, taking so much care with both as she slides them into a gift bag, and hands it to me along with the one containing my maid of honor dress.

It's like finding a message in a bottle. And now I have to decide what to do with it.

24

TWO HEADS ARE BETTER THAN ONE

REMY

I don't hesitate the second we're in the car. I turn to Lake. "Do you want to go to Puzzle Me This?"

He tilts his head, his blue eyes sparking with surprise. Like he kind of can't believe I asked that. "Yeah, I do."

His answer is emphatic and clear, and a feeling of calm spreads through me, chased by anticipation as he drives through the city at night, expertly navigating the stop and start traffic till we reach the Haight. A minute later, he's holding open the yellow door of the shop while I clutch my bag that holds an unexpected treasure—the unknown bride's wish list.

We pass the families assembling puzzles with cows and ducks, the friends sliding pieces of the Eiffel Tower into another, until we reach the drink counter. "Is it matcha month now? Latte week? Are you still in your chai days?"

I'm touched that he remembers. I study the chalkboard menu for several seconds, considering too many options. What is the right drink to talk about a list of five things to do before you say I do, even though you didn't get to say it? A sugary drink feels a little wrong. Something warm and comforting seems right.

And this bout of overthinking is brought to you by my too busy, too controlling brain.

"Surprise me," I say.

He turns to the barista and orders two vanilla lattes, each with extra caramel.

"That's a good surprise," I say.

"Had a feeling you'd like it."

When they're ready, Lake carries the mugs to a table—the same one as last time, only there's a different puzzle on it now. Instead of the Golden Gate Bridge, the Formica's home to a puzzle of signs with sayings—hit the road, get your ducks in a row, two heads are better than one.

He slides a piece of a head of lettuce into the *two heads are better than one* section. I spot a duck's bill and slot that in as Lake takes a drink, then gives an approving, "Damn this is good."

I try mine. "It really is."

But the hot beverage love fest ends there because this list is serious. It's poignant. It's full of hope—but hope that never came to be.

I overthink everything: the kiss in the car, asking Lake to be my plus-one, even my potential proposal in the twenty-four hours before it didn't happen. All this overthinking has left me feeling a little jumpy, a little tightly wound. What would it be if I let go a little? If I stepped outside of my normal life and let someone else's plans guide me?

"I should do this list."

He squints, tilts his head. "I don't think I heard you right."

Spreading open the piece of paper next to the half-done puzzle I speak a little louder. "I think I should do this. Is that ridiculous?"

His answer is instant—stern too. "Yeah, it's ridiculous."

My brow knits. Why would he say that? Lake's an athlete.

He's trained to take chances. This feels like a risk I should take. "Why is that ridiculous?"

It comes out like a challenge since, well, it is.

He sets down the cup with a decisive clink, his eyes locked on mine. "Because it is."

I scoff. "Seriously?"

"Yeah." He holds my gaze, his eyes darkening with frustration.

Well, I feel the same. I cross my arms. "It's not ridiculous."

He arches a brow. "It's ridiculous that you said *I*." He points to the paper but doesn't touch it. He treats it like it's a piece of art, something precious, something he doesn't want to sully. "*We* should."

We.

The word echoes. It vibrates inside me. I didn't see that coming. Should I have? I take another drink, processing his reaction. He wants to do this too? What would that look like? Him and me tackling a list of date-like experiences? A bucket list of romantic wishes? My breath catches with excitement, but I swallow down a healthy dose of worry too. It feels dangerous.

He breaks my thoughts with a question. "Remy, why did you think I bought the dress? Like, right away offered to buy it?"

I meet his determined gaze, focusing on his questions, not the million running through my head. "Because you want to be a good fake boyfriend? The whole 'be the best rebound ever' thing?"

Blowing out a frustrated breath, he leans back in the chair and drags a hand through his now very short hair. "Because it clearly touched you. Because it matters to you. But also, we found it together. It's like finding a wallet on the street. You'd try to return it, right?"

"Yes!"

"Or a dog who didn't have a collar or tag. You'd help the dog, right?"

"Of course. I'd take him to a rescue. Or give him a home if he needed one."

"The list is the same. We can't return this list. We can't give it back to her family."

"And we can't leave it undone."

He nods a few times. "There's only one thing to do with it. And maybe we weren't looking for it, but it found us. We're the guardians of this list now."

My skin feels tingly. My heart, bubbly. Maybe this drink is going to my head. That's the only explanation I have for why I say exactly what's on my mind. "I thought you were something of a secret poet," I say in a whisper, like a confession, "when we were texting the other day."

He scoffs. "I'm not."

"You say you're not good with words. But I say you are. Everything you just said is...kind of soulful."

He rolls his eyes, mumbling, "It's the right thing to do."

"You say you're rude and you're not. You're sweet." I spot another piece of the lettuce and attach it.

"Okay, now you need to stop."

But I don't. Apparently, when I stop overthinking I'm a little unleashed. "The last time we were here you admitted you were secretly sunshine."

He narrows his eyes, then scans the pile of puzzle pieces. "I never admitted it."

I lift the cup, not quite stifling a smile. "You didn't have to."

He snags a light green piece, adds it onto the one I just locked into place. "Enough of your poet theories. We have work to do," he says, all stern and bossy as he leaves the puzzle alone. He pushes up the sleeves of his Henley a bit, revealing taut forearms, strong and sinewy, with a smattering of dark hair. And the owl, perched on a tiny branch, watching me.

My chest rises and falls as I imagine reaching out a hand, touching those forearms, tracing the fine lines of his tattoo.

He points to the list, all sexy business.

I fight off a smile as I look down the list, reading the five items again. I think it's doable. I slip into planning mode, since now's the time. This list—it feels like something a romance designer would craft. It's like a series of experiences for a couple to complete before they walk down the aisle. A list of challenges for young lovers. A road map of where to go next.

I wish I knew who she was. I don't even know her name. But as I study this list, the pieces slide into place like a puzzle.

She liked dresses that are simple but with a little flare. Her handwriting is neat but she writes her y's with a flourish and dots her i's with panache, so she was orderly but artsy. I know, too, she had something of a romantic, adventurous heart. She was a dreamer and a doer.

I get her. I really do. I look up, fueled by this understanding. "We can do this whole thing before my sister says I do."

I brace myself for pushback, for questions. This list is a lot. It'll take time, and we only have a little over a week. It's too much to ask, perhaps.

But Lake simply nods a few times, like he's considering it. "Yep. It's a plan."

It's that easy with Lake, and I like that. Maybe I even need it.

As if this is an event I'm planning, I rub my palms together and get down to business. "We don't have much time. Item number one on Five Things To Do Before I Say I Do—play a truth-telling game." My stomach twists. That's exciting, but daunting. There are things I don't love talking about. But then again, we all have things like that. "Should we try Two Truths and a Lie?"

He scrubs a hand across his beard, momentarily distracting me. His hair is shorter on his head, thicker on his jaw. I kind of like the shift. That beard is making me think about how it might feel against my thighs.

I clench them as he shifts his gaze to the shelves in the store. He pops up. "I've got an idea."

I tuck the letter away in my bag as he busses our mugs quickly, then offers me a hand, like it's the most natural thing in the world.

It feels natural, but it also feels delicious in a way that makes my bones vibrate. That makes my pulse skitter. And that somehow calms my strung-tight nerves.

For now at least, but I'll take it.

We walk to the shelves, stopping at the card games. He scans the offerings, then grabs The Naked Truth with his free hand.

"Feels apropos."

He slides his thumb along the crease between my thumb and forefinger, a slow, smooth slide. I have no idea what I'm getting myself into, but I jump into the unknown of the list. "Sure."

We head to the counter and he buys the game. Before we leave, I hold up a finger. "There's something I need to do."

I head back to the table, remembering where I spotted the final piece for the *two heads are better than one* lettuce, then slide it into place. "I like this puzzle. Would your dad like it?"

His eyes flicker with vulnerability. "Yes."

I grab it and rush to the counter to buy it before he can stop me. When we get to his car, I hand it to him. "You can give it to him."

"Thanks. Seriously." He sets the puzzle and The Naked

Truth down on the back seat next to my garment bag and the gift bag with the wedding dress. "This means a lot."

This whole night has meant a lot. "You're welcome."

He turns on the car but doesn't make a move to go. He stares straight ahead at the street unfolding in front of us, clearly thinking before he turns to me. "It means a lot, especially since my dad's still around, you know?"

My throat tightens. "I do."

"Clem told you?"

"Enough. I know your mom left?"

He sighs heavily. "When we were in high school. Gavin was in college. She was just done."

My heart aches for his family. "I'm sorry. That sounds terrible."

He drags a hand across his beard. "It kind of sucked."

That's an understatement if I've ever heard one, but I'm learning he doesn't share easily. When he does it's the bare minimum. But sometimes the bare minimum is enough. "Do you ever miss her?"

He scoffs lightly, shakes his head. "Nope. My dad is there for me for whatever I need."

I can't not touch him right now, so I reach out and squeeze his biceps. "I'm glad."

"Me too, Remy." He taps the gas, and pulls into traffic. After we cruise through a few green lights, I return to the topic du jour. "When do you want to play The Naked Truth?"

I half want him to say tonight, but I also don't know that I can excavate any more of my emotions today. I hold my breath, waiting for him to answer.

"Tomorrow. Yeah, tomorrow. That work for you?"

He has a game in the late afternoon. I need to be at the arena too. I'm conducting a VIP tour for a local youth sports and mental health charity that we partner with prior to warmups. "Before the game?"

"Yeah, I was thinking since we picked up your dress today, why don't you come over to my place? You can help me pick out a suit for the wedding. I've got a lot."

But all I hear is *why don't you come over.*

Lake's inviting me to his apartment, in the city, before a game. He wants me to look through his clothes. Like a girlfriend would do. Then, play The Naked Truth.

My chest is lava.

My throat is a desert.

He's been in my home, so I don't know why this feels different. But maybe it's because of the way he kissed me today.

Maybe it's because of the things he said in the dressing room.

Or possibly it's because he wants to do five things with me that a bride and a groom were never able to do.

"Sure," I answer, but my voice hardly sounds like my own. This is the real danger, and I'm walking right into it.

As the buses and the buildings and the city streak by, I try to tell myself it's just his home. It's just a project. It's just a thing two people going to a wedding together would do.

But it's also a card game, a list, and a night where we held hands.

We're both quiet as he drives me home, grabs the dresses, and walks me to my door. I unlock it and open it slightly. I hardly want the night to end. "The Ruby Glow? It's doing great," I say, stalling.

His gaze sails down to my lips once again. They feel tingly under his stare. "Because you take good care of it."

"I'm just good at following directions—that's all."

He scoffs, looking me in the eyes again. “Nah. It’s more than that, Remy.”

I buy some more time. “Is it?”

“Yeah. You’re detailed. You remember things. Not everyone can take care of a plant.”

“It’s not a dog. Or a cat.”

“But someday it will be, right?” It’s a reminder of what I told him—that my plants would become real pets.

“See? You’re the one who remembers things. But yes, someday it’ll be a dog keeping me company as I plan dates for my clients. For now it’s plants,” I say, and I’m doing it again. I’m trying to extend the night. I force myself to shift gears. “What time tomorrow?”

“How about noon?”

“Perfect,” I say on a rough swallow. “I have to be at the arena two hours before the game. And you need to be there two and a half hours early, so it should all work out.”

There. That was businesslike.

“Yes, I’ll text you the address, but you should know I always take a nap on game days. So, bring your nap blanket.”

I go inside with a black dress for me and a white dress for someone who never got to wear it, but all I’m thinking about is a small, soft fleece.

25

THE NAKED TRUTH

LAKE

"Called it," I declare once I round the corner into the kitchen, spotting my dad assembling the border of the Signs with Sayings puzzle.

He shoots me a look that says calling it was child's play. "Yes, like it's a surprise, too, when Thor rubs his face on the catnip banana."

I stop in the doorway, arch a brow. "Did you just compare your love of puzzles to the cat's obsession with a catnip banana?"

He stops, stares at the ceiling with a puzzle piece in hand, then shoots me a smug smile. "I did."

As if on cue, Thor rounds the corner and leaps onto the table then skids, sending a handful of pieces skittering onto the floor.

"You are such a dick," I say to the big boy, but I pick him up and scratch his chin.

He permits five seconds of contact before ejecting himself from my arms and onto the floor where Dad's kneeling to pick up the scattered pieces. I bend down and help him out.

When he returns to the table, he slides a piece in, then nods to the stove. "You want some breakfast? I can make you something."

Shaking my head, I grab a banana from the hanger on the counter, then a bowl. "Nope. Just gonna have some cereal then take off. I've got morning skate."

"And a game this afternoon."

And...something in between. Something like a date. Or maybe a date-ish. But that reminds me of something else. As I peel the banana and slice it into a bowl, I say, "Dad, I forgot to tell you the puzzle is a gift from..." I pause, since I'm not sure how I want her name to sound coming out of my mouth. Affectionate? Fond? Fucking obsessed? *The latter, dickhead, since it's the truth.* "Remy."

His smile looks positively feline. "That so?"

I head to the pantry to grab the granola. "Yeah, she thought you might like it."

His smile widens. "She sounds like a lovely lady. When do I get to meet her?"

I freeze, the box of granola in my hand. How the hell can I picture the path of the puck down the ice during a game, but I didn't see that coming? Telling my dad I'm seeing someone is easy since it's true enough. Introducing him to a woman I'm having a fake real rebound with is something different.

"That's a good question." I return to the bowl, pour the cereal, then add some oat milk. I shove some cereal into my mouth to buy some time before answering. I chew and think, then when I finish I say, "Soon, Dad. Soon."

I eat as fast as I can then harness Thor so we can take off. I'll need him for the nap.

* * *

Morning skate ends right on time, and I couldn't be happier. I shed my practice gear so fast, and am hightailing it out of the locker room when Miller nods my way. "Want to get some lunch?"

"It's early," I say, since it's barely eleven.

"When did the time ever stop you from eating?" Riggs says with a laugh.

Fair point. "Just have some things to do at my place," I grumble.

"Some things with your hand," he tosses back.

I roll my eyes, but I'm grateful for the crude joke. I make a jerking gesture with my fist. "Don't want to mess with a streak, boys. It worked for the last game. So on that note," I say, and then I escape from the tribunal.

I hop in my car and head to my apartment, where I already dropped off my cat this morning. I even got him a new cat tower but haven't finished assembling it yet. Dude knows how to make do though—the trouper's got his own catnip banana here and he's basking with it in the windowsill of my place in Russian Hill, at the top of a building, overlooking the bay, the sun uncharacteristically shining in a bright blue sky.

Perfect.

Checking the time, I head to the closet where I keep my game day and travel suits, checking that everything's in place and the card game is on the table.

I stop in the middle of the bedroom suite, my Alaskan king dominating the room, the rays from the sun warming my shoulders. I should feed her. It is lunchtime. Pretty sure she's a vegetarian, so I google vegetarian options nearby, then shoot her a text.

Lake: Want some lunch? There are some veggie places nearby, and I can place an order.

Remy: I love lunch.

No idea why this detail about her makes me smile. But it does. Maybe because it feels so honest, and I get the sense that Remy doesn't always, or often, like to let people in. So even a detail like adoration of a meal feels like a secret.

Lake: I'll make sure it has perfectly squishy avocado.

Remy: Now I'm practically running.

I place an order. The food arrives a few minutes before she does.

And fuck me.

Remy looks good in a hoodie, in a skirt, in jeans, and in her casual attire. Black sweatpants, rolled at the waist, and a white sweatshirt that is mercifully, beautifully, fucking enticingly sloping off one shoulder.

She carries a canvas bag with the blanket in it, and her hair is swept up in a ponytail I just want to tug on.

I don't say anything for a beat. I just stare at the beauty at my door. She's here and I know this thing is only a rebound, a fake romance with an expiration date, a chance to show her what she deserves, but it's also all mine.

My chance.

And I'm going to make the most of it.

* * *

I finish the last bite of a power bowl with salmon, squash, and quinoa, set down my fork, and grab the box of cards.

"All right. Let's do it," I say.

"For the unknown bride. Ask away." She pushes her mostly eaten bowl of quinoa, tofu, and perfectly squishy avocado into the middle of the table.

I fish out a card and read the first question. But nope. Not going to ask that one. "Let me put this one aside," I say, setting down the card.

She gives me a look. "C'mon. We have to do this fairly."

"It's a bad question."

"I can handle it."

She probably can but I'm selfish. I want today to go well. I want it to feel date-ish. "Remy." It's a warning.

"Lake," she presses, more urgently, then reaches for the card I don't want to read.

Ah hell. If I play keep-away, I'm a dick. With some reluctance, I let her take the card.

She reads it, her expression hardening. She swallows, looks up, and says, "What's the most embarrassing thing to happen to you on a date?" She lowers the card, shoots me a sad smile and says, "I think you know. I think the world knows."

My shoulders slump at the mention of the Jumbotron incident. "Does it still bother you?"

She screws up the corner of her lips, like she's giving it some thought. "No. Not really."

"Which one?"

"Well, both." She blows out a breath. "I see a therapist pretty regularly. I saw her a few days ago when you were on the road trip. We talked about a bunch of things, but also that."

I had no idea she was in therapy. "Did it help?"

"She talks about moving on, helping me practice self-compassion."

"How do you do that?"

"I try to be nice to myself. Sometimes that means getting a face mask—standard self-care. Sometimes it's time with friends. Other times it's reminding myself that I'm not just the woman who got dumped. That I can learn from what happened."

"What do you think you learned?"

She sighs, thoughtfully. "To be less controlling. To let things happen at their own pace."

She's suddenly an open book, and I can't stop asking questions. "How were you controlling?"

She shrugs, maybe a little sheepishly. "I like things to go a certain way, to be right. For dates to go well—those that I plan of course. But also my own. For nights out to go well. Things with my family. I need to try to be okay with things not being perfect."

There's so much in there about Remy. That she wants to relax, but that it's hard for her. Maybe even that she needs time to deal with her breakup.

"She sounds really smart," I say.

"She is. I'm glad I see her." She lifts her chin, all proud and tough. "So you didn't have to protect me from that question."

"I would have though. If you'd wanted me to."

She's quiet for a beat, then nods. "I know you would."

"Glad you know that." But I'm not ready to move on to another question yet. The door's been pushed ajar by her truth card, so I kick it open farther. "Do I need to protect you from seeing him outside of the wedding events? Does it hurt when you do?"

"No," she says, and the speed of her answer makes me want to kiss the sky. "I'm all good there. Sure, I've kind of questioned all my life choices because how was I ever with him? But seriously, it's kind of amazing how something like that makes you realize you are better off without someone."

Fuck yes. I fight off a shit-eating grin but can't quite smother a small smile. "Good. You're so much better off without him."

"It only took a Jumbotron incident for me to learn that." She digs for a card, shooting me a playful glance. "Now it's my turn to ask you something."

I brace myself as she reviews the card.

"Would you date your college crush today?"

Oh, shit. Is this game holding up a mirror to my black soul? I swallow uncomfortably, thinking of Heather, the bold, confident athlete I met my freshman year at the college rink. We hit it off, connecting instantly with our passion for the game.

But something changed after we got married right after graduation. We were both so focused on our worlds as pro athletes that we stopped focusing on each other. We were all hockey all the time, and it felt like there was no space to grow, or change.

I think I changed.

I meet Remy's gaze, earnest and open, making it hard to lie as I pull myself back into the here and now. "I don't think I would."

Her lips part, soft, full of concern. "You wouldn't?" It comes out staccato, concerned. But also clear. She knows what she's asking. She's asking if I'd marry my late wife all over again.

I'm keenly aware this answer doesn't make me look good. But she told the truth and I ought to do the same. This isn't quite admitting Heather and I weren't in love—I'll keep that terrible truth locked up, but I nod and say, "I think I want different things now."

"What do you want?" she asks tentatively.

To take care of the people I love. But I say something else true. "I don't want to fail the people I care about."

She gives a soft, small smile. "I doubt you are."

I think of my dad staying inside all the time. I wonder. I wish. And I hope.

I move on, too, by grabbing another card. "What's your biggest fear?"

"Easy. Snakes," she says, but there's something in her eyes —a shift—that tells me she's afraid of something else more than slithery creatures. Maybe something deeper, more emotional. Especially since she turns the question around with a quick, "You?"

"Is that your card?" I tease.

"No, I just want to know."

"Hurting someone I care about," I say, a variation on my theme today evidently.

She nods, like she's taking in that info, then she tilts her head. "For what it's worth, you're not hurting me."

I breathe a sigh of relief. Did I think I was? No. But do I want to? Hell no. "I'm glad."

We play a few more rounds, the air a little softer, the sun a little warmer. Thor wakes up as Remy tackles the question of whether she's ever used a fake ID—the answer is a defiant no. The cat jumps from the sill and sashays past the unfinished cat tower and me to my bedroom as Remy asks one more question: "How are you really right now?"

I'm nothing but truth as I say, "Fantastic."

Once Thor and his white paws are out of sight, she sets down the cards, checking the clock in the kitchen—a wooden owl cutout with moving eyes. "I don't want to cut too close to your nap. Do you want me to check out your suits?"

And I'm honest, too, as I say yes.

26

MY, YOUR CLOSET IS SO BIG

REMY

I have serious closet envy. It's not the size of Lake's closet though. It's the organization. Every single thing is neatly arranged. Dress shirts hang crisply on metal rods, wingtips and sneakers alike rest on clean white shelves. Cubbies display pristinely folded shirts and workout shorts. A small wooden watch box sits open on a shelf, showing off a velvet padding cradling several watches.

"I didn't think you'd be so neat," I say, looking around.

He scoff-laughs. "You've been in my car. It's not messy."

"True, but I guess I wasn't expecting *this,*" I say, though I'm not entirely sure why.

"You're the one who once said I was—your words—*adorably, superstitiously organized.* Why did you think I'd be a slob?"

He's got me there. I did say that about his pre-game superstitions. "I didn't think you'd be a slob. Just...chaotic."

He arches a brow, looking like he doesn't want to let this go. It almost feels like we're still playing The Naked Truth. Like this matters deeply to him. "Why?"

I consider him before I answer. His hair is neat. His beard

is trimmed. His clothes are never adorably rumpled. His home is clean. "I'm honestly not sure."

He hums, low in his throat. A doubtful sound.

"What's that for?" I ask.

"You know why you thought I'd be messy."

"I honestly don't," I say.

He pins me with a knowing stare. "Because you think we're opposites."

I stop everything for a second, standing still. I feel a little see-through. "Maybe I did think so for that reason. You like surprises. I don't. You're decisive. I turn things over twenty thousand times. You go with the flow. I take copious notes."

"And yet, we both have neat closets," he says, entirely amused now.

"Hey, were you spying in mine?" I counter.

"Yes. Remy. I was super focused on the shelves and all the folded sweaters that day."

The memory of that haircut, and looking in the mirror after, sends a dart of lust down my spine, and I lick my lips, then glance around at the glorious organization in here. "I guess you surprised me then," I say softly. "But maybe it's a good surprise that you're so neat."

My attention returns to the watches. They glint in the light. "These are from your watch sponsor?"

"Yeah. Victoire gave them to me," Lake tells me, a little apologetic, like he's embarrassed he has an endorsement. Or more likely that they give him such expensive goodies.

"They're gorgeous," I say, hovering my fingers near a shiny silver watch, then a matte one that's subtly classic.

"That's titanium," he says. "Supposed to be lighter, hypoallergenic, good for diving."

"You dive?"

"No interest. Too slow."

I shudder at the thought of being underwater for so long. "You'd never catch me diving either."

"See? Not opposite."

I shake my head. "Definitely opposite. It's not the speed. It's that I don't like activities with a high chance of death. Skiing, diving, bungee jumping..."

He laughs. "Scuba diving is actually low risk."

I turn to him, pressing my finger to my lips. "Shh. It seems like it has a high chance of drowning, so let me believe that it does. Also, there might be snakes underwater."

He cracks up. "That's pretty rare in places where you'd scuba dive."

"But it's not out of the realm of possibility."

"You have me there," he says, still chuckling.

"But it is a nice watch," I say while studying the elegant look and style of the timepiece. "It's seriously pretty."

"You can touch it," he says, urging me on. "They're supposed to be worn."

"You don't wear them," I point out. "I'm not sure I've ever seen you with one."

"Checking out my wrists, Remy?"

Well, lately I have been. His forearms. Dear god, his forearms. "Yes, all the time. Wondering why you don't wear a watch," I tease, since it's easier than admitting I catalogue every detail of my fake boyfriend.

"No need. I mean, the time is fucking everywhere," he says, and that's so Lake. A thing should be functional for him.

He reaches past me, his strong arm brushing mine, making my skin spark, my heart jump. I swallow as he grabs the titanium watch, tugs it from the velvet box, and flicks the clasp open, dangling it in front of me.

"Give me your hand," he says.

I stick out my arm.

He takes it. When his fingers graze along my skin, my breath catches. My chest flips as he slides the watch onto me, inch by delicious inch. He's not speedy. He's slow, purposeful, dusting his fingers along my hand as he puts the titanium on me like it's foreplay. By the time he reaches my wrist, I'm not sure how I'm still standing—every touch is so electric, so charged.

Is it this way for him too?

He meets my eyes, and the look in his is raw and hungry. It's such a good look that I ache everywhere, a slow, thumping pulse that settles in my core. He flicks the timepiece closed, tightening it on my wrist, but it's still loose on me. "The case diameter was designed for me," he says.

An explanation, but one that hardly matters as he takes his time adjusting the loose watch, like he wants to make sure it's worn in just the right way.

He finishes, then meets my gaze.

"It's like a bracelet," I say, holding up my wrist, letting it slide up and down.

Lake stares at my arm like he's mesmerized, then swallows roughly. "Yeah, it does look like one on you."

"It's so light," I say, then study the timepiece for a beat or two. It's elegant and sophisticated and fun to play with. But it's just play. That's all. These watches are well over five figures. "Thank you for letting me touch it."

"It's touching *you* now," he says, his voice a little husky, and it's then that I realize Lake's staring at the watch on me with something like jealousy, or maybe even longing in his eyes.

Like he's jealous of...a watch?

A watch that's been kissing my skin.

But that's a ridiculous thought.

A ridiculous thought that's making my heart cartwheel dangerously. I really need to focus on the reason I'm here.

I un-hook the watch and set it back in its soft case. "Thank you," I say, then catch the time. It's running out. "That's a reminder I need to get to work picking out your wedding attire."

I walk toward the back of the closet with the suits. "They're as pretty as the watches."

A charcoal three-piece suit. A midnight blue blazer and matching trousers. A maroon suit with a clever plaid pattern that screams cutting-edge-athlete hot.

"You can touch them too," he says.

There's a sultry subtext to the invitation. The permission.

He doesn't need to tell me twice. I coast my fingers along the fine fabric of a dark brown suit, the color of chocolate. I travel along the arm of a forest green jacket with the faintest of checkmarks on it. I move to the pants next, touching the expensive-looking material. My head spins with choices. My pulse thunders with possibilities. I'm picturing Lake in the smoky one, the midnight blue one, the one the color of an evergreen.

I linger on the last one for a few seconds longer, closing my eyes, imagining it on him.

"You like green. You like earthy colors," he says from behind me.

I turn around. "I do. But that's for me," I say, then look him up and down, with his short dark hair, his cool eyes, his strong jaw.

But I'm always returning to his eyes. To the beauty in them, like cool blue gems. "This feels like you," I say, gesturing to the midnight blue suit.

"Yeah?" He sounds like he's questioning me.

"Definitely."

"You sure?"

I can't tell if he's teasing or truly doubtful. "Yes," I say, adamant.

"I should make sure though," he says, the corner of his lips twitching as he grabs the suit from the rack, then nods to the door. "I'll be right out."

He's going to put it on? But of course he is.

"Right. No problem," I say, flustered, but trying to cover it up.

Did he think I was going to stay while he changed? He must have thought that. Am I misreading him again?

It's kind of your thing, Remy. "I'll be out here," I say stupidly, then race out, shutting the door behind me.

I stand in his bedroom, but is this even any better? Since I'm now checking out his bed.

Right there in the middle of the room. Alaskan king and inviting with all those pillows, and the cream duvet.

I'm trying to think pure thoughts of sleep, but it's hard when the rustle of fabric drifts past my ears, the zip of metal. He's changing in there, and my mouth is dry. My lips, too, come to think of it.

"Be right back," I say to the closet door, then head to the sunny kitchen, grab my bag from the chair, and root around for lip gloss in the side pocket. I need something to do. I land on metal first and tug out my lipstick. That'll do. As I return to his bedroom, I'm slicking on ruby red lipstick right as the closet door swings open.

He emerges, all glower and growl in his midnight blue suit and icy eyes.

I freeze, momentarily stunned by the sight of Lake in the perfect shade for him. The pants hug his strong thighs. The white dress shirt stretches deliciously across his firm pecs. The jacket kisses his muscular arms.

He smooths a hand down the lapels, then adjusts the

jacket, and I somehow regain the power of movement. I finish applying the color right as he meets my gaze.

His lips form a ruler. His hands tighten into fists. His irises are locked on my mouth. A low, barely audible rumble seems to escape his lips, and when the sound stops, neither one of us says a word. We both just stare. He's a tiger, and I'm waiting for him to pounce.

All the questions that haunted me are answered.

The man wants me. And I want him.

Except, I don't want to be pounced on. I want to be in control. I cap the lipstick tube, set it in the pocket of my sweatpants, and tilt my head. "All you need is a tie."

He nods toward me, commanding, authoritative. "Pick one for me."

I stride into the closet again, tossing him a flirty glance as I make my way to the tie rack, flicking through the options quickly, powered by this fresh rush of confidence, before I settle on a silvery number. "It'll provide a nice contrast to the blue of the suit," I say, but I sound breathy, like my mind is elsewhere.

Because it is.

He moves behind me, the fabric of his slacks swishing with each step before he stops. "But how will it go with your maid of honor dress? Or should I wear a black tie?" he asks, far too casual, reaching past me for a plain, simple black silk tie. He grabs it and holds it up, dangling it in front of me.

Like a taunt. Like he's the one in control of the color choices. It's a good choice he's making though—lush and dark and seductive.

"That's better," I say, then turn around so I can fully face him. I take the neckwear from him, taking back the moment too. I toss it around his neck, adjusting the ends as my fingertips brush briefly against his shirt.

My whole body is lit up. Every cell, every molecule is shimmying.

I'm contemplating tying the tie but Lake's staring so hard at my mouth, and he's so shameless about it I'm not sure if there's any point in completing the knot.

"Your lips," he rasps out.

The heat in his eyes tells me everything I've ever needed to know about these last few weeks with him.

The flames in them feed me.

The spark leads me on.

There are too many reasons why this is a bad idea. My breakup is too fresh. His hurts run too deep. We work together. I'm friends with his sister. I can't risk the wedding, or my sister's brand deal, or anything.

I shouldn't cross another line. I know—and I ought to know better than anyone that now *is* a time for overthinking—but no one has ever looked at my mouth like that.

I'm so tired of thinking. I'd rather *do*. "I guess we should try the real lipstick test."

27

THE SIXTH LESSON OF NAP DATES

REMY

He groans, tossing his head back briefly. It's enough of a pause for me to do something else daring. I drop to my knees. When he lowers his gaze, his eyes flare.

"Remy," he warns. But he sets a hand on my shoulder, asking, "You sure?"

I lick my lips first, the tip of my tongue sliding across them. "Do I look unsure?" I counter as I shrug my right shoulder, shaking the sweatshirt fabric down farther, exposing my collarbone.

And his weakness. He lets out another groan. This one is more resigned.

"No," he says, the sound of a man giving in. "You don't look a damn bit unsure."

I slide my hands up his legs, along his thick thighs, toward the zipper.

His right hand curls around my shoulder, the left running gently through my hair as my fingers reach for the button. I undo the button and Lake closes his eyes, like this is all too much. Good. I want him to be overwhelmed. He's overwhelmed me in the best of ways. It's my turn to show him I'm not just a taker.

That I can give.

I slide down the zipper. A naughty grin tugs at my lips as I think of him last night zipping up my dress, and now I'm doing the opposite.

When it's undone I push the fabric of his tailored slacks open, exposing tight black boxer briefs that leave little to the imagination. Lake's hard-on strains against the material, an ambitious erection that's making all its wishes known. The best part? The wet spot at the top of the cotton.

A wild pulse beats between my thighs as I stare at that revealing little spot. The evidence I need. I nibble on the corner of my lips, then peel his briefs down.

His cock says, *It's really fucking good to see you*. Long, thick, hard, with more liquid arousal beading at the tip. A spark slides down my chest, a hot pulse that finds its way between my thighs. I clench them, my whole body melting. Hell, my mind is on fire as I wrap my hand around the base.

The skin is soft, his cock is hard, and I'm riding a roller coaster of thrills.

Lake seems to be too, since he grunts out a rough and dirty, "Fuck yes."

From that. Just that. My hand on his dick.

Ha. I can do better than that. I dip my face, dart out my tongue, and lick the drop, savoring it.

I moan at the taste—salty, musky, masculine. And clean.

"Yessss," he says, sounding a little lost already, and I've barely tasted him. But I want to make him feel as incredible right now as he's made me feel these last few weeks. Squeezing the base, I drag my tongue around the crown, licking the head, then playfully sucking it past my lips.

I drag the tip into my mouth. Just the tip though as I take

my sweet time, making sure he's watching me, making sure he's losing his mind as I execute the true trial for this red lipstick.

"How's it holding up? The color?" I ask ever so innocently, then wrap my lips around the tip of his dick again.

"Not sure yet. Better try a little harder."

"Harder, you say?" I ask, letting him fall from my lips. And since I want to ace this test, I drag my hand up his length, keeping the pressure on as I watch him.

"Yeah," he says on a strangled grunt. "And wetter."

I laugh, but I comply. Oh yes, do I comply. With my hand wrapped around his pulsing cock, I draw him back into my mouth.

I'm nice and slow, easing him in, playing as he goes. By the time he's halfway in my mouth, Lake is groaning loudly, then wrapping a hand tightly around my skull. The sounds that fall from his mouth are pure caveman grunts. Filthy groans. Needy sighs.

His excitement is like the carnival game where you hit the hammer. And bam. The bell is ringing. He's gripping my head and rocking into my mouth and breathing so hard already that I feel like the queen of the world. Or really of *his* world, here on my knees, with my panties outrageously wet as I tease him into my mouth.

Every moan he makes sends a direct line of pleasure straight to my core. I'm aching as I draw him in another inch.

"Fuck, Remy," he moans, gazing down at the sight of me with his dick nearly down my throat. "Your mouth. Your perfect fucking mouth."

I think I'm glowing from the praise.

I'm certainly soaked from it.

But I also want to make some things clear. I let go for a brief second. "Fuck my perfect mouth then," I urge.

He blinks. Parts his lips. Shudders. Then shakes his head. "No."

No? *No*? What just happened? "Why?" I ask, and I hate that I sound terrified.

He grips my chin, strokes it with his thumb. "Because if you take me in your mouth for another second, I'm going to blow. I'm going to come in two seconds. And that is *not* going to happen the first time."

First time. Those words vibrate in the air. They shimmer with the implication that there will be a second.

"You will?" I ask, a little enchanted. I kind of want to know what that's like.

He lets out a harsh, ragged breath. "I fucking assure you I'm *this close* and it's not okay."

This close.

His heated words echo. *I'm this close*.

I didn't know that was what I needed to hear today—that naked truth. But I did, and I fight off a smile as he tucks his *this close* dick back into his boxer briefs.

I wish he'd let me finish, but it's such a wicked thrill to wield this kind of power.

He offers me a hand, and I take it, letting him tug me to my feet. He's standing in front of me in his dark sapphire suit, pants zipped, looking sophisticated and sexually frustrated. It's such a good look. He drags a hand through his hair, then blows out an irritated breath.

But maybe not that irritated since he tilts his head, dips his face toward mine, and presses a gentle caress of a kiss to my cheek, before whispering, "My turn."

I picture myself spread out on his bed, a midday meal for him. It's heady, but also scary since there's no way I'll finish quickly. If at all.

I won't be the reason his focus is off on the ice this afternoon. “No. You have a game day nap to take. So get this suit off and put your shorts back on.” I pause, tap dancing my fingers along the open waistband of his pants. “It’s time for my nap lesson.”

“You bet it is.”

I hustle out of the closet, head down the hall, and pop into the guest bathroom. My panties are a mess, but I do my best to straighten up. When I leave the bathroom, I grab the blanket he gave me and return to his bedroom as he’s shifting pillows around the bed, making room for us.

He’s wearing only a pair of tight boxer briefs, and my fingers ache to explore every groove of his abs, every muscle in his chest. To trace the tiny running horses on his biceps. To explore the cat on his abs. “Get over here,” he says, beckoning with his finger.

It’s funny how he’s trying to take charge again. I don’t mind obeying though. Padding across the soft beige carpet with the sage green blanket in hand, I join him at the side of the bed.

The next thing I know, I’m staring at the ceiling. Lake scooped me up in his arms with zero warning. “Good surprise?”

I’m catching my breath but laughing as I say, “Yes.”

He drops me gently onto the bed with the blanket in my hand. He settles the soft fleece over me, resting it at my breasts. “Rule one. You don’t go all the way under the covers for a nap. Not the duvet, and not the blanket itself.”

He’s so serious about it. I could poke fun at him, but he seems to really want to impart this knowledge. “Why?”

He leans over me, hands on the mattress, his weight making it sink slightly. “Because then you sleep too deeply.”

“I sleep hard at night. I’m out in like two seconds,” I say, bragging, like an out-like-a-light skill is some kind of superpower. “What’s the second rule?”

He lifts a brow, moves around the bed, and hops in on the other side, scooting over to me. "Naps are better with a..." There's a pause, like he's weighing what to tell me before he settles on, "*friend*."

The word is warm—a little unexpected too. As he inches closer, it doesn't feel wrong; it feels like a euphemism and he knows it.

"Is rule three you should make room for that *friend* under the blanket?" I ask, a little giddy about getting close to him again even after that heated moment amongst his suits.

"Yes," he says as I lift the blanket, inviting him to cuddle. He RSVPs to the hilt, sliding right next to me.

"Rule four."

"There's more?"

"Yes. Set an alarm. Otherwise your nap might turn into an all-day affair."

"An all-day affair sounds a little risqué."

"It does. Which is why I've set mine already. For forty-five minutes."

I groan. "That's so long."

He laughs, then kisses my shoulder. "Rule five. Turn on your side. Let me wrap my arms around you."

My heart shimmies. But why? Why is a nap exciting to me? I don't know. It's just a silly nap. But this lesson is also as organized as any date I've ever planned for a client. Only it's a new kind of date—an intimate one.

Lake wraps his strong arms around me, then nuzzles the back of my neck. That's not entirely relaxing, so I blurt out, "Are you always a cuddler?"

I'm not sure why I'm asking either.

"Remy," he says, just shy of exasperated.

I wince. "Sorry. You probably want to sleep."

"No. Well yes, but also—" he hesitates, then exhales heavily. "I haven't napped with anyone in a long, long time, so I really don't know. I just want to hold you."

My heart springs in my chest. It's a little uncomfortable the way it's bouncing around in there. "Okay," I say.

It feels like giving in, like letting go, and it's terrifying.

Especially when he shifts a little, then blows out a slow, steady breath. Again and again and again. He's asleep in seconds, his big, warm body holding mine close.

I close my eyes, but I'm not sleepy. Not one bit.

I try to relax. To think of breathing exercises. Of sleep techniques that I've never needed at night and never tried during the day since, well, naps are not my thing.

Is a nap date my thing though? I'm not sure either. There's not much room to spread out. There's not much room to do anything.

I try to just be in the moment. Surely, that's what my therapist would tell me.

I hear Elena's voice saying, *When you get too much in your head, try to just be in your body. Look around and focus on the here and now, not what you need to do next, or do better, or do tomorrow.*

But I'm pretty sure she wouldn't advise me to blow the hockey player I'm fake dating, the hockey player I work with, no less. *And* doing it a few weeks after a painful, public breakup.

My chest tightens. Not with regret, but with worry. I'm not sure what happens next, and the uncertainty makes me feel itchy.

The dip of the mattress catches my attention. I lift my head a few inches. Thor pads across the covers, stopping inches from Lake, then settling into a cat ball and closing his eyes.

Thor!

That's it.

Carefully, so as not to wake man or beast, I ease away from Lake. I hold my breath, hoping he won't wake up as I escape his arms, then scoot over to the edge of the bed, swing my legs to the floor, and survey the scene.

Relieved that the big hockey player and big Siamese furball are sound asleep, I pad quietly out of the room, snicking the door closed. I head to the kitchen, where I spotted the half-assembled cat tower earlier.

This is my happy place. It's easy-peasy, and I can finish it in way less than forty-five minutes. I root around in my bag for the Swiss Army knife I keep with me, then get to work assembling the rest of the baskets, perches, and shelves for the cat. When I'm done with time to spare, I step back, admire my handiwork, and close the knife. I listen for sounds from the bedroom and hear none.

Good.

I slip back into the bedroom, where Lake's asleep on his side. *And folks, the challenge for perfectionist Remy Hatmaker is sneaking back under the blanket without disturbing either occupant.*

Deep breath.

On tiptoes I cross over to the bed and slowly lie back down. The mattress groans slightly. Lake stirs, but he doesn't wake.

Like I'm a puzzle piece, I slot myself carefully back into place, lifting his heavy arm and setting it around my breasts again, the owl watching my every move.

And she nails the dismount!

With a victorious smile I keep to myself, I let out a soft breath and close my eyes.

Pretty sure it's been about forty minutes of nap avoidance now when Lake's hand coasts down from above my breasts to below them. His arm's wrapped around my waist, and soon his fingers are traveling lower.

He's taking a slow, sensual path that makes me feel a little shimmery. A lot tingly as his hand drifts even lower. I can't help it—I move a little closer to him. He shifts behind me, wedging against me, and I haul in a breath. He's impressively hard. And he's letting me know, pressing his erection to my ass.

A soft breath ghosts past my lips.

I squirm around a little, seeking some relief from this sweet ache. If I were home, I'd reach for a toy, watch a video, imagine a scenario.

I try to breathe past the pleasure, to ignore the desire. I can deal with this tonight when I'm alone. There's no time right now. But when his fingers skim down my stomach and he's playing with the waistband of my pants, my brain short-circuits, then goes offline. Impulsively, I reach for his hand, cover it with mine, and urge him a little lower.

A groan rumbles past his lips, deep and hungry.

All the risks flash before my eyes again. All the consequences. But I'm stretching my neck, easing closer to him, and getting so, *so* lost in this sensation. It feels like it's been forever since I've been touched, though that's not true.

But maybe it's been forever since someone touched me like *this*. With words, and deeds, and talented fingers that inch underneath my pants.

"Oh," I gasp.

"Mmm," he murmurs against me as his fingers travel down the front of my white panties. He dips one strong finger between my thighs, pressing it firmly against the wet fabric.

I can feel, rather than see, his satisfaction.

"This is so unfair," he murmurs, stroking the damp cotton.

"What's unfair?" I ask on a rough pant.

"Leaving you like this."

I tense for a second. Is he going to just...take off? Then it hits me. His alarm is going off. Oh. Right. He has to go. I'm about to make this easier for him and bolt out of bed when he lets go of me, twists around in the covers, and grabs for something on the other side of the bed.

His phone.

I swallow, pushing off the blanket so I can get out.

But the man isn't the fastest skater on the team for nothing. When he hits the off button on the alarm, he reaches for me again, jerks me against him, replaces the blanket, and says in a low, commanding tone, "Rule six. Waking up is fun too."

His hand slides between my thighs, where he cups me.

The sound I make is obscene. A desperate, greedy whimper. I try to hide my face in the pillows. But as he slips his fingers inside my panties this time, his throat rumbles. "Let me hear you."

This man is barely touching me and he's already assuming I'm going to be loud?

"So cocky," I say, but the words are muffled when he strokes my wetness, a slick, tempting slide of his fingers.

"Yep," he says with a grin in his voice. He wraps his other arm around my chest, locking me against him, his face buried in the crook of my neck as he draws dizzying circles on my clit. "Show me why, Remy. Show me why I'm so cocky."

He strokes me with a steady, thorough rhythm that has me rocking gently against his fingers. He brushes his talented mouth against my neck as he touches me. Then along my collarbone as his fingers tease, then push.

I gasp.

"That's it. You've fucking got it, baby."

I shudder out a breath, my hips picking up the pace, seeking more of his fingers. He reads my every move, tapping my clit with his fingers, then stroking me through all my wetness. I'm slick and hot, and it's too much.

It's almost embarrassing how much I want this and how much I want to hide from it too. The admission of it—the intensity—is terrifying.

But Lake's kisses are breaking me down as he drags that beard across my neck, as his lips travel across my collarbone, as his fingers stroke and glide and then speed up. He's following my lead, chasing every move I make, urging me on.

Then, he crooks his fingers inside me, and I tip over. Everything's shiny and bold as pleasure bursts, hot, fast, demanding. I cry out.

I can't see straight. I can't think. I just shake and moan, my vision a lovely black blur as he strokes me through my release. In the corner of my mind, I'm aware of his groans and grunts, deeply sexy sounds that thrum through me right along with my pleasure, still hitting me. Then I feel the push of his hard cock against my ass, our clothes a barrier.

But a barrier that's not stopping Lake. He's gripping me tight, holding me close and...rubbing against my ass.

Oh.

Ohhhh.

His breathing is ragged, and as I come down from the high of my orgasm, I register my surroundings again. My eyes blink open right as Lake eases his hand out of my panties and lifts his fingers to his lips.

I crane my neck, catching a glimpse of him behind me, grinding against me—no, rutting against me—as he licks the taste of me off his fingers.

And moans.

Low, ragged, salacious.

"Fuuuuuck," he grunts, then pumps his hips against my ass again, panting like he's running a race.

Or, really, finishing it. His face twists as he bites out a groan, shuddering. His pumping stops. He gives a slow, final thrust, a wind-up toy winding down.

I want to ask so badly. I want to say the words *"Did you?"*

But I don't have to. His breathing slows, his eyes float open, and the glassy look in them starts to fade away.

He lifts a hand, drags it through his hair, and shakes his head, like he can't believe what just happened. His gaze drifts down to his boxer briefs. And he rolls his eyes—at himself.

I bite the corner of my lips, shift around a bit in the bed, and steal a glance. Well, it's not every day you get to see the evidence that someone's into you. And I like what I see.

I roll my lips together, sealing in all sorts of pride, all kinds of satisfaction.

He breathes out hard again and cuts through the tension with a few words. "Told you I was *this close*."

I laugh, feeling on top of the world.

He grabs my face, turns me toward him, and gives me a hot kiss that makes my head swim and my heart sing.

But it only lasts five seconds. When he breaks the kiss, he says, like it pains him, "I have to go."

He needs to get ready for the game, and I need to go home and change. "You probably need to shower too," I deadpan.

That earns me a smack on the ass.

28

THE EXES IN THE BUILDING

REMY

Technically I don't have to be here for the game, but when Mabel texts me that she's got her Knight jersey on and is bringing the "family"—Clementine, Skylar, and Trevyn—that's reason enough to stick around. I've finished the VIP tour and some prep for the week, so I put my work aside now that it's time for warmups.

Speaking of, I'm *still* warm from the sixth rule of napping. I haven't stopped thinking about what happened under the sage green blanket.

As I head down the corridor toward the rink, I replay those moments again. Who even was that woman grabbing his hand and shoving it between my thighs?

Let me hear you.

Other things repeat too.

I'm this close.

All those ragged words of his echo in my mind, and I swear I can feel his beard whisking against my shoulder, his firm lips pressing open-mouthed caresses to my neck, his magic fingers finding that spot inside me.

I make a tiny noise in the back of my throat that I should

not make in public. A quick glance around confirms I'm alone. But *still*. I need to get my thoughts together. I clench my thighs as I walk—which, for the record, is kind of hard to do. I try though, like I can squeeze out the desire. News flash—I can't.

Best to avoid all the player haunts then, so I dart around a corner, ducking into another hallway that doesn't pass the workout room, the locker room, or the tunnel. I circle all the way around the arena, avoiding any possibility of bumping into a growly hockey star who made me come hard and also admitted he wouldn't date his college crush today.

I stop for a second by the escalators, letting that confession hit me again. And it hits me even harder than his moans, than his dirty commands. Lake Axelrod doesn't want to hurt the people he cares about.

Like me?

Yeah, I think he meant me.

My head spins from all this new information. I've got to get a handle on my thoughts, so I try to sort them into neat boxes as I resume my pace up to the ticketing level. I don't know if there will be an extra seat near my friends right now. But as I weave past the early crowds on the counter, a text lands from Clementine that she's running late.

I should be able to steal her seat for a bit. This'll be good. Time with my friends will reset me. Settle my overactive mind. I dart past a gourmet sandwich stand, then a thirty-flavors-of-pretzels vendor, before saying hi to the ushers at the top of the bowl.

As I head down toward the ice, I'm strangely glad Clem isn't here yet. I'm not sure how to face her after what happened earlier today with her brother. From the truths we shared with words and hearts at the table, to the ones we shared with lips and hands in his bedroom.

I don't know how to organize any of this.

How to sort it.

Understand it.

Lake's both my fake wedding date *and* my partner in trying to complete a bride's unfinished bucket list. He's also the guy who wants to show me how a good boyfriend treats a woman, with honesty, with passion.

Passion like Lake's grunts. Like the sounds he made when he lost control once I came—once he tasted me. Heat climbs up my neck from the memory of his fingers in me, then in his mouth, right as I reach my friends. Trevyn, Mabel, and Skylar are huddled together in a row, talking and laughing, Skylar's freckles dancing across her pale complexion, Mabel's brown eyes sparkling with laughter, Trevyn's witty smile coasting across his warm brown skin. When he spots me standing in the aisle, he snaps his gaze my way, and arches a knowing brow. "Why do you look like you just got some?"

Are you kidding me? It can't be that obvious, can it?

I sink down next to him, acting all cool. "What are you talking about?"

He pats my hand placatingly, then swings his gaze to our friends. "Have you ever seen our girl's cheeks so flush before?"

Mabel shoots me an assessing look. "Not since she started *vacationing*."

Shoot. I am obvious.

"Oh, is that a euphemism for a little hockey action?" Trevyn asks.

Skylar hums appreciatively, then gives me an *I know what you did* look. "I told you hockey butts were the best. Did you find out for yourself about the perfect squish?"

This is bad. This is so bad. I'm so transparent they can already tell my fake date is real banging me.

"Yes," I whisper, motioning for them to lower their voices. "But don't talk so loud about it."

"Why?" Trevyn asks innocently, but speaks in a whisper. "Everyone thinks it's real with you two. And if it were real you'd be climbing his hockey body like you're evidently doing, you minx, you. Ergo, it shouldn't be a secret you're getting the D."

"And you deserve the D," Skylar adds, "especially after that cad of an ex of yours, who I just walked past at his beer stand and hissed at. Which, for the record, represents serious growth. I had previously considered hiding a carton of rotten eggs under the beer taps."

"Major growth," I say, approvingly.

Skylar preens. "Thank you. I think so too. But back to you and your D face," she says with a naughty glint in her eyes.

"Yeah, I don't recall you ever showing up for a game looking like this," Mabel adds as she waves her hand toward my face, since I must be wearing my thoughts on it. "You must be getting it good."

It's a compliment. Really it is. And the zing in my body confirms it. But I also feel so flustered, and I'm not sure why.

Before I can say another word, the lights dim and the ominous voice of the announcer booms over the sound system, taking everyone's focus off me and onto the ice as purple strobe lights flash on the slick surface.

The deep baritone tells the tale of a fearsome fox who defended his den, like the Golden State Foxes will defend the net. When the light show finishes, the spotlight swings to the tunnel. "And now...your Golden State Foxes."

Mabel hoots and hollers when Corbin hits the ice. Once it's Lake's turn to fly out of the tunnel, I cheer, but my friends nudge me like they expect me to behave like Mabel. To be all lovey and exuberant.

But is that my place as a fake girlfriend? My stomach dips and rolls, and that's the answer to why I'm out of sorts.

Because I don't really know what my role is—how far to go, how deep to fake, who to fool.

I'd thought I was controlling the narrative, but I don't know what string to pull or button to push.

By the time Clementine texts that she's finally here at last, I'm grateful to slip away. I definitely can't face her right now since not only did I blow her brother today (he's complicated, she warned me), I also bought a gift for her dad last night—since her dad is Lake's dad of course.

I'm buying gifts for my friend's dad. I'm hooking up with her brother. Who's also my fake boyfriend.

My stomach dips. Every molecule in me feels stretched too tight, like I don't fit in my body anymore.

I need some time alone.

I trot up the steps, then do something I haven't done before—avoid a friend. I head the other way to avoid running into her. But that other way means I'm walking right past Jameson's beer stand.

What a stupid move. But I keep my focus forward, blinders on.

"Remy!" he calls out, and I try to avoid him, giving him a quick wave and walking on. But he rushes around the counter, leaving it to one of his servers, and catches up with me in the concourse.

"What's up?" I ask.

"I was thinking it'd be nice to get coffee and chat."

He's really milking this friendship BS. "Why would that be nice?"

Oh wow. Did I say that?

"Because I bet you've got a lot on your plate with the wedding," he says, totally missing the bite in my tone. "And I'm your friendly expert when it comes to libations. I can recommend some beers for the reception."

He's so relentless in his fake friendship project. I'd really like to tell him to stop using me to get to my sister. But if I say what's on my mind, I might rock the boat. Caroline wants everything to go smoothly for the wedding. Everything includes me, so I bottle my snappy retorts up.

I flash him a fake friendly smile. "I can't do coffee, but I will totally think about your offer," I say with a wave, then waggle my phone, the universal sign for I need to take a call.

I hustle off, but once I round the corner and dart into the personnel hallway, my heart is beating too erratically, my mind racing to too many places. I stop, set a hand on my chest, and try to calm down.

Since now I have another thing to worry about, and it's not how far to go with this fake dating.

It's what happens when I run into Lake like this when our fake romance is over? How the hell am I going to handle having two ex-boyfriends in the same building?

I close my eyes and sink to the floor.

29

GOOD LUCK NUTS

LAKE

It's good to be the rebound guy. On and off the ice. I snag two goals—one on a breakaway, the other off a rebound that I collected before their D-men did, shooting it right back into their net.

Man, it was beautiful.

"You can all thank me. My superstitions did it," I say to the guys as I rip off my jersey at my stall after the final buzzer.

Miller peels off a leg pad. "Nah. Pretty sure it was me and my superstitions."

I stare down our goalie. "Because you started imitating me."

"And we started winning again. So yeah, that means I'm the fucking good luck charm," Miller says, patting his chest.

Riggs hums thoughtfully. "Guess that makes you a squirrel, not a fox."

Miller jerks his gaze to Riggs, who's not even looking at us. Just tugging off a skate as he doles out animal facts.

"Explain," Miller demands, but I know why he picked a squirrel.

Riggs looks up, expression thoroughly even-keeled as he tugs off a skate. "Squirrels organize their nuts. Like you organized your gear. C'mon, we've been over this."

Miller grabs his crotch. "Organize this."

Ivan chuckles from his stall, then pumps his hips like he's about to perform a striptease. "Besides, *these* are the good luck charms."

I groan, waving a dismissive hand at the D-man, and the rest of my guys. "And you've all officially cured me of my superstitions."

"It's about time," Corbin shouts as he wings his undershirt into the laundry basket. "It's teamwork, men. Not superstition or good luck nuts."

"Oh, I definitely have good luck nuts," Miller shouts back at Corbin.

"Men, that wasn't about luck." The cool, commanding tone of Coach Ahmed cuts across the locker room shenanigans. He strides in, polished and proud in a sharp suit, and we snap our attention to the man in charge. "You played hard, you executed, you did your jobs."

He spins toward me and tosses the game puck my way.

I catch it, and turn it over in my hands. Maybe I'll give it to Remy. She could tell this story at the next wedding event, the shared shower or the spa or what-the-fuck-ever is next on the list. I don't even care. But she could say I gave her a game puck and it'd be as true as the foxes and the succulent, and all the other stories of our romance. Like the cat tower she built for me this afternoon. The little sneak. I didn't notice it till she'd left, but I'd like to thank her for it. Ideally with my tongue between her thighs. But a simple thanks with words will work too.

"And I expect you to do your jobs in Evergreen Falls as

well," Coach continues. The reminder of our schedule snaps my attention back to the here and now. Our crosstown rivals, the Sea Dogs, have a new minor league team in the Christmas-y town near Lake Tahoe about three and a half hours away. Sometimes they host games there to draw more attention to their affiliate.

When he mentions the plan, and the date for the team bus departure for the road trip, my thoughts race again. To the next item on the Five Things To Do Before I Say I Do list.

It's about a road trip.

What if we could hit the next item on that list with the Evergreen Falls game? My fingers itch to text Remy but I do my best to give Coach all my attention.

He deserves it, and hockey deserves it too, since hockey saved my scarred and empty heart three years ago. I was a damn good player before then. But I hit a new level after Heather died. More goals, more points, more speed. The game gave me everything I needed in the aftermath of her death. It was an escape from the things the press said about me. The things the public thought they knew about me.

Things I've started sharing with Remy.

When Coach is done, I whirl around to my stall so fast, and I text her, asking to meet here at the arena soon. She doesn't respond right away, but I shower fast anyway, feeling confident she will.

But as I button up my dress shirt ten minutes later, there's still no note from her.

Hmm.

That's not entirely like her. She's responsible to a T. Maybe she's busy.

Well, of course she is. She has a fucking life.

I toss my tie around my neck but don't knot it as I pocket

my phone and head out, determined to find her. Maybe she went home already, but we've got an animal rescue photo op tomorrow at a local shelter—or so I heard the other guys saying. I bet she's still here, still working.

I should make sure she has a ride home.

I head to the stairwell, bound up the steps, and march down the corridor. It's a little pushy to show up at her cubicle, but I'm a little pushy.

Only when I scan the marketing department, it's empty, like I'd expect in the evening after a Sunday afternoon game.

No one's here—not even a tall, leggy brunette working overtime.

My chest hollows out. A question rushes through my brain—is this too much? Is this that love-bombing shit guys do?

No one likes that.

Well, fuckhead, you're standing at her desk, looking for her on a Sunday night. If the shoe fits...

I drag a hand roughly through my short hair—still getting used to it—and get the hell out of the marketing department.

I can't be this guy. She wanted a fake boyfriend, not a real stalker.

Except as I retreat, heading down the corridor to the players' lot, I ask myself—is it truly stalking to check in on a woman who went down on you unexpectedly in your closet? Is it obsession to ask her if she needs a ride home? I mean, it'd be ruder to leave without saying goodbye.

And if I know Remy, and I'm starting to, she's probably planning a date for someone.

In seconds, I'm marching through the concourse, empty now. All the fans have gone home. Most of the vendors have shut their stalls. I circle around the arena, heading straight toward the plant wall.

And my Remy radar was right.

One tall, leggy woman sits in front of the ferns and evergreens in a chair made of reclaimed wood. Her brunette hair cascades over her shoulders in soft waves. Maroon headphones cover her ears. She nibbles on the end of a pen as she stares at a notebook in her lap.

Fuck, she's beautiful and fierce, and she made me a cat tower. My heart thumps dangerously hard as I stride closer.

The echo of my wingtips on the concrete floor grows louder. The sound must penetrate her headphones, since she snaps her gaze up, flinching.

"Sorry. I know you hate surprises," I say, as she takes off the headphones.

"Hi." She sounds distant. *Because you're chasing her too much.*

"You okay?"

"I'm fine. I just came here to plot a date for a new client. Someone from my podcast. They didn't even mention the breakup. Yay," she says, but she sounds unenthused.

She brandishes her notebook. It says *World Domination* on the cover—so her, so fucking her—but when she opens it she shows me a mostly blank page with just the words:

First date night in two years since their kid was born.

And the only other words are *maybe a paint and sip*.

Hmm. That doesn't seem inspired, but what do I know about the kind of fancy date planning she does? "It's a good start."

She shakes her head. "It's really not."

I scratch my jaw, unsure what to say as I crouch down to her level. "I'm sure you'll come up with something."

"Maybe," she says with a heavy sigh.

She's really off tonight. Is it from this afternoon at my place? I should ask, but I'm not sure I want to know. "That animal rescue thing tomorrow? You still need players?"

"You're always welcome there," she says, a smile shifting her lips at last. A real one. "It's pretty simple anyway. Hockey players holding dogs and cats looking for homes."

"I can do that," I say impulsively.

"Yeah?"

"I can."

She arches a questioning brow. "Are you just doing this because—"

Because I like you? Fuck yes. But that's not a good answer. "Because I'm your *boyfriend*?"

"I don't want to look like I'm, I don't know, using you to get ahead?"

My chest twists. I hadn't thought of all the ways she'd be perceived or misperceived. But I should have since I know what that's like. "You're not," I insist, since that's all I can do. "I want to be there."

"You never used to before," she adds, gentle, but a reminder.

"I do now," I say, then try to figure out what else is going on. But maybe she just has a lot on her mind. "Thanks for the cat tower. That was a surprise."

Another real smile comes my way. "You liked it."

"Yeah. I was going to finish putting it together," I say, scrubbing a hand across my jaw. "Eventually. But it was nice to wake up to." Something nags at me though. Something I know the answer to, but I ask anyway. "You didn't nap?"

She shakes her head. "No."

"You just slipped back in when you were done?"

She nods. "Sorry."

I'm not mad though. She's clearly telling me the truth, and that's all I've wanted from her. But I also want to help her. She's got a lot on her plate, and I can take some of the burden off. "The next thing on the list?"

"Number two? Go on a road trip before you say I do?"

"Yes. We have this Evergreen Falls game coming up this week. Do you want to—"

"Take a road trip there?" She sounds so enthused, and it's the first true spark I've heard from her tonight. "Like, go up a day earlier?"

More than I want to win the cup. "Let's do it," I say. "I'll handle all the plans."

"I'm in," she says, and my chest doesn't feel so hollow anymore.

Until she nibbles on the corner of her lips, and furrows her brow. And shit. We're not good after all.

"What's wrong?"

She sighs heavily. "I ran into Jameson during the game."

I look around, ready to pummel that jackass. "Where is he, and when do you want me to fuck him up?"

"I wish. But also you'll need to get in line. Caroline offered to murder him a few weeks ago."

"I'm down with that. With anyone who hurts you."

"He wanted to talk about his beer, of course. And I said something vague and left, but I kept thinking...someday, someday soon, I'm going to have two exes in this building."

Something turns sour inside me. I hate everything she's saying, especially because she's not wrong.

"And I worry about that," she adds.

"I get it."

"I worry that if we...do anything again," she says, then makes a rolling gesture with her hand, "like this afternoon, that it'll just be too complicated."

My heart sinks like an anvil's tied to it. But I can't be a little prick and whine that she doesn't want to let me bury my face between those sweet thighs of hers. I need to be a mature adult. "It would be complicated," I say, speaking the plain truth.

"Right?" Her voice is wobbly, a touch desperate. Like she needs the confirmation from me.

"Definitely."

"I just think maybe we should focus on the wedding and this list. I don't want to make things harder when they end."

My bones chill with the clear reminder—maybe the one I needed—that this fake romance will finish.

I'm frozen, but this icy feeling is for the best. I was getting in too deep. I was too obsessed. Thank fuck someone pressed the brakes.

I swallow, pushing down my feelings far, far away. "I don't want to hurt the people I care about. But I do want to give you a ride home."

"You don't have to."

"But I do."

She gathers up her stuff and walks with me to my car. I'm just being a good fake boyfriend. That's all.

The drive is quiet. We're never quiet. But neither one of us seems to have anything to say as I cruise through the foggy night. When we reach her porch, mist still curling around us, she gives me a resigned smile. "Thanks again for understanding. I don't want to mess things up for my sister, for work, for everything. You know?"

Right. The fake romance needs to be airtight.

"Don't worry about a thing," I lie, smoothly. Because I'm sure as hell not going to tell her that I can't stop thinking about her.

I'm a good fake boyfriend too the next morning when I show up at Little Friends and pose for a picture with a frosty-faced old Papillon mix with wise eyes, big ears, tufted paws, and one tooth. Judy looks at me like she can tell why I'm here.

To impress a woman.

But she's not going to rat me out.

"Smile, Lake Onion," Miller calls out in between giving hugs to a Malinois mix that seems to have his number.

I try to smile with Judy. Maybe I even manage a hint of one. But I'm pretty sure it doesn't reach my eyes.

30

CAT DADDY AD

REMY

When Caroline arrives at my door five minutes before Lake is due to pick me up, I know she's feeling better by the pace of the knocking. Strong, rapid, but not five-alarm fire level. Still, you can't ever be too cautious, so I shout that I'll be right there then dart into the kitchen, yank open a drawer, and grab a hospital mask. I pull it on and open the door.

She tilts her head and gives me a *c'mon* look. "Are you serious?"

"It was only three days ago when you were on death's door."

"I was not on death's door. I was just too sick to make out on camera with my husband-to-be."

I shrug. "Sounded like death's door to me."

"I'm feeling so much better. I did the floral mockup yesterday with Margot, thank you very much. And I was even at work today. I hosted my show."

"Well, I hope you were generous with your employees and handed out masks for them too. Or mind vises perhaps. That would be a great wedding favor for your guests."

She parks her right hand on her hip. Her left holds a red canvas bag. "I'll have you know I have a clean bill of health."

"And as far as I'm concerned, you can never be too safe," I say, holding my germaphobe ground. "Seeing as I have to get on the road with a hockey player, I can't be responsible for making him sick. What if the team loses because he can't play?"

"You're seriously ridiculous." Rolling her eyes, she thrusts the red bag my way.

"What's this?"

"It's a reusable bag. You use it to pick up the candy. You put it in the bag and voila."

I shoot her a challenging stare. "I know," I say. When she learned I was heading to Evergreen Falls, she asked me to swing by a specialty candy shop there to pick up the wedding favors in person. One less thing to ship is less of an eco footprint, and we're both all for that. "But I have my own reusable bags."

"Well, you can't be too safe," she says with a smirk.

She turns to leave, then stops and must think better of it because she turns around. "You and Lake are traveling together. Things are moving...quickly with him?"

I tense at that word, the implied judgment in it.

She holds up a stop-sign hand. "That's not a bad thing. It's nice that things are moving quickly. You seem happy. This thing with him is promising?"

Her voice pitches up with hope, and my gut twists so hard, as if someone is squeezing it like a washcloth. "It's just a rebound. That's all it's going to be," I say, squashing that hope.

She won't be vanquished. "You never know. Love doesn't always happen on your schedule. And there's no mandatory time period for moving on. You get over someone when you get over them, and good for you."

"Caroline," I warn.

But she's already in go mode. "And just in case the rebounding is going super well," she says, then dips her hand into the pocket of her crisp, perfectly pressed slacks. Out of the corner of my eye, I spot Lake turning the corner, walking down the path to my little porch while my sister pulls out a sleeve of condoms.

Tension shoots sky-high in me. "Caroline!"

My cheeks redden.

As Lake heads up the steps, Caroline swivels around. "Oh! This is perfect."

She wings them his way, and he catches them. Seconds later she's gone, and Lake is holding a sleeve of protection and I'm wearing a mask.

He gestures to me. "Are you sick? Do you need anything?" It's asked with genuine concern, but I don't need help.

I rip off the mask. "Just a precaution. Since she says she's over her cold, but you never know. I don't want to get you sick. As then you couldn't play and..."

The sentence dies as the awkwardness expands. I'm explaining my germaphobe excuses while he holds condoms we won't use. "I'll just grab my bag."

He gives a tight nod, and I hustle inside, snagging my overnight bag—well, for two nights—then roll it out.

I'm locking the door, ready to wheel it toward his car when he snags it from me with the kind of stealth he'd use when snagging a puck.

"Lake, I can roll my own suitcase."

But it's a futile argument, since he's already carrying it in one hand like it weighs nothing. It's only when we get to the car that I realize he's still holding the condoms too.

"I can put those back," I stammer.

"Right," he says, glancing down, like he's just remembered he was holding them.

He hands them to me, and this is the most awkward game of hot potato I've ever played. Do I take them back to my house, which might imply I'd use them there? Or give them back to him? Pack them away with a saucy wink and 'That's for later, big boy'? I spot a pair of big blue eyes staring at me from the back seat, so I jam the condoms in the side pocket of my suitcase. "Thor looks like he's ready to go."

"He sure is," Lake says, and he's a little inscrutable.

But maybe that's what happens when you tell a guy the new rule of fake dating is no real touching. This is going to be the longest short road trip ever.

I slide into the passenger seat, greeted by a hearty meow from Thor. "Hey, cutie," I say, stretching around and offering him a scratch on the chin.

Once Lake slides into the driver's seat, I pull my hand back, like if I can't touch him I shouldn't be touching his cat. What are the rules now? My chest is taut, like there's a steel band around it, and I wish I knew. I reach for my necklace, fiddling with the sun charm. Yes, be sunny. Be upbeat.

I fill the uncomfortable silence with words as he pulls away from the curb. "Is Thor coming with us?"

"No, I need to drop him at home. In Cozy Valley. That cool?"

"Yes," I chirp. "Of course."

If I'm agreeable, that'll smooth over the new tension I created, right? Maybe it will help to acknowledge my sister's wingwoman-ing. "That was awkward timing, right?" I ask, pointing my thumb behind us as he weaves into traffic.

He shoots me a curious look before returning his gaze to the road. "What was?"

He's not making this easy.

"The condoms," I say uncomfortably.

He stays quiet for a long, painful beat. Finally, he breaks the silence with, "And the ambition. She thought we'd need so many."

I laugh, high and forced. "But wrong. Especially since we decided we're not doing it."

He hesitates before he answers with a casual, "Yep."

Hmm. He seems content with our decision to pull back. He went along with it easily the other night. Maybe he was thinking the same thing—that we shouldn't do anything again —and I simply said it first.

I breathe a small sigh of relief. Yes, that has to be it. And for a while I don't worry about the silence as we cruise over the Golden Gate Bridge. But when the wonder of the modern world is in the rearview mirror, he says, "Do you have a fear of getting sick?"

"Yes, but it's not because my mom didn't take good care of me when I was sick. Or my dad. I know that's a question that therapists ask to figure out if you were unloved—who took care of you when you were sick."

"Whoa, I wasn't saying that."

I close my eyes. I overreacted. Because he hit a nerve when he saw a part of me I rarely show others. "I don't like being helpless," I admit, even though it makes my chest ache to say it.

"I hear you." Then he drums his hands on the wheel and says thoughtfully, "I didn't realize that was something therapists ask."

"Mine did. I think she was surprised when I answered that my parents did. Take care of me when I was sick."

"Why did that surprise her?"

"Because I probably seem like someone whose parents don't like weakness," I say with a shrug, maybe a slightly defensive one, maybe because it's a little true. My mom does prefer it when everything works out, like with her wedding planning, like with her marriage, like with my dad. She was determined to help him when he struggled with depression. Falling apart was not an option.

I exhale heavily, then try to push past my own roadblocks, since he's clearly trying. "And yes, I do want everything to be just so. But I'm trying to ease up."

"You mentioned that the other day."

I lower my face. "I'm not doing a good job."

"You're hard on yourself. You're doing fine. Also, I don't think sickness is a weakness, Remy."

I close my eyes for a second. He's being so nice to me even when I'm not sure I deserve it. I really need to get the focus off me. I open my eyes. "So we're going to your ranch right now to drop off Thor? Do you want me to stay in the car?" I ask gently, since that might be easier for him.

His hands curl tight around the wheel. "You can come in." He hesitates then adds, "My dad doesn't go outside."

"I know," I say softly. "Clem mentioned he has agoraphobia. How has that been going?"

Lake sighs, then clenches his jaw. "I really don't know. Not well, I guess," he says, then blows out another breath. "But he wants to meet you. Since he thinks..."

My heart squeezes, and I hate that we're probably going to disappoint his father too. "Will he be sad when this ends?"

Lake shrugs, but that sure feels like a yes.

* * *

The car bumps its way over a long, winding gravel driveway till we round a final curve and on the other side of a green hill, a sprawling property emerges with a rustic sign that reads *Big Steps Ranch and Bird Sanctuary* in a cutout style.

In the distance, under the blue sky, a handful of people work with horses and kids in a ring, and there's a huge home too—a big white farmhouse, then acres and acres of land. It's peaceful here, bucolic even with the warm sun, the bright skies, and the meadows stretching out to a stream and beyond.

"I've never been here before," I say as I step out of the car, quickly adding, "I mean, there was no reason. Clem tends to stay at her place."

"She does. It's good for her there," he says, and that sounds like it means something but it's probably a family thing I don't need to know about.

After Lake unclips Thor from the car seat, he sets him down on the ground, and I beam. His cat's still wearing the harness, and Lake's holding his leash. "It's like the picture you took," I say, unable to contain my glee. "You two are so cute."

That's fine to say. It's not flirty. It's just reality.

Lake shoots me a searing look. "Not cute."

But he's wrong. Lake's a walking ad for cat daddy right now—the big, burly hockey player heading up the steps with his trained cat.

I wish I were enjoying this moment for real. That he was mine. But I do my best to push all my wishes and wants out of my mind. The time isn't right. There's too much at stake.

I head inside, leaving my wishes behind. The house is light and bright, with shiny, clean wood floors and a rustic feel, but with a touch of a modern look. I don't know why—maybe because I know his dad doesn't leave—I was expecting a musty place.

It's the opposite. Fresh and sunny, and it smells like oranges and home.

Nerves bounce in my chest as Lake calls out, "Thor's home. Are you decent?"

"Of course I am," a voice calls from the living room, and when we enter, an older man stands and strides toward us. He looks a lot like Lake, but with a weathered face, graying hair, and clever blue eyes. There's a library book on the table. A *Damon Cross.*

"You must be the lady my son's so crazy about."

My pulse jumps up and down.

"Dad," Lake seethes.

"Oh hush," his father says, as he reaches me and offers a hand for shaking.

I shake back but inside my mind pings with questions. Did Lake tell him he felt that way? Or is his dad just giving him a hard time? Or is this his dad's best guess?

"So nice to meet you, Mr. Axelrod," I say.

"Call me Nicholas."

"Nicholas," I say with a smile, setting my questions aside. They're not important anyway. "Your son clearly got his good looks and charm from you."

He waves a hand, then says to Lake, "She's a keeper."

Lake looks away, inscrutable once more.

His father's not though. The man is clearly happy to see his son, and, I surmise, me. "Your place is beautiful. The horses are majestic. I can't wait to check out the birds someday. I hear there's an owl box," I say.

He strokes his chin. "I wonder if there's a baby owl yet."

"Did you know an owl's eyes make up five percent of their body weight?"

"I did not know that," he says, then tilts his head. "You an owl expert?"

I shake my head. "No, I looked it up when I learned Lake likes owls. He sent me a picture of the owl box."

With a pleased smile, his father turns to his son again. "Like I said, a keeper."

This time, Lake meets my gaze and he looks...a little bit sad.

* * *

When we're back in the car, after Lake showed me the bird sanctuary at his father's insistence, the mood feels heavy again. Awkward. I wonder if Lake and I can return to the way we were—friendly, supportive, playful—before I dropped the *we can't do that again* rule.

I don't know, but as he pulls out of Cozy Valley, the wooden sign for the town with an illustrated squirrel curled up asleep in the V fading in the rearview mirror, I ask the inevitable question. "How long has it been since he left the property?"

Lake lets out a heavy sigh. "About five years."

"Did something happen? I did a little research into agoraphobia and learned that sometimes there can be a triggering event."

"You researched it?"

I nod. When he told me his dad was keen on him dating, I figured we might eventually meet. "I wanted to understand him better. And you."

Lake seems to sit with the info for a minute or two as he drives. I try to read his expression, but his gaze is focused on the road. "He was in a car accident. It was his fault. He hit someone. A woman, but she's fine. Just minor bruises, but it was enough for him to not want to drive again."

My chest aches with sympathy for everyone involved. "Understandable."

"He retreated. Had serious PTSD over it. Would not get in

the car. But he liked to walk. And Gavin, Clem, and I thought he was getting better, going for walks on the property. He liked to go with Heather and me," he says on a rough swallow. "It was nice to see him outside. Then Heather was killed by a car, and that was it. Instant. He shut back down because the world is 'unsafe.'"

"Oh, Lake," I say, my heart sinking like an anchor in the ocean. "That's so hard. I'm so sorry he has to deal with that. And you."

"Yeah me too. I wish..."

"That you could help him?"

He nods. "Yeah."

I give that some thought, trying to find an answer. "Sounds like he has a lot to unpack. So many things wrapped up in each other."

"I try to encourage him. Ask him if he wants to join me with the birds and Gavin with the horses. But he never does."

My throat tightens with emotions. "Clem said it's been a while. I know she hoped he would go to her bookstore at one point."

"That was hard for her. Not being able to share the grand opening with him. To just show him pics." He exhales, long and steady, like he's releasing some of the pain. "I felt some serious hope for a while, but then it was just gone. And this is now his normal."

My heart hurts for Lake, like there's a deep bruise on it. I wonder if this has to be the norm. If there are other things to be done. But I know, too, these conversations take time, and that he would have tried everything he could think of to help his father. "I appreciate you sharing that."

He gives a tight nod as he drives. "I don't really talk about it much. Not with the guys. But, um, thanks for being cool about it."

"Of course." I replay the last convo, grateful we could share. Maybe this is *our* new normal? "I feel like we're friends. Like we can talk about things."

It's only when the word *friends* makes landfall that I remember how Jameson broke up with me, how that word cut to the bone. "I don't mean it like *let's just be friends*," I say backpedaling.

His brow knits. He stays quiet though.

"I just mean," I continue, trying to fix things, "that we are. That I want to be."

And I don't know if I'm helping anything at all.

His shoulders seem to tense, and he swallows, but then says, "Friends."

But we don't talk much the rest of the drive.

And I don't know if that means we are or aren't friends.

By the time we finally drive by the Welcome to Evergreen Falls sign, we haven't even talked about why we're here. Not the candy we're picking up for my sister or the road trip the bride couldn't make.

And why it's one of the five things you should do before you say I do.

THOR

31

BITE ME

LAKE

If I'd thought surviving a penalty kill was hard, it's got nothing on this road trip. Being in close quarters with a woman who smells like flowers and all your fantasies, and not being able to tell her you think about her all the time is more brutal than being undermanned on the ice.

But I last somehow, and when we pull into Evergreen Falls, I can breathe again. It's late afternoon. We'll check into the hotel soon, grab some grub, and then call it a night, and when that's done we can check this off the bucket list.

Only three more items and a wedding to get through.

That's all.

But as I come around to her side of the car and open the door, I remind myself that I said yes to her request to be her plus-one because I want to help her. When I offered to show her how a man treats a woman—with passion and honesty—I did it because she deserves it.

Not because I want to lay her down on the bed and kiss every inch of her skin. Worship her entire body. Make her toes curl and her fingers grab the sheets.

Though I really fucking do.

"Let's get that candy," I say. Hell, maybe some sugar on my tongue will distract me from my vastly inappropriate thoughts.

She gives me a smile—one that says she's trying her best to be normal. "Thanks again, Lake, for doing this."

This presumably being running errands for her sister. Going through the bucket list. Taking a road trip.

I blow out a breath and glance briefly down the street of the town that's known for going all out for the Christmas holidays but also doesn't seem to hold back on spring decor either. The streetlamps are decorated with flickering pastel lights, and the stores are dressed up with illustrations of flowers, birds, and butterflies in the windows.

It's all so festive, and I hate it on principle.

Oh shut up, you grump. Remy probably loves it. Bet she'd enjoy a bouquet of flowers or some chocolates just to celebrate that spring is almost here. And you'd enjoy giving them to her.

Great, now my brain is calling me out on my hypocrisy.

We go inside The Candy Cottage. The smell of sugar smacks me in the face.

Remy's eyes pop as she looks around. And she's, yup, the kid in a candy shop, and this is a new bit of intel about her. I file it away in my Remy list, along with the succulents, the spreadsheets, the notebooks, the strappy shoes she wears, the off-the-shoulder sweaters she likes, and the watches of mine she admires. I file it beneath the therapy she goes to in order to work on her need to feel in control, even though I think she's fucking amazing as is, but I admire the hell out of the fact that she wants to improve.

What kind of candy does she like best? I try to read her as she drinks in the shelves of nostalgic candy like Lemonhead and PEZ, then the glass jars stuffed with all kinds of gummy bears, gummy worms, gummy monkeys, Swedish Fish, raspberry treats, and gummy soda bottles, all with signs that say *Vegan AF*.

I snap my gaze to the register. "Are they normally not vegan?"

A woman behind the pink and white counter with curly black hair and warm dark skin says, "Actually a lot of candy has gelatin, which is made from beef."

I cringe. "So I've been eating beef candy all these years?"

"Well, not if you get it from here," she says, gesturing to her shop. "We're proudly meat-free. But yes, gelatin is common in a lot of candy from licorice to gummy bears."

I cringe. "I don't ever want to eat licorice again."

"Or just eat this licorice," she says, patting a jar with vegan licorice, next to a discount red basket full of Valentine's candy, all marked *Vegan AF* too.

Remy strides closer to me, her gaze curious. "Do you have a thing for licorice, Lake?"

"Until I learned I was eating meat when I thought it was sugar."

Remy pats me on the arm, her brown eyes twinkling. "Let me help you. I'm kind of a candy aficionado."

Before I know it, the candy lover is scooping up the wedding favors, and buying up the licorice, and something about the competence she displays in breezing through the store irks me—like it means she's already and easily moved the hell on from the other afternoon when she fell apart in bed, my face buried in the crook of her neck. But the way she sails through the store excites me too.

That's the problem with obsession.

You just can't hit the off button so quickly. Especially when she buys up discounted Valentine hearts that say things like *bite me*.

That's totally not going to make me think of what I'm not having with her.

* * *

As the sun dips low on the horizon, we pass the North Pole Nook and Tavern and turn down a side street, then I pull up to the Chestnut Inn. Since this town's bread and butter is Christmas, there are chestnuts roasting on the sign in the yard but no snow on the ground, or the hint of it in the air.

Good—I don't need to get snowed in with her, or anything fucking romantic like that. Just need to get checked in, eat dinner, and get some alone time, so I'm not stuck with her and this going-nowhere attraction.

I grab her bag. "I managed to upgrade our room to a suite—two bedrooms and a living room. Couldn't get an extra room tonight. Too many people in town for the game."

"Sounds perfect."

Inside the inn, we head to the main desk, and an older man with a pale face, a goatee, and red hair snaps his gaze to us from the screen. "Welcome to the Chestnut Inn. How may I help you?"

"Hey there, Cedric," I say, reading his name tag. "I'm checking in. I've got a suite for tonight. Last name is Axelrod."

"Fantastic. I'll just look you up right now," he says, then studies the screen. Studies it for a few more beats than I'd expect.

"That's a suite for tomorrow night?" he asks with some concern, looking up.

"Nope. Tomorrow is just a regular room for me."

"And tomorrow I have my own room," Remy chimes in, then gives her name. "But for tonight we're sharing."

"The suite?"

"Yes. Tonight's for the suite. Since there're two of us. Two friends," I add, for Remy's sake, since that's what she wanted.

Cedric swings his gaze from Remy to me, like he's adding up the details of us. "Right," he says, squinting at the screen, then clucking his tongue.

Cedric looks up with an apology written in his eyes. "See, it looks like the suite upgrade was for tomorrow night. Tonight we just have the one room. A regular room with a king-size bed though."

He fastens on a smile that seems to say *I really hope that'll do.*

"That's all you have for my friend and me?" Remy asks, voice squeaking.

And shit.

That was a rookie mistake I made, introducing us as friends. We're supposed to be faking it as boyfriend and girlfriend. *Everywhere.* What if this guy knows someone? Like Jameson or Caroline? What if he rats us out? Is that why he was clocking us seconds ago? *Probably, you dumbass.*

"We're fully booked," he says.

"Are there any other hotels?" she asks in an even higher tone. She's totally forgotten we're supposed to be in character too. I've got to fix this, stat. I take a step closer to her, getting in fake boyfriend territory as she fiddles with her necklace. Clearly she didn't notice the gaffe. Maybe Cedric didn't either. A man can dream.

"I'm afraid the whole town is booked," Cedric continues.

She gulps. "So it's just the one room tonight?"

"For you and your friend," he confirms, and he heard us loud and clear. "But it has a bed and a very comfy couch."

Which I'll be sleeping on since there's only one bed. But Cedric doesn't need to know that. I drape an arm around

Remy and plant a kiss to her cheek, punctuating it with a smack. Time to sell this romance. "Sounds perfect for us."

Cedric blinks, then furrows his brow even more. "Oh, so it's all good?"

Remy tenses, but then relaxes, or perhaps she wills herself to relax. "Yes, it's so perfect."

With that problem fixed, I grab the key card, thank him and walk toward the stairs. We say nothing on the way up.

Once we reach the room, I unlock it and say, "I'm sorry. I just forgot. There's no excuse."

"I forgot too," she says, then flashes a hopeful grin. "But it'll probably be fine. It's not like Caroline's here, or my parents, or Jameson, or the team yet. And besides, I think you fooled him there at the end."

I swallow past my self-loathing. "I won't let it happen again."

She sets a hand on my arm. "I won't either."

But even that gesture, her hand on my arm, feels good. She must realize it, since she takes it off too quickly. The door swings open, and Cedric wasn't kidding about the one bed. It takes up three quarters of the room.

And the couch? It's more like a love seat. There's no way I'll fit on it.

I can't be in this room for long, brushing up against her, stealing glances at her, so I use the workout excuse. I head out as soon as I can for a run, and then a session at the hotel gym. When I'm done, we meet up for dinner in town, grabbing sandwiches and fries at the Candy Cane Diner. She tells me she worked out in the fitness center while I was out for a run and already showered so there's no need to worry. "You can have the shower to yourself tonight," she says.

And now I'm thinking of showering. With her. Great. Just

great. I take a bite of the fake chicken sandwich like it'll make me stop picturing her naked.

When we return to the room, it's nearly nine. Close enough to bedtime but not quite.

The door shuts with an ominous *thunk* and it's just her, me, and my unchecked longing for the rest of the night.

"Want dessert?" Remy asks.

You.

"Got some in your pockets?" I tease, trying desperately to make light of the situation.

"No," she says, laughing as she gestures to her bags. "I have the Valentine's candy."

Oh, right. "Sure," I say.

"And the licorice for you."

She fucking bought me licorice.

"Let's do it, then I definitely need to shower," I say, gesturing to my gym clothes.

"You look cute in sweaty gym clothes," she says. And that is not helping. And she must know it since she mutters, "Sorry."

"It's okay. I do look hot," I say, owning it.

"Well, yeah."

But that won't help either, the admission that she's still attracted to me, and I am to her, and we're not doing a thing about it.

Because it's complicated, you ass.

I really need to get away from her, but I'm a glutton for Remy, so I settle in on the floor and she sits on the couch, and we crack open the Valentine's candy. As I pop in a *bite me*, Remy asks if I want to watch a show.

"Sure," I say, since it'll pass more time.

We agree on *Top-Notch Boyfriend,* a series based on a book from a writer named TJ Hardman. It's about an American guy who meets an Englishman and falls fast and hard for him but circumstances pull them apart, and it's a little addictive.

So addictive, we plow through two episodes and a box full of *kiss me*, *hug me*, and *touch me*.

Soon enough, she's yawning and has clearly come down from the sugar high. "I should go to bed."

"And I should finally shower," I say, grateful we've survived. Well, almost. There's still that matter of the one bed.

"Lake," she says, standing and stretching. "You don't need to sleep on the couch."

"Thanks. I don't think I'd fit."

She pauses, swallows, then lifts her chin, like she needs to stay on point. "We can share the bed. Right?"

The *right* is doing a lot of work there. The subtext is clear—we can share it and it won't end the way the nap lesson did.

"Right," I say.

After she brushes her teeth, she emerges from the bathroom. She's wearing sleep pants and a T-shirt that do nothing to help me escape all my desire for this woman.

But she's also sporting a pair of red glasses that make my heart kick, and I don't even know why. "You wear glasses," I say, the words thick in my mouth.

"Only when I remember to take my contacts out. And they were bugging me, so I took them out."

My desire is bugging me. Wish I could remove it just as easily.

32

SO HARD TO SEE

REMY

I'm stuck outside in a storm. The wind whips around me. The clouds are angry. The rain pelts me everywhere.

I've just got to get inside, and I trudge to the door on heavy feet that barely move, trying to yank it open, when my eyes blink open.

Oh. I was just dreaming. It's raining outside though, and wow, is it loud.

All I want is to go back to sleep but my eyes feel sticky from my mascara, a reminder that I forgot to wash my face. I drag myself out of bed, squinting in the dark. I stumble toward the bathroom door, which looks fuzzy without my glasses, but I can tell it's ajar. A yawn takes over me, as I push on the door the rest of the way open. It's so bright in here and so loud. What kind of monster would leave all the lights on in the bathroom?

In a flash, the rain stops. I yawn again, but something scratches at my brain as I fumble for the light to dim it.

It's. Not. Raining.

Don't look, don't look, don't look.

I don't listen to the voice in my head. I turn to the shower, and I look right at the gorgeous hockey player as he slides open the steamy glass door and steps out.

Without glasses or contacts I can't see objects that are far away, but I can see well enough up close, and right now the object is a very close, very wet, and very naked hockey player as he reaches for a towel from a nearby hook.

I make a sound. Something like a whimper.

I've seen him naked-ish. I've had his cock halfway down my throat, but I've never experienced the man in all his naked glory. And even with my flawed vision, the man is still glorious. Muscles for days, dark hair on his chest, and that impressive cock, half hard, with a drop of water sliding down it.

My mouth waters, and I should go. I *really* should go. "I..."

But have I ever spoken before? Do I even know how to make words? How to move my feet? They're currently glued to the tile.

Lake doesn't seem fazed. He's amused as he lifts the towel and runs it over his hair. His hair! He doesn't even attempt to cover up his birthday suit. Just lazily dries his locks with the white terrycloth as I stare at all of him, ink and skin and muscles.

"If I'd known you wanted to join, I wouldn't have gotten out yet."

The easy rasp. The hint of a tease. The cocky assurance.

It snaps me out of my six-foot-two naked hockey player haze.

"Sorry, I thought it was raining," I blurt out, then spin around and hightail it out of the bathroom, and dive into the bed alone with my mortification.

And, unfortunately, my arousal.

I pull the duvet over my head, willing myself to fall asleep.

C'mon, brain.

I even bragged to him about being able to fall asleep fast. Now would be a really good time to show off that skill.

But nope, my overactive, overthinking, overeager brain is caught in a loop.

A loop of Lake with droplets sliding down his strong chest. Lake with a roguish smirk. Lake sporting all the confidence in the world.

Ugh.

I squeeze my eyes shut, failing miserably in my quest to nod off when the door creaks open.

Is he still naked? I don't look. I can't look. He caught me gawking at him shamelessly.

Footsteps pad across the carpet. The rustle of soft blankets floats past me. The mattress dips.

I try not to inhale him, but I catch the clean, soapy, masculine scent of him as I burrow under the covers, pretending to be asleep.

Breathing in, breathing out. My stomach flips again as I draw in the intoxicating smell of him.

I just love the scent of a clean man.

He says nothing, but I swear I can feel his satisfied grin burning a hole through the atmosphere right now.

He sighs, a big, loud one, chased by an even louder yawn. "I'm so tuckered out," he says, like he's muttering to himself.

Oh my god. The fucker is taunting me.

I dig in, keeping my body as still as possible under the duvet, my breathing as steady as if I were asleep.

"What a day," he adds in another hearty sigh.

He shifts a little, then punches a pillow. Again and again.

"There. That's better," he says to his audience of one.

I grit my teeth, but I am committed to my role too.

"I'll just close my eyes and go to sleep," he says.

Please, please, please go to sleep and I can pretend I'm not turned on to the moon and back just being near you.

"Good night, Remy. It was nice seeing you today."

Ugh.

I can't be this person. I blow out an apologetic breath. "I'm sorry I walked in on you."

He doesn't even have the courtesy to laugh. He just says, "Are you though? You didn't seem sorry."

How dare he!

I yank off the duvet from over my head and flip over. "I am," I insist, the moonlight casting the room in a dim glow. "I couldn't see. I thought it was raining. I didn't have my glasses on. I'm sorry."

He smirks again, but then it vanishes. "I'm not."

And I burn everywhere. Flames lick my bones, my hair, my heart from his words.

I part my lips, but what do I even say? I'm the one who pumped the brakes on us. Everything feels so complicated, our lives entangled in ways that make a bedtime tryst a bad idea. My breakup is still so fresh.

But the pull toward him is so strong. It's so much. There's a drumbeat inside me and it's pounding out a rhythm to his name. This longing to touch him is consuming me. It's eating me up. It's taking me apart.

Nerves are throttling me though. How do I make the next move? Do I even?

He lifts a hand, like he's about to touch me, maybe to tuck a strand of hair behind my ear. I hold my breath and hope.

But he just slides it through his hair, the consummate picture of a patient man. A man who's willing to wait for it.

To wait for me to say something.

"Lake," I begin, my resistance starting to melt away.

"Yes?"

"I'm not that sorry," I say, and my lips twist into a naughty smile.

He shifts to his side, studying me. "You did want to join me, didn't you."

It's not a question. It's a statement. And the unspoken words, *admit it*, hang there at the end in the charged, dark air, the moonlight slicing across his lovely skin.

There's no point pretending anymore. There's just none.

"Maybe I did. A little bit," I say.

His smile could light up the night sky. It's a goddamn star twinkling. He leans closer, and I think—no, I hope—he's going to pin me down and kiss me senseless.

But instead, he dusts a too-chaste kiss to my cheek.

All the air whooshes from my lungs. A pulse beats between my thighs.

Whispering, "Good night, Remy," he breaks the kiss, pulls back, turns the other way, and pulls up the covers to his sturdy pecs.

No.

Just no.

That is not happening. Powered by lust and weeks of pent-up desire, I grab for his shoulder. "Don't you dare go to sleep."

He climbs over me, and kisses the breath out of me.

33

SHUT UP AND FUCK ME

LAKE

Remy doesn't melt underneath me. She roars. She grabs. She claws. Her nails scrape through my hair, and I didn't know I liked long nails until she dragged hers across my skull. It's fucking possessive and needy.

Electricity crackles down my body as she kisses me back just as hard, just as fiercely as I kiss her.

It's everything I've ever wanted in a kiss.

There's just one big problem.

This goddamn duvet between us. I wrench away from her, breaking the kiss to tug the cover off her and toss it to who even knows where.

And damn. Here she is in that sleep shirt and pants, all rumpled and twisted and unbearably sexy because they're on her.

I tug on the bottom of her shirt, and I'm this close to pulling it off her, when I stop.

"Can you see okay?"

She laughs, then nods. "I can. Up close is fine."

"Like my dick was after the shower?"

She growls, curls a hand around my neck. "Shut up and kiss me."

"With so much pleasure."

As I slant my mouth to hers, I run a hand along her neck, up into those chestnut strands. My other hand brackets her face. Her lips chase mine, hungry and needy. Her hands slip around my bare back, grabbing at me, then traveling down to my ass. I'm just wearing boxer briefs, and I really fucking hope that changes soon.

Remy doesn't waste a second. Her hands are inside my briefs, and she's grabbing my ass, and my skin tingles.

Everywhere. Just fucking everywhere.

I'm like a city grid lit up at night. I could power the whole country when she spreads her thighs and invites me closer.

Hello, dream girl.

I grind against her.

She arches her back. Moaning into my mouth. Seeking my tongue. Rocking up against my erection.

It'd be better though if we were naked, and she seems to agree since she's pushing off my boxers.

I stop so I can help her along, stripping to nothing.

She groans her approval.

I kneel between her thighs and pull down her sleep pants.

And wow.

I didn't expect anything less than something perfectly put together for my perfect planner, but this? White lacy panties with a red bow right at the center? My dick thumps its approval.

"I really hate that I have to take these off," I say on a rumble.

Her breath comes in a harsh pant. "Take them off."

My three favorite words. I slide them down her long, toned legs, slipping them off, then just admiring the sight.

Even in the dark, I can see enough of her, and I want it all. I want to bury my face between those thighs, lick and suck her pretty pink pussy. Make her grab my hair and scream my name as I eat her up.

But when she flings off her shirt and sits up, I'm greeted by full, creamy tits, and my brain scrambles.

"Every inch of you is beautiful," I say, wishing I had more words, better words, but I hope those are enough.

She meets my eyes and her expression is so vulnerable and so aroused at the same time, it makes my heart squeeze. Her gaze drifts down to my legs. "Your dick is beautiful."

This woman. I dip my face and brush a quick kiss to those red lips. "Who knew such a good girl had such a filthy mouth," I say, then hop out of bed and head to her suitcase. "Good thing your sister was ambitious."

"Because you are too?"

"You bet I am," I say, grabbing the sleeve, then tearing off one as I return to the bed and settle between her thighs. Her hands are back on me in a nanosecond. Running up my thighs, traveling over my abs where she stops at the cat, tracing its tail, its ears, then darting down to my cock.

She gives me a pump.

"So fucking eager for my dick," I muse. "Who would have thought?"

"Just shut up and fuck me."

"Don't worry, beautiful. I'll give you every inch of what you want tonight." As I open the condom, I don't take my eyes off her, and she never takes her hands off me.

I roll on the condom, then notch the head of my dick against her sweet, wet center, and I haul in a breath. I'm not even pushing inside her. I'm just rubbing against her and I'm shaking. It's that fucking good.

I've got to keep it together for her. I pause, rub a hand up her belly, travel to her breasts. "It's been a while," I confess.

She smiles softly. "It's okay. I just want you."

And hell, if that isn't the sweetest thing anyone's ever said to me. I sink inside, and my world spirals away for a white-hot minute. The feel of her. My god, the incomparable, incredible feel of this woman.

She's warm and tight, and she's arching her back already. I ease out as a hot wave of pleasure shoots down my spine.

Her lips part as she looks up at me. "More," she whispers, urging me on.

"Whatever you want," I say, then sink back into her again.

She gasps, then grabs my neck, holding on tight.

I clench my jaw, narrowing all my focus to her, just her as I rock my hips. Finding a rhythm. Seeking the right pace for my woman.

Doesn't take long to discover it since Remy's roaming her hands into my hair, and whispering, "*Faster, harder, yes.*"

And I obey. I piston my hips, pumping faster, reading her cues.

Her hair's fanned out on the pillow. Her breasts are heaving. Her arms are locked tight around me.

Funny, I didn't expect her to be so...bold. There's so much of her that seems to hold back. She measures her words, and makes sure everyone else is okay, including me.

Like when she wanted to suck me off.

But tonight, in the dark, in this small-town inn where it feels like we're the only ones in the world, she's giving in to her desire.

And somehow...that's me.

With every moan, every cry, I move faster, I sink deeper, and I hold off. I don't stray from the mission of her.

As her breaths come faster, turning more ragged, I ask, "What do you need, beautiful? Want to get you there."

She grabs my right hand, and like she did in bed the other day, she shoves it between her thighs.

Well then. I can definitely do that. "It'd be easier like this."

In seconds, I flip her over, and we readjust so she's on top of me. "Ride that dick," I tell her, as I slide my hand against her clit, my other one holding her hip.

Like that she rises up and down on my cock, as I stroke her lovely clit till she's gasping, shuddering, then calling my name.

It's the sexiest thing I've ever seen. The woman I've wanted for the last year, falling to pieces on top of me.

And that's all it takes.

I'm right there with her, my whole body one giant spark as my thoughts spin out of control and I finally let go, following her.

A few minutes later when I can think again—one stark realization is clear. Once with her won't be enough.

34

WHEN SQUIRRELS FLY

REMY

I'm up well before Lake. Morning breath is my mortal enemy, and I will do anything to vanquish it. I've scrubbed my teeth and brushed my hair, taken a quick shower, and applied my makeup, all while replaying the way Lake took me apart last night.

I've watched that twenty times.

I've memorized it.

If I were on a flight, I'd sit back in my seat, close my eyes, and binge watch my new favorite show in my head—the Great Only One Bed Fucking at the Chestnut Inn.

For now though, my contacts are back in, and I'm setting my packing cubes back in my suitcase, ready to go. I don't want to presume we're staying together again. I mean, why would we be? It's not like he's going to crack me like a lobster every night. I have my own room tonight, and a busy day ahead.

I have a lunch meeting with the publicist for the minor league team that normally plays in the arena, then we have a promo event at the arena tonight before the game. Players from both teams will warm up with some young hockey players to raise awareness for Total Teamwork, a youth sports mental health organization.

Which reminds me—I really should replay that episode in my head again so I'm not doing it at lunch or later, at the warmups.

As I squat down to zip my suitcase though, I don't replay last night. My mind annoyingly skips ahead to tonight. To after the game. My chest tightens slightly, like there's a belt around it. My palms feel sweaty, so I rub them down my slacks. I check the time on my phone. I could go get breakfast. I could grab a coffee. I could plan the next date for my new client—

"Morning, beautiful."

I jump.

Spin around, stand up. "Hi."

It comes out high-pitched, but I don't think Lake notices, since he's stretching then threads a hand through his sex-rumpled hair. My attention snags on his biceps. They're so biceps-y and big, and my mouth waters, and I think I love biceps, and the ink of the tiny running horses makes me want to lick it.

My gaze drifts down to the ladder of his abs and the bird there. Lake is covered in animals and the fact that he's chosen to ink his body with creatures great and small is doing funny things to my heart.

Scary things. I jerk my gaze up to his face right as he pushes up on his elbows, the duvet snaking down to the V of his abs. "You leaving?"

"No," I say but my voice squeaks. I wasn't leaving. I was just...trying to protect myself from being left.

"Remy Hatmaker. You little liar," he growls.

"What?"

"Don't make me get out of bed and get you."

My eyes widen. "That's an option?"

But evidently it is since he flings off the cover, strides over to me in his glorious nakedness, and grabs me, scooping me up again, like he did that day at his place. He brings me back to bed and drops me down. Then he climbs in next to me, resting on his side.

Is he horny again? Well, we did have sex again in the middle of the night. It was fast and hot and good. I suppose he might be ready to go another time.

"You love lunch. Do you love breakfast too?"

What a weird question. "Um, sure."

He nuzzles my neck. "Have breakfast with me."

It's just a meal. It's nothing. But it makes me unreasonably happy.

"Okay," I say, when my attention snags on his ass, exposed.

Is that...?

"Do you have a squirrel tattoo on the side of your ass?"

He twists around, like he needs to confirm it. "What do you know? I do."

"Lake," I say, amazed.

"You didn't see it last night."

"Well, yeah, I was touching your ass, not looking at it."

"You love my ass."

I roll my eyes, but I do, I really do. "It has the perfect squish."

The covers sit right below his cheeks, and like this I have a perfect view of the little squirrel, and it's holding a hockey stick. It's a different style than his other ink—which is more fine-line work. This is cartoonish and I have a feeling he didn't choose this tattoo.

"Did you lose a bet with the other guys?"

"That obvious?"

I hold up a thumb and forefinger. "A little. What was it over?"

"I said I'd finish with twenty-five percent more points than anyone else. And that didn't happen. I had twenty percent more, but it motivated those fuckers to work harder so it was a win–win."

"Who picked the squirrel?"

"Riggs, but they all voted on it and it was unanimous."

"It's adorable."

He narrows his eyes. "I'm not adorable."

I squeeze his muscular glutes. "But this is." I move to his owl. "And this is because you love owls. Is it because they're wise that you love them?"

"No. Because they're stealthy. They have serrated feathers so they barely make a sound when they fly. Also, have you ever seen one fly?"

I give that some thought. "I'm not sure I have."

"I highly recommend it."

I laugh. "I'll just camp out beneath a tree then and wait."

"It's worth it. It kind of makes you realize how impressive nature is. And other species. And the planet. And how precious too."

"There's that secret poet side of you."

He rolls his eyes. "Yeah, I'm a secret poet since I want to save the planet from climate change and human destruction."

"We should all be secret poets then." I travel up his body to trace the tiny horses on his biceps. I kiss one of them, and he shudders. I look up. "And these are for the ranch. Your family?"

"Yeah, my dad was a PT focusing on equine therapy. Gavin and Mira are now."

"That's a nice way to honor them." My hand slides down his body to the tiny cat on his abs. "For Thor?"

"And the next one, and the next one."

"Already planning to adopt more cats?"

"Of course."

"Such a cute cat daddy."

Like an owl flying, his hands dart out without a sound and he grabs me, hoisting me above him.

"Lake!"

"Spend the night again."

I barely register what he says, since I'm laughing and kicking my feet while he holds me with arms straight up, like this is easy. But my laughter fades as I look into his eyes. They're flashing with vulnerability. "Will you stay with me again?"

My heart does the tango. It's outrageous how much I want that. How quickly that tightness in my chest vanishes. How much I crave time with him. "Yes."

He lowers me, swallowing roughly as he sets me gently down on his chest, my body aligned with his. "And whenever you can. Maybe until the wedding when this ends." It sounds like there are stones in his mouth. "But until then, what if we just...give in? I can really show you the full boyfriend treatment."

"Fake boyfriend. Real dick?"

He laughs. "We know how much you like to ride my cock."

I swat his chest. But he's right, I really do.

So I say yes.

35

DREAMING OF MY BERRY BAR

LAKE

Always have a strategy.

That's what my college coach taught me, and it feels especially apropos right now.

Because I've had the wrong strategy for the last couple of days and I only just realized it. Hey, maybe the sex last night knocked some sense into my brain. Maybe I need to have more sex to get more sense knocked into my brain.

No shit.

Either way, I should have been getting to know Remy even more these last couple of days instead of pulling back after she said we should cool things off.

But no time like the present. As I drown my pancakes, slathered already in a heaping serving of strawberries, blackberries, and blueberries from the berry bar, I say, "So the list. You've got it, right?"

"Of course." She digs into her purse, sitting next to her on the red vinyl booth at the Candy Cane Diner on Main Street where we're having breakfast. "What do you take me for? Someone unprepared?"

A stupid grin threatens my mouth. "You've probably

already entered everything from it into a spreadsheet," I say, setting down the syrup and taking a bite.

As she grabs some kind of bag from within the bag, her eyes spark with excitement. "That's a good idea. I am going to add that to my to-do list."

I roll my eyes. "It wasn't a suggestion."

"But it's a good suggestion," she says, then sets the pouch thingy on the table. It's a beige color and there's a tiny dog illustration on the bag in the same sort of simple line work of most of my tattoos. For a second, I think that's kismet.

But no. I don't believe in kismet. A cartoon bubble sits above the dog's head saying, *Your dog is cute.*

I nod toward it. "Is that a bag within a bag?"

"Yes. How else would I keep the list safe?" she asks, nonplussed.

"No idea," I say, then take another bite to hide my grin because that's so her.

But wait. I'm following a new playbook and with that new strategy in mind, I chew, swallow, then meet her gaze. "That's so you."

I say it instead of keeping the thought to myself.

Her smile is like the sun, and it warms me from head to fucking toe. "Thanks." She sounds so pleased, so happy to be understood.

She opens the list from the unknown bride, setting it far enough away from her plate of tofu scramble to remain pristine. "Number two, take a road trip together." She mimes checking off the item. "I don't want to actually cross it off since it's her letter, you know? It feels sort of wrong."

"I get that."

"Like it's ours to do, but not to change?"

"Makes sense."

She screws up the corner of her mouth, clearly thinking.

"Why do you think it's on this list of five things to do before you say I do?"

"I've been wondering that myself. And honestly, I've been wanting to ask you," I say, and wow, that feels like stretching a muscle that's been dormant for a long time. Like a hamstring that you haven't given enough attention to. The honesty muscle. The openness muscle. Hurts like hell but it's a good kind of pain.

She tilts her head. "You have?"

I stretch it some more. "I have. I want to know what you think."

I want to know what you think about everything.

There's honesty, and there's also too much honesty. So that last thought stays locked up.

She glances toward my plate. "You love berries, right?"

I'm not entirely sure where she's going but I jump on the train anyway. "So much I'm going to get a berry bar installed at my house."

She takes a beat. Her tone is thoughtful and wise as she says, "I think *that's* the reason for the list."

"For me to get a berry bar?"

"The road trip. Why it's on the list. For details like *that,*" she says, pointing at me. "For learning things like you love berries. And that you love to tease me. That you're so confident about how you play hockey that you make ridiculous bets with your teammates, but you're so loyal that you go through with something like getting a squirrel tattooed on your ass." She pauses. "That you wish there's something more you could do for your father. That you told your dad nice things about me."

I don't move for a few seconds. It's like someone just peered into my medicine cabinet and learned that I take ibuprofen sometimes, and that my toothpaste tube's a mess, but that I like to use body butter on my hands so they're soft since they're usually so dry from hockey.

It's like she knows...me.

Maybe I was wrong when I thought I'd pulled back these last couple of days. Turns out I was still getting to know her all along, and she was getting to know me.

"Because you learn these things about each other on a road trip?" I ask at last.

"And that has to be good for a couple getting married, so that's why it'd be on her list. But also because road trips bring problems you have to navigate through. Like awkward tension," she says, looking at me with kind eyes, but ones that say *yeah, I know there was tension.* "And only one bed."

My fork frozen midair, I give that some thought. "But we worked through the issues."

"I suppose we did, in a way."

I set my fork down, lean a little closer because she is so much fun to play with. "I guess the road trip helped you work through your little issue."

"Fine, I'll bite. What's my little issue?"

"The way you want my dick."

She tosses her napkin at me. "Shut up."

I catch it easily. "Oh, my bad. I meant the way you want my dick all the time."

"You're the worst."

"The way you want it more than you've ever wanted anything in your life? Is that better?"

"You're in trouble."

"Fine, fine. I guess you don't want it. I don't have to give it to you again then."

She crosses her arms. "Good. I don't want it anymore."

I blow out a long sigh. "Such a shame. I had so much planned for you with it."

She smirks, then takes a breath, like she's gearing up to say something hard. "Because I want your tongue."

My brain stalls. It just stops working for a white-hot second or fifty. As I absorb everything she's saying, then devise a brand-new game plan—one that consists of two words.

"Check, please!"

But she shakes her head. "Tonight. I need to get some work done before my meeting."

"Like I can wait."

"Good things come to those who do," she says, and holy fuck. Who knew she was so flirty, so dirty?

"I'm going to be so fucking good at waiting today," I say, then before it gets too heated here in the diner, I gesture to the bag within the bag. "What do you want to do next? On the list?"

I'm avoiding number five. It scares the hell out of me. Maybe she is too. Because she says, "Three or four."

I study the list, peering closely at those two again, even though I've memorized the list already.

3. Camp under the stars
4. Make breakfast together and clean it up

"I think we could easily do number four back in the city after this road game. The one about making breakfast together in the morning."

Her shoulders tense. "Okay."

Not sure why that stresses her out, but I've got a feeling, seeing as how I woke up this morning to her dressed and ready to go. "You don't like waking up next to someone."

She shrugs. "It's okay. I just like to brush my teeth and, you know, freshen up."

I could tell her she doesn't need to worry about that with me, that I find her sexy with dragon breath, but that's not what she needs to hear. "Then we'll make sure you get to do that."

Her smile is one of relief, then she moves on. "But I don't know how the hell we're going to do number three. Camping under the stars?"

"There are campgrounds everywhere."

She shudders, then leans closer, cupping the side of her mouth like she's confessing. "I don't know how to break it to you, but I don't camp."

I laugh. "Right. Snakes."

"Exactly."

I stare at the ceiling for a beat. "How about glamping?"

"Maybe," she says, but it's a hopeful maybe.

That twinkle in her brown eyes makes my pulse spike. It's a little ludicrous, this effect she has on me. Making her happy just does it for me. Too bad I only have a few days of this kind of happiness left.

But I try not to linger on that. She doesn't want to see that side of Lake Onion. I zero in on practical matters. "I'll look into glamping. And we can fit the breakfast easily around the wedding shower and the spa day. Did your sister ever pick a date for that kind of torture? I mean, that kind of relaxation?"

She gives me a sharp stare. "I saw you get a massage in the training room."

"That was for sore muscles."

"Yes, they work on sore muscles at spas too," she says, then clicks on a link on her phone—a spreadsheet no doubt—and gives me a date.

I swear I'm not grinning when I say, "I have a game that night."

She sighs mournfully. "I was really looking forward to seeing you with cucumbers on your eyes. I was even going to take a picture."

"Dream on, beautiful," I say.

"Oh, I will, Lake. I will."

After I pay for breakfast, we head back to the hotel, and walk by the front desk where Cedric's working. He gives us a wave, then a knowing sort of smile. "Hey there. Looks like everything worked out okay?"

Right. I have to keep making sure it's clear that I didn't fuck up yesterday when I first said we were friends. I tug Remy closer. "Sure."

"Glad to hear that, and go beat the Sea Dogs tonight."

"I see we have a hockey fan in our midst," Remy puts in.

Cedric swings his gaze to her, studying her for a second or two, then adding, "Absolutely. And...I think I saw you on the broadcast too."

She cringes, but he shakes his head quickly, then gestures to Remy. "Nice to see you happy."

"Thanks," she says, her smile fading as we walk away.

His remark is similar to what the woman at that dress shop said. "When people recognize you from the Jumbotron video," I say as we head up the steps, "does that bug you?"

She draws in a breath, like she needs to steady herself. "At first, it did a little. But I try to look on the bright side. It's nice to have so many people rooting for you to move on."

My gut twists with the reminder that she's still very much in the moving on phase. And I'd do well to remember that.

36

JUST A TASTE

Lake

Hockey.

Just hockey.

Only hockey.

That's what goes through my head the rest of the day as we practice at the Evergreen Falls Arena.

Since Remy will be moving on when this ends, and I'll have to as well. Don't want to move on from her. Don't know how to convince her to move on *with* me. Hockey though? That's what I'll never move on from.

I remind myself of that as we shoot press photos with the Sea Dogs for The Sports Network before the game. Our first line heads to the ice as if we're facing off against theirs. Wesley Bryant, their hotshot right winger, Asher Callahan, their veteran left winger, and Miles Falcon, their center. Since it's a promo shot, our goalies are here too at center ice, looming ominously.

Miller's next to me, mask on, game face tight for the

cameras. But once the cameras are off, he grins like an excited kid. "This is going to be so fun."

"'Cause you like losing," Wesley tosses out.

Miller shakes his head. "Nah. It's going to be so fun to beat you here just like we did on your home turf earlier this year."

Wesley snarls. Miles deals us an ominous stare.

But Asher just gives a shoulder shrug. "Miracles do happen, boys," he muses like nothing can bother him.

I know that feeling too when I'm on the ice. The ice is the place where nothing can hurt me. Where emotions don't touch me. Where I'm one with the puck.

"It's not going to take a miracle," I drawl as I skate away. "It's just going to take me."

Maybe I've put a target on my back, but I don't care. I want to beat our crosstown rivals as much as I want to beat any team, but I especially want to tonight.

We might not be a real thing, but I promised Remy I'd show her how a good man would treat her, and I'll do that till the planned end. I'll do it as well as I play the game I'm obsessed with. There's something about winning in front of the woman you want to impress. It's hot, plain and simple.

Once we're in the locker room, taping up before the game, I turn to the guys, starting with Miller. "A thousand dollars for every goal saved."

He scoffs, "You don't have to bribe me. I'm going to fucking save them anyway."

"Consider it an extra incentive." I switch my attention to Riggs and Corbin. "And a thousand for every point you fuckers score."

"Love it when you pay us extra to do what we were already going to do," Riggs says, then points his stick at me. "But don't forget we still have a grand on you falling in love."

I wince at the reminder of the bet. At the way it makes my

chest squirm. Love is for other people. Love is for other times. Someday when she's ready, Remy will find a man who gives her the world—someone who knows how the hell to make love work.

When we hit the ice, both teams join some local kids all suited up in skates and gear. It's part of an effort to drive awareness of mental health for young players. As I stretch out the hammies with some teenagers, I briefly wish my father would take his mental health as seriously as these young athletes do, but I've suggested that in the past to him to no avail.

You can't make someone you love get help. All I can do is still love him. And I show him that at game time when I tap my left shoulder for him. Then I look to the press box where Remy is and I give a chin nod. Mouthing the word *presume*. So she knows that gesture is for her.

Even if this is all going to end after the wedding, she deserves the full boyfriend treatment now. Like I promised.

At the face-off I jostle for the puck, snagging it from Bryant, then flying down the ice with it. I spot an opening, line up at just the right angle for a sharp, precise wrist shot, and bam! It sails past their goalie and lands in the twine with a satisfying *thwap*. Victorious, I give a fist pump, then shoot Bryant a look like *told you so*. After the scoreboard boasts of our early lead, I dig in, and focus on each second, and keep playing at the top of my game the whole night.

And as promised I enjoy destroying the Sea Dogs very much. When the scoreboard flashes with a W, I turn my attention to the press box once more, and I feel like the king of the ice when I spot Remy cheering.

* * *

When we're back at the hotel, I'm so amped up from the win that my hands are aching to touch her. I want to peel off our clothes in the hallway as we walk back to the room—no need for a suite tonight, after all, so I kept this room. By the time we reach the door I'm kissing the back of her neck, roaming my hands up her sweater, whispering filthy things in her ear.

She shudders and says, "I can't even concentrate and open the door."

"Let me," I say, taking the key card, sliding it over the pad, and pushing the door open. Once we're inside, I strip off her sweater in no time, but then stop since she's staring at something behind me, pointing. "You got us champagne?"

I just spin around, spotting a bucket of champagne and two flutes on the table in the corner. "Actually, no," I say, feeling a little sheepish that I didn't. Maybe I should have.

She walks over to the bucket and picks up the card next to it. "*Thank you so much for staying at the Chestnut Inn. Come back anytime. Best wishes, Cedric.* He must have felt really bad for the one room thing."

"And clearly wanted to make up for it."

Remy flashes me a naughty grin. "He hardly has to. You're going to make it up to me with your mouth," she says, then steps closer and drags her thumb along my bottom lip, making me forget my fucking name as my skin lights up.

But the star of the show tonight is her.

"Get naked and get on the bed."

"If you insist."

"I do," I say, then open the bottle. When she's down to nothing, I tug off my shirt, leaving only my jeans on as I climb on the bed, champagne in hand. It's not lost on me that she bought champagne for her ex and didn't get to drink it. This champagne isn't going to waste.

I drizzle some of the bubbly on her breasts, then spend a

good long time worshiping those gorgeous globes, licking the champagne off her flesh, sucking her nipples till she's writhing and I'm aching. Grabbing at the sheets with one hand, she pushes my head lower with the other, practically begging me to eat her up. I set the bottle of champagne aside and then kiss my way down her body, reaching her hips.

I pause for a second or two, amazed I get to do this. I get to touch her. It's such a privilege.

I can't believe that the woman I crushed on from afar is so much better in real life. More fun, more caring, more kind than I'd imagined. And for a few more days, she's all mine. As that heady thought roars through me, I settle between her thighs.

But she presses a hand to my shoulder, stopping me. "I have to warn you, I don't come this way easily."

She gives me an apologetic look, but there's nothing to apologize for. This isn't a problem. This is something we can figure out together.

"Is it that you don't like it?"

"No, I like it. I mean, I think I like it. It's just that it's sort of hard to let go."

I could say something cocky like *it's because whoever was with you wasn't doing it right,* but now is not the time for crowing. Now is the time for listening. "Do you want to let go?"

She pauses and shrugs. "I don't know."

"Then how about this? I'll just go down on you for a few minutes. No pressure. Come or don't come—whatever works for you. And when you want to stop, I'll fuck you instead just the way you like it."

"Okay," she says, sounding breathy, and sounding happy too, like that was the right answer I gave.

Thank fuck.

I'm not some kind of expert in the mind or intimacy. But if

she's worried about letting go, maybe the most important thing is to let her know she doesn't have to with me. She can just be herself.

I slide my hands under her ass, scoop her up, and bring her close to my mouth. And then I kiss and lick and suck. I flatten my tongue, dragging it slowly, luxuriously up and down. I savor every single taste of her, flicking her clit with the tip of my tongue. Letting her know with my hands digging into her ass, with my sounds, moans, and grunts that come from the center of my filthy soul how absolutely fucking good it is whether she lets go or not.

And I kiss her pussy more deeply, like I'm French kissing her. Like I can't get enough of her taste, her scent, her pleasure as I listen to her every sound.

As she starts to whimper, as she arches her hips, as she grabs my hair, I don't stop. I pick up the pace a little bit while the pleasure runs roughshod through my veins. She grinds against my face then lets out the sexiest little squeak, digs her nails into my skull and then shouts, "Oh my god."

Like it surprised her. Like she wasn't expecting the orgasm to take her hostage.

She rocks up into my mouth as pleasure seems to take over her body, and I kiss her through it as lust barrels through mine.

When I let go, she's panting, breathing hard, running a hand through her hair, basking in the letting go, and it's a stunning sight. Made even more so when her eyes flutter open, and she looks both satisfied and powerful. And like a woman with a plan.

She scoots up a little on the pillows, then pushes her tits together. "Come on me."

I'm not saying no to that.

I rip off my jeans and boxer briefs, then drag my fingers

through her sweet, wet pussy, and lube my dick with her orgasm.

She gasps.

"Knew you could do it, beautiful. I fucking believe in you, my horny, dirty woman."

"Lake," she says, but it comes out like a needy rasp.

"Don't worry. I'll give you what you need," I say, then slide my fingers through her one more time, watching her shudder, then shudder again as I stroke myself.

I straddle her chest and slide my slick cock between her breasts, give a few quick pumps, then stop when she darts out her tongue. "You want a taste of me?"

"I really do."

I move higher, offering her my dick.

She parts her lips so perfectly, so seamlessly. Yes, she's letting go indeed.

I give her an inch, and she takes it, flicking her tongue all over the head. My thighs are shaking. My brain is scrambling.

"I'm close," I mutter, then shift back down to her tits.

She squeezes them again, offering me the fantastic valley between them. And I take, and I fuck, till I'm eaten alive by pleasure and coming all over this woman.

When I collapse next to her, both of us a sticky mess, she runs a hand along her breasts, drags her fingers through my release, then brings it to her mouth. She sucks me off her fingers, closes her eyes, and moans.

And right now, nothing feels fake between us.

37

THANKS FOR THE EARMUFFS

REMY

"Drop you off at your place, the arena, a sex toy shop, or some, I don't know, glow-in-the-dark neon paint and pottery shop you're testing for a date?"

Lake poses the question as we cruise across the Golden Gate Bridge the next day, the Pacific Ocean unfurling endlessly to the right, with choppy waves cutting through the dark water.

I give him a playful look. "Just dropping 'sex toy shop' in the middle of them." Is he trying to tell me something? Like, he wants to use one on me? The zip of electricity through my body is saying, *You know you want him to.*

"Sex toy shops are always a good idea." He smirks. "For dates and all."

"Ah, so you're just being oh so helpful and suggesting I recommend it for clients," I say, nodding a few times like *right, of course I buy that.*

"Yup. I bet it'd be a big hit," he says dryly. Then in a curious tone, he asks, "Have you ever had a client that wanted that? Like a sexier type of date? Maybe a strip club, or something like that?"

"I actually planned a sex toy shop tour for two women, and they said it was the best date night of their lives."

"If you want to test it for yourself, you just let me know, Remy," he says with that familiar confidence in his tone.

Is he asking me on a date of sorts? Maybe but I'm not entirely sure. This might be like the nap lesson, or it might be an offhand remark about sex toys. I don't want to read into it or assume he's suggesting something when he's not. "Noted. But also, if you know of a glow-in-the-dark neon paint and pottery shop and are holding out on me, you're in big trouble."

"Nope but I'm sure there is one somewhere, someplace," he says, a smile shifting his lips.

Lake's smiled more these last couple of days than I've seen in the past. He looks good when he smiles. I like that maybe I'm responsible.

"No doubt," I say, then return to his original question. "My place is fine. I have to meet Caroline at the shower venue so we can review the setup. And then I'm going to the arena for a meeting with Daniel."

"Busy day," he says, his smile slowly slipping away as we cruise off the bridge, the road dipping down toward the Marina. He slows at a red light, his brow furrowed, then turns his gaze briefly to me. He doesn't speak right away. Just flexes his hands tighter around the wheel, then loosens them. Clears his throat. "I had a really good time, Remy."

Sounds like it cost him something to say that. Looks like it did too. My heart softens, and a part of me—the part of me that's taking up a lot more space lately—wants to plan *all the dates* for us.

Wants to find that glow-in-the-dark paint and pottery shop.

Is chomping at the bit to plot a risqué night of sex toy shopping.

Craves planning a simple night out at a bird supply store to check out feeders and baths, then take him to a cat café. He'd like that, I bet. All of it.

But I have to rein in all those desires. Silly, pointless desires that have no place here. It's only been a month and a half since I thought I was being proposed to. This thing with Lake is fake. It's a rebound by design. It has an end date that's coming right around the corner on the calendar.

I want to show you how you should be treated. Before, during, and after a relationship. I want to be the best rebound you've ever had.

With that reminder, I squeeze his biceps. "Me too. I had a great time," I say, and that's all true. Nothing fake there.

He drops me off, and I rub my knuckles against my sternum, trying to relieve the pressure. It feels a little hollow as I watch him drive away.

After I unzip my suitcase and put everything away in record time, I check the hummingbird feeder and quickly freshen up the sugar water. Like it was waiting for a drink, a tiny greenish-gray bird appears, wings flapping, beak drinking.

I sneak a picture. I'll send it to Lake later. For now, I need to catch the next bus to Alamo Square Park.

Caroline's doing a final walk-through of one of the Painted Ladies, which has a gorgeous backyard garden area for her non-traditional shower.

On the bus ride, I flip open my World Domination notebook and turn to the page I've marked for a new client—a self-proclaimed video game nerd who wants me to help plan a proposal involving games. I tap my pen against my chin, wondering if I could involve the puzzle store Lake and I go to.

I stare out the window at the hills and the homes, picturing a date. A latte, a Golden Gate Bridge puzzle, a list.

And...shoot.

I'm daydreaming about Lake. *Again.*

I snap out of it, but I'm already at my stop. I close the notebook and hop off the bus. There will be time to deal with it later. I trot over to the pink house, following Caroline's orders to head to the backyard.

I rap on the wooden gate on the side of the house as my sister groans a loud and irritated: "Are you kidding me?"

The gate's unlocked so I push open the door, and walk along the side of the house and into the yard, dotted with outdoor furniture and minimalist landscaping.

Caroline shoves a manicured hand through her lush blowout, heaving a frustrated sigh. My mother's here, dressed impeccably in a cranberry silky blouse and designer jeans, and she's talking to someone I don't know—a man in a blue shirt that gives off caretaker vibes.

"There's really nothing to be done?" my mother asks.

"It's going to take a few days to fix this," the man tells her, his voice calm, making it clear that this isn't his first irritated client rodeo.

Caroline's jaw is set tight, and she paces across the stone path. "Isn't there any plumber that can fix this sooner?"

"We can't get anyone out till tomorrow," he says.

I stride over, ready to help however I can, though with the two of them at the helm, I'm not sure what I could contribute. I don't know any plumbers who'd show up at the drop of a hat.

"What's going on?" I ask, keeping my tone calm, trying to soothe Caroline since I can at least do that.

She whips around, her frustration transforming into the threat of tears. "A pipe burst inside," she says, her voice wobbly. "We can't have the shower here tomorrow since there's no bathroom."

That would be a big problem. "What about your place?"

"There isn't enough room for the guests and the camera crew," she says, and my jaw ticks at the mention of the crew.

"We need another venue," my mother says, calmly. "Someplace that can handle twenty-five guests and catering and the cameras for Fresh Face."

Part of me wants to punch Fresh Face in the mouth, if it had one, but I set that wish aside as Caroline and my mom toss out options. The Happy Cow isn't big enough, Parker's parents' home is too far away, and Caroline's favorite bistro with the garden is booked, because of course it's booked.

But as they talk, I'm mentally filling in the spreadsheet for the event, adding a cell here, a row there, adding it up, then sending a text to Lake.

Crossing my fingers.

He writes back quickly with a **Yes.**

"I have a place," I announce, excitement sweeping through me, and the hope that they'll like my idea.

"The hockey arena?" Caroline asks, her voice pitching up with doubt.

"No. Better."

I tell them, and Caroline throws her arms around me. "Your brain is fabulous."

I do feel pretty fabulous today, for many, many reasons.

* * *

Daniel shoots me a sharp-eyed stare when I walk into his office an hour later.

"Yes?" I ask tentatively.

He taps his pen against his reclaimed oak wood desk, shaking his head. "I'm confused about something."

That doesn't sound good.

My neck prickles with dread. "Okay, what is it?" I ask as

evenly as I can, even though my mind is racing back to Evergreen Falls, to the Chestnut Inn, to the game. Why is my pulse shooting through the roof, as if I've made a terrible mistake? "Did something happen with Total Teamwork? Were they unhappy with the warmup?"

I try to strip any worry from my voice. I am ready to slide into problem-solving mode, like I did with my sister earlier today.

"Yes, something happened. Total Teamwork reported a fifteen percent spike in donations last night."

My brow knits. I'm baffled. "So that's good?"

"No, Remy, it's not *good*. It's great."

But my heart is still beating too fast. "What's the confusion, then?"

He shoots me an even more serious stare. "The confusion is how come you're more efficient than anyone else I've worked with?"

I breathe a huge sigh of relief. "You had me there for a minute."

"Sorry, Rems. I basically wanted to know how we could replicate you," he says with a grin, then clears his throat. "The Neighborhood Works coffee shop day drove an increase in volunteers and other organizations signing up to offer job training. Plus, Little Friends said they cleared the rescue thanks to the hockey players' visit."

"They did?" The back of my eyes sting with happy tears. "Judy and Cornelius and Bea and all the others found homes?"

"They sure did."

"I was rooting for those little dogs so bad," I say.

Daniel sets down his pen. "Based on these results, I'm hoping you could take point on the Hockey is for Everyone initiative. It'll still fit within your thirty hours a week," he says.

"So you haven't posted a listing for my job?"

He laughs. "It's yours till you leave me. But Brinkley has some interest from a podcast network, so we may need to advertise for more help soon," he says, mentioning the other part-time manager. "Anyway, for now, we want to put together theme weeks to show that the Golden State Foxes celebrate diversity. We'll select local business leaders for Women's History Month, Black History Month, Disability Pride Month and so on."

He explains more, like events for Pride Month too, and I let go of my worries since my synapses are firing on all cylinders with excitement. I'm picturing different events, a range of partnerships, social media opportunities, and players to involve.

"I'd love to," I say, thrilled for this chance.

"Great. But you can't use Lake for everything," he says, wagging a finger. His tone is deliberately playful but it slices through my excitement.

"I won't. I promise," I say earnestly. "I won't give him special treatment."

I won't even be involved with him when this initiative starts. We're racing so fast to the end of us.

"I know. I'm just teasing," Daniel says, rolling his chair closer around the desk, like he needs to remove the barrier between us. "As a friend though, how's it going?"

I hesitate for a second or two, a twinge of guilt stabbing me. No, that's more than a twinge. That's a freaking basketball of guilt. "Great," I say, then realize I'd better hedge my answer. Our *romance* is going to end soon. "Everyone needs a rebound now and then," I add, using his prior line.

"Truer words," he says as his smile disappears. "I haven't seen the media make much of it yet. But that might happen, you know?"

I remember his words about the media's obsession with the grieving widower, and it hits me how little I know about Lake's relationship with his late wife.

Well, why would I know much? There's been no need to discuss it.

"I'll be ready," I say with a bright, peppy smile, but when I leave his office, my gut churns. I feel nauseous from the little lies I'm telling him.

Daniel's my boss, but he's a friend too, and I hate that I'm not telling him the truth.

But I can't, right? Once you let the truth out, it can snowball. And really, Lake and I only need to keep up the lie for a few more days till the wedding.

There's one person I need to tell the truth to though, and I can't wait much longer.

Someone I avoided the other night.

Someone whose father I just met.

Someone who thinks her brother is broken.

I call Clem.

* * *

There aren't enough pages in my Notes, Complaints, and Existential Crises notebook for all the possible outcomes involved in telling Clem I'm banging her brother. But Elena would be proud of me for doing this—listing all the different things that might happen when I see my friend. That is, if I ever tell Elena about the fake dating. But first, I focus on Clem. I write out the outcomes on the bus ride home from the arena. It helps with my worry that things might go wrong when I talk to her.

I *think* I know how to smooth things over though.

Before I catch the next bus, I pop into a store in the Marina that has everything, find what I need, then hop onto a bus out of town.

Once I arrive in downtown Cozy Valley, I feel ready. I let the fresh air center me and yes, the cozy vibe centers me too. I pass Whiskers and Kisses where the store's tuxedo cat bats lazily at a stuffed mouse from the top floor of his tower. Would Thor like a mouse like that? I'm tempted to pop in and grab a toy, but I have to remind myself I'm not here for Lake. I'm here for his sister.

Up ahead, The Meet Cute comes into view. That's the bookstore Clementine opened a couple of years ago. A brick wall along the side of the store is painted neon pink, showing off the spines of popular books from the last few years—like *Top-Notch Boyfriend*, *The Twelve Hate Dates of Christmas*, *When You Kiss Me Like This*, and other fan favorites.

I open the door as Clem calls out a question to a group of a dozen or so avid readers, draped across the couch in the shape of lips and several pink folding chairs.

"And for the grand prize and the chance to call yourself the Trivia Smut Queen—what did Lucy from *Bangable* proclaim was the wildest place she'd ever banged her enemy?"

A woman with tattoos of books dancing down the bronze skin of her arm darts up a hand. "The hot-air balloon as it flew over the food festival in Lucky Falls."

Clementine picks up a silver bell from the counter and rings it. "All hail Mariana Valdez."

Mariana stands and takes a bow while the others clap and cheer for her.

Clementine grabs a sparkly tiara off the counter, waving to me when she spots me. She's wearing a shirt with an illustration of a cat reading a book on it, and the words *Books. Because Murder is Wrong*.

She bestows the tiara on Mariana. After that, I busy myself

checking out her sticker collection and hoping the confession goes as well as I believe it can.

Once the trivia club has filtered out, Clem shuts the door and locks it, leaving just me and her little dog, Fern, all frosty-faced, who glances up from her heated bed behind the counter and gives me a look that seems to translate as: *Did you bring me a biscuit? If not, I don't care about you.*

"I don't have a biscuit, Fern."

The cutie sighs the most dramatic dog sigh of all time, then curls into a ball on her bed, looking the other way.

"You're dead to her," Clem says, as she joins her little critter behind the counter.

"I'll do better next time," I say to the pup then glance around the shop, hoping to ease into the convo. "Looks like trivia night was great."

"We have a blast here." There's a wistful note in her voice, and I wonder if it's because she always wanted to open a shop in the city, not a little town.

She shakes it off, then pins me with a curious stare as she sweeps around the counter and starts folding the chairs away. "But I suspect you're not here about trivia."

There's a tease in her voice, but also a no-bullshit edge to her tone. Which is one of the reasons I adore her. She doesn't like to beat around the bush.

"I'm not," I say, and her words from earlier repeat in my head. *I always support you. Even if it involves my weird brother.*

But other words do too. Lake's words: *She likes to give me gag gifts. Last year for my birthday she sent me my face on a potato.*

I dip my hand into my bag. Some conversations just need lubrication.

I hand her a gift wrapped in pink paper.

Arching a brow, she sets down the folding chair in her hand and takes it. "Gifts are the way to my black heart."

"It's not black," I chide.

"No, but my soul might be." She rips it open, then laughs. She slides the fluffy pink earmuffs onto her head, covering her ears with the gift I picked up at a shop in the Marina. "Go ahead now and tell me you're"—she stops to gag—"banging my brother."

It's a relief, her reaction. Her amusement. Her sarcasm. I still need to say it though. I speak crisply and clearly, so she can read my lips even though she might not be able to hear me well. "I had sex with your brother."

She cringes. We're talking the full-body kind. When she stops doubling over, she raises her face and asks loudly, "Are you done? Is it safe to remove them?"

I nod.

She slips them off her ears. "Was it as gross as I suspect? Wait. Don't tell me."

I laugh, grateful for the outcome—the one I was hoping for with the earmuffs she requested.

"I won't tell you a single detail, I promise," I say, grabbing a folded chair and carrying it to her stock room. She grabs one too.

"Good, but also, I knew."

My jaw drops. "How?"

"Girl, you ran away when I joined everyone at the game the other night. I put two and two together. Also, he cut his hair. And I saw that kiss online from the dress shop."

"You watched the lipstick test?" I'm glad she has no idea about the *other* lipstick test.

"I did, and yes, it was as weird as I expected. But look, I'm the person who watches horror movies, so this should not be a surprise."

"Fair."

"And it was horrifying. But also telling," she says as we return to the shop to grab more chairs.

My heart speeds up, liking that the kiss told some kind of story. "How could you tell it was real?"

"He pretty much made googly eyes at you then and was all *I'm gonna kiss you now*," she says, in a faux deep voice before she gags again.

I laugh but inside butterflies are taking off.

And I should not like the way they feel so much. I focus on my friendship with her—not my blooming feelings for her brother that are going nowhere. "I didn't want to lie to you. I hate lying. I hate lying to my boss and my parents and even Caroline in a way."

She gives me a sympathetic look. "I know. It's anathema to you."

"It is."

"But, also if you're"—she pauses, like she's bracing herself to say it—"smashing, isn't it real?"

My heart twists, wishing I could say yes, but knowing I can't. "It's just temporary. And it's fine, really it is. It's just a rebound. That's all it can be. I'm fresh out of the land of the dumped and he's, well, he's complicated."

She tilts her head, as if she's mulling that over. "Does he seem complicated when he's with you?"

It's a valid question and the answer's a resounding no, but also we don't always let other people see our complexities. I certainly don't. And I'd be wise not to fool myself again.

"No, he doesn't," I answer truthfully. "But I remember what you said. I deserve a man who isn't so...shut down."

She gives me a sympathetic smile. "Maybe he's not so shut down anymore. I don't know. But I know this—I don't want you to get hurt," she says gently, then pauses and adds, "or him."

I flinch. I didn't expect her to say *that.* Could I hurt him? It hardly feels like I have that power. But I suppose we all can hurt each other. "I don't want to hurt him either. That's why we have rules. So no one gets hurt."

"I love my brother. He's a pain in the ass and a weirdo who's obsessed with owls and his cat and free food, but he also cares deeply for a few people. He'll go to the end of the earth for them."

Something warms inside my chest. "I believe that."

She reaches for my hands. "And you're a beautiful, brilliant, tightly wound optimist who believes in love—and in doing things at the right time, in the right order, the right way."

It's her way of saying *take your time.*

"I don't want either of you to get hurt," she adds again.

"I know," I say quietly then I hug her.

I stay a while and help her close, catching up on her customers' latest requests for stories about aliens with five dicks, and cinnamon-roll hot nerds who are secretly obsessed with their curvy best friends, and rival chocolate shop owners who have to compete in the town treasure hunt. As we reshelve books, I feel lighter and freer now that she knows things aren't entirely fake with her brother.

But there's someone else I should tell.

On the way home, I tap out an email to Elena. *I wanted to let you know I've been fake dating my friend's hockey-playing brother to stick it to my ex, but along the way the lines started to blur.*

Ugh.

I try again. But as I re-read each draft, something sticks in my gut. It's the sinking realization that I can't confess this behind the shield of email. I'll have to say it in person, especially since I've been avoiding it.

I slump down in the seat. Sometimes adulting just really sucks. Like when I walk into my place, feeling both better for having told the truth to Clem at least—and a little achy, knowing that both this fake romance and the real fling I'm having with my friend's brother is cruising toward its inevitable end.

But I'm going to enjoy the ride.

38

SOME PEOPLE

REMY

No one needs a new set of napkin rings, or napkin rings at all. No one needs an ice cream maker, or soup tureen either.

But cookware? Gently used woks? Dutch ovens? Never-been-used blenders?

Pretty much anyone can use those. Which is why I'm beaming like a proud mama as Caroline's friends arrive at Lake's family's equine therapy ranch, and make their way to the edge of the bird sanctuary—escorted by Gavin and Mira—where we've set up picnic tables to collect the secondhand items.

By the time the Something Shared Shower is underway, the table is stacked high with all sorts of kitchen gadgets and household items that Caroline and Parker are going to take to a local charity that helps foster kids set up their own homes when they age out of the system. Caroline came to me for suggestions of charities and this was my top pick. The videographer circles, capturing the scene for Fresh Face. Good. I'm glad the brand is capturing something meaningful on camera.

"I told you it wouldn't be like a traditional shower," I say to

Lake, pleased that Caroline kicked that old-fashioned tradition to the curb, choosing instead to give back.

We're standing by the fence at the edge of the property as guests mill about, snagging appetizers from The Green Pantry, a Cozy Valley bistro where I placed a last-minute order yesterday.

He leans closer, his shoulder brushing mine. "Spoiler alert: I've never been to a traditional shower."

I tense for a second, but then decide to seize the moment. The afternoon sun is bright, highlighting his strong jaw, his cool eyes, and his intensity. An intensity I want to know more about.

"Did you have one for your wedding?" I ask, gripped with the curiosity to understand his past more.

He shakes his head. "No. It felt weird to ask people to give me gifts when I'd just gotten a good contract with the pros."

"I hear you," I say, liking that he was thoughtful.

"It was a pretty simple wedding too. I'm not that into..."

"Appearances?" I ask.

He shrugs. "Yeah. Some people would say I'm an asocial grump."

I laugh. "Are you some people?"

"You know, I think I am," he says, a little evilly, like he's embracing this side of himself. "You're the opposite though."

He's not wrong. "I'm definitely social. I like groups, like this," I say, feeling calm and centered as I survey the scene—friends mingling, people laughing, guests admiring the blue herons and the bride and groom. It's a serene setting here in the meadow, a stream gurgling, the blue sky stretching as far as the eye can see. "I'm glad we pulled this off, thanks to you."

"All I did was say yes. You did this, beautiful. This is all you. Your idea, your planning. You made it happen."

I stand a little taller, loving the praise. "It was fun. Like a puzzle," I say.

He wraps his arm tighter around me, takes a beat, then clears his throat, waving to the crowd here. "Would you...want one like this?"

The question comes out so earnestly, a man trying to understand a woman. It makes my heart squeeze.

"I definitely don't want household gadgets, new or gently used. I don't really cook much anyway," I say, and briefly wonder if it's too much to bring up a future wedding shower with a man I'm fake dating and real flinging with. But I found the courage to talk to his sister last night and tell her the truth. In for a penny..."I think I'd do a volunteer shower—where you ask your friends to do a beach cleanup with you, or plant some trees, or walk dogs together at the local shelter."

Lake's smile is soft, thoughtful. "That's very you."

"Why do you say that?"

He meets my gaze. "Plants, dogs, the earth. They're kind of your things."

I glance around at his bird sanctuary, where an owl watches over from the owl box and where wood ducks and black-crowned night herons splash in the stream. I nudge him with my elbow. "Same to you."

He lifts a brow, teasingly. "*But* I wouldn't want a spa day."

"Yes, I'm well aware," I say dryly. "And I swear you engineered tomorrow's game so you don't have to go to it."

"I was looking forward to seeing you in a cute little bikini," he jokes.

"Did you think I was wearing a bikini at a spa?"

"More like hoping."

"Try bathrobe."

He makes a show of peering at my breasts, like he would if I were wearing a robe. "I can work with a robe."

I lift my chin. "You don't get to see either. You'll be too busy napping before the game."

"And missing you as I nap," he adds, so easily, so casually that my cells feel a little fizzy.

Since he's being so direct with me, I choose to do the same with him. Maybe I'm on a kick today. "I saw your sister last night. I told her we were..."

"Fucking like the world is on fire?"

A laugh bursts from me. "Lake!"

"My bad. You told her we were having the best sex of our lives?"

Sparks shoot down my back from the compliment. "And shockingly I didn't say that either."

"Fine. You told her how much I like to eat, right?" His eyes glimmer with dirty thoughts of me.

I swat his shoulder, and he grabs my hand, brings it to his mouth and nibbles on my palm.

I laugh. "You're the worst."

"So you told her I was a god in bed? That I make you come hard and often? That I'm totally obsessed with your pleasure? That I want to take you apart over and over?"

It's official. I can't breathe I'm so turned on. "Stop," I whisper, but it's hardly a protest. It comes out feathery, needy.

He brushes his cheek against mine, turning his face and whispering in my ear, "Are you wet right now? Imagining me turning you around, telling you to hold onto the fence when everyone's gone, then fucking you out here, beneath the wide open sky, just the birds overhead watching as you call my name? Or am I slipping a hand into those panties and getting you off hot and fast when no one's looking?"

I roll my lips together to seal in a gasp. I close my eyes, breathe out, then open them and meet his heated gaze, ready to give as good as I get. "I believe the answer is..." My gaze drifts down to his jeans, the bulge in them. "You're rock hard."

He growls, a low, sexy rumble, as he tugs me closer. "You know I am," he murmurs then drops a kiss to my cheek. It's a kiss that says he's thinking of doing unholy things to me. It's passionate, lingering, and chased with a desperate groan from his throat that makes me feel...adored.

Yes, that's how this man makes me feel. And I don't think I realized how very much I wanted to be adored until him.

I want to bask in this affection, even though it's temporary, so I let myself enjoy his kisses on my neck for another several seconds until I catch sight of an undercut and a vest.

I groan.

Jameson's arrived. He's striding over to the gift table with his date, a woman with curly red hair, a boho skirt, and an ankle bracelet that jingles.

"Never thought I'd say this, but I'm glad to see him," I mutter.

Lake lets go of me and jerks away. "What?"

"Because I was about to climb you," I quickly explain.

But that doesn't seem to satisfy Lake. His jaw tightens, and he breathes out hard through his nostrils. "I hate how he treated you." He turns to me, his eyes hard. "I can't believe I have to act like I'm okay with him being here."

Where is this coming from? He's been so...chill the whole time we've been here. "Lake. You don't have to talk to him."

He drags a hand through his hair, jaw still tight. "I know. It's a good thing. Because I'm not sure what I'd say. Or do."

I grab the collar of his shirt. We need to get something straight. "I was joking when I said I was happy to see him."

"I know," he bites out, but he's not looking at me. He's staring at Jameson like he wants to tear his limbs off. It's a little hot.

Okay, *a lot.*

But it's also throwing me off. Lake's so cool, so in control, even when he's dismissing Jameson with a quick *I don't share* comment.

This is a fiery side of him, and I wasn't expecting it today. "He should be thrown out of the wedding party for being a fucknozzle," he bites out.

"He's friends with Parker."

"Then fuck Parker too," Lake says, huffing. This is out of character, this level of hotheadedness.

"Are you okay?"

My concern seems to shake him from his bull-seeing-red moment. He blinks, turns to me, exhales. "Shit. Sorry. I'm a little—"

He swallows, but doesn't finish the sentence—just stares hard at the enemy as Jameson places a set of Jameson's Brew glasses, complete with his logo, on the table of donations. I roll my eyes. There's nothing he won't make about himself.

Even so, I won't let him ruin the shower or the moment with Lake.

I turn back to the hockey player. "A little what?" I press, needing him to say the word—*jealous, ridiculously, over-the-top jealous.*

But Caroline swings by and squeezes my arm. "This is so much better than the Painted Lady. It's totally the right vibe," she says, then turns to Lake. "Thank you for saving the day."

"Glad you're happy," he says to her, his voice cool again.

"I am. And now I need to steal my sister away."

She tugs my arm and I join her, but my heart is with the man I left by the fence. The man who's wearing his red-hot emotions on his sleeve.

39

THE DRAGON AND HIS GOLD

LAKE

This is why I don't do romance. I failed at marriage, I'm a fucking sham at being a widower, and I swore off love when my mom took off years ago. Some people aren't wired for it. *Me.* I'm some people. I'm not wired for love.

But I can't let Remy think she's messed up, because I know those thoughts eat away at her.

She waves goodbye to Caroline from the driveway. The second her sister's car—piled high with secondhand items they're going to donate—pulls out of the gravel driveway, I push past the tight ball of dread in my chest.

"Jealous," I blurt out to her from a few feet away.

Remy turns around, tilting her head. "What?"

"I'm jealous," I say with a frustrated sigh. "That's why I acted that way."

She strides across the driveway, joining me at the stone path edging the front yard as twilight falls, casting shadows over us. "You mean like a dragon protecting its gold?"

If the shoe fits. "Yes. But in my defense, I want to show you how you should be treated. And the corollary of that is someone treated you badly, so therefore, I hate him. I just do, and I'm not sorry about it."

She laughs. "I can tell. Although it was kind of out of the blue. You're normally so...cool about everything."

Is that how she sees me? Cool is the last thing I am around her. White hot is more like it. "Trust me, there's nothing cool in me when it comes to your ex. But still, I shouldn't get so worked up."

"I don't know. I kind of liked it," she says with a shrug. A damn flirty one at that.

And hello, plot twist.

I advance closer to her. "You like a caveman, Remy?" I never would have expected this. She's so put together, so thoughtful.

"Evidently."

I run a hand down her arm, stopping at her wrist, sliding my thumb along the top of her hand. "Good to know," I say as she shivers. But at the same time, she deserves an explanation, so I let go of her. "Look, like I told you in Evergreen Falls, it's been a while. Not just for sex, but for...everything. Dating, this romance, the whole thing," I say, waving a hand at her and me like that covers broadly what's happening between us, even though I have no clue what that is. "I shouldn't have gotten pissed that he's here. I knew he was coming. I just..."

Felt like protecting what's mine.

"Just what?" she asks, as if she's dying to know.

And fuck it. "I want to protect you from him. I don't want him in the same space as you. You're fucking mine for now, okay?"

"Okay," she says, but she's smiling, having too much fun with my response. "And for the record, you're pretty damn good at the dating thing."

"Yeah?"

"Great, I'd say." She reaches for my hands, squeezes them, and *fuck me*. She should not be reassuring me. I should be reassuring her.

"Remy, you don't have to say that. It's my role to tell you how amazing you are."

"Maybe it's mine too. Maybe we both need to know from each other that we're doing okay."

I don't want to be vulnerable. I really don't. But she's doing so much, so I crack open my chest and ask, "How'm I doing?"

"Much better than okay. I'm pretty sure you deserve good things too."

My heart slams hard against my rib cage, like it's trying to break out. I want to wrestle the organ, shove it behind the door, lock it up. This woman is doing things to me that I wasn't expecting. She's breaking down walls that I'm not sure I wanted knocked down. But I also don't want her to stop.

I thread my fingers through hers and try to focus on the here and now. "Tonight, I want to show you that you deserve good things. Will you let me?"

She nibbles on the corner of her lips. "What do you have in mind?"

"Spend the night with me again." I tug on the waistband of her jeans, pulling her close. "I can make you breakfast in the morning. Number four on the list."

She pretends to give that some thought. "Will it involve a berry bar?"

"If that's what you want." I'll go out tonight and hunt through all the grocery stores in the city to get her every type I can find.

"You're the one who wants the berry bar," she tosses back.

I roam my fingers across the soft material of her sweater, covering her waist. She lets out a surprised breath, a shuddery one. I fucking love how simple touches undo her. "I want berries, and I want you."

She inches closer to me. "We're supposed to make breakfast together."

"Then you can wash the berries and I'll eat them."

She swats my chest, but I grab her hand quickly and kiss her palm. "I'm hearing a yes."

She glances at the house, then up at the sky, the stars peeking out in the twilight. "If Thor can come."

I laugh, dropping my head to her neck. "You like me for my cat."

She slides a hand down the front of my jeans, squeezing. "And this."

I snap up my gaze. "Let's go. Now."

Eager for the rest of the night to begin, we fly up the steps, then rush inside. My dad's sitting on the couch in the living room, feet up on the table, reading a book, and petting Thor on the cushion next to him.

"Hey, Dad. I'm just going to steal him from you and get out of here."

"Sure, take an old man's cat. Real nice," he says dryly.

"Lake, you're so mean to take the cat," Remy chides.

"See if I'm mean when he wakes you up at five-thirty, knocking things off counters, asking to be fed," I say.

"Fair point. You can have him," my dad says.

But before I can grab the feline, Gavin strides through the house, nodding my way. "Can you help me with the grain bags in the stables before you go?"

"Course," I say, even though I'm itching to get the hell out of here.

"Good. I can chat with my son's new girlfriend while you do *strapping man* things," Dad says, and my heart twists with guilt. I'm going to disappoint him when this ends. But I'll deal with that when it comes. For tonight, I need to show Remy I'm more than a caveman, more than a dragon.

But first I head out to the stables and help my brother move some fifty-pound grain bags. Gavin can lift them solo, but it's safer to carry them with someone than to risk injury.

When that's done, I return to the house, where my dad's saying to Remy, "So he showers you with gifts. That's very good to know."

"He's an excellent gift-giver. Like your daughter."

Dad's smile is fond. "She sure is." He looks up, seeming reluctant, but also a gentleman. To Remy, he adds, "It was nice chatting with you. About everything."

"The pleasure was all mine."

I leash up the cat, then steal the cat and the woman away. A dragon hoarding its gold indeed.

As we pull out of Big Steps, I ask, "What was that about?"

"I told him you gave me a Ruby Glow."

"The other part. The *about everything*."

"Oh, he was curious about Jumbotron-gate, as he called it. I said I was holding up well. I said my friends helped, therapy helped, and you helped."

"That's all I wanted to do. From the first swing at a stuffed fox."

"You were insistent, and I'm glad."

Maybe I'm not so bad at romance after all. "Me too."

This time I don't focus on my dark feelings about her ex. I don't dwell on the past. I reach across the console for her hand and hold it, focusing on the present.

* * *

When we get to my place, I unleash Thor and he tears off after the catnip banana. Perfect.

I take Remy to my bedroom and bring her to the mirror. I've been thinking about this. Picturing it. Want it badly. With her standing in front of me, I admire the view of my woman, her lush hair falling in waves, her eyes bright, her mouth soft.

"Do you know what I see?" I rasp out.

"Tell me."

I run my hands down her arms, nice and slow, taking my time, watching her reaction in the glass. She shivers as I touch her, and it's breathtaking.

"I see a brilliant, clever, caring woman who pulled off something amazing today. You saved the day for your sister. You made her shower happen and made it better than she'd planned. Hell, you pulled off an event with barely any notice," I say, then kiss the back of her neck. "You're a star. And look at you, how strong you are, and how good you are at everything. How fucking capable."

She preens under the praise, and that's good. That's so damn good.

I move her hair to the side, kissing her neck, sliding my hand up her stomach, over her breasts to her throat.

"But I want to see how good you are at everything," she says, her voice vulnerable, full of need. "Will you show me?"

"I will. Under one condition."

"What is it?"

"Don't look away from the mirror."

40

MIRROR, MIRROR ON THE FLOOR

REMY

Lake moves in front of me and drops to his knees, sliding his hands up my thighs.

He means it. He wants me to watch him do...whatever he's got planned.

I've never done this before. Never watched someone, or watched myself. I'm not sure where to look. At him, or the reflection of him as he starts with my shoes, undoing the little strap across the top of my foot. Sliding it out. Then the next one.

He reaches up to undo the button, then the zipper on my jeans, slowly tugging it down tooth by tooth, like he's enjoying the sound of it being opened. The look in his eyes—filthy delight—sends a shiver down my chest. I help him along, pushing the jeans down, letting the denim hit my ankles.

He helps me step out of them, then takes the jeans and folds them neatly, stretching out an arm and setting them on a nearby chair.

I nearly come from that—from the care.

"Now I'm really aroused," I tease.

He returns to me, hands on my thighs. "That makes two of us."

My smile vanishes as he presses his face against my center, dropping a quick, hot kiss to the outside of my panties.

A ragged breath escapes my lips. I reach for his hair, sliding my fingers through it as he moves his face lower, kissing the panel of my panties.

"So wet. Just like I said you'd be," he murmurs.

"So cocky," I toss back.

"And right," he says, then flicks his tongue against the soaked fabric. "So fucking right."

I try to protest, but what's the point? I'm warm everywhere, my cells all shimmery as he teases me with his talented tongue. I give in, tugging him closer. "Take them off."

He stops, wrenches away, then looks up at me. "You're not watching though."

My legs shake. "I was watching you."

"In the mirror, Remy," he says, stern and commanding. "Watch in the mirror. I want you to see how fucking sexy you are."

My pulse beats between my thighs, where I ache. "I'll try."

He hooks his index finger in the top of my panties. "Good girl."

The panties vanish in a flash. His hands roam up my thighs and he rubs his nose against me, drawing a deep inhale.

Sparks shoot through me, and I want to close my eyes, but I obey, watching in the mirror as this big, strong man kisses my wet center.

"Oh god," I murmur.

He grips me harder, clearly liking that sound. "Mmm. You taste so fucking good," he says, then flicks his tongue down me and back up.

I gasp, grabbing at his hair. My eyes float closed for a second, but then he stops.

"Follow the plan, Remy," he instructs and damn him. Damn him for using me against me.

I open them, and he's flashing that evil grin.

"Don't deviate then," I say.

"I won't." He dives back in, and I...stare, giving in to the voyeurism plan.

Or is it self-voyeurism?

I don't even know, but it's surreal to watch his head bobbing up and down, to witness him burying his face between my legs, to see my own reaction.

Lips parted, breasts heaving, fingers roped in his hair.

My nipples harden, visible through my sweater, and that's new too—seeing the evidence in real time of my response.

He licks faster, sucks harder, rubs his beard against my thighs, and...yes. The roughness of his stubble, the softness of his lips, the focus of his tongue.

I breathe out hard, swallow, then moan again. All for me to witness. And I don't look like the woman who likes to be in control, to plan and to prepare and to organize. I never thought I'd look that way as I was driven wild by pleasure, sure, but a thrill shoots through me at my reflection. I look... wild. Beautiful.

Then, he kisses me more deeply, and I wobble. Grabbing his shoulders, I dig in, trying to hold on.

That stops him. And in no time, he's rising, scooping me up and carrying me to the edge of the bed.

"Sit. Spread your legs for me."

My butt hits the mattress. I part my thighs.

He crosses his arms. "Wider. And use your hands. Spread them open for me."

Nerves spark inside me, but so does heat. This is the in-control Lake. The man in charge. The man willing to wait for it.

And for me.

I slide my hands down, spread my legs open.

"Oh, fuck. Look at you. Fucking look at you." He drops down to his knees again, then devours me.

There's no other word for it.

He's fucking me with his mouth, his tongue, his lips, even his beard it seems. He's eating me up like I'm the last thing he's ever going to have.

Like I'm the only thing he wants to have.

And I'm grabbing his skull, digging my nails in, yanking him closer.

And...watching. I'm staring at us, as I take and he gives, and soon I lose control.

Soon, the pull of pleasure becomes too much.

It tips me over, and I'm coming apart on his mouth. He moans through it, loud, hungry sounds like a man feasting, like a man licking every last drop from his fingers, a man savoring the taste.

When I come down from my high, he's standing again, ripping off his shirt, toeing off his shoes, then undoing his jeans.

And I want his nudity, more than anything, but I also want...this.

I dart out a hand, covering his, stopping him. My voice still breathy from the orgasm, I say, "Turn around. Strip in front of the mirror."

His smile—it's the stuff of dirty legend. It's crooked and hot.

He turns in slo-mo, like he knows he's sexy. I stand, half-naked, just my sweater on, sloping down my shoulder. Moving next to him, I lock eyes with his reflection as he pushes his jeans down his thighs, to his ankles, then off. I bite my lip, excitement racing through me.

My gaze strays to his black boxer briefs. There's a wet spot on them, and his hard-on strains against the fabric.

"Off. Now," I direct, and holy shit. The hair on my arms stands on end. What even is this feeling inside me? This power. This thrill. It's addictive.

He sheds his briefs in a flash, tossing them to the floor. The fact that he treats them differently than my clothes excites me too. Maybe everything does about Lake.

But what thrills me most of all is the way he's so shameless in the mirror, stroking his hard cock, his eyes pinning my reflection.

He gives a long, slow tug, squeezing the head. A drop of liquid beads out.

I let out a hungry cry, my mouth falling open, and I don't even care how obvious I am.

"Want that, beautiful? A taste of me?"

I nod. "So badly."

He swipes it off, lifts a hand, then says, "Suck it off in front of the mirror."

I reach for him, circling his wrist with my hand, bringing the thumb to my mouth, and rubbing the drop of him on my lips. His growl is unholy. Deep, dark, and filthy. Like his eyes right now.

I draw his thumb farther into my mouth, sucking on it as he stares at me, eyes glimmering with heat. I let his thumb fall from my mouth, then lick my lips. "Just the way I like it," I say, and that's enough for him it seems, since he grabs me, yanks me against him, and kisses the breath out of me.

We're all teeth and tongue, lips and moans. We're limbs and heated skin, smashing into each other. He deepens the kiss while also somehow tugging my sweater off, stopping only for the second it takes to get it over my head. I'm down to just my bra, but he divests that in seconds. When he breaks the kiss, I see he's got my clothes in his hand. He doesn't fold them this time, but he sets them on the chair, then turns back around.

"On my bed. Hands and knees. Facing the mirror."

I scramble and get in position. He's behind me in seconds, kneeling, lining up with his dick in his hand.

But he stops, gritting his teeth. "Need to get a condom."

I reach an arm out, stop him. "I'm negative and on protection."

His eyes flare. "I'm negative too."

He notches the head against me, and I tremble from head to toe. "Yessss," he groans as he pushes in. "You're so fucking wet. So fucking perfect."

I feel perfect, but in a whole new way. In a way I haven't arranged or organized. I feel perfect because this moment is him kneeling behind me.

Me on all fours.

Us unable to look away from our reflection as he slides in, eases out, then drives back into me.

His fingers dig into my hips, and I bite the corner of my lips. He pulls out, then slams back in, tension lining his jaw, desire etched in his eyes.

My breasts sway. His biceps ripple.

My hair swishes. His Adam's apple bobs. And he fucks me. Sinking in, pulling out, then picking up the pace.

It's hot and it's X-rated. It's like watching our own dirty videos. A live sex tape as the jealous, possessive secret poet of a hockey player fucks the tightly wound perfectionist, the sunshine to his rain. His fake girlfriend who's somehow become another person after dark with her fake boyfriend.

I'm someone who can let go.

Because that's what I'm feeling most of all. The giving in. I give in to pleasure, to the sensations whipping through me, to the kick of bliss in my belly, to the insistent ache between my thighs, and most of all to Lake Axelrod as he fucks me in front of the mirror. I don't dare look away anymore. I enjoy the show as I thrust a hand between my legs, helping myself along till I'm gasping, moaning, begging for *more, harder, yes, now*.

I break, shattering as I fall apart, my head dropping, my back arching.

I can't keep my eyes open as I come. Who could? But I don't close them for long. When I open them, and raise my face, there's Lake. He's grunting, shuddering, his gorgeous face twisted in pleasure as he comes deep inside me.

And I get to see him lose control.

It really is its own kind of perfect.

41

ACQUIRE ME

LAKE

"I have only two eggs," I announce in the morning as I stare at the fridge, frustrated with the barrenness of it. "Hmm. I didn't think this through."

Remy's right next to me, peering into the appliance too. "I've noticed there's no berry bar either."

"But there *are* berries," I say, grabbing the blueberries, blackberries, and raspberries I ordered from the grocery store last night. They arrived sometime after her second or third orgasm. It's a haze. I'm not sure when.

I hold up the basket of blueberries like it's Simba. "Behold."

She laughs, her cheeks flushing as she sweeps strands of hair from her face.

My heart stutters.

She looks good here in my kitchen, the sunlight streaming past Thor at the top of the cat tower, illuminating her pretty face. She looks good and right. Like she belongs here.

Like she ought to be here every damn day.

And...where the hell did that thought come from? From the berries? The fridge?

No, from your head and your heart, dipshit.

But she's not ready for that. Hell, I'm not ready for that. Except, is that still true?

Am I?

My damn heart is thundering as I stand here in the kitchen, frozen in place, hoisting up blue fruit the morning after an intense night with the woman of my dreams. Who's looking cozy and happy to be here...with me.

"We can just have berries," she says, breaking me from my dangerous thoughts of a future that's not in the cards.

Or is it?

I shake my head, rooting myself to the here and now.

"But that's not what's on the list," I point out, sticking to the rules. "We've got to follow the list. Number four of Five Things To Do Before I Say I Do is *make breakfast together and clean it up.*"

She shoots me a challenging stare. "Why don't berries count as breakfast?"

I set the carton down on the counter, forcing myself to focus on something other than the absolutely inconvenient realization that I want something more than a fake girlfriend. The list.

"Hold on," I say, then I duck into the bedroom, grab a sweatshirt, and tug it on. I race back out to the kitchen, snag my phone, and say, "Be right back."

"Where are you going?"

"You'll see. Back in five."

I shove my feet into sneakers I keep by the door, trot down the hall, punch the elevator button and zoom to the lobby, then out onto the street. I run down to the corner, pop into a bakery, and snag a loaf of fresh sourdough.

Like it's a football and I'm running it into the end zone, I race back inside, up the elevator and to my penthouse in four minutes and thirty seconds.

"Behold again!"

She's at the sink, washing berries, because of course she's doing something. My heart caves as the memory of her the night of the Jumbotron flashes before me. Remy, pushing the cart of stuffed foxes. Remy, working. Remy, hiding under a hat she didn't want to wear.

Only this time, her hair's twisted in one of those messy buns that is incomparably sexy, and she's wearing *my* T-shirt. She's making herself at home in *my* place.

It's a whole new Remy, and that heavy feeling vanishes like smoke. It's replaced by something else entirely—something like hope.

"I am beholding it," she says as she shakes a colander, the water dripping into the sink. She went through my cupboards and helped herself to a colander, and I fucking love that she didn't think twice about it.

"Have you ever had the world's most greatest toast?" I ask.

"I don't know. Have I, Lake?"

That challenging but warm voice of hers makes my heart fucking shimmy again. It's just toast. Toast and berries and the simplest possible breakfast we could make, but it's also her and me in my kitchen honoring someone else's list together. Coming up with solutions, working with what we've got—two people who don't love to cook are making food.

Ten minutes later, she's set the table and I've made regular toast, avocado toast, and peanut butter and banana toast drizzled in honey. I put the plate down on the table. "It's a toast flight."

"A toast flight and our very own berry bar. I feel like the bride would be pleased," she says, but her brow furrows. "We should give her a name."

"Good point. I think we should too."

She pauses, her gaze locked on an unseen point in the distance. "I'm picturing her dress. It had lace on the bodice. Why don't we call her Lacey?"

"Works for me," I say, and offer Remy first dibs at the buffet.

"It's almost impossible to choose," she says, but she grabs a slice with banana and peanut butter.

Surprise, surprise. "I would not have pegged you for a banana and peanut butter person."

"Why not?"

"Banana's kind of an acquired taste. Not everybody likes it, especially on toast, especially with peanut butter."

She gives me a pleased look, lips quirking, eyes twinkling. "Well, you're an acquired taste, aren't you?"

I laugh. Maybe I am.

She bites into the toast, hums in pleasure, then meets my gaze and says, "And I guess I like you, Lake."

And that's it. That's just it. Might as well wave the white flag. I don't deserve her. I'm shit at relationships. But I'm pretty sure I am falling head over fucking heels for my fake girlfriend. And I want to tell her *"Then acquire me."*

But that is a thought that needs a strategy, a careful plan—a strategy for convincing this incredible woman to go on a *real* date with me.

She motions to the bread. "Which one's your first choice?"

I pick up the one with banana and peanut butter and take a bite where she left off. After I chew and finish it, I say, "I guess I just wanted to get a little closer to you."

I lean in to give her a kiss across the table, when there's a soft thud, the scrabble of paws, then a naughty Siamese cat skidding across the table, hell-bent on our food.

Thor lands right at the edge of the plate, then meows at

the top of his lungs and does that cat thing—he freaks the fuck out. Spins around, knocking the plate off the table, leaping in the other direction and racing off, peanut butter and honey in his paws as the plate clatters and breaks.

It all happens so fast that I don't move. I just look at the remains of the plate on the floor, then Remy, then the broken plate. And we both burst into laughter.

"I guess maybe that was the point of number four for Lacey," Remy says. "You never know what might happen when you make breakfast together."

We clean up, and when we're done with breakfast number two, Remy wipes her hands on a towel, then her gaze lands on her bag, hanging on a chair at the table. "Wait. There's something I forgot to show you." She hurries to the bag and pulls out her phone. "I took this picture the other day, and things got crazy."

She grabs her phone, flicks her finger across the camera roll, and then stops. "It's a hummingbird," she says, then shows me the picture. "I saw it the day we came back from Evergreen Falls. It made me think of you."

She's always doing things for me. My heart acts up again. But it's not just thundering. It's expanding, and it's a little uncomfortable. It tries to take up space that I haven't allotted for it, and I don't want to give in to this unexpected expansion. I don't want to give in to the way it's threatening to overtake the other organs, but the heart wants what the heart fucking wants, and it wants her.

This woman who took a hummingbird photo for me, not for the first time, not for the second time, not even for the third time. She's been sending them to me whenever she sees them. And she did it again.

I stare at the pic as this hazy, heady feeling spreads through my cells.

"That one's a ruby-throated hummingbird," I say, my throat feeling tight.

"It's so pretty," she says, gazing at the picture.

"Like a jewel," I say, but I'm staring at her. This woman I want more with.

"You were right. I like hummingbirds," she says softly.

"Me too," I say, a rough whisper.

There are other things I want to say, like *go out with me*, and *let's give this a shot*. But as I'm trying to form those words, she's busying herself with taking out the list from the bag, then the pouch she keeps it safe in. She mimes checking number four—make breakfast together and clean it up—off. "And then there were two."

The mood shifts. It feels somber as I look down at the list and the two remaining items—number three, which is camp under the stars, and then...number five.

And that's when I know. If I want anything more with her, anything that might feel remotely real, there's something else I need to do. Something I need to say. Something I've held onto for a long, long time.

I didn't think now would be the moment to say it, but as I'm sitting here with her doing something as pedestrian as having breakfast and cleaning it up, I'm sure there's no time like the present.

Since this is number five: Share a secret.

I look at the list, then at the woman across from me.

"I wasn't in love with Heather when she died. We were getting divorced."

42

MY PROTECTOR

REMY

Even if I had my Notes, Complaints, and Existential Crises notebook handy to map out potential outcomes of this conversation, I'd never have picked that one. That Lake and his late wife were divorcing before her motorcycle crash. But he did tell me when we played The Naked Truth that he wouldn't have dated her again.

I just didn't think they were breaking up back then. Why would I have?

I'm thoroughly unprepared for this moment, but I desperately want to say the right thing. Judging from the way he's leaning closer to me, holding my gaze, nerves flickering in his beautiful blue eyes, that wasn't easy for him to say.

I can hear the clock ticking. More so, I can feel it in my chest. "I don't know what to say."

But that might be the exact wrong thing because he rolls his lips together, then nods. His expression turns hard and eerily familiar. This is the Lake in control. This is the Lake who's inscrutable, broody, a closed book.

The Lake *before*. I don't want him to go back to being a

closed book. I try again, reaching forward, taking his hand. "But I want to understand you," I say.

His shoulders relax. His jaw unclenches.

I keep going, wanting to help him along this uncharted road. "You don't really tell that to anyone, do you?"

He scrubs a hand across his bearded jaw. "I don't."

"Not even your dad?"

"Especially not him. He liked Heather. I didn't want him to take on another worry. He was rocked by her death, by how it happened. I didn't need him to deal with my guilt or my feelings or whatever. I was trying to help him deal with his own stuff."

Oh, this poor man, keeping it together for everyone else—his family and, I presume, the world at large.

"What about your teammates? Or your brother? Do they know?"

"With Gavin, I maybe said something offhand to him once while we were working, like things were rough there at the end. But that was it. With my teammates, there was no point. Once you say that, it's out there."

Boy, do I ever know what that's like—for everything to be out there. "I hear you, but it's a lot to carry."

"I had to carry it. It was one of the last conversations Heather and I had, and she also said she wanted to keep it quiet. Wanted it to be as private as possible while we were going through it. Then she died unexpectedly the next day and all at once the media and fans immediately constructed the story of my *grief*. It seemed wrong to say anything else then. What would be the point? Just to correct the public record? *Hey, Heather Axelrod was killed today, and guess what—she and her husband were splitting up?* No one needed to know that. The media had already decided I was the grieving widower." He takes a second, looks away, then back at me.

"Which was maybe selfish too. I didn't need to be held up as some fucking sad saint. But what was the alternative? She didn't want our split to be a big thing while she was alive, so I didn't want to turn it into a thing once she'd died. It seemed like a mean thing to do to her family too, you know?"

That makes perfect sense. "That's why you don't like talking to the press?"

"Exactly. I only want to talk about hockey. That's it. I didn't want the image they foisted on me, but the truth felt worse. Both were selfish choices, but exposing the truth felt more selfish. So I kept it to myself."

This man is such a protector. Sometimes he does it quietly, like for his late wife. Sometimes publicly, like for me when he knocked the stuffed foxes into the stands, and then drove me home.

"You've always been the protector, haven't you?"

He tilts his head, as he's giving that some thought. "Maybe."

"You were protecting her after death. Her memory. Her legacy. You didn't want to share personal details that she probably wouldn't have wanted shared."

"She was a good person. We just fell out of love. We grew apart. That was all."

"Do her parents know the truth?"

He fidgets with the napkin on the table, shaking his head. "I had dinner with them when I was in Colorado. They like to talk about her. I listen."

I give him a sad smile. "That's a really lovely thing to do. If it gives her grieving parents some comfort, there's nothing wrong with that."

"I hope so."

But something gnaws at me. Since I care about him. I lean closer. "But what about you? You keep that all to yourself. But who protects you?" Then I force out a laugh. "I mean, what do I know about keeping things quiet? Everyone knows how my last relationship ended. I'm the opposite of private."

He manages a small laugh. "Maybe we are opposites. But I'm fine. It wasn't hard. I just kept my mouth shut and let others tell the story. I didn't want people saying shit about her after her death. I didn't want to make her seem...unloved. Know what I mean?"

My throat tightens. "I do. So why now?" Or really, why me?

He scrubs a hand across the back of his neck then shrugs, a little helplessly, like he's giving in to something. His expression gentles even more. "You're the first person I've really wanted to understand me," he says, a quiet confession and one that makes my heart beat wildly. He shifts his gaze to Lacey's list. "But also this list. Lacey never got to do all these things. The road trip, the breakfast, the secrets." He pauses, then seems to backpedal. "But actually, now that I say that, I think I've always been doing this for me—the list. To spend more time with you."

That wild beating turns chaotic. It's like a riot in my chest, and I don't know what to do about it except keep the focus on him. Maybe I can protect him in a way—with how I treat him. "You deserve nice things too."

"Thanks," he says, and there's relief in his features. He seems...lighter.

"I'm sorry that you've been carrying this guilt. And I'm sorry that you were splitting up with Heather. Mostly I'm sorry you felt you had nobody to tell that to. But I'm glad you told me."

"Me too."

We're both quiet for a minute. It's tough to know what to say next after someone unburdens themselves with a secret they've been storing in a locked safe. I chew on my lip for a second, then say, "There's something deeply ironic about the fact that everyone knows my business and nobody knows yours."

But perhaps that's why my chest is racing, and something tugs on me—the wish to share with him too. It's not easy since my dirty laundry was broadcast on the Jumbotron, but there are still things I keep close to the vest.

One look at number five on the list and I feel the suffocating weight of another secret press against me. A secret I've only started to unpack over the last few years. Something I've been wondering every time I've tried to plan a date for someone else, especially recently.

Here goes.

"I don't know if I'm a romance designer for the right reasons," I admit.

43

NO ROSES OR SYMPHONY

REMY

This feels a little like flinging open the door on a warm summer day and drinking in the sunshine.

And also like turning down a dark, creaky corridor late at night.

"Talk to me," Lake says, both a calm command and a gentle invitation, which is sort of his style. And maybe that's why I'm saying this out loud first to him and not to Elena.

The thought has flitted past my mind when I've written down topics for our sessions. But I haven't quite voiced it.

I feel safe with her, of course.

But with Lake I also feel seen. Maybe because I let him see me.

And so, I take the next step.

"Lately I haven't felt inspired. I'll try to work on dates, but my mind just wanders," I begin. "It's like I have romance-planner's block. But I don't think I really have that. I don't think that's a real thing. I think it's because—" I stop, pausing to take a deep breath because this is as uncomfortable as being on an exam table at the doctor's office but you know you have to do it anyway. "I think it's because I've always done it."

He nods, which surprises me. "Is this to do with what your parents said at the picnic? About the dates you planned for them?"

Tears prick the back of my eyes. My throat tightens. How did he notice that? But then again, that's what this man has done. From the night at the arena when he found me wearing a hat, then insisted on giving me a ride home, then declared he was going to be my fake date, he's always been finding me. "Yes," I say. "How did you know?"

"The way you reacted. You tensed up; you shifted to another topic right away."

"And you gave me a look. A curious one," I say, recalling that too. A look I didn't want to acknowledge then. But I do now.

"I figured you'd talk about it when and if you were ready." He drags his chair even closer to me, so close our knees knock. It's reassuring, the knee connection. "What's going on, Remy?"

Now it's my turn. I'm the only one who can do the rest of this excavation. "When I was younger my dad went through this whole period of depression and honestly, not even wanting to be here on this planet at times," I say, then I choke up at the mention of his struggles. "And my mom was there for him and she helped him, and they went to therapy alone and together. He always felt like he was bringing her down. He felt like his sadness was ruining her happiness. And she just wanted to show him that she loved him. That he wasn't bringing her down. That she wanted them to stay together, even if he struggled with his...mental health."

I swipe at my cheeks and keep digging. "I didn't want them to split up either, so I would make dinner for them. I would plan a game night. I would set up candlelight and music and everything," I say, my throat raw as I tell him the story. "I saw everything my mom was doing to try to help him, and I started doing it too, but for them."

Lake rubs a palm on one of my knees, soothing me. His touch is so comforting—almost as much as the way he listens is. "When I plan dates now, it's fun and I like it, but I think," I say, then wince, because facing all your childhood issues is like scraping your skin against a jagged rock, "I'm just doing it out of this fear that if I don't, somebody will split up. Like if I can create all the right vibes and the mood, people can stay in love." I stop, replay what I just said. "Now that I say that out loud, it sounds ridiculous."

"No." His voice is strong and certain. He reaches for my hands and holds them tightly. "It's not ridiculous. It's not ridiculous at all. Those things do matter. But what you want also matters. That's a lot to take on as a kid, and you don't have to keep taking it on as an adult."

Something heavy in my chest lifts even as a tear slips down one cheek. "I don't think I want to take it on."

A smile shifts his lips. "If it's not what you want to do, then don't do it. A date doesn't have to have roses or a symphony to be special. A date can just be two people hanging out."

Like this.

I want to say the next thing. I'm dying to say the next thing. That this list from Lacey has shown me that what matters in romance are the little moments. The unexpected. The challenges. Trying to make breakfast and failing. A cat breaking a plate and cleaning it up together. Helping someone's parent. Volunteering for the other person's event. Taking a road trip when you're not even sure what to say to the other person. Dealing with a misunderstanding at the hotel desk. But if I say all that, then I'll say something even scarier—that I'm falling for my fake boyfriend.

And that's not in the rules we clearly laid out. Sure, I want to believe he feels something real. But I've been fooled before, not long ago.

I don't want to make another mistake.

I pour all my focus into the one thing I'm sure of right now, and I say it with my whole heart. "I'm going to shut down Romance By Design," I say, and wow.

My hand flies to my mouth, like I can't believe I said that. But I'm so glad I said it. That is what I needed. That's the step I needed to take. And now I do feel like it's a summer day, and I'm lifting my face toward the sky.

I lower my hand. "Today! I'm going to do it today."

"Proud of you," he says with a gorgeous smile, one that floods my whole chest with lightness. I think I needed that kind of support. That kind of encouragement.

He squeezes my hands and that emboldens me. So I do something bold too. I cup his cheeks and I lean forward. I kiss him, soft, slow, and tender. Like I can tell him with the caress of my lips how much this *fling* has meant to me.

He's done exactly what he promised he'd do. Shown me passion, honesty, and respect. And I try to say with the slide of my mouth, the stroke of my hand, the softness of our kiss what that means to me.

What he means.

Maybe later, maybe at another time, when I'm feeling braver, I can say it with words.

44

A GOOD A LOT

REMY

A little later, I'm ready to leave. After that emotional moment, I need to recalibrate.

Maybe he does too. Sometimes we need time apart to process.

There's also the practical realities—I need to hustle back to my place and get ready to work for a couple of hours. "I have to help out with a VIP tour in a bit," I say as I reach the door, my bag slung over my shoulder. "One of our charity partners has some VIPs in town, and Miller is going to be the tour guide."

"That should make the tour last a couple of hours," Lake jokes.

"And then I have the"—I pause to adopt a spooky tone and horror movie fingers—"*spa day.*"

He frowns, almost believably. He's far too pleased about this timing. "Such a shame it's a game day. Because I will be napping. I need it after this morning."

He doesn't mean the sex we had. Glad he feels the same.

"And I think I need cucumbers on my eyes to process all

that," I say, waving my hand to the table, the scene of all the unpacking. "That was a lot. But a good a lot."

"It was definitely a good a lot."

Where do we go from here? The wedding tomorrow, of course. There's also the list. I don't think either one of us expected to knock off two items today. We're pretty much done, and the ending of the list looms even bigger than the wedding.

The quiet grows, and I should try to make it better. But maybe it's okay that it's awkward.

Lake swallows roughly, then says, "Will I see you tonight?"

The way he asks—vulnerable, like it's hard for him but worth doing—stirs something inside my soul. Makes me want to write our plans in ink for the evening. Throw my arms around him and tell him he's making me feel far too much far too soon. "I hope so," I say.

"I'll call you after the game."

"Good. You better," I say.

"Promise." He tugs on my sweater, then drops a poignant kiss to my lips.

When he pulls apart, he sneers at my sweater. "This won't do."

"Why? This is a cute sweater," I ask, then rattle off its attributes. It's burgundy, it's soft, it's secondhand.

But he's striding back to his bedroom and once he's around the corner, I turn to Thor, who perks up an ear from the cat tower. A second later, he drops his head back, returning to his slumber, uninterested in humans. "You have no guilt over the broken plate," I say to the cat as he covers his eyes with white paws to show me exactly how uninterested in me he is.

Lake returns with a purple and white jersey draped over

his arm and a cocky look on his face. He closes the distance between us, then tugs the bag off my arm.

I'm smiling stupidly as he sets my bag on the floor, since I know what's coming.

He drops the jersey over my head. I shimmy it on the rest of the way over my sweater. I'm swimming in it. I run my polished nail along the number 7.

"Wear this to spa day," he instructs. "It's hot, like you. And it says you're mine."

Heat rises in me at the same time my heart dares to flutter. I dip a toe in emotion-infested waters, but just a toe. "We haven't finished the list."

The unsaid corollary? There's no way we'll have time to go camping before my sister's wedding.

He smiles. "We'll figure it out."

That feels like a promise. That maybe the list's inevitable ending could be a new beginning. I swivel around to go, but he clears his throat. "Remy," he says, his voice hoarse.

"Yes?"

"You're like a hummingbird."

It's the highest of compliments from him, and I want to cup it in my hands. "Why's that?"

"You make me happy."

It's a miracle I'm able to leave without melting into a puddle.

* * *

This time on the way to work I don't stare out the window and avoid planning dates as I daydream of Lake. Nope, I face my romance planner's block head-on. By grabbing the loose thread, I unravel the sweater I've been making for the last year.

Or really, my whole life.

I'm giddy as I email my current clients I've been planning proposals, anniversary celebrations, and special nights for, telling them I'll finish up their dates, and then I'll be stepping back.

I go to my website and I disable the submissions form. I go to socials, and I flip the sign to closed for all intents and purposes, writing "not open to new clients." Exuberance, thy name is Remy.

And as the bus trundles toward the arena, the fearsome fox statue growing bigger and bigger, I pop into the group chat with my friends.

Remy: Attention. Your resident type-A, tightly-wound, spreadsheet-nerd, turns-over-ten-thousand-iterations-of-everything girlie has an announcement.

Trevyn: You finally got that nipple piercing?

Skylar: You adopted a dog so Simon will finally have a cousin? *inserts praying paws emoji*

Mabel: Dude? Where did you find a praying paws emoji?

Skylar: I made it myself. Have you heard of the Internet, Mabel? You can do pretty much anything on it.

Clementine: Like respond to a friend WHO SAID SHE HAS AN ANNOUNCEMENT. Remy, I've got my earmuffs on since I presume this is about my brother. If you're going to mention you got that new life-changing toy I told you about last month, I'm going to see myself out of this chat.

Trevyn: As if you could ever see yourself out of anything, Miss Has To Know Everything.

Mabel: And I believe you just described all of us! Anyway, Remy, is it that you nabbed some superstar celebrity client? Ooh, I bet that's it, and I am so proud of you! I knew you could do it. I bet it's one of the female hockey players! Their stars have been rising ever since they won the championship last season.

I'm walking past the fox statue by the time I finally respond. But I'm laughing, feeling a little over the moon. Nervous, of course. But in a good way as I head into the great unknown. I stop at the statue to reply, pushing my bag back up my shoulder. I pat it for good measure—I have my jersey in it that Lake gave me. I can't wear it on the tour, but I'm yanking it back on the second I hit the spa. Let Jameson squirm.

Remy: I shut down Romance By Design! And I couldn't be happier. I'll tell you more when we play pickleball again, but I wanted to let you all know. Also, wish me luck. I think I'm going to go talk to my boss about the job I really want.

Mabel: Holy shit, you have ovaries. That's big.

Clementine: Sometimes knowing what you don't want is as important as knowing what you do.

Trevyn: Girl, that is not what I expected, and this is much better news than a piercing. And you should still get a piercing to celebrate.

Skylar: We all need to celebrate you. Let's do something fun after pickleball. Ideally, involving frothy drinks rather than exercise. And good luck with the boss. He'll be a fool not to hire you.

I push open the door to the arena, stop at security, then pass the giant posters of the hockey players. I smile, a private one as I walk by Lake's, and his words at the door echo in my mind. *We'll figure it out.* Maybe soon, we can figure out if our little fling can turn into something more. If it does, I won't even need to tell Daniel we split up. I won't need to tell anyone it's ended.

The list, the finishing of it, the what comes next. *We'll figure it out.*

I clutch those four words tight in my hands, a precious sentence, a promise. They give me an extra boost of confidence as I march through the arena, ready to tell Daniel I'm closing my burgeoning business. It's a little bittersweet to believe something will be your special thing and it turns out you just don't love it.

But there is something I do love. Helping. Charity. Giving back. And planning events that celebrate those things.

With a fleet of nerves docking in my chest, I trot up the stairwell to the second floor, figuring Daniel will be working today, since we have a game tonight. I also saw the schedule for the day and there's an interview with the general manager, Theo Llewelyn, on a prominent sports podcast, so that'll keep my boss busy pre-game. I march down the hall toward his office, spotting him at his desk on the phone. He motions for me to come in.

"Sounds great. Love Anna Piper over here. I'd put her toe-to-toe against any of the guys on the team," he says to someone on the phone, then mouths "*Hi*", and nods to a chair.

I grab a seat, even though I'd rather stand. Too much energy. But I wait as he finishes up his call. When he ends it, he says to me, "Try not to be too excited, but Anna Piper is joining the VIP tour today."

My jaw drops. "The play-by-play announcer for the Vancouver team, and one of the greatest players ever?" I ask, even though of course I know who she is.

"Yup. She'll be here anyway with Vancouver and thought it would be fun to see the arena. She's as good a sportscaster as she was in skates."

"Queen. She's a queen," I say, and I can be a queen too, in my own way. By taking ownership of my choices.

"What can I do for you? You're all set for the tour in thirty minutes? Early of course."

"I always am," I say, then take a breath, and wait one second for another flurry of nerves but they don't come. Maybe figuring out what you want gives you a newfound calm, something I rarely feel. "I wanted to let you know I can plan that birthday celebration for you and your hubs, but I need to do it as a friend. No fee."

His brow knits. "Oh, why? Everything okay?"

"Everything's great," I say, bursting with excitement. "Because I'd like to take you up on the offer to work full-time. I'm not going to do romance design as a business anymore. Turns out I actually love this job more."

He blinks. Rolls his lips. Blows out a heavy breath. "Remy," he says, his voice even, and my heart sinks. This is bad. Whatever's coming next is bad. "I posted the job listing. Brinkley is leaving and with all the extra work we have and you wanting to do your own thing, I decided I needed a full-timer in addition to you. But you can apply for it."

Oh. I thought he'd want me just like that.

Just like you thought Jameson wanted to marry you.

But I don't let on I'm thrown off. I fasten on a smile and say, "Of course I'd love to apply."

"Look, I have to keep it open for a week. Corporate and HR rules and all." Then he glances at the door and makes a show of lowering his voice. "But you'd be a leading candidate for sure."

"Great. Thank you," I say, even though I'm parsing his words—*a* leading candidate, not *the* leading candidate.

"Of course," he says, then furrows his brow, "I wasn't expecting this. But I want to hear all about this decision. Let's do lunch tomorrow, and you can tell me everything. We can catch up then."

"Sorry, I can't do tomorrow. My sister is getting married. How about the next day?"

"It's a working lunch then," he says, then rubs his hands together. "World domination, here we come."

That sounds promising, but I wish I didn't feel so...let down.

What? You thought he was going to hand it to you on a silver platter?

I did think that. But I'll need to earn it, and that's okay. That has to be okay. I'm about to leave, but something is rooting me here. This buzzing in my brain that says *Don't stop. Keep going. Say more.*

I found the courage this morning to tell Lake about the way I tried to fix my parents' marriage. I opened up to him and my friends about my business, and then Daniel. I can take this newfound openness a step further. I can share a secret with Daniel and tell him that Lake and I are fake. But that I'm hoping it can be real.

After all, we're figuring it out.

It only seems right to control the narrative of how we started. The wedding is tomorrow, and really, Daniel deserves to know. I told Clem. I can tell my boss.

"There's just one more—"

But there's a knock at the door. Devon pokes her head in, bright and upbeat. "Daniel, we have that interview with *The Competitive Edge*. Mr. Llewelyn wanted you to join him. They're all set up in one of the media rooms."

Daniel pops up in a flash. "I don't like to leave Theo waiting."

"Of course not," I say, disappointed as Daniel takes off.

And I head to my cubicle with a new plan forming. I'll tell him at lunch. He'll appreciate the honesty. Maybe it'll even make me stand out more in the job quest.

In the back of my mind, though, I'm hoping for another outcome entirely—that somehow this thing with Lake will become real and no one will ever know it was fake.

But there will be time for matters of the heart later. I have a job to do, and it turns out it's the job I love most. I head to the entrance of the arena, scanning for Miller. I always like to chat with the players beforehand when they are going to be helping with a tour, even though Miller never needs much guidance. Talking is his favorite hobby so he's a dream on these things. He'll often regale VIP guests with tales of his minor league days or pranks the guys have played over the years. On tours, he's a bit of a fabulist, telling ghost stories about the spirits of made-up hockey legends that supposedly haunt this arena.

I texted him letting him know I'd meet him by the life-size posters in five minutes. I should arrive before him, but when I reach the posters a few seconds later, he's already resting an elbow on the ledge of the escalator to the arena, chatting with none other than our other VIP, Anna Piper.

I don't normally get awestruck around hockey players since I work with them, but she's something else. She won a gold medal and a championship before a knee injury took her down, and now she's made herself indispensable as a play-by-play announcer for the Vancouver team. She looks like a superhero, all tall and strong in a maroon pantsuit with high heels and a white silk blouse that makes her red hair—the shade is a striking rose gold—stand out even more. She's tough to look away from—foreboding and stunning.

I march right over to her, flash her a smile, and say, "I hope Miller isn't already talking your ear off. I'm Remy Hatmaker. So thrilled to meet you."

"Anna Piper," she says, shaking my hand. "Thanks for letting me tag along. This is a treat."

Miller turns to me with a friendly smile, then swings his gaze back to her. "And for the record, she likes it when I talk her ear off."

Anna rolls her pretty green eyes. "Always so full of yourself."

Always. That's interesting.

"Oh, do you two know each other?" I ask, since I was getting a vibe.

"We went to college together," Miller says. "We've been friends forever."

"How did I not know this? Why didn't you ever tell me you had cool friends, Miller?" I demand.

"Maybe I was keeping it a secret."

Anna laughs, then says to me, "Miller likes to be mysterious sometimes." She leans in closer and gives me a conspiratorial whisper, like we've been friends forever. "He thinks that's part of his whole goalie mystique."

"Hey now," he says, inching closer to her. "I don't have a goalie mystique—I *am* the goalie mystique!"

She pats his arm, laughing. "Yeah, keep telling yourself that."

It's friendly, the way she treats him, but when Miller glances down at his arm like he's treasuring the spot where she touched him, my romance instincts tingle. No, I'm not dying to set them up on a date. But I've got a feeling Miller has a crush on his longtime friend.

But that's a thought I need to tuck aside for now. I spot the head of the charity striding into the arena with her VIP donors.

"All right. It's showtime," I say.

45

HOPTIMISM AND OPTIMISM

REMY

On the tour, Miller charms the donors with his fabricated ghost stories in the Golden State Fox's locker room, then his tales of a haunted equipment room before ending the tour with everyone's favorite part—a photo opportunity on the Zamboni.

He motions for Anna to join him at the end, then slips his arm around her waist as I snap a pic, all while smiling like I know what's coming next for them.

When the tour is over I thank everyone and wish both Miller and Anna good luck for the game tonight. Anna will be commentating in the booth, and Miller on the ice.

I head upstairs to my cubicle to finish a few things before I slip away for the spa day. I'll miss seeing the game this evening. Part of me feels a tug in my chest at the thought of missing it, even though I had never planned on going to it. But there's no way I'm missing the spa session, especially since I've got this jersey to show off.

When I reach my cubicle, Devon's setting a small ruby red bag on my desk with a ribbon around the handles.

"Oh, you got another gift. Is this from your boyfriend?" she asks as she spins around.

"I don't know," I say, feeling tingly and giddy all over, and I sure hope it's from him.

But I also feel a little queasy when she says *boyfriend*. At the way the word sticks in my chest, like heartburn.

At the way it still feels like a lie not only on my tongue but on other people's tongues, especially as Devon adds, "I bet it is, and your boyfriend is seriously a king."

"He is," I say.

When she spins around and leaves, I swallow down the guilt. One more day. One more day and we'll figure it out.

For now, I rip open the bag and gasp when I see a midnight blue velvet box I recognize instantly. It's from Victoire.

I tug it out, along with a card on it.

It just says—*It should fit you now.*

My breath catches. With excited fingers I click it open then. My heart is beating so fast. This feels so unreal as I stare at the elegant timepiece that I tried on at Lake's apartment.

I can't believe this. He's giving me the watch I modeled for him, and it's just for me. He had it resized...for me.

Delicately, I tug it out of the box, and I'm about to slide it on my wrist when I spot something on the back. It's been engraved with the words *For you.*

I clutch it tight for several seconds as something dangerously close to happiness floods my chest. Not for the watch. But the gesture. Then, I click it open and slide it on. It fits perfectly, and I can hear what he said the day I tried it—*it's touching you now*.

Like he wanted to. Like he did. Like he's still doing. And in ways I never saw coming but now desperately want.

* * *

For the record, I *am* a spa kind of person. As soon as the scent of lavender and the sound of soft waves greets me when I swing open the door of DeLaTour Spa in Russian Hill, my muscles relax. My mind breathes more regularly.

Maybe I've always needed the mandatory calm that the permission slip of a place like this affords.

Sure, I need to be *on* as the mistress of spa ceremonies this afternoon—maid-of-honor duties are no joke—but I also get a massage and facial for it.

That's winning.

I'm fifteen minutes early, so I head straight to the counter and tell the attendant I'm checking in for the Hatmaker party.

When that's done, I wander around the entryway, soaking in the ambiance of the plants hanging over the front counter, the photos of serene beaches, the soothing scents of the candles, lotions, and potions.

I peruse some bars of soap, sniffing each one.

For the first time in a long time, I don't feel wound tight. I'm not checking and re-checking every detail to make sure everything is going to be okay.

Maybe everything is going to work out just fine. Caroline's wedding will go smoothly, Fresh Face will be happy, I'll get the job, and I'll swim into a new romance, no one the wiser that it started as a revenge scheme.

I set down a candle as the door groans open.

"A bakery that serves beer. Right? Wouldn't that be a perfect combo? It was my idea."

All the good feelings are washed down the drain as Jameson walks in with a boast and a lie.

"Hmm. What about a brewery that serves baked goods?" a cheery woman asks.

And yes, that actually makes way more sense than Jameson's new *concept restaurant* as she lands on a better business model than him easily.

I want to tell him his concept is another ridiculous idea, but when I spin around, I'm struck with one thought—gratitude.

I'm so immensely glad he dumped me for the world to see.

Let his new girlfriend deal with his ludicrous ideas. Let her manage his hoptimistic ambitions. He's not my problem anymore.

"Hi, Jameson. Hi, Chelsea," I say, since I recognize her from the shower.

"Hi, Remy! Thank you so much for including me in this," she says, enthusiastic.

"Same here," Jameson says, then looks around, peering behind me. "Where's your other half?"

"He has a hockey game," I say.

"Bummer he couldn't make it," Jameson says, but he hardly sounds bummed, especially since his eyes flicker with plans. "But maybe we can chat about an idea I have for the wedding tomorrow for the best-man toast."

Oh for fuck's sake. I'd like to throw him into the sauna and let him bake and then give a toast about that.

I give him my best "so sorry" look. "Wish I could, but I need to greet all the other spa guests. Oh look, I see the bridesmaids right now."

I don't spot a soul but I leave anyway, choosing to wait outside for my sister.

When she arrives, sans Fresh Face, I'm inordinately happy that she's free of her entourage. They've been like her wedding homunculus. I hug her and say, "Everything is going to be great tomorrow."

And I believe it.

"It is," she says, then motions for Parker to come inside. "Let's go treat everyone to some relaxing."

"Anything for you, babe," Parker says, then drops a doting kiss to her cheek, and soon the rest of the party is here, ready to be pampered.

* * *

I'm lounging in a comfy spa chair, wearing a fluffy bathrobe, my glasses, and a face mask, a manicurist artfully applying a soft shade of pink to my toenails.

"Would you like some cucumbers for your eyes?" another woman asks.

I flash back to the conversation with Lake earlier today when I told him I needed these to process the day. But I feel pretty good about everything. Still, I might want to put these on when the pedicurist is done. Besides, I may as well make the most of my contact-lens-free time. "Thank you. I would but I'll put them on myself," I say, since that's one thing I like to feel in control of.

"Of course," she says and sets a plate of sliced cucumbers on the arm of the chair.

As she offers cucumbers to the bridesmaid next to me, Jameson appears again out of nowhere. He's wearing a robe and some kind of muddy goop is slathered on his face. He strides straight to me.

And those cucumbers sound real good right now. I grab two slices and drop them on my eyes before he can say a word.

Yes, these definitely help process my ex, that's for sure.

When I peek past them and see he's safely out of range, I snag my phone—it's on airplane mode but I have it for pics—from my pocket, and take a selfie, then sneak it back into the bathrobe pocket.

A little later, I'm getting dressed in the ladies' locker room and once I pull on the jersey again and place my contacts back in, I send the selfie to Lake.

Remy: Hope you had a good nap while I had cucumbers.

He'll be busy on the ice, but he'll find it later. I'm tucking my phone in my pocket when Caroline pulls me aside and says, "Guess what I just worked out with Fresh Face?"

For them not to come to the wedding? "Tell me," I say, doing my best to muster enthusiasm for her brand partner, even though I kind of can't stand them.

More than kind of.

I'd like to put them on Clem's hate list.

"They're going to live stream the wedding," she says, giddy, and she's never giddy.

Kill. Me. Now.

But this is also the true test of my faking skills. I paste on a smile and say, "That's great."

"I know. Views have been so good for the content. It's all working out," she says.

I'm happy for her, but when I leave the spa, I'm ready to go home and see Lake later.

When I check the score in the hockey game and see it's still the second period, I have a better idea.

46

WHAT PRETTY TOES YOU HAVE

LAKE

We're down by one, but there's still time. That just means we have to make every second count.

Coach knows it too. In the locker room during the second intermission, as I change into a new undershirt since mine is sweat-soaked, and Riggs ices his shoulder since he always ices his shoulder, Coach Ahmed prowls up and down the stalls. "We've been on a tear lately, boys. It's easy to get caught up in that feeling. But that's when you need to dig in and play harder. Don't get complacent. Don't expect a win," he says, spinning around at the ears at the top of the Foxes logo on the carpeted floor, then pacing back the other way, locking eyes with Corbin, who's retaping his stick. "You've got to get out there and earn it. Every single second on the ice. I know you can do it. Get out there and fight for the two goals we need."

Corbin lifts his stick toward the rest of us. "You heard him, boys. Let's get it done."

"Let's get it done," the rest of us say, echoing him.

After I tug the rest of my gear back on, then snap on my helmet, I hit the ice with my team, ready to dig in.

Because that's what I do.

That's what I've always done. After Heather died, I channeled all my focus, all my emotions into the game, and I leveled up.

I can do it tonight. And then I'll see Remy, and soon, I'll ask her out on that real date.

But as I take a lap around the ice, a traitorous thought lands in my skull.

What if she says she's not ready? Will you be able to handle that too, you cocky ass?

Something hard and brittle wedges into my heart. A reminder not to get too close.

But even if it hurts when Remy moves on, I'll just follow my playbook again. I'll pour everything I've got into the game. I'll keep myself locked into the sport that never lets me down. The game that deserves all my emotions.

I glide behind the net, when my attention snags on the first row behind the glass.

And the beautiful brunette who's standing, cheering, making a scene of rooting us on as she wears my number. And not just my number but *my jersey*. The one I gave her.

Fuck, she looks so damn right there that the brittle edge in me softens.

She came to my game. She's cheering for me. And as my vision narrows to her for a quick second, I spot a glimpse of silver on her wrist.

She's wearing the watch too.

Maybe just maybe, I don't suck at romance after all.

I line up for the face-off, flanking Corbin, ready for anything, taking nothing for granted.

We pounce, and Corbin gets the puck so fast he's like a goddamn cheetah on blades. He cruises toward the net, and I'm right there with him, open for a pass if he needs me.

When their defenders swarm him, he feeds the puck to

me, and I race around the back of the net, flipping it to Riggs, who slams it right past their goalie.

Bam.

Just like that, the score is tied.

"That's the way we do it," I shout to Riggs.

"It fucking is," he says back, and as we make our way to the boards, I can't help it. My focus turns to her again, and when I see her hugging the person next to her, as if she's losing her ever-loving mind over the goal, another piece of the ice surrounding my heart breaks off.

She came to the game for me.

I've only ever been playing for my dad, and that's been enough for a long, long time. Making him happy. Boosting him up. Connecting with him.

But I didn't realize how much I wanted someone in the stands for me till she showed up.

"Uh-oh. It's happening," Ivan says, his voice an ominous warning on my left.

"And I want to get in on the bet," Riggs puts in from my right as they talk across me.

I furrow my brow, tearing my gaze away from Remy. "What are you two clowns talking about?"

Ivan flashes a grin my way, his eyes flickering with satisfaction. "I'm winning the bet. You're falling in love."

What the fuck?

Riggs points his stick at Remy's row. "Yup. You've been making lover-boy eyes at Remy. God, it is going to be so fucking fun when Ivan collects."

I roll my eyes, to get them off my back. Don't need anyone in my business, even my friends. "Fuck off."

"And you didn't deny it," Riggs says. "I bet you loved going to the spa day."

How does he know about that? I shoot him a *what the hell*

look? "That was today. So no, I didn't go. Also, how do you know all this shit? Are you stalking me?"

He scoffs. "I watch her sister's show. It's pretty inspiring, if you must know. And we're all going to be watching the live stream tomorrow at Corbin's home."

The wedding's being streamed now? "Are you kidding me?"

Corbin laughs, tossing his head back. "We've even got snacks ready."

"We'll probably place bets on when *your* wedding will be," Riggs adds.

Maybe someday, I won't mind telling these guys what Remy means to me. But first I need to figure out how to tell her. I turn away from them, putting my glower on, zeroing on the game like Coach told us to do. When it's time for another shift, I hop over the boards, so fast, ready to attack the ice.

I push all thoughts of Remy, the wedding, and my teammates out of my head.

And I do what I do best. Put my heart and soul into the one thing that never lets me down.

The game.

By the time the last second ticks off the scoreboard, we've got a W.

As we skate toward the tunnel, I try, I swear I try—not to look at Remy. Don't want to give my teammates any more ammunition.

But she came to my game.

On her own.

Fuck it.

I spin around, peel away from the pack, and fly the other way across the ice, right to her.

She's on the other side of the glass, of course. But when I reach her, I yank off my helmet.

"Hey!" I shout over the noise.

"Hi," she says right back.

"I'll drive you home," I say.

She nods. "See you soon."

Then I lean closer, like I could kiss her through the glass. No doubt someone's taking pictures. No doubt the cameras are on us. But I don't care.

She blows me a kiss.

I give her one right back, wishing the glass weren't between us.

Soon, it won't be.

* * *

I get showered and dressed at Mach speed, texting Remy that I'll meet her at the players' entrance to spend the night with her.

Can't wait is her reply.

Same here is mine.

I fight off a grin, but it's hard not to smile at her reply, and at the pic she sent me while I was playing. It's perfect, the shot of her at the spa with cucumbers on her eyes—perfect because she took it. Perfect because she sent it to me.

I shove my arms into my suit jacket, raring to go see the woman who sends me quirky photos that let me into her world.

"See you kids in a couple of days," I say, grabbing my tie and tossing it over my shoulder, then tucking my phone into my pants pocket.

"Have fun at the wedding, lover boy," Corbin calls from his stall. "And have fun paying Ivan."

I don't even know where Ivan is, but I crane my neck

around to flip them all the bird as I head to the door and walk straight into a hockey stick.

"Oof," I blurt out, as it lands across my stomach.

Which joker did this? My vision goes dark when the joker tosses a jersey over my head.

"You're not missing the spa day now."

It's Miller, his voice laced with amusement as my world flips upside down. One of them hoists up my arms, the other my legs, and someone ties my hands with my own goddamn necktie.

I've been kidnapped.

Again.

* * *

They don't tell me where we're going as they toss me into the back seat of someone's car. They keep the jersey over my head, using it like a pillowcase.

But unlike the first time they did this earlier in the season and dragged me to play lawn games, I'm antsy. A little worried. And frankly, annoyed I have to say this.

But I do. I fucking do.

"Guys, I need to text Remy. I was supposed to meet her."

"Aww, so cute. I texted my hubby too, and told him I'd be home late," Ivan teases from the front seat.

"Seriously. Untie me."

"Only if you let me into the bet," Riggs says from next to me.

"You need a grand that badly? Why don't I just give you the name of my money guy so you can manage yours better," I counter. Because I can't just give in.

"Sure, if it means I can bet on you falling for the woman you've been obsessed with for more than a year."

I growl. "Why are we fucking friends?"

"Are we?" Riggs asks dryly.

"Whatever," I say, then tug hard on the tie, but these assholes probably took a knot-tying class just to do this.

"I'll text her for you," Riggs offers.

"The fuck you will," I say.

But it's too late. He's dictating into his phone. "Hey, Remy. It's Riggs. We kidnapped your boyfriend since he needs to get his balls waxed before the wedding tomorrow. Says he wants to be beautiful all over for you. He'll see you later with his good luck nuts all nice and shiny."

I'm going to kill him.

* * *

They free me at the spa, some place called Haven on Fillmore Street that Ivan goes to for massages. He knows the owner and asked her to keep it open late for a private party.

I wouldn't exactly call it a party, but I also know better than to try to escape a team prank. That'll only make them prank me harder next time.

The second the tie falls off my wrists, I'm grabbing my phone and texting her.

Lake: I'll come over as soon as this spa torture is done.

Remy: Good luck with your nuts 😊

I roll my eyes and pocket the phone. I've got to find a way to turn the tables on them. And if it involves me doing something I hate, so be it.

Once we're in the locker room, I clear my throat. "Listen up, boys," I say, and the guys turn toward my voice. Ivan, Riggs, Miller, and Corbin. "You can all get in on the bet under one condition."

"Name it," Riggs says.

Twenty minutes later, they're all in bathrobes, parked in lounge chairs, and having their toenails painted purple—our team color.

It's so goddamn satisfying.

On many levels, because even though these guys are a bunch of clowns, they're my clowns. My family. My brothers on the ice, and, I suppose, off it.

The spa kidnapping doesn't end in the chair. Before I know it, I'm flat on my stomach, getting my sore muscles worked over.

At least this part isn't so bad, except it's getting late. I'm growing antsier. It's probably past midnight. Even if I can see Remy, it'll be too late to *talk*. To *figure us out*.

She'll probably be asleep when I arrive at her home. I'll just slide into bed with her and hold her.

That would be enough. You shouldn't have important conversations late into the night anyway.

As the masseuse digs her thumbs into my lower back, I map out a plan. After the wedding. Yep, that's when I'll ask Remy out for real. As I'm twirling her on the dance floor in that mouth-wateringly sexy stunner of a dress she'll have on.

And...why the hell am I still on this massage table?

I pop up, grabbing the sheets around my waist so I'm not indecent but still startling the massage therapist. "Sorry, I have to go."

"Oh, okay," she says, then scurries out of the room. I wrap

a towel around my waist, and march back toward the locker room, passing a room on the way where my teammates are gathered around a chalkboard, picking options for facials.

"Gotta go," I announce.

They spin around. Words like *what the fuck* and *no you don't* fall from their mouths. I hold up a hand.

"Love you guys," I say, speaking louder, cutting through the noise, saying that to them for the first time—these assholes I'd go to war with and for, and I do in every single game. "But I'd rather be someplace else."

And with that admission, they stop protesting.

They wave me out of there.

47

MAKE IT LAST

LAKE

I don't bother returning to the arena to get my car. I catch a Lyft and head straight for her place, texting to see if she's still up.

Remy: Barely. But come over anyway. Here's the code.

She sends it next and it feels like Christmas morning. She gave me the code to her house. She made me a cat tower. She came to my game. She sent me hummingbird pictures. She gave my dad a puzzle. She talked to him about hard things.

My heart skips ten beats on the ride, and it's nearly one when I arrive, sprinting out of the Lyft to her porch, tapping in her code, creaking open the door so it doesn't wake her. I toe off my shoes at the entrance, and set my jacket and tie down at the hall table. Her place is quiet, the lights dimmed. Only a night-light in the bathroom illuminates the way home—to her.

Unbuttoning my shirt as I walk quietly in my socks, I'm half undressed by the time I reach her doorway.

My chest tightens, squeezes hard when I see her. She's curled up on her side, chestnut hair spilling across the pillowcase, moonlight from the window casting a soft, silvery glow across her face.

Her eyes are closed, and her breathing is slow and steady.

And my head feels fuzzy. My body feels light. My fingers tingle. It's ridiculous the way she makes me feel. *Alive.*

Everywhere.

But most of all in this organ in my chest that's been on ice for so long. It's thudding painfully against my rib cage, but it's a good pain. A pain I want as I strip off my pants, take off my socks, and set my phone down on the other nightstand.

I slip into bed, sliding under the covers where it's warm and welcoming, and I get to be near her. I inch closer, and my breath halts.

She's wearing my jersey still.

She's wearing my goddamn jersey, and she smells like flowers and clean laundry and every single morning and every single night.

I can't resist. I wrap an arm around her, needing to hold her, wanting to have her. I bury my face in her neck, dropping a soft, barely there kiss to her perfect shoulder.

She stirs, shifting, making a low, humming sound.

Shit. I didn't mean to wake her up.

Yes you did, you liar.

"You won," she says.

"You came," I say.

"Were you surprised?"

"Yes, and I loved it," I say. *And I think I love you.*

"Good. I wanted to give you a good surprise."

"You're the best surprise," I whisper into her ear, but guilt at waking her digs into my chest. Tomorrow's her sister's wedding, and she needs to be *on*. "Go to sleep, beautiful."

"I will," she says, soft and a little slurry. She takes one breath, then another, and something must perk her up since she says, more clearly now, "But I have another surprise for you."

Before I know it, the beauty in my jersey turns around, climbs over me, and pins my wrists. "This is a much better kidnapping," I murmur.

"I'd like to kidnap your dick with my mouth," she says, then shimmies down the bed, yanks off my boxer briefs and wraps her lips around my half-hard cock in seconds flat.

My brain sizzles. My body sparks.

"Fuck, Remy," I moan, gazing down at the sight of her with my cock—now rock hard—down her throat. "Your mouth is incredible."

She lets me fall from her lips. "Fuck my mouth then. You know you want to."

"More than anything," I say, then I give in to this midnight moment. To this woman kneeling between my spread thighs, sucking on my dick, playing with my unwaxed balls, making me feel like a goddamn king.

I don't deserve her.

I really don't.

But I'm going to do everything I can to show her she deserves the world.

I thrust my hips up into the paradise of her mouth while she runs her hands along my thighs, her nails trailing through the hair on my legs.

She sweeps her tongue across the head, then licks a long stripe down the underside, and I'm lost.

I'm moaning, low and loud as she taunts me with her tongue, teasing my dick before she devours me again.

And colors burst in front of my eyes. Ticker-tape parades kick off in my body. A comet launches.

It's fucking incredible. No idea what this sorcery is but I don't want it to end.

Except, I do know what it is—it's her, in the dark, wanting to make me feel incredible.

And she *is* making me feel out of this world.

But I didn't come over in the middle of the night to get serviced.

I tap her shoulder, then bite out, "Enough."

She lets go, raises her face, and meets my eyes with a concerned look in hers. "Are you okay?"

"I will be when I'm inside you."

"Then do it. And make it good," she says, an order.

She's so giving and so confident in bed. It's the headiest combination. It's like she's free here to be this bold person who demands the pleasure she deserves. And I'm the lucky man who gets to answer to her.

I flip her so she's on her back. She peels off the jersey in seconds, and my world stalls. She's already naked. Not even wearing underwear.

I drag my thumb down the soft skin of her hip, then drop my face and suck on her right there, drawing out a moan before I let go.

"You wanted me in the middle of the night, didn't you?" I ask, staring at the sight of her all long and lithe with nothing but starlight across her skin.

"What do you think?" She tips her knees open.

And I need a minute. The way she offers herself to me knocks me out. The way she talks to me stirs my chest, my dick, my mind.

That's the problem. If I go too fast, this'll be over far too soon. I only have one goal—make it great for her.

I lower myself so my palms bracket her face, my hard cock pressed to her stomach, our bodies together. "I'm going to make it so fucking good. Because I'm going to take my time with you, beautiful. Want to make this last."

She arches her back, wraps her ankles around my ass. "Better start now."

My entire body is a live wire. Cells are buzzing; nerves are firing. I'm already on the knife's edge of lust. But I didn't ease up tonight in the game. No way am I checking out early here either.

Gripping the base of my cock, I notch the head against her sweet pussy. A groan is ripped from my chest as I touch her. No, from the center of my fucking soul. "You're so wet, beautiful."

She's slick and hot, and she feels like heaven already.

Her hands curl around my shoulders, her nails digging into my flesh. I hope she leaves marks. I hope they never go away.

"I'm a little turned on," she whispers, a playful confession, a naughty glint in her eyes.

"Yeah, same here."

I sink inside her so easily, parking my right hand back by her face. My gaze is locked on her. The way her neck stretches, the gasp that crosses her lips, the twist in her features.

The feel of her heat.

Her legs hook tighter around me. Her fingers dig into my shoulders. Her ruby red lips part, then a word passes from them, all ragged and hungry. "Yessss."

That's it. One word. The only one I want to hear.

I ease out, then take my time filling her, driving deeper. Her hands slip down my body, traveling over my ass, lighting me up. I swivel my hips, then sink back inside, nice and slow and sensual.

We find a pace, one that's lingering, one that's like a slow, dirty song you want to dance to all night.

One that has us both gasping, moaning, reaching. Soon, we're just hands and breath and bodies that don't want to let go as I slow-fuck her into the night, edging her close, and closer. But never quite sending her over.

She shudders, then grabs my face. "Please," she says, her voice wobbly, her eyes glittering with need.

"Please what, baby?"

"Please stop teasing me."

I still my movements right as I ease out of her, leaving her empty. "This better?"

"No," she cries out, grabbing my ass even tighter. "Make me come."

I smile. Fucking love her orders. I dip my face and kiss her neck, but don't press into her again. "You sure?"

She pouts. "Do it now!"

"Say my name. You know you want to," I demand and tease.

She groans in frustration, but she's arching her back, asking for more of me, begging with her body. "Lake, please make me come."

I rise up on my knees, push on the back of her thighs, then thrust into her. I bring my thumb to her sweet, hungry clit.

She tosses her head back and moans to the sky.

I don't slow-fuck her anymore. As she chases her orgasm, I do everything to find it for her, fucking her deep and passionately, using my fingers and my cock. Giving her everything she's shown me she likes till her breathing is staggered, uneven, and then it's just a long, keening sound as an orgasm wracks her body.

It's gorgeous, the way it crashes over her.

I try to memorize the way she looks, record in my head how she sounds, wanting to keep that with me forever.

But my thoughts break apart as my thighs shake and I follow her there.

It's never been like this for me—this connected, this intense, this...real.

It's terrifying how much I want it to be the same for her.

48

MY BEST LIFE

LAKE

She might be done being a romance planner, but that doesn't mean I'm throwing in the towel on planning romance with her.

I'm at the house in Cozy Valley, trimming my beard to get ready for the wedding this afternoon, barking questions at my phone to tackle number five on the to-do list.

"Where is a good place in Northern California to take someone glamping?"

"Wine country is considered by many to be a glamorous location," the cool, modulated voice answers.

"Glamping," I say, over-enunciating as I run the buzzer under my chin. "Where do I take someone glamping?"

"Experts recommend an Airstream, outfitted for luxury. Would you like a list of Airstream dealers?"

Rolling my eyes, I groan. "No, Alexa, I don't. I want you to actually answer a question correctly."

"I can answer a range of questions, such as the size of the universe and what wine goes best with pasta," she says, as Thor leaps on the bathroom vanity, skids across the marble, and whacks my beard brush into the sink with a *thunk*.

I swing my gaze to the dastardly cat. "Are you kidding me?"

"I would suggest a Merlot," Alexa puts in, oblivious to the mess my cat is making of the sink.

Thor doesn't care either. He's more disturbed that my hair is on his precious cat paw, and he's fastidiously cleansing it of all human contact.

"Stand down, Alexa. I'll do it myself."

After I finish trimming my beard, I tap some options into my phone and—yes. That one. That'll be perfect for Remy. I'll ask her to go next weekend in between games. I'll pack a picnic of her favorites. I'll bring a new jigsaw puzzle and a card game. And maybe we can go sex toy shopping for another date. Then I can take her to the succulent gardens for another.

Damn, I'm brilliant. I've got three dates planned.

All this training as a fake boyfriend is going to make me an excellent real one.

I pat some cologne onto my face, then grab the suit Remy picked out for me and put it on so I can meet her shortly at the hotel at the Presidio, where she's helping her sister get ready.

She doesn't need me to pick her up, of course, since she's been busy all morning doing...whatever maids of honor do.

I head downstairs, my cat following, then racing ahead of me, to trip me at the bottom of the stairs, I expect.

No, to hide around the corner and stick out a paw.

But I evade the little stinker, turning into the kitchen to find my dad making a sandwich. A gourmet one by the looks of it, with avocado, some kind of artichoke spread, and then—I squint—is that fake meat?

"Dad, are you eating fake meat?"

He turns around, flashing a clever grin. "I'm trying this plant-based bologna. Remy recommended it."

"When were you and Remy chatting about fake meat?"

"After the shower, when you were helping your brother." Right, she mentioned when we left that they talked about *Jumbotron-gate*. "Fake meat, Jumbotrons, the dog she wants to adopt," he says, then smiles. "She's a good one, son."

Something softens in me even more. I'm grateful he sees it too. Glad he's enchanted, in his way, with the woman who's captured my scarred heart.

I won't need to break his heart again either.

If, buddy.

My chest clenches with an unwelcome tightness. Don't assume the final score. It's big to ask her to date me for real. She might need more time. She might want to be alone. She might not feel the same way I do, and I've got to be able to handle that.

But I handle fearsome defenders on the ice, and I won't back down from this either.

"I hope you enjoy it," I say, then ruffle his hair. "I should head to the wedding."

And I hope this won't be the last time he thinks I'm going to see her.

"Have fun. Take some more pics. That was a nice one at the game last night," he remarks.

I turn around, arching a brow in question. "What was?"

"Picture of the two of you at the boards. Someone there took it, and it looks like it wound up on her sister's feed too."

"Aren't you just a social media bug today?"

"Nah. Not me. Gavin and Mira showed it to me."

Ah, that makes sense now.

I take off, but curiosity grips me when I get in the car. Before I leave, I need to see this pic. Want to see the evidence that he sees. I toggle over to social and hunt for it. I find it on Caroline's feed, and there are a ton of comments already, including one from Jameson. I ignore that, in particular, and focus on the pic. It's me looking like I'm blowing Remy a kiss and Caroline's words: ***Look at my brilliant, amazing sister, living her best life.***

And hell, if that doesn't feel like an endorsement of my plans too. I'd like that best life to include me.

49

ASK ME ANYTHING

REMY

Already, Caroline's broken the heel on her satin pump. I fixed it since superglue was already stocked in my bridal emergency kit. She's lost the barrette hair clip. I tracked it down in her car, under the spare tire kit.

The tasks keep me from worrying too much about my life.

Right now, I'm focused on the makeup artist, who arrived early. She's applying Caroline's Fresh Face foundation here in the bridal suite at The Luxe hotel in the Presidio, with a breathtaking view of the Pacific.

The main videographer's here too, naturally, capturing the makeup application for the live stream. So is Fallon, with her hair cinched back in a tight ponytail. She's dressed in peach today, like the camera crew, and it's weird to see her in that color. She's only ever worn black, but she said she wanted her team to blend into the champagne roses so it'd be like they were not even here. "NEH," she'd said.

I won't mind *that* part of the wedding being over at all. No more acronyms. No more Fallon, skulking around.

But one more day, I keep telling myself. The pressure will end tomorrow.

With her tablet in hand, Fallon reviews what's next on the live stream with Caroline. "Our research shows your viewers are connecting with the MOH, so we'll follow her as she checks on the seating and the floral setup in a few," she says, the direction itself recorded live, all part of Caroline's efforts to show authentic behind-the-scenes content.

"Of course they love her." Caroline beams, clearly proud of me. "My sister's incredible."

"Remy put this all together like that," my mother chimes in with a snap of her fingers, facing the lens. She's polished and put together in a mauve mother-of-the-bride dress that shows off her toned arms, because of course she has toned arms.

I wave a dismissive hand, not wanting or needing the praise, especially on camera. "I just want it to go well for you," I say to my sister.

"And it will. Because we planned for it. Everything is set up perfectly in the waterfront ballroom," my mother says as the makeup artist sweeps highlighter over Caroline's cheekbones. "Just like we wanted."

Perfect. That word pokes at me. A reminder of how often I try to be perfect. But I have to be okay with just being me, however that looks, Elena would say.

Elena, who I need to tell about my fake boyfriend.

But I can't focus on me now. Tomorrow is for me. "I'll do the floral review shortly. I already checked the flowers in the reception room as well as the seating arrangements. Everything there is great too," I say, then lean closer to Caroline. "I also peeked in on the live stream on my phone when they were in the groom's suite, and the guys look good."

I didn't even see Jameson trying to horn in on the shot with a bottle of beer in hand, and that was a nice surprise.

"I can't wait to be married to Parker," Caroline says, with a rare sort of girlish vulnerability in her voice that's lovely to hear. She turns to the videographer next, looking the lens dead-on as she talks to her audience. "And my sister is the reason everything is coming together. She's helped me with every detail. She is a badass babe who lives life on her terms, just like I tell you all that you should do. Live the life you've imagined." She turns back to me. "Remy, are you living the life you imagined?"

Oh. I didn't know she was going to toss that question to me on the live stream, but I do my best to catch it.

"Answer honestly," Caroline continues, then turns to the camera again. "You can always tell my sister is bluffing if she blushes."

"Like beet red," Mom says, playfully ganging up on me.

My face isn't blushing at all when I say, "Can confirm."

It's true enough.

I *am* finally chasing the job I can imagine myself in. But there's that little matter of the lie of my romance, and the reason for it. I glance away from the camera, lest my cheeks pinken from the thoughts of the falsehood I'm fabricating for them.

I run a finger along the smooth metal surface of the watch Lake gave me—a reminder that appearances can become real. It settles my nerves.

I turn back to my sister, my mother, and Fallon, scanning their faces for any evidence that they saw through me.

I don't see it.

"I should go meet Lake," I tell them, since he texted me a few minutes ago that he was almost here. "I'll pop into the ballroom on the way back for the floral check."

"One of the videographers will be there in the doorway. She'll be in peach."

"Of course." I smooth a hand over my black maid of honor

dress, then leave to meet my plus-one. It's a relief to escape the cameras for a bit.

I dart down the hall, lined with champagne roses as far as the eye can see. Pulling up my skirt, I race-walk to meet Lake at the front entrance when Jameson pops out of the groom's suite, uncharacteristically wobbly on his feet.

"Hey, Remy. Would now be a good time to talk about the best-man toast?" His words are a little slurry, but his smile still friendly. Or performatively friendly. "You were busy yesterday at the spa."

I flash him a smile that I don't mean. "I'm still busy."

"I totally get it," he says, laying on the charm. "But listen, I know this wedding is a big deal with the live stream and all, so I just wanted to let you know I'll be giving the best man speech with my own brew." He taps the bottle in his hand.

Screw smiling. "No!"

"Remy," he says, all playful and too sweet. "I didn't have to ask for permission. I'm doing it to be nice. And who cares if I use champagne or beer, right? Everything will still go perfectly. I know that's important to you, so I wanted to give you a heads-up. Cool?"

My blood boils. He thinks by giving me a heads-up that I'll play along? Like my desire for things to go smoothly is stronger than my protection of my sister from being used? He dumped the wrong woman then.

"The answer is still no. Caroline has a sponsor for her wedding, and it's not your brewery. This isn't about product placement."

He tilts his head. "Can't we talk about it as friends and all?"

"We're not friends, and we don't actually need to talk."

He waggles his phone at me. "Don't we though?"

What is he going on about? "Jameson, you can't do this. It's that simple. I need to go get Lake."

"I imagine you do," he says with a knowing smirk I want to wipe off his face.

I snap my gaze away from him, beelining to the front entrance and trying to shake off that uncomfortable encounter, and this foreboding feeling nipping at my ankles. And I do forget it momentarily as Lake pushes through the revolving door.

My heart speeds up. He's so staggeringly handsome in his dark sapphire suit that hugs his muscular frame, his short hair that he cut for me, that trim beard that sends sparks across my thighs when he rubs it against me, and his cool blue eyes, intense and vulnerable and locked on me.

Memories of last night crash back into me, and I reel from the emotions that rushed through me as we came together. Maybe Caroline was right. Maybe romance can happen on its own terms, in its own time.

Maybe a rebound can become something more.

I hope.

I walk right over to him, grab the lapels of his suit jacket, and speak from the heart. "You look amazing."

His eyes roam over me. "So do you," he says, his voice a raw scrape. "You're just...wow."

I reach for his hand, and he sighs happily. Like all he's wanted is for me to take it. We walk back through the hallway.

"I need to slip inside the ballroom where the ceremony's being held to check on things," I say, "and then it'll probably be a little chaotic."

He stops walking, spinning me around and tugging me toward him.

"What is it?" I ask.

He's quiet though. Just squeezes my hand, like he's sending me a private message. A new sense of calm floods me. This is the man I shared a secret with. This is the man I learned to trust. This man makes me feel...like myself.

I squeeze back and he draws a deep breath, squares his shoulders and shakes his head as he looks me over, like he can't believe his eyes. "I was going to wait till tonight, but seeing you now—I can't wait to ask you something."

My pulse spikes, half in worry, half in excitement. I swallow past a knot of tension. "Ask me anything."

"Would you like to go—"

A harsh laugh slices through the air. I jerk my gaze away from Lake, whirling around to face the noise behind me.

My ex leans against the wall, in the corner of the hallway several feet away, holding a beer bottle and his phone while sporting a closed-mouth smile that reeks of arrogance.

The hair on the back of my neck stands on end, but I try to ignore it and to ignore this twisting in my chest.

"Let's go," I say to Lake.

"No, let's stay," Jameson says, pushing off the wall. "So I can hear what you two have planned for your next performance. I've been dying for this moment since I saw the comments on the photo."

I freeze, all the color draining from my face.

"Oh, you're probably wondering how I know, right?"

"What are you talking about?" I ask, my neck flushing hot as I lie.

"Maybe stop talking," Lake cuts in, stepping closer to Jameson.

My ex cackles, his breath smelling of beer. "A picture's worth a thousand words. Or really, a comment is." He shoves his phone toward us. I study the image of Lake and me from last night at the game, him blowing a kiss my way. When my gaze swings to the comment, I haul in a stuttered breath. There's a comment from Jameson saying *That's so interesting.*

And it's right under one from Cedric.

The innkeeper in Evergreen Falls. The guy who checked us into the Chestnut Inn. We claimed we were friends, then told Cedric we'd become more.

With dread swirling in every cell I read Cedric's comment. It's harmless, really. A sweet, supportive remark. But I gulp because the damage is done.

Love this! And pretty sure I'm the guy responsible for taking these guys from friends to lovers! When they checked in at the Chestnut, they were definitely just friends...but like many of our guests, they left as something more.

I look up, my face hot.

Jameson grins, clearly pleased he's caught me in the act. "You were faking it with him all along, weren't you?"

I'm sick that he found out. That he, of all people, put it together.

Lake drops my hand to wrap an arm around me, holding me close. "There's nothing fake here," Lake says, firm and commanding.

Jameson rolls his eyes. "Touch her all you want. It's clear it's fake. Because why, Remy? You wanted to show me up? Prove you could get a date for the wedding before I did? Some friend you turned out to be."

He's awful. Absolutely horrid. What did I ever see in him? I scoff, ready to tell him off but another voice cuts in from behind me, stitched with worry and disappointment. "Is this true, Remy?"

My mother. My shoulders fall, and I go fire engine red as I whisper a feeble, "No."

But my mother's seen through the lie, and my own tell. She knows me too well. She raised me, after all, to fix relationships, so she can spot all the cracks too.

"It is true." She clasps a hand to her mouth, devastated I'd do this. Ashamed I'd trick her and my whole family.

"It's not fake," Lake says, squaring his shoulders, standing up for me over and over again.

But I feel even worse now that he's piling a lie upon a lie.

My mother lowers her hand, ignoring him, turning to me. "Why would you do this? You can just be honest."

Sometimes, you have to stop doubling down. You have to stop lying. You have to stop pretending. No matter how much a man defends you.

I take a breath, ready to face the truth. "Because—"

"You want to know why we faked it?" Lake cuts in, letting go of me, closing the distance between him and Jameson and getting right in his face. "Because *I* insisted on it," he bites out, taking all the blame once more, protecting me again. "Because you were such a dick to her. You're such a selfish ass all the time. Who does this? Who breaks up with someone on a Jumbotron? Who tries to be friends to pitch his beer at her sister's wedding? Who claims he wants to help make dating profiles? Then turns around and does this shit? Who shoves his stupid fucking beer in every picture? No one wants you crashing every photo. No one likes you. You're a fake and a fraud, and guess what, buddy?"

"What?" Jameson asks, apparently unable to shut up when he's buzzed.

"No one in the entire world wants beer at a bakery."

Jameson lunges for Lake, headfirst into the hockey player's chest, like he's wrestling. With barely an ounce of effort, Lake peels him off, pushes him back, and holds him at bay easily with one hand.

It's sexy as hell but also the exact opposite of what I wanted to happen today.

I'm the scene. I made a mess of my sister's wedding. This is the antithesis of a preemptive strike. I struck myself and my sister and my whole family.

But when I catch a flash of peach, my stomach drops. I turn around slowly, dread curling tight inside me as I spot the videographer in the ballroom door. She must have migrated down the hallway, blending in with the flowers, as she caught the authentic behind-the-scenes moments with Caroline's viewers' favorite subject—me.

She caught everything. And live streamed it for Caroline's audience.

It's official. Nothing in my life is private, and I just ruined my sister's wedding and, probably, my job prospects all in one short, heated minute.

Even worse? I've hurt Lake too. He's trying to protect me, but now his sweet, wounded father will know he lied. The man who doesn't leave the house. Who's facing his own demons. The man who's been rooting for the two of us.

In that one short, brutal minute, the tender piece of my heart that hoped a fake romance might become real breaks off. Once again, I'm the fool, but this time it's all my doing.

50

THE WORST MAN

REMY

It's official. Of all the worst-case outcomes I've ever envisioned, this one definitely takes the cake. But I'm a planner. A fixer. I've got to solve this problem, and that has to start with getting the half-drunk best man out of the way.

With my nerves frayed and my emotions raw, I lift my chin and say to the guy I'm so glad I'm not marrying, "Even if my romance was all fake, you need to go."

Okay, that's something. That's a start. I can keep fixing things for my sister.

But as the sound of shoes clicking down the hallway grows louder, Jameson rolls his eyes. "Yeah, I'll get out of here. I can't wait to tell Parker what you were trying to do to me. Bro code."

He wheels around with his stupid beer still in his hand and runs smack into...the bride.

I gasp as he wobbles, then plants his wing-tipped foot right on the train of my sister's wedding dress. He tumbles forward, ripping the train off her dress with a loud tear, his beer bottle toppling to the floor with a splash.

My heart craters. Just when you think things can't get

worse, the universe says, *Hold my beer so I can fucking spill it on a wedding dress.*

"Leave," I seethe as the commotion in the hallway grows. More footsteps.

Caroline stares down at the beer-stained dress with venom in her eyes. Then, as cool and collected as I've ever seen her, she looks up at him and whispers in a deadly voice, "I'm going to do something I should have done a long time ago."

Her groom appears, pulling up at her side. Parker's brow is furrowed; he looks pissed. I didn't know he had any expression on his face besides worship of my sister. He points to the dress, then to Jameson, then the dress again, and he says, "Did you just spill beer on my bride's wedding dress?"

Lake clears his throat, helpfully adding, "He also ripped the train."

Parker licks his lips, breathes out hard, then says, "You ruined our wedding and Caroline's dress. Also, I just watched the whole fucking live stream. What the hell is wrong with you? Get out."

Jameson whines, "But I'm your best man."

"No, you're officially the worst man," Caroline corrects coolly.

"And I will gladly see you out myself," Parker says, standing firm.

Lake raises his hand. "I could toss him out for you. I'd be happy to help."

Parker smiles again. "Thanks. Why don't you do that? I need to tend to my bride."

Lake grabs Jameson by the collar of his dress shirt and drags him down the hall as Caroline turns to Parker and says, "Sweetie, I should've told you a long time ago—but your best friend is a jerk. Also, that was the hottest thing you've ever done."

"I'm sorry I didn't do it sooner."

"I'm sorry I didn't do it when he broke my sister's heart," she says to him, and they're so loving, so doting, so clearly in love that it makes my heart soar for them but ache a little more for me.

"But now I need to fix this dress, stat," Caroline says. "Where's Margot? Fallon? Someone has to—"

I raise my hand. I do have a solution. "I have a dress for you."

51

A GOOD CRY

REMY

But I won't let myself bask in my sister's delight. Once we slip into the back of a town car with Mom, the cameras off, Fresh Face left behind, I take the next step. It's one I should have taken a while ago.

"Everything Jameson said was true. It was a fake romance. I'm sorry I didn't tell you the truth, but I wanted everything to go smoothly for the wedding. I didn't want the Jumbotron dump with Jameson to cause problems. But I was wrong," I say to them, and this excavation hurts, like someone is scraping out my insides. "In the end I did cause problems. Your dress, and the live stream, and lying to you both. And I'm so sorry. I wish there were something else I could say, but I made a mistake."

I'd like to say it's a relief to tell the truth at last. But mostly I'm sad. Disappointed. And heartbroken. I'm tired, too, of always keeping it together.

Across the seat, Caroline reaches for my hand and sets hers on mine, her huge diamond glinting in the sun streaming through the car windows. She tilts her head, her expression unusually gentle. "Why did you feel you had to fake it with me? Because of your ex?"

I wince, heat crawling up my neck. I don't want to lie again. "It seemed...easier."

"What do you mean?" She's soft, so rare for her.

"How could it be easier?" my mother chimes in, confusion in her eyes.

I half want them to be mad. But I'm so grateful they're not that a sob works its way up my chest. "I wanted to look like I was moving on," I admit, as my breath hitches, my voice breaking.

"Why didn't you just say that?" my mother asks, reaching for me too, setting a hand on my arm.

That's a good question. One I've asked myself often enough. I had ample opportunities to tell them it was fake. And I could answer them in a number of truthful ways. I could say I didn't want the secret to leak out. I didn't want Jameson to know. That once one person, aside from my best friends, knows everyone will know. Case in point—today.

But deep down, that's not why I kept the truth hidden. I face my fears head-on. "I wanted you all to think I was fine, to think I had it together. Like you two."

"Oh, sweetheart," my mother says, her lower lip quivering. "I hardly feel like I have it together at all."

I whip my gaze to her, arching a brow. "Come on, you do your brain games. You work out. You're retired from a successful business. You helped manage this wedding. You have everything together. You even got it all together with Dad," I say, then turn to my sister. "And you have the ultimate power-woman life. Your show, your employees—even your hair is perfect."

Caroline shakes her head. "Oh, Remy, I make mistakes every

day. I lost my shit on camera a few minutes ago, but that's just part of life. I've learned not to let those things get me down, and I'm sorry I told you to get a plus-one. I'm sorry I didn't handle this from the beginning by kicking Jameson out," she says, her eyes pleading with me. "I told you to strike first without thinking what it might turn into. I'm the one at fault. I pressured you to be responsible for my wedding going smoothly. That's on me."

Oh god. She's right. She does own her mistakes, immediately and completely.

"It's not your fault," I whisper, exonerating her.

"But it is," she says. "I treated you like a member of my team. I gave you a role to play. I expected key performance indicators. I'm so sorry."

My heart softens, even though it was never very hard toward her. I love her too much. "I didn't say no to you. I let my wishes for everything to go perfectly get the better of me. And I wanted it all to go so well today." I shift to my mother, as the car cruises closer to the Marina, the site of the wedding dress. And with everything out there, I share the hardest part of all —the part I haven't really ever said to her. I swallow roughly. "Just like I wanted everything to work out for you and Dad. Like when I was trying to keep you together as a kid. When I planned all those dates for you, the dinner and the candlelight and the games. All I have ever wanted was for you guys to stay together. I knew you were struggling."

It feels like rubbing sandpaper against my heart.

My mother frowns, shaking her head. "Oh, sweetheart, I'm sorry I made you feel that you had to do that. And I know maybe it seemed like we stayed together because of all of your planning and your dates, but honestly it was because we realized we'd raised such great kids and that they were a team worth fighting for. It wasn't because of the candlelight, the games, or the dinners. It was because of the hard things. And

I've probably been hard on you, and I'm sorry for that. I truly am."

My heart doesn't feel like it's being scoured. It feels like it's being held by someone who cares.

"It's okay. We can start over."

She wraps an arm around me, hugging me in the back seat of the car, Caroline getting in on it too as a good group cry turns into a group hug.

* * *

I hold my breath as I zip up the dress.

"Let this be my glass slipper moment," Caroline whispers, adjusting the lacy bodice.

I reach the top of the zipper and my shoulders relax since it's nice and snug. It fits perfectly.

I turn her around and gasp. "It's even better."

My mother nods. "She's right. It's simple and lovely."

"And it doesn't smell like beer or have a train," Caroline says, then sighs like she's settling into a bubble bath.

But it hardly lasts. She jerks her gaze to me. "Why did you have this again?"

That's a whole other story, but as she hustles to my bathroom and fixes her makeup, I tell them about the store, the estate items, and the list. "I think I wanted our relationship to be real," I admit quietly.

"Well, why can't it be?" Caroline asks, since of course in her world she'd march up to Lake and say, *"It's real. Deal with it."*

But I'm still me. I'm not her. You don't change that quickly. "Because it was fake. Things don't work out that way. Sometimes you get a dress and it fits perfectly. But most of the time, fake romances don't become real."

My mother squeezes my shoulder. "Maybe it could be."

Maybe, but truly for now, I need to focus on them. My final romance design. "I quit being a romance designer," I tell them, since this is evidently the day of confessions.

As Caroline brushes on pretty pink blush, I tell them more.

And once she's done, we take turns touching up our makeup.

"For what it's worth, you're pretty great at events," Caroline says.

"I'm *not* going to be a wedding planner," I say.

My mother laughs. "It wasn't the worst job."

"But it would be for me."

"And that I understand. Now let's get your sister down the aisle."

And we leave, but when we return to the hotel, Caroline holds up a finger and says, "There's one more thing I need to do."

She marches over to Fallon and says, "Cut the live stream."

Then she walks down the aisle in front of friends and family and marries the man who adores her while I steal glances at the hockey star in the front row, wishing I could do what Caroline would do.

But Lake's words from earlier repeat in my head. *You want to know why we faked it? I insisted on it. Because you were such a dick to her.*

He finally admitted it was fake in front of everyone to save me. But he didn't say it was real. Maybe someday I'll be strong enough to walk over to him, grab his collar and say *be mine* like I mean it.

But not today.

* * *

That night, as the DJ plays a Frank Sinatra song, Lake asks me to dance. I take his hand, my heart aching with so much longing. So much wishing.

He brings me to the dance floor, among the other couples: my mother and father, Parker and Caroline, and so many others. My throat tightens as I meet his blue eyes. They're searching mine, like he's looking desperately for something, hoping to find it.

But what?

As we sway, he parts his lips, and says, "That was…a wild day."

"It was. And you have been the best fake boyfriend ever. So thank you."

He tenses for a second or two. Maybe more. Then he presses a kiss to my forehead, his voice tight as he says, "You deserve everything."

But what I want most is you. And I want so badly for him to ask me to stay the night at his place. Just one more night where we're together.

But his motivation to fake date me is gone.

And now my heart is breaking for real.

It's shattered in a fresh and painful way, so much worse than when I was dumped on a Jumbotron.

This time, I ache everywhere.

I keep those thoughts locked up, where they're safe.

52

THE TIME I WENT ON TOUR

REMY

I peel off my maid of honor dress before midnight and hang it up in the closet, finding just the right spot, then running a hand down it since I don't want to let go of it.

I miss Lake so much. But I have to move on.

Turning around, I tug on a T-shirt and leggings, but I don't get into bed.

I get to work.

I worked after Jameson broke up with me publicly.

This time, though, I don't need work for a hideout. I need it for a future. I stay up late, researching, outlining, planning.

Rome wasn't built in a day, and this PowerPoint won't be either.

But I can start a new foundation, even while this missing burrows under my skin.

* * *

I'm a bit of a broken record, but I have to answer for the con job. The next day I sit across from Daniel at lunch at Happy Cow, a restaurant in Hayes Valley, and say the words that might as well be tattooed on my tongue. "I'm sorry I didn't tell you."

Daniel drags a hand through his sleek hair and laughs. It sounds self-deprecating. "I gotta say, I have a pretty good bull-shit detector, and I didn't see that coming."

Yeah, I thought it was going to be real too. "I should have told you. As a friend. Not just as a boss," I say, wishing I didn't have to produce so many *mea culpas*, but knowing that's the price I have to pay.

He holds up a hand. "Actually, you don't need to tell me if it's fake or real as a boss. That's not really anyone's business at work. But you're right. I think of you as a friend, and I feel a little misled."

I take that on the chin. "That's fair. I understand," I say, folding and unfolding the napkin on the table.

"Make that a lot," he admits quietly, his brow knitting. "I was rooting for you two. As a couple, I felt like every time we talked about it, we were..." He sighs, his mouth turned down, "Speaking the same language. I gave you advice. I wanted to see it work out for you because I care about you. I asked how it was going as a friend."

His disappointment is the sharp edge of a knife. I let so many people down. "I know. And it probably doesn't matter that it felt like I was speaking the truth. Since even though it started as fake, it became real for me."

"Oh, Remy," he says, shifting gears, his voice filled with sympathy. "That's rough."

But this meeting isn't about him feeling bad for me. My throat tightens and tears prick the back of my eyes, but I hold my head up high, choosing honesty over perfect appearances. "I could've told you the truth. I don't have an excuse, except that it was fake and we were trying to make sure nobody would find out. I was going to tell you all this the other day, including that I had feelings for him, but I didn't, so my intentions don't really matter."

"I get it. Love is...hard. Really hard."

A mirthless laugh escapes me. "It honestly is."

There's a pause, heavy, uncomfortable, as servers circulate around the table, depositing plates of pasta and sandwiches and taking orders. Doing all these normal things, while I try to claw my way out of a hole that I shoveled myself into.

"I guess we should still talk about the job though," he says, but his voice sounds flat. This lunch feels obligatory. Daniel is a man of his word. He promised he'd talk to me about the full-time position and he's doing just that. That doesn't mean I'm going to get the job. Or keep mine.

Still, he's here, and the floor is mine. "I'd like to be considered for it," I say, because you can't always clean up your messes before people see them. Sometimes you clean them up in front of other people. "I understand you probably aren't even considering me now, but I want you to know I've already put together all the concepts for the Hockey Is for Everyone initiative. I finished it last night."

He blinks a few times. "You did? I only told you about it a few days ago."

"I was excited. I worked on it in between other things. I'm very efficient." I started it right away, working on it the night he told me about the initiative, then the next day, right through to last night. "It's not complete, but I think it'll give you a good start. I know this is just part of my regular job, and I hope that I can keep that too, but even if I can't, even if you need to let me go, I believe in the mission and I want whoever gets the job to be able to execute this initiative," I say, and then I take out my phone and I hit send. "It's yours now for whatever you want to do with it."

After an awkward meal, we return to the office and go our

separate ways. I try not to look at the locker room, the rink, the equipment room. Not that I'd see Lake anyway. The team flew to Los Angeles today for a game tomorrow afternoon. It's for the best.

If I ran into him here, I don't know what I'd say or do. Instead, I work, keenly aware the whole time that it might be one of my last days in this arena.

And the whole time, I'm missing Lake and what I thought we were becoming.

* * *

I'm almost done with my tour of truth. That's what Clem and Mabel call it in our group chat.

Clementine: Are you doing it today?

Mabel: We should celebrate afterward.

Remy: Oh yeah, I'm totally in the mood to celebrate.

Mabel: Cookies are always a good idea.

Clementine: Facts.

Remy: And yes, I'm ready. I'm at her office now.

It's Tuesday afternoon. I've finished work for the day, and the team is losing to Los Angeles. I've heard nothing from Daniel all day about the job, and I'm pretty sure he's been interviewing other candidates based on the tailored blouses and slacks and sports jacket attire I've seen from those heading into his office on and off throughout the day.

I can't control what he decides.

But I can control what I do next.

And when I sink down on Elena's cushy gray couch, my gaze straying briefly to the painting of the snowy cabin above her head, I rip off the Band-Aid.

"I haven't been truthful with you."

"Oh?" The question is asked with curiosity and without judgment.

And I tell her everything about my romance with Lake, how it started, and how it ended.

A small, pleased smile shifts her lips.

"Why are you smiling?" I ask.

"Because you're being upfront. That's how we start."

A start. A real start. "Okay. I'll keep being honest."

"Not just with me though. With others. Like Lake. Do you think you were honest with him?"

It's like a kick in the gut even though I don't think she meant it that way.

Because the answer is no.

53

SUPPOSED TO BE

LAKE

My lungs are burning, my thighs are screaming, and my shoulders want to murder me. I've been knocked into the boards more times than I want to count, and I've got nothing to show for it. We're still scoreless in a rough, messy game. I've missed shot after shot.

I chase the puck with one minute left on the clock, hoping for a goddamn miracle—both in the game and in me. But I don't know that I can do what I've done in the past: Put all my emotions into the game. Because there's someplace else they want to be. *With her.*

She's where I want to be.

But I'm here on the ice, so I line up and take a swing. Their goalie blocks it like it's nothing. The clock eats up the rest of the minute, and we trudge off the ice to the visitor locker room. I toss my gloves on the bench, yank off my helmet, and try to rub out the knot of tension in my neck.

Riggs pats me on the back. "We'll get them next time," he says.

The guys have been nice to me. Because they know. They

saw the blowup, the admission, the beer on the dress. They watched the stupid live stream.

I've barely said a word though. I grumble something like "thanks," then hit the shower, stewing in my aloneness once again.

I'm good at that. Being alone.

It's where I've been for the last three years.

I'm an expert at going solo. I could teach a master class. So I should be able to handle this—the inevitable end of a fake romance.

Too bad my chest is hollow, and it aches more than my bruised body.

Soon I'm boarding the team jet so we can fly back to San Francisco, but as I slog up the steps to the plane, dread coils in my stomach. I have to face my father for the first time since the wedding.

He doesn't know what happened. Shocker: he doesn't watch advice shows that are live streamed. He likes the *Property Brothers* and sports.

When I reach the cushy faux leather chair in the second row, I sink down into it, my jaw tight, my mind a traffic snarl.

Corbin pops up behind me, Miller in front of me, Ivan in the aisle, Riggs by my side.

"Is this a clown car?"

No one takes the bait.

"Dude, what are you gonna do?" The blunt question comes from Miller. And it's a valid one.

And I could blow them off, make a snarky comment, grump my way out of the conversation.

But I'm tired of being lonely, I'm worn out from my own inner grouch, I'm exhausted from thinking only of her. "Besides pay all you assholes?"

It's an admission, all right. They won the bet. I fell ass over skates in love.

Ivan gives me a wise look—the look of a happily married man. "You could just tell her."

Is she even ready, though, for all these fucking feelings inside me? Does she need a guy like me who's madly, outrageously, ridiculously in love with her when she's a mere month and a half out of a toxic relationship? I can't just be a rebound with her. I can't take it day by day. I can't be casual. I want everything. "She broke up with that fucknozzle less than two months ago," I say, like that proves my point. "And the night of the wedding, she thanked me for being a good boyfriend—that was it. She acknowledged it was fake. I was only ever supposed to be a rebound."

Corbin gives a so-what shrug. "'Supposed to be' doesn't really matter, does it?"

Hmm. Maybe he's onto something.

"And maybe let her make that decision about what she wants," Riggs says.

And dammit. He has a point too.

"Pretty sure she can't do that though unless you tell her," Miller adds.

And I hate that they're right.

* * *

But first things first. I pull into the gravel driveway late, clocking that the light's on in the living room. A weight settles into my gut, but I have to tell my dad now. I have to let him down. He'll be so destroyed. He liked Remy so much.

Well, get in line.

I'm heading up the porch steps, mentally prepping, when

somebody inside opens the door. Holy shit. It's my father. He never opens the door. It's too close to outside.

"What is going on?" I ask with some trepidation.

He gives a cheeky grin. "I wanted to open the door for my son. Anything wrong with that?"

Something dangerous like hope swells up inside me, but I tamp it down. I've been hopeful before. I don't need to be hopeful again. "How's everything going?" I ask, stepping inside.

"I'm okay. But are you? That was a tough game."

"Yeah, it was," I say, and then I shut the door and follow him to the kitchen table. He gestures to two plates, each one holding a sandwich on thick, seeded bread—my favorite.

"Figured you'd be hungry. Made you a sandwich," he says, and I'm pretty sure it's the fake bologna Remy turned him onto. For some reason, that makes my heart hurt even more.

"I'm ravenous," I say, then bite into it. "This is good," I admit.

"Told you so."

No matter how good the sandwich is or how hungry I am, I need to face the music. I set the sandwich down. "Dad, I'm not with Remy anymore. We were just faking it for her terrible ex-boyfriend."

His brow furrows. "Faking? Is that a new thing your generation does? Like 'situationships' or 'cuffing' or something?"

A smile tugs at my lips. I can't believe my dad is using those words, let alone knows them. "No. My point is I was lying to you all along. She's not my girlfriend. We were doing it for her sister's wedding. To stick it to her ex," I say, but that's hardly the truth. Ah, hell. This is harder than I'd thought. "And I wanted to make you happy. I knew it would make you happy if I were seeing someone."

He pauses, giving that some thought. "Bullshit."

I blink. "What?"

"Bullshit you were doing it for me."

This is not how this was supposed to go. He was supposed to be disappointed. Instead, he sits taller and looks me right in the eyes. "I don't think you were faking it."

I swallow awkwardly, unsure what's happening. "You're not going to give me a hard time over lying to you?"

"No, because you weren't lying to me."

"I was, Dad," I insist.

He shakes his head. "I saw the two of you together. You can say you were faking it all you want, but you weren't. You fell for her, and I'm pretty sure she fell for you too."

I can't resist picking up that last one. I'm such a sucker for her. "How do you know?" I ask, my voice pitching up.

"She wanted to meet your father. She gave you a gift to give me. She talked to me at the house. She talked to me about her ex. And she talked to me about how to be brave."

That kernel of hope wiggles through me. Tempting. Alluring. "How?" I ask, quiet, careful, like if I talk too loud, the fragile possibility might disappear.

"I made an appointment to see a therapist."

It's a rocket that just launched me into another galaxy. This thing I've been wanting for years. My heart soars. "Are you serious?"

"It's an online appointment. I'm going to start that way, but she talked about how she likes to control her environment, how she tries to make sure everything's just right. But how therapy helped her to face her stuff." He stops, closes his eyes like this pains him, then opens them. "That forced me to realize I'm doing the same thing. And I need to face my fears."

I reach across the table and wrap my arms around him, choking up. "I'm so proud of you."

"It's about time," he says, his voice breaking too.

"You're brave," I tell him as I let go.

He's quiet, as if he's giving that some thought. "You can be brave too."

I flash back over the last month or so. The date at Costco. The puzzle shop. The haircut. The kiss in the dress shop. The list. The nap date. The road trip. The secrets we shared. The way she talked to me, the way she trusted me, the way we came together.

She's done more than build me a cat tower. She's shared her secrets; she's let go with me. And, most of all, she's helped my father.

She's the most real thing to happen to me in years.

I've always operated on instinct on the ice. Off the ice, I've protected myself. But maybe I ought to trust my instincts because I know—I absolutely *know* there was nothing fake between us.

If I do nothing, I'm just one of those guys who's not worth the effort.

But Remy is worth all the effort. And I'm not one of those guys.

54

A GLASS SLIPPER

REMY

Elena's question shadows me that night, and into the next morning as I wake early. I'm not due at the arena for a couple of hours, but I might as well head over soon. I have a few VIP tours to lead today, so that'll keep me busy as I ponder Elena's words.

I hop on the bus, but on my way to work, a powerful feeling stops me from stepping into the arena.

Something unfinished.

Something I've held close in a bag inside a bag for more than a week.

The list.

I peer outside at the street signs, then quickly google the hours for the dress shop. The store is already open for the day. I pull the cord, then hop off the bus and race-walk through Hayes Valley to Champagne Taste. I push open the door, the soft floral perfume drifting past my nose, and the torch singer tunes floating past my ears.

The shopkeeper looks up from her work at the counter, recognition in her eyes. "Hi, love. How was your sister's wedding?"

I pause, thinking on that. "It was great in the end. She had the wedding she wanted."

"Wonderful." A pause. "And the list?"

She's so warm and so direct. I walk over to her, like there's an invisible line connecting us, like this store is the final stop on my *tour* and I didn't realize it till this morning.

"We did the list. Well, four out of the five items."

"That surprises me. You two seemed just right; that's why I left it for you," she says, her eyes flooding with sadness.

I stop in my tracks. "You mean it wasn't random? Finding the dress?"

She shakes her head. "No, love. It wasn't happenstance that *you* found it. I left the dress out for you two. I saw the video from the arena. And when you walked into the store with him, and he went to the dressing room and kissed you like he meant it—I just knew. And I wanted my niece's list to wind up in the right hands."

My heart lurches. The breath leaves my lungs. "She was your niece?"

"Yes. Her name was Katrina," she says, her voice catching.

Not our made-up name of Lacey, but Katrina. A real name for a real person with real wishes.

"She died before she could get married. Before she could do those five things before she said I do. I wanted the list to go to someone who understood...well, love."

"I'm so sorry for your loss," I say before I can even process her words about us and love.

"Me too. She never got her chance to do all those things."

But I'm here. I have the chance. I can't waste it. "I think I needed to know that," I whisper, and even though we haven't finished the list, I understand what's unfinished for me.

Before I go, I need to help this woman move along on her

journey. I take out my phone, click to the camera roll and say, "My sister wore the wedding dress from Katrina. She looked beautiful. It saved her wedding day. Do you want to see the pictures?"

The woman chokes up, nodding through tears. I show her the images of Caroline and tell her the story. "It fit like a glass slipper."

She manages a smile through her grief. "Like I said, it wasn't happenstance. It was meant for you."

And I'm pretty sure Lake is meant for me too.

On the way to work, I call my friends—one big group call. "How do I do it? How do I tell him?"

Clementine laughs dryly. "This from the woman who just gave up planning romantic moments."

"Yes, exactly. Ironic, isn't it?" My hands tremble. This is putting myself out there for real. This is the big risk. "But seriously. What do I do? Or say?"

Mabel jumps in. "You just have to wing it. Embrace your new inner impulsive side. Let the anti-planner in you take over."

"What she said," Trevyn adds.

"Do I even have an anti-planner in me?" I ask, meaning it.

"I vote for doing it after work. Keep it simple. Go to his house and tell him there," Skylar says, laying it out like it's a set of IKEA furniture assembly instructions—this anti-planned moment.

But really, that's the key. "It's time to stop overthinking," I say.

"Ding, ding, ding," Clementine says, like she's proud of me.

"I can do this," I say.

"Of course you can," Mabel adds in that supportive tone of hers.

"Girl, we'll be cheering you on," Trevyn says.

I picture them doing just that. And it's a great image.

The fear of being fooled rears its head, but I'm stronger than my fears. Tougher than my anxiety. And finally ready to take a chance.

His house. Tonight. No more planning.

55

A NEW ROMANCE DESIGNER IN TOWN

LAKE

A man can't win a woman's heart all by himself. Sometimes, he needs help. Like a whole team.

And someone else too. The second I arrive at the arena after a very busy morning taking care of some important stuff, I head straight to see Daniel, making sure to avoid the entrance to Remy's work area. Don't want her to see me yet, especially since I have no reason to be at the arena, with no game or practice scheduled.

Well, no reason she knows about, anyway.

I stop for a second outside his office, smoothing a hand over my shirt. It's a dress shirt—the color of the suit I wore to the wedding. The color she loves. But this is so weird. I don't ask for help. I need it though, so even if I feel like I'm wearing shoes too tight, I knock on his door.

He looks up, brow furrowed. I've never come to his office before.

He quickly smiles, always the professional. "What can I do for you?"

I sit down, blow out a breath, scrub a hand across my beard, then say, "Think you can help me with Remy?"

His eyes twinkle. “How?” His tone is dripping with intrigue.

Remy might have moved on from being a romance designer, but she still loves romance. More so, she deserves it. “Is she doing a tour today?”

“Yes, a few.”

“I had a feeling. I saw the schedule for tours by the locker room. And I need this to be big. I need her to know she’s the one. I need you to keep her in the arena after her last tour. Can you do that?”

His lips twitch. “So I’m like the romance designer now?”

If he wants a title, he’ll earn it with what I need him to do. “Yes. Daniel the romance designer.”

He leans forward, wiggling his fingers. “Give me the brief.”

After I tell him the details, he nods like a soldier, and says, “I’m on it.”

That’s just the start though. After I thank him, I head downstairs, my phone buzzing with a text.

I grab it so fast. It’s Remy, and my heart jackrabbits.

> Remy: Are you around tonight? I was hoping to come over after work.

I don’t know if that’s good or bad, but the answer is always yes. I send a reply letting her know I’ll be at the apartment, then find the guys in the locker room and give them their assignments.

“Can I watch?” Miller asks. “Since I came in on my day off.”

“Me too,” Riggs says.

"Same here," Corbin adds.

"I'm totally watching," Ivan adds.

I roll my eyes. "Obviously."

But that's okay. I asked them for help, and they're giving it. And hell, do I ever need it.

56

A LITTLE HUMMINGBIRD TOLD ME

REMY

"And that's how you ride a Zamboni," I say, as cheerful as ever, even as I try to subtly shoo the VIP guests from the literacy organization out of the rink. "So glad you enjoyed the tour."

I motion for them to head to the tunnel when I catch the silhouette of a man entering it. Is it Lake? But he's not even here today.

The figure steps out to the ice—it's Daniel.

"Thanks, Remy," he calls to me. "I'll escort them back to the exit. If you can just wait for me behind the players' bench, that'd be great."

I blink. Why would he want me to do that? Is he going to can me? Give me a talking to? I don't know that I want to face another hard thing today when I'm already planning on facing the hardest thing of all in, say, an hour when I head to Lake's home.

Nerves tap dance across my skin, but I try to ignore them as I say, "Of course."

Like I've been chastened, I return to the ice alone, walking carefully across it to the gate that leads to the stands. I climb up into the seats, picking a row behind the players' bench.

And I wait.

I don't dare look at my phone. I don't want to be distracted when Daniel returns to talk to me. I just sit, the chill enveloping me. I fold my arms across my chest and look around the arena at the suites on the upper levels, the press box, the food concourse, the ice itself.

Wait. Is that Miller over by the home team's tunnel?

He's wearing his jersey and jeans. I lift a hand to wave, but he's turned the other way, his back to me.

Okay, weird.

Is he going to be here for my chat with Daniel? I squint at the other tunnel. Riggs looms in it, his back to me as well.

My gaze swings around the arena, and I spot Ivan and Corbin guarding other entrances.

What is going on? My pulse speeds up, not with worry, but with questions. Why are they here?

The cut of blades through ice slices through the silence as someone flies onto the rink in jeans and a jersey. It's Lake speeding onto the rink in skates, stick in one hand, a sack of some sort tossed over his shoulder.

My mouth falls open and my skin warms. He's here.

"Lake!" I call out. Maybe I'll tell him now. Maybe I'll tell him here. No time like the present.

He's quiet though. He stops at center ice, nods to me, then dips his hand into the sack. One by one, he takes out several stuffed foxes.

My breath catches.

I roll my lips together.

He lifts his stick, takes aim at the first one, and launches it right to me.

I'm not athletic, not at all. But I manage to grab it in the air, and study it. The fox is holding a card with one word written on it.

Go.

I clutch it tight to my chest, hope sparking inside of me.

He lines up for another shot. Swings his stick. Sends it to me.

On.

I smother a smile but then stop hiding it. I can be happy. I can let him see I'm giddy. I can encourage him.

"More!" I shout, hope spiraling high.

He seems to fight off a smile too, as he sends the next one my way.

A.

"Another," I say, elated.

He hits one more, then the next one in quick succession. I rip open the cards.

Real.

Date.

"Yes," I call out, even though there are several more foxes.

"I'm not done," he says, the first words he's uttered.

"The answer is still yes."

His smile fills my whole entire soul. It's rare to see, and usually it's just for me. I cherish it like I cherish him.

He hits the rest of the foxes my way, and when he's done, I'm over the moon as I read them all.

Go on a real date with your ex fake boyfriend who loves ***you.***

The second I open the *you* card, I'm up and rushing to the ice, climbing over the row, racing to the bench. "I love you. For real. It's all real. I want us to be together."

He scoops me up in his arms and pulls me onto the ice, sets me down, and wraps his hands around my waist. "I love you so much, Remy. So much I don't even know what to do with all these feelings. I hope it's not too much for you. But god, I just want to love you. Let me. Please let me."

He sounds so desperate, so hopeful, and it's such a gift to receive all his love.

I cup his cheeks, and it's been just a few days, but it's been too long. I've missed his stubble, his scent, his mouth, *him.* "You're all I want."

I kiss him, soft and tender and real, showing him that everything is real for me.

When I break the kiss, he looks woozy, drunk on me. "I should have said something at the wedding. It's been hell without you."

"I should have too. I'm sorry I didn't. I was so scared I'd misunderstood what was happening."

"Fuck, I've missed you. I love you. I need you," he says, then tucks his finger under my chin, like he did that first night. "And just so it's clear..." He stops talking and lifts up the hem of his jersey. My hand flies to my mouth. On his stomach is a brand-new tattoo. A pretty, delicate line work of a hummingbird. "For you."

And I fall even more in love with my very real boyfriend.

57

NUMBER FIVE

LAKE

Remy can't stop staring at my new ink as she rides my cock. She rises up and down, owning my body and my mind as she admires the new lines on my abs. It's mind-bending: the feel of her, the heat of her, and the *care*. The way she's mesmerized by the tattoo, all while she chases her pleasure.

The bed shakes. The headboard creaks. She moans. I growl. Electricity shoots down my spine, like a fuse is lit and crackling. Just a few more moments before it explodes.

I grip her hips, pull her down tighter, harder.

She rocks her hips, taking me deeper and nearly touching the hummingbird the entire time.

The makeup sex is almost, *almost*, worth the three miserable days apart.

"Love this," she mutters as she gestures to the bird's wings.

"Love you," I bite out.

I slide my hand between her thighs, helping her along.

Her breath hitches, then she cries out. A shudder wracks her body, and she plants her hands flat on my pecs as she comes, her hair spilling across my chest.

It's breathtaking, soul-stealing. It's the best thing I've ever felt. *Her.* Letting go for me.

"Need to get closer to you," I mutter as I flip her to her back, slide back in, and sink to my forearms, bracketing her face. "Wrap your legs around me."

She complies, giving me what I need, hooking her ankles around my back. Yes, this is what I need—her as close as can be. The edge of pleasure slices through me, sharp and hot.

We're limbs and heat and sweat as I move in her till an orgasm seizes all my thoughts, taking me hostage to the only place I want to be—with her.

I collapse onto her, panting, moaning, and still needing so much more.

I press quiet kisses to her neck, inhaling her scent, memorizing her again and again. "I meant it, Remy," I say, the words spilling out.

"When you said you loved me?"

"Yes, but also the night I hinted I'd been into you," I admit, then ease out of her. "Early on when I drove you home one night and told you my friends knew I liked you."

"I remember. When you said you *could be...into me*?" she asks, a soft surprise in her voice.

"I think I was trying to tell you something then but failing."

She runs her fingers down my slick back, making me shiver. "You just weren't ready then, and that's okay. I probably wasn't ready to hear it."

"You are now?"

She nods, a bright, buoyant smile tipping her lips. "Very, very ready."

Timing is a funny thing. You think you can control time, you think you can manage your emotions, you think you can protect your heart. But then someone comes along and knocks your world off-kilter. Challenges you. Accepts you. Loves you. I should tell her those things. Not just let them kick around in my brain. "You're it for me," I say, a bare admission.

She holds my face, her eyes shining. "Thank you for insisting on me."

"I always will." I let out a contented sigh, then glance down at us. "Better clean up."

"Might as well shower together."

That sounds like an excellent idea.

Twenty minutes and a couple more orgasms later, we're back in my bed, Remy in a T-shirt of mine that hits near her knees. It's perfect. I roam my hand down her arm. "So about that real date."

She turns toward me, happiness flickering in her brown eyes. "What about it?"

"It'll be number five on the list."

She tenses, then lifts a finger in warning. "It better be glamping."

I drop a kiss to her forehead. "Beautiful, I know you."

She ropes her arm around my neck. "I know."

Then she settles into my arms, breathes easily, and says, "I still don't like naps."

I laugh, kiss her head, and say, "And I know that too."

I hold her close, and for the first time, I'm aware that hockey isn't my one true love. She is.

My mind starts to drift when there's a clatter in the other room, then the scrabble of paws against hardwood, and a few seconds later, a big Siamese flies onto the bed, knocking pillows out of the way.

"Way to make an entrance, Thor," I say.

"He's really not subtle."

"It's definitely not his strong suit," I say, as the creature curls up on Remy's pillow, wrapping himself around her head. It's a claiming, like he's saying *she's mine.*

I get it, Thor. I really do.

* * *

When Friday rolls around, I pick her up at the arena at the end of her work day. We had a game last night—we won, thank you very much to me for the game-winning goal. And I've got a night off before we need to leave for a road trip. So I'm taking the love of my life to finish the list.

She hops in the car, her overnight bag already packed. Thor is hanging out with my dad, likely messing up his puzzles and landing on his plates.

"You look stunning," I tell her, drinking in the sight of her lush chestnut hair, her bright smile, her kind eyes. I reach for her silver sun charm, touching it, touching her.

"So do you," she says, then drops a kiss on my lips.

It's like a shot of happiness straight to my veins, and with it fueling me, I drive up the coast to a little town where we check into a treehouse hotel in the middle of an old-growth forest.

I gesture to the small cabin several feet above us, nestled high in the redwoods. "See? It has indoor plumbing, a shower, and a deck."

She turns to me, grabs my collar, and kisses me hard. "You're the best boyfriend ever."

"That's true," I say, without any sarcasm or irony. It is true. I am. Because she deserves the best.

That night, we settle into sleeping bags on the deck, under the stars.

"We did it," she says. "We finished Katrina's list. I wonder why she had this one on it."

She told me about the time she returned to the store,

learned Katrina's name, and the story behind the list. But we don't know the *why* behind each item. I noodle on her question as I run my fingers through her hair. "Maybe because it gives you perspective on what really matters."

She turns to me, her hand on my chest. "The people you love."

We're quiet for a minute or two, just listening to the sounds of nature as the night sky covers us. Out of the corner of my eye, I catch something. The flicker of wings. A silent flight. "Look," I whisper with urgency, pointing to a branch twenty feet above us where an owl has landed silently, stealthily.

"You summoned an owl," she says.

And I laugh. "Yes, Remy. I'm an owl whisperer."

But I lose interest in the owl when she tugs me closer and pulls me on top of her, her bright eyes flickering with naughty thoughts. "There's something I want to do under the stars."

And she's not at all silent as we enjoy the best benefit of sleeping under the stars—not sleeping.

EPILOGUE: MY PLANTS HAVE LEGS

REMY

I'm ready. Whatever the answer is, I'm ready. If I lose the job, I'll find another one. It's all going to be okay. I blow out a steadying breath, then rap on the open door to Daniel's office a few days later. He asked me to come see him this morning. That's all he said, and I'm trying not to read anything into it.

"Good to see you. How's everything going?" He gestures to the chair.

I take the seat, perched on the edge of it. "It's great. Lake and I stayed in a treehouse hotel on Friday night. And there were no snakes."

He laughs, amused. "Good to know."

"Thank you again for helping him the other day. That was amazing of you," I say, so grateful Daniel played a role.

"Maybe there's a new career for me as a romance designer," he says, then lets his smile vanish. "Remy, I've given a lot of thought to how things went, and I want to reiterate that you don't ever owe anyone information about your personal life. You can do whatever you want in your relationships. And no one but you and your partner should ever have any say."

"Thank you," I say, eager for him to get to the next part, whatever that is.

"And honestly, being able to fake a relationship isn't the worst skill set in this job. We work in marketing and publicity. Appearances matter. But I also want you to know I care about you as a friend, and I want you to be able to come to me if you have any problems."

"I do know that," I say, then my brain replays what he just said. *Come to me*. He's speaking in the present tense. He's speaking about the future. I'm practically holding my breath as I ask, "Does that mean…?"

His smile is pleased, proud even. "Your work speaks for itself. The fact that you went the extra mile to plan the Hockey Is for Everyone initiative clinched it for me. I need someone who's an overachiever."

Fireworks shoot in my chest. "That's definitely me."

He stands, extends a hand, and says, "Welcome to the Golden State Foxes full-time."

I shake his hand accepting the offer, moving forward into a bright, new future that fits me so much more than the one I left behind.

* * *

When I leave work that night, I walk through the concourse, passing the now empty beer stand where Jameson used to work. I guess he wasn't able to renew his lease here without all his unearned product placement. Boohoo.

Later at my place, I break out a bottle of champagne I bought myself almost two months ago. Lake's here in my kitchen, and we're celebrating my new job. "I made you a promise I'd crack this open when I was over that jackass. But I've been over him for a long time," I say, filling a flute.

"I know," he says, leaning against the counter, his stance casual, his gaze locked on me.

"How do you know I've been over him for a long time?"

He shrugs, cocky, confident. "Because you have me."

I laugh, rolling my eyes, then I swallow some champagne. It tastes like how happiness feels. "I do have you."

My sister was right. There is no mandatory time period to get over someone who hurt you. You move on when you move on. You date when you date. You fall in love when you fall in love. And it's best to let it happen, rather than fight it.

He lifts the glass to his lips and knocks some back, then sets it on the counter. "And now I'll drink some off you."

Lake Axelrod tosses me over his shoulder, carries me to my bed, and strips me down to nothing, showing me once again his favorite way to drink champagne.

The next day in the kitchen, I take another step forward. As I water my succulents, I say to him, "I think I'm ready for something else too."

"What is it?"

I turn my gaze to the plants, then give him a knowing look.

He growls like a warning, maybe even an order. "I'm going with you."

But he doesn't need to issue a command. I always planned on taking him. "You sure are."

* * *

After Lake's game, we go to the Little Friends rescue, where I visit with a young Terrier named Pearl, a fluffy middle-aged Pomeranian mix named Frito, and an older Chihuahua mix named Minnie.

Her tan fur is dusted with silver, her eyes with white fur.

She's not the fastest dog, but she walks to me with purpose, then lifts her chin and asks for pets.

I oblige happily, then pick her up.

She lets out one of those little dog sighs and curls up into my arms.

Sometimes you just know. I take her home and name her Katrina. After she's settled into my home, Lake swings by, a car seat buckled into the back of his car just for her. I clip her in, and we drive up to Cozy Valley, turn into Big Steps Ranch, then bump along the gravel driveway till we reach the big farmhouse.

I hop out, unclip Katrina, and set the little old lady on the ground. She takes her sweet time sniffing everything on the way to the porch. When she reaches the steps, she lifts her face, surprised, I suspect, to see someone waiting there for her on the porch swing.

It's Lake's father, and he's sitting outside.

Katrina trots over to him, and they sit in the sun, listening to the birds. My heart is full.

* * *

A few days later, I return to the podcast studio to record another episode of *How We Met*. I might have given up romance planning, but I still love romance and telling stories of the cutest of meet-cutes. But today I'm not sharing a meet-cute from a listener.

Instead, I have a special guest. "I'm here today with Lake. You might also know him as my real boyfriend," I say, playfully.

"That's my job title," he says, dry and deadpan.

"And we have something to share with all of you. We

spend so much time talking about how couples meet, but how do they stay together?"

"That's an excellent question, Remy. Do you have a plan for that?"

This is my favorite plan. "I do. I have five things that you should do with the one you love, and today I'd like to challenge all of you to do these things."

I read the list so I can pass it on, sending more love out into the world.

When we leave, Lake takes my hand and we walk down the streets of San Francisco. "We should keep adding to it—that list. Since I'm going to ask you to marry me someday. Figured you wouldn't want me to surprise you so I'm giving you a heads-up."

My heart soars. "That is a very good secret you just shared with me."

Curious how the single dad hockey star Corbin fell hard for Mabel, his best friend's sister, when they opened a bakery together? Download Just Breaking the Rules for FREE in Kindle Unlimited! Miller's and Anna's forbidden, friends-to-lovers, he-falls-first romance comes next in Just Scoring With Love!

You can binge the entire Love and Hockey series starting with The Boyfriend Goal, a roommates-to-lovers, he-falls-first, teammate's little sister romance FREE in KU!

For more Remy and Lake click here for an extended epilogue or scan the QR code!

Bonus Scene Just Playing for Keeps

Want to be the first to know of sales, new releases, special deals and giveaways? Sign up for my newsletter today!

Turn the Page!!

EXCERPT: JUST BREAKING THE RULES

Corbin

She holds up her hands, but she's not defeated. Her words crackle with a spark that hasn't been snuffed out from a rough day. "Let's see what you've got."

"Game on," I say and reach for the clip in her hair, letting her waves fall in a dark mess, a contrast to her fair complexion. I wet the end of the towel under the faucet and dab the frosting off the strands near her face.

As I touch her hair, she shudders in a breath, then goes quiet, and I work steadily.

I wet the towel once more, then clean the sugar and cake bits from the back of her hair. I check the time. She's due out in eight minutes for the picture. "Done."

"Is it all gone?"

"Yes. But your hair's damp now."

"Does it really matter? No one's going to be looking at the llama-kissing ex," she says with a snort.

I spin her around, shaking my head. "You're wrong. They will."

Her look says she doesn't buy what I'm selling. "To stare at the five-car pileup on the side of the road?"

The question hangs in the air, taking up the very small space between us.

The mere inches between us.

It's the first time I've been *this* close to Mabel. I've seen her a few times over the years. At hockey games. At barbecues. In the diner, when she stops by Cozy Valley to see her family.

With her shiny hair, her expressive eyes, and her bow-shaped lips, Mabel Llewelyn's always been pretty. I've thought so ever since the day I met her at a fundraising event for the local fire department in Cozy Valley—her hometown, and now mine too.

But I knew it in an empirical sense.

Now I take a beat to drink her in, and the answers to her question are clear and bright.

Why? Because freckles dance across the bridge of your cute nose. Because your lips are so lush. Because your eyes shine with fire and humor. And because you're so fucking brave.

"Because...you're you," I say at last.

There. That's safe enough. Just because I'm thinking things about her for the first time—or, really, the first time since I learned who she was—doesn't mean I'm going to say them out loud. Let alone act on them. Our lives are too... connected. It'd be messy, and I hate messes.

But helping her right now? That's easy, so I keep going. "Which means you're going to have the best French braid ever. Now, turn around."

"Yes, sir." Mabel spins around once more. I take the clip and run the teeth of it through her hair, combing out the wet strands, then separating them into three chunks.

Checking the time on my watch, I put the clip on the

counter, then grasp the right chunk in my hand. Her breath hitches.

I weave that handful over the middle section, then loop in the left chunk. I gather more locks on the right, add it to that strand, and weave it into the braid. I do the same on the left side, then slowly, steadily work my way down her hair, crafting a tight French braid.

As I go, I sneak a whiff of her sugary scent. No surprise—Mabel smells like the treats she makes. It's the best kind of smell, like candy and butter, with a hint of vanilla.

When I reach the nape of her neck, my thumb slides across her pale, creamy skin. I don't want to stop touching her, and this is a problem.

A problem I like far too much. My chest heats as I steal another touch, grazing her neck once more.

She stifles a gasp, and I pause, absorbing the realization that she likes the way I'm touching her hair, maybe even the way I have to pull on it to braid it. When I near the end, she goes still, as if she's holding her breath. I fight the urge to tug on the end of her braid. But I focus on finishing, neatly looping one strand over the other until I'm down to the middle of her back with little hair left.

I grab the clip once more and use it to secure the end of the braid. "Done. And with four minutes to spare."

She turns around, and there's something in her brown eyes that wasn't there before—curiosity with a touch of heat.

"Thank you, Corbin." She lets out a laugh, then adds, "I should bake you a cake to show my appreciation."

"That's not necessary. I'm just glad I was here."

"You don't like cake?" From her tone, indifference to cake would be blasphemy.

"I ate some off your arm a few minutes ago."

"But did you like it?"

I'd have thought that was proof. "Of course I like cake."

"Why of course?"

"Because I like things that taste..." I pause, trying not to look at her mouth, but failing, "really fucking good."

Maybe that came out a bit naughtier than it sounded in my head. Maybe I'm flirting with my best friend's little sister.

"Like what?" she counters.

This woman doesn't back down. And there are so many reasons I shouldn't answer that question. Her brother's the acting general manager for my hockey team, filling the role after the longtime GM retired last season. As if that's not enough, with the season barely underway, a rough end to last year's playoff hopes, and my daughter extremely busy with middle school in the city, my life is complicated enough.

But there's something about the space in this trailer, or the lack thereof. There's something about the flirty way Mabel asked, *Like what?* And there's definitely something about the way she's waiting for my answer like she *needs* it.

My gaze drops to a tiny bit of frosting still left on her forearm, then returns to her eyes. "Things like frosting."

Read on...

BE A LOVELY

Want to be the first to know of sales, new releases, special deals and giveaways? Sign up for my newsletter today!

Want to be part of a fun, feel-good place to talk about books and romance, and get sneak peeks of covers and advance copies of my books? Be a Lovely!

I've written more than 100 books! **All of these titles below are FREE in Kindle Unlimited!**

The Love and Hockey Series

The Boyfriend Goal

A roommates-to-lovers, teammate's little sister hockey romance!

The Romance Line

An enemies-to-lovers, player and the publicist, forbidden romance!

The Proposal Play

A brother's best friend/marriage of convenience romance!

The Girlfriend Zone

A coach's daughter romance!

The Overtime Kiss!

A single dad/nanny romance!

The Flirting Game!

A neighbors to lovers, fake dating romance!

Hockey Ever After

Just Breaking the Rules!

A brother's best friend/workplace/one who got away romance!

Just Playing for Keeps!

A grumpy sunshine, fake dating romance!

Just Scoring With Love

A friends to lovers hockey romance!

Darling Springs

It Seemed Like a Good Idea!

An only one-bed-in-the-room, forbidden, small town bodyguard romance!

I've Got a Crush On You!

A grumpy sunshine, workplace romance where the boss has a secret identity!

Holiday Romances

Merry Little Kissmas

Fake dating my brother's best friend at Christmas!

My Favorite Holidate

Fake dating the billionaire boss at Christmas!

The My Hockey Romance Series

Hockey, spice, shenanigans and cute dogs in this series of standalones! Because when you get screwed over, make it a double or even a triple!

Karma is two hockey boyfriends and sometimes three!

Double Pucked

A sexy, outrageous MFM hockey romantic comedy!

Puck Yes

A fake marriage, spicy MFM hockey rom com!

Thoroughly Pucked!

A brother's best friends +runaway bride, spicy MFM hockey rom com!

Well and Truly Pucked

A friends-to-lovers forced proximity why-choose hockey rom com!

The Virgin Society Series

Meet the Virgin Society – great friends who'd do anything for each other. Indulge in these forbidden, emotionally-charged, and wildly sexy age-gap romances!

The RSVP

The Tryst

The Tease

The Dating Games Series

A fun, sexy romantic comedy series about friends in the city and their dating mishaps!

The Virgin Next Door

Two A Day

The Good Guy Challenge

How To Date Series

Friends who are like family. Chances to learn how to date again. Standalone romantic comedies full of love, sex and meet-cute shenanigans.

My So-Called Love Life

Plays Well With Others

The Almost Romantic

The Accidental Dating Experiment

A romantic comedy adventure standalone

A Real Good Bad Thing

Boyfriend Material

Four fabulous heroines. Four outrageous proposals. Four chances at love in this sexy rom-com series!

Asking For a Friend

Sex and Other Shiny Objects

One Night Stand-In

Overnight Service

Big Rock Series

My #1 New York Times Bestselling sexy as sin, irreverent, male-POV romantic comedy!

Big Rock

Mister O

Well Hung

Full Package

Joy Ride

Hard Wood

Happy Endings Series

Romance starts with a bang in this series of standalones following a group of friends seeking and avoiding love!

Come Again

Shut Up and Kiss Me

Kismet

My Single-Versary

Ballers And Babes

Sexy sports romance standalones guaranteed to make you hot!

Most Valuable Playboy

Most Likely to Score

A Wild Card Kiss

Rules of Love Series

Athlete, virgins and weddings!

The Virgin Rule Book

The Virgin Game Plan

The Virgin Replay

The Virgin Scorecard

The Extravagant Series

Bodyguards, billionaires and hoteliers in this sexy, high-stakes series of standalones!

One Night Only

One Exquisite Touch

My One-Week Husband

The Guys Who Got Away Series

Friends in New York City and California fall in love in this fun and hot rom-com series!

Birthday Suit

Dear Sexy Ex-Boyfriend

The What If Guy

Thanks for Last Night

The Dream Guy Next Door

Always Satisfied Series

A group of friends in New York City find love and laughter in this series of sexy standalones!

Satisfaction Guaranteed

Never Have I Ever

Instant Gratification

PS It's Always Been You

The Gift Series

An after dark series of standalones! Explore your fantasies!

The Engagement Gift

The Virgin Gift

The Decadent Gift

The Heartbreakers Series

Three brothers. Three rockers. Three standalone sexy romantic comedies.

Once Upon a Real Good Time

Once Upon a Sure Thing

Once Upon a Wild Fling

Sinful Men

A high-stakes, high-octane, sexy-as-sin romantic suspense series!

My Sinful Nights

My Sinful Desire

My Sinful Longing

My Sinful Love

My Sinful Temptation

From Paris With Love

Swoony, sweeping romances set in Paris!

Wanderlust

Part-Time Lover

One Love Series

A group of friends in New York falls in love one by one in this sexy rom-com series!

The Sexy One

The Hot One

The Knocked Up Plan

Come As You Are

Lucky In Love Series

A small town romance full of heat and blue collar heroes and sexy heroines!

Best Laid Plans

The Feel Good Factor

Nobody Does It Better

Unzipped

No Regrets

An angsty, sexy, emotional, new adult trilogy about one young couple fighting to break free of their pasts!

The Start of Us

The Thrill of It

Every Second With You

The Caught Up in Love Series

A group of friends finds love!

The Pretending Plot

The Dating Proposal

The Second Chance Plan

The Private Rehearsal

Seductive Nights Series

A high heat series full of danger and spice!

Night After Night

After This Night

One More Night

A Wildly Seductive Night

Joy Delivered Duet

A high-heat, wickedly sexy series of standalones that will set your sheets on fire!

Nights With Him

Forbidden Nights

Unbreak My Heart

A standalone second chance emotional roller coaster of a romance

The Muse

A magical realism romance set in Paris

Good Love Series of sexy rom-coms co-written with Lili Valente!

I also write MM romance under the name L. Blakely!

Hopelessly Bromantic Duet (MM)

Roomies to lovers to enemies to fake boyfriends

Hopelessly Bromantic

Here Comes My Man

Men of Summer Series (MM)

Two baseball players on the same team fall in love in a forbidden romance spanning five epic years

Scoring With Him

Winning With Him

All In With Him

MM Standalone Novels

A Guy Walks Into My Bar

The Bromance Zone

One Time Only

The Best Men (Co-written with Sarina Bowen)

Winner Takes All Series (MM)

A series of emotionally-charged and irresistibly sexy standalone MM sports romances!

The Boyfriend Comeback

Turn Me On

A Very Filthy Game

Limited Edition Husband

Manhandled

If you want a personalized recommendation, email me at laurenblakelybooks@gmail.com!

CONTACT

I love hearing from readers! You can find me on TikTok at LaurenBlakelyBooks, Instagram at LaurenBlakelyBooks, Facebook at LaurenBlakelyBooks, or online at LaurenBlakely.com. You can also email me at laurenblakelybooks@gmail.com

www.ingramcontent.com/pod-product-compliance
Lightning Source LLC
Chambersburg PA
CBHW011929050726
47591CB00009B/2407
* 9 7 8 1 9 6 4 0 4 8 5 1 2 *